GUARDIANS
OF THE FLAME:
LEGACY

Baen Books by Joel Rosenberg

The Guardians of the Flame
Guardians of the Flame: Legacy
Guardians of the Flame: To Home and Ehvenor
(forthcoming)

Paladins (forthcoming)

GUARDIANS
OF THE FLAME:
FLAME:
LEGACY

JOEL ROSENBERG

GUARDIANS OF THE FLAME: LEGACY

The Heir Apparent © copyright 1987 by Joel Rosenberg; The Warrior Lives © copyright 1988 by Joel Rosenberg.

A Baen Books Original Megabook

Baen Publishing Enterprises
P.O. Box 1403
Riverdale, NY 10471
www.baen.com

ISBN: 0-7434-8829-6

Cover art by Monty Moore

First Megabook printing, June 2004

Library of Congress Cataloging-in-Publication Data

Rosenberg, Joel, 1954-
  Guardians of the flame--legacy / Joel Rosenberg.
    p. cm.
  "A Baen Books original megabook"--T.p. verso.
  ISBN 0-7434-8829-6
  1. Role playing--Fiction. 2. Friendship--Fiction. I. Title: Legacy. II. Title.

  PS3568.O786G834 2004
  813'.54--dc22

                                                                    2004004243

Distributed by Simon & Schuster
1230 Avenue of the Americas
New York, NY 10020

Production by Windhaven Press, Auburn, NH
Printed in the United States of America

10   9   8   7   6   5   4   3   2   1

CONTENTS
Guardians of the Flame: Legacy

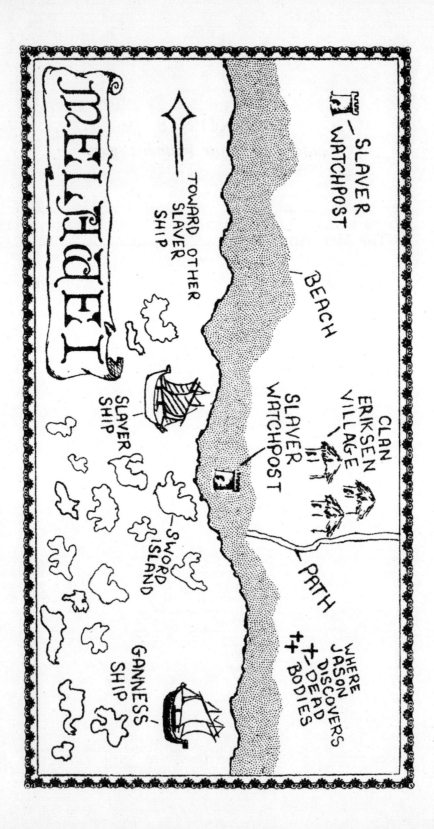

The Heir Apparent

Vol. 4 of

*The Guardians
of the Flame*

I'd like to thank the people who made it possible for me to write this one: Harry Leonard, my favorite quibbler; Kat Martinez, cat-sitter extraordinaire; all the able people at Bulldog Computers; Bob Wallace, for inventing PC-Write; Ron Pastore, who keeps the mill; my agent, Richard Curtis; my new editor, John Silbersack, who has proved himself both remarkably capable and inhumanly patient; and my friend and former editor Sheila Gilbert, who still watches out for me.

As usual, I'm particularly grateful to my cats Bubbles, Squish, and Amy Surplus—who don't understand why—and my wife, Felicia, who does.

This one is for the Student Union Rats:

Marty,
Spring,
Bob,
Frank,
Laurie,
Paul,
Sherry,
Dori,
Harry,
Norm,
John,
Bill . . . and me, for that matter.

DRAMATIS PERSONAE

Karl Cullinane—Prince of Bieme and Emperor of Holtun-Bieme

Andrea Andropolous Cullinane—wizard, teacher, Princess of Bieme and Empress of Holtun-Bieme, Karl Cullinane's wife

Tennetty—warrior, Karl Cullinane's bodyguard

Ellegon—a young dragon

Garavar—general of the House Guard

Arrifezh, Baron Arondael

Thomen, Baron Furnael—Biemish baron; judge

Beralyn, Dowager Baroness of Furnael—Thomen Furnael's mother

Enrel—Thomen's bailiff

Vilmar, Baron Nerahan—Holtish baron

Kevalun—Biemish general, military governor of barony Nerahan

Ranella—master engineer

Nartham—soldier of the House Guard

Aravam, Bibuz—journeyman engineers

Kethol, Pirojil, Durine—warriors of the House Guard

U'len—chief cook at Biemestren castle

Jimuth and Kozat—U'len's assistants

Jayar—senior journeyman engineer; engineer duty officer at Biemestren Castle

Garthe, Gashier, Danagar—three of Garavar's sons, soldiers

Hivar—Furnael family retainer

Listar, Baron Tyrnael—Biemish baron

Kirling—a minor noble of barony Tyrnael

5

Yryn—Slavers' Guildmaster
Ahrmin, Lucindyl, Wencius—master slavers
Doria, Elmina—members of the Healing Hand Society
Ahira Bandylegs—dwarf warrior
Walter Slovotsky—part-time farming consultant to King Maherrelen, part-time warrior, full-time smartass
Geveren—dwarf soldier fealty-bound to Maherrelen, assigned to Walter Slovotsky and Ahira
Arthur Simpson Deighton/Arta Myrdhyn—lecturer in philosophy, master wizard
Jason Cullinane—Karl and Andrea Cullinane's son
Louis Riccetti—mayor of Home, the Engineer
Bast—Home resident, journeyman engineer
Petros—Home resident, farmer, deputy mayor
Daherrin—dwarf warrior, Home raiding-team leader
Valeran—semiretired soldier in the service of the Cullinane family; Jason's teacher
Bren, Baron Adahan
Aeia Eriksen Cullinane—Karl and Andrea Cullinane's adopted daughter, part-time teacher
Samalyn, Danerel, Mikyn—warriors on Daherrin's raiding team
Artum, Habel—Wehnest soldiers
Vator—Wehnest hostler
Falikos—rancher
Kyreen, Ceenan—drovers from Wehnest, employed by Falikos

CHAPTER ONE:

His Imperial Majesty

A cardinal virtue—perhaps the *cardinal virtue—of hereditary rule is that you may—may—get a reluctant ruler. The
trouble with the usurper is that he usually wanted the job. I
said* usually; *I'm an exception.*
*Wanting to rule—as opposed to being willing to govern—is
clear evidence of a diseased mind; the only person who should
be allowed to make decisions for anybody else ought to be
someone who doesn't want the job.*
*Note: Pretended reluctance to rule isn't an effective
substitute.*
*Additional note: Not wanting the job isn't a sufficient
qualification, just a necessary one.*
Short form of the above: Life can be a real bitch.
—Karl Cullinane

Baron, you're an asshole, Karl Cullinane thought as he approached
the keep, crawling on his belly through the tall grasses.

If Baron Arondael was going to try to explore the possibility
of rebelling against his prince and emperor, at least he could have
had the goddam consideration to have his goddam groundskeepers
mow the goddam lawn so that the goddam prince and emperor
couldn't quietly sneak up on him, thereby forcing said goddam
prince and emperor to come up with some plan either more
straightforward or more devious than creeping through the goddam
grass on his goddam hands and knees.

He paused for a moment and rose to his knees to rub at the stubs that were all that remained of the three outermost fingers of his left hand. After all these years, he had gotten used to managing with thumb and forefinger; he rarely missed them—

Matter of fact, you can count in base seven better than anyone else I know.

—but grass made the stumps itch.

Baron, you are going to pay for my itching stumps.

That seemed only fair. The stumps weren't Arondael's fault; the itching was.

Good, good, the sarcastic voice echoed in his head. *Worry about what a jerk Baron Arondael is and how you'd rather just walk up to the castle. Much, much better to think about what you'd rather be doing than to concentrate on what you are doing. Why not worry how Jason's lessons at Home are coming along?*

Ellegon—

Maybe you could concentrate on Jason's incompetence in long division instead of the admittedly more minor issue of whether or not somebody's going to shove a sword through your guts.

Sarcasm doesn't become you.

Stupidity doesn't look good on anyone. Do you know the technical term for the children of stupid soldiers?

Okay, I'll bite: What do you call them?

Orphans.

To his right, General Garavar and the six soldiers strung out beyond him pretended that Ellegon hadn't included them in his mental broadcast.

There was one exception. And a carefully pitched snort of derision that couldn't have carried farther than a few meters.

Tennetty says that I'm right, as usual, by the way.

"Be quiet, all of you. We've got a job to do."

"Your majesty," Garavar whispered, "I say again: Emperors don't do this sort of thing."

"I said to shut up. I don't want to attract attention." Yet.

Garavar was a soldier of the old school, Bieme style, where loyalty counted more than obedience.

Still, when Karl glared as Garavar opened his mouth again, Garavar shut up.

Karl had to admit that Garavar did have a point. A good one, at that. Not that this was particularly a bad idea, but it shouldn't have been Karl Cullinane leading it.

It shouldn't be me, Karl thought. It should be someone good at a quiet sneak, it should be somebody like Walter Slovotsky trying to creep in close. This was Walter Slovotsky's sort of thing, not Karl's.

There is nobody like Walter Slovotsky. I take it you miss him.

Good guess. Slovotsky would already be well inside the castle, have seduced one or more pretty girls, filled his pockets with coins and jewels, set himself up with another bed partner or two for later, stuffed himself on rich food in the castle kitchen, uncorked and imbibed the best bottle of wine available, and had the baron up against the wall, fully frisked and intimidated by now.

Without raising a sweat, probably.

*Hmmm . . . I wonder if he has such an overinflated opinion of your abilities. By the way, you *could* have done this like a normal kind of person. You have heard of normality?*

The standard way to get a recalcitrant baron out of his castle was for a detachment of his neighboring barons to show up at his door and invite him to accompany them to the capitol.

That was almost completely safe: no baron would want open combat with his neighbors unless he was certain his life was already forfeit; fighting his neighbors was certain to get him killed. Even if he did order his men to attack such a delegation, his soldiers would be likely to mutiny; princes and emperors tended to frown on such attacks and express their disapproval with axe and gibbet.

Relay to Garavar, Karl Cullinane thought. *I didn't get where I am today by doing things the standard way. And speaking of which, it's my understanding that generals don't usually go creeping around through the grasses, either.*

There wasn't an answer to that.

Although Tennetty quickly provided one anyway. "There are some people," she whispered softly, "who are a bit concerned about your tender hide."

Ellegon provided another. *And since when are you so happy about where you are today?*

Shut up. I've got to think.

Oh—a new trick!

Shush!

There was a time when Karl Cullinane would have gone on a

raid without worrying about the welfare of the people he was raiding, but that was in the old days, when he was the leader of a Home raiding team, and the victims were slavers in caravan.

Now, it was different: The guards here were his subjects— although he did not like the word—and an emperor didn't just go around killing innocent subjects.

Hmmm . . . it was just as well that the baron clearly didn't expect trouble this quickly; instead of paying attention to what they were doing, the two guards were chatting about what a bastard the new guard sergeant was as they approached. Karl eyed their path and didn't like it. It looked like the guards were going to come too close to his squad.

We don't need a whole lot of alarms being raised. Relay: Ten, what do you think of the idea of taking the one on the left while I take the one on the right?

From Tennetty: "What do I think? I think that's just about the dumbest idea you've had this year. Aren't they going to get a bit suspicious when the two of us pop out of the grass? We need a diversion, not a brace of panicky soldiers crying for help."

Ellegon, can you read them well enough for a mindscream?

Yes, but I'm not close enough to be sure it would really stun them.

Wonderful. Karl shrugged mentally. *Okay, back to basics. Relay: Tennetty, you take that skinny kid—*

"Hoften."

—Hoften, and work your way around behind them. When I get their attention, jump them, and do your best to silence them, without killing. Understood?

"Understood. Without killing."

Karl didn't like it, but he'd have to count on Arondael's military commander being as sloppy about training as he was about peacetime discipline.

As the two closed to within barely five yards of where Karl lay, Karl Cullinane leaped to his feet, a flintlock pistol in one hand, his saber in the other.

"Halt in the name of the emperor," he hissed, as the others rose up beside him, Garavar with a throwing knife balanced, the others with sword or crossbow ready.

That stopped them for a precious second; a second was all that was needed. Arondael wasn't on a war footing; neither guard had time or inclination to make an outcry in the second before Tennetty and Hoften were on them.

"Who . . . ?" the larger of the two started, the word trailing off to a gurgle as Tennetty snaked an arm around his throat, gently setting a knifepoint against his windpipe.

"Please don't scream," she said politely, "or I'll cut the sound in half before it leaves your throat. Now, open your mouth slowly," she said, jamming a gag in it when he did.

Hoften had silenced his quarry by the simple expedient of jamming his own arm into the man's mouth; the boy gritted his teeth against the pain as the guard struggled for the moment it took until Karl was upon him.

Karl Cullinane uncocked and holstered his pistol, then reached out and grabbed the guard by the front of his tunic.

"I said," he whispered, " 'Halt in the name of the emperor,' " setting the point of his sword against the guard's throat.

Wide-eyed, the guard relaxed his bite.

"Better. Would you prefer I said, 'Halt in the name of me'? I don't normally like incidental killings, but if you don't get your damn teeth out of that boy's arm, I'll make an exception. Good.

"Now, I want tonight's passwords."

Wearing the guards' livery, Karl and Garavar approached the guard station, muttering the night's password under their breath.

As the sleepy-eyed corporal of the guard snicked the bolts aside and opened the door, Garavar took a step inside the gate and brought a cocked pistol up to the corporal's head.

"You know," he said conversationally, while Karl guided the guard into the shadows, "there comes a time in a man's life when he has to make a decision. You've got one to make right now. You can either give out an alarm—in which case the emperor will be most irritated with you—or you can help us get close to the baron."

"Emp—"

"That's me," Karl said, reaching into the cloth bag at his waist and pulling out the silver crown of Bieme. He set it on his head. "The one and only."

Now, I want a broad relay to everyone in the castle.

Station Kay Ay Ar Ell, the voice of the Emperor of Holtun-Bieme, is now on the air, Ellegon answered back, as the dragon landed noisily on the ramparts above them.

"My name is Karl Cullinane," he said quietly, knowing that Ellegon would add the proper volume as he relayed the thoughts. "I am Prince of Bieme, conqueror of Holtun, and Emperor of Holtun-Bieme, and I want to see Baron Arondael, now."

He unbolted the door and kicked it open for Tennetty and the rest to follow. "And in case anyone has any foolish idea, I've summoned a sufficient force to tear this castle down to the bare stones. Anyone who gets in my way is dead."

Next step. Karl closed his eyes.

Here goes. A dark shadow passed high overhead, only to be relieved by dazzling brightness as Ellegon's flame lit up the night.

Relay: "Into the courtyard, everyone. Now."

In moments, the entire keep had stumbled out, soldiers numbly clawing for their armor and weapons, servants and children in their night tunics.

Including Arrifezh, Baron Arondael.

The rapier-slim man rubbed a gnarled fist against eyes that hadn't yet noticed they weren't sleepy anymore.

"Good morning, Baron," Karl Cullinane said, raising his voice. "And good morning all. Every man, woman, and child, regardless of rank, who is not in rebellion against their prince and emperor, will now kindly lay down any arms and kneel." He sheathed his sword and folded his hands over his chest. "I said *now.*"

Tennetty brought up her rifle and took careful aim at the middle of the baron's nose. "Starting with you, Baron," she muttered in a low voice. "We start with you, one way or another."

Karl's soldiers following the baron's example, the several hundred people in the courtyard bent like a sea of wheat in the wind.

"That's fine. Up, all of you."

Garavar drew himself up to his full height. "My apologies, your majesty," he said to Karl. "You were right; I was wrong. It worked."

"As usual," Karl said.

"For those born luckier than they've any right to be," the general shot back. And then added: "Sire."

But he was smiling. And that was usual.

Karl returned the smile, then sobered as he raised his voice and turned to Arondael. "Baron, I'll need to speak to you privately at your earliest convenience—as long as your earliest convenience is right now."

✧   ✧   ✧

Arondael had recovered most of his composure as he sat in his high-backed chair, a cup of hot tea warming his hands.

Karl wasn't thirsty, he'd said.

Actually, without his wife or a reliable cleric to check for poison, he wasn't about to trust Arondael's food.

Ellegon, from his perch on top of the keep, might be able to probe the baron's mind, but there was no guarantee that some subject of Arondael's might not decide to ingratiate himself with the baron by poisoning the emperor, and Karl wouldn't have wanted Ellegon to subject himself to the odious task of probing hundreds of minds simply so that Karl could have a cup of tea.

"What I don't understand, majesty," Arondael said, sipping nervously at his tea, "is the necessity for all this . . . commotion."

"Did you get my letter of last tenday, Arondael?"

"Yes, of course, sire—a response is on its way to the capitol."

"You'll notice that I asked that you visit me at Biemestren yesterday, Baron."

"Your majesty, as I said in my response, things have been so busy here that—"

"I want all my barons visiting me regularly, when summoned."

There wasn't a better way to prevent treachery than to insist that Karl's nobles show up at the capitol every now and then, effectively surrendering themselves to his mercy.

"Maybe the trouble, Baron, is that you're thinking of me as your prince."

"Which you are, sire, in law and in fact. As well as my emperor."

"What I mainly am, Baron, is a usurper; I wasn't born to inherit the throne, but I do intend to keep on ruling. And I do intend to be obeyed. Kapish?" he said, immediately switching back to Erendra and correcting himself to "Understood?"

"Of course."

Karl nodded. "Good. Officially, our explanation—what you'll tell your people—is that you were concerned about the readiness of your guard, asked that I have them tested, and, as a sign of my great respect for you and love for your people, I've honored you and them by doing it personally. Agreed?"

"Yes, sire." Arondael didn't smile at the absurdity of it. Despite the fact that Karl had publicly suggested that Castle Arondael was in rebellion, Arondael didn't see anything strange in agreeing to a cover story that everyone in the castle would know to be false.

I guess he doesn't think that, say, a twelve-year-old boy might point out that the baron's story leaves his butt uncovered.

You mean that the emper—make that baron—isn't wearing any clothes?

Something like that.

Then again, maybe the baron felt that a twelve-year-old calling out that the baron's cover story left him bare-ass naked might be the reason that they invented the gibbet, Ellegon suggested.

That could be part of it, too, "You're sure that's acceptable, Baron?"

"Yes, sire."

This is starting to feel like a Platonic dialogue.

What do you mean? I don't see a whole lot of wisdom flowing around.

No, no, not the wisdom part. I'm not that egotistical.

Nah. Not you. But you were saying?

In the Dialogues, *Socrates has all the good lines; the rest just get to say "Yes, Socrates" and "It would surely seem so, Socrates" and "How true, Socrates."*

"So we do have an understanding?"

"Of course, sire."

Very good, Socrates. "Rules, as we say, are rules, Baron." Karl gave a genial smile. "I don't mind your testing my authority, once. This was once, understood?"

"Yes, sire," the baron said.

How clever, Socrates.

He's wondering what would happen if you happened to disappear here tonight.

Karl sighed. Sometimes these damn barons were so predictable. "Mmm . . . I know you have grievances against the Holts. I know about how Arondael was taken by the Holts during the war."

The baron's face clouded over. The Holts hadn't been as gentle conquerors as Karl Cullinane had—somewhat later—insisted that the Biemish be; men, women and children had been chained, hauled off by guild slavers. Some had made their way back in the nine years since the end of the war; most had not.

And then there was the baron's family. . . .

Karl didn't like thinking about the baron's family. "Well, Baron, like it or not, we're all part of the same empire now. Granted, the

Biemish barons have more independence; Furnael can run his barony as he pleases—"

"As his mother pleases."

Karl Cullinane stared long and hard into the baron's eyes. "I believe I was speaking?"

"Sorry, sire."

My mistake, Socrates. "Better. As I was saying—we've had to be very restrictive of the Holts. Baron Nerahan, like the rest of the Holts, hasn't been allowed to have even a small detachment of soldiers under his own command; they've all been occupation troops."

"As well they should be."

"Until now, Baron. Like it or not, Nerahan and his people have been the most loyal of the Holtish; I've rearmed them, and ordered the occupation troops into Nerahan's service. And unless I—personally—stop them, an army under Barons Nerahan and Furnael—"

And—ahem—me.

"—and Ellegon, which is even now marching on Arondael, is going to lay siege to your keep, bring down the walls, and not leave a stone standing on a stone." That wasn't true; there was no army marching on Arondael. But it could be made true, quickly, if need be.

Arondael's face whitened. He opened his mouth, worked it silently for a moment, closed it.

"Or," Karl Cullinane said as he rose to his feet, "you and Nerahan, under General Kevalun's overall leadership, will jointly carry out the first joint Holtun-Bieme military maneuvers."

Karl had planned that, but the next thing out of his mouth surprised even him. "I'm about to call a barons' council of both Holtun and Bieme. I want to see some cooperation between an opposite pair of baronies before. It'll make me look good."

The baron bit his lip, then shrugged.

"Spit it out, Arondael."

"A joint council? Are you sure that is wise?"

"If I wasn't sure, I wouldn't call one, would I? You're stalling, Arondael; take your pick, Baron. Joint maneuvers, or do we flatten your keep?"

He's geeking.

Surprise, surprise.

"I'll take the second alternative, sire," Arondael said calmly, pleasantly, as though he'd been offered a choice between two sweetmeats.

I'll take one from Column B, Socrates. Still, Karl had to admire Arondael's composure; under the proper threat, the baron had simply folded his hand, giving no apparent look of regret toward the pot Karl was sweeping in.

Best to remind him of the pot. And of the penalty for overbetting. But first things first.

"Very well," Karl said. "Now, the thing I'll want you to concentrate on—both you and Nerahan—is making sure that no fights break out. None. Even a fistfight won't look good." Karl rose from his chair and deftly plucked the cup from Arondael's hands. "Do you mind? The tea does look good." He sipped at it. A bit more honey than he would have put in, but better leaf tea than he usually had at Biemestren, if not quite the sassafras of Home.

Not to mention coffee.

He tried not to mention coffee, not even to himself; he hadn't really had any for close to twenty years, although he could still almost taste the imaginary cup that Arta Myrdhyn had served him, almost ten years before.

"Understood, sire." Arondael deliberately suppressed a knowing smile. "I'll happily take another taste, if you like."

"Not necessary, Arrifezh. And now that we're friends again, I'm Karl, when we're alone."

"Very well, Karl," Arondael said, rising to pour himself another cup of tea. "You were saying about the maneuvers?"

"It wasn't all that long ago that you and Nerahan's people were at war with each other, and I'm not foolish enough to expect that your men and his will get along, so I want you to make sure that each and every one of your men understands that there's to be not only no fighting, but no name-calling, no insults. If anybody steps out of line, I want him slapped down immediately—you see to that personally, understood?"

Arondael nodded. "Understood, Karl."

"One more thing," Karl said, drawing himself up to his full height as he drained the last of Arondael's tea. "Don't test me again. Don't let me think that there's a trace of disloyalty left in Arondael. Or I'll yank you out of this keep and give it to Nerahan."

He turned away from the baron, forcing himself not to tense the muscles of his back until he heard the choked words:

"Yes, sire."

Good. Karl had pushed Arondael's self-control far enough. "No, make that 'Yes, Karl'—remember, we're friends again."

"Yes, Karl. I understand."

"And next time I send for you?"

"I will be where you require me to be, when you require me to be there, or I shall die trying."

"Good point." Karl looked at him for a long time. "A *very* good point."

CHAPTER TWO:

Before

Two Years Before, in Pandathaway:
Ahrmin and the Guildmaster

*Your offer is rejected, Guildmaster Yryn. I don't see the need
for a truce, since we already have you defeated.
Individually, both Home and the empire outnumber your
vicious band of flesh-peddlers. Together, we are stronger than
you and all your allies. If that wasn't so, you would have
long since destroyed us. As things stand, your guild can't
operate at all in Holtun or Bieme; your slavers are easy prey
in Khar and much of Nyphien; I have heard of caravans
being assaulted in Sciforth, and near Lundeyll and Ehvenor.
Eventually—count on it!—we'll cut into your seaborne raids
onto Salket and Melawei. Even sooner, raiders will be
operating at the gates of Pandathaway.
Or perhaps inside the gates of Pandathaway?
We are going to overrun you. If not in my generation, then in
my son's or my grandson's. The only question is how and
when you will be defeated, not whether.*

—Karl Cullinane

Karl Cullinane, Ahrmin thought. *I can't take a breath without
having to worry about Karl Cullinane.*

He was angry with himself. If only Ahrmin had been a bit cleverer, Cullinane a bit less lucky the last time.

If only the rest of the guild hadn't stayed his hand since the last time.

"Masters, friends, and brothers," Slavers' Guildmaster Yryn said, his slate-gray eyes flashing as he shook his massive head slowly, "hidden in this overpolite scorn is a sad truth." He paused, likely more for effect than anything else. "And that sad truth," he went on, "is that Karl Cullinane is almost correct—I say again: almost." He turned to Ahrmin. "Which is why, Master Ahrmin, by order of the council, permission to attack him is again denied."

"No—"

"Yes." Yryn tapped a thick finger against the parchment scroll, then drummed his nails on the age-smoothed oak of the table while most of the other dozen masters nodded in agreement. "You will leave Karl Cullinane alone," Yryn said. "For the good of the guild."

"For the good of the guild." Ahrmin carefully kept the scorn in his voice to a bare minimum as he repeated the words. The others respected calm and self-control; a display of temper would only, could only, lower his status in the Slavers' Guild Council.

Turning the ruins of the right side of his face away from the others, he sat back in his chair, forcing himself to be calm. Anger wouldn't help.

It was tempting to let it flow. The idiots—even after all this time, they didn't understand. Despite the raiders who had, only a few tendays before, hit a caravan only a day's ride from Pandathaway.

And despite the blatant provocation of Cullinane's letter, they didn't understand.

Well, he thought, *then I will* make *them understand.* "We must kill Karl Cullinane, Guildmaster. He is too dangerous."

"He *is* too dangerous," Lucindyl put in. "And that is precisely the guildmaster's point, Ahrmin." He was the only elven master slaver present, and tended to fawn over the guildmaster; he was far too willing to support Yryn, no matter what the right of the situation. "He is too dangerous. You have crossed swords with the emperor—"

Ahrmin started to slam his fist down on the table, but caught himself. *Be calm, be calm.* He raised his hand up before his eyes and examined it, as though for the first time.

"That dog," he said quietly, his voice barely louder than a whisper, "has no more right to the title of emperor than a Salke peasant has." He lowered his hands to his lap and folded them together with exquisite gentleness as he looked away, shrugging away the half-hood of his robes and bringing the horror of the right side of his face into view.

Even Yryn shuddered.

Ahrmin didn't, not after all these years, not even when he looked at himself in a mirror. For years, he had forced himself to stare at what Cullinane had left of him: the puckered scars where the fire had burned away flesh and seared the bone beneath; the tattered ridge of callus that was all that remained of the ear; the raw-looking welts that were the right side of his lips.

"No." Yryn swallowed, twice. "He has the right, my friend." Yryn shook his head and settled himself more firmly back in his chair. "He holds Holtun-Bieme by force of arms, and by force of law—"

"His law."

"—*and* by popular support, it seems. At least among the commoners and 'freemen,'" Yryn finished, pronouncing the Englits word like a curse. "Though I understand that some of his barons are not so pleased." He shrugged, dismissing the subject.

"But some are, no? And he is well liked among the lower classes—for an emperor," Lucindyl added, raising an eyebrow. "A very popular man, this Karl Cullinane."

Wencius, a young man whose dark slimness was almost effeminate, toyed with his glass of wine, dipping a manicured finger into the purple liquid, running his fingertip along the rim of the glass until a bell-like note momentarily sounded. "He is very popular, Ahrmin. Or were you too . . . distracted to notice?"

"And as I was saying, Master Ahrmin," Yryn said, glaring Wencius and the elf to silence, "each time the guild has come up against Karl Cullinane, we've emerged the worse for it. First, it was your father losing to him in the Coliseum. Then, after Karl Cullinane had freed the sewer dragon, when Ohlmin attempted to capture him, Karl Cullinane killed him, and more than twoscore good guildsmen. And again, in Melawei, when—"

"I know all this, but—"

"—and the time when Thermyn thought he had trapped Karl Cullinane outside of Lundeyll, and . . ." The guildmaster leaned back in his chair and took a thoughtful sip from his water goblet. "Worst was the last time you went up against him, when you tried to use the Middle Lands war as a source of supply—"

"Which it should have been."

"Indeed, it should have been," Wencius said, his very agreement infuriating.

Yryn pursed his lips. "But it wasn't, Master Ahrmin. Instead of a profitable venture, we stood a sizable loss: powder, guns, and more good guildsmen than I care to think of—"

"Then let me hire mercenaries! I—" He raised his hands to his face and bowed his head into them. "I apologize, Guildmaster. Please continue."

Yryn smiled. "Now, both Bieme and Holtun—and increasingly the rest of the Middle Lands—are closed to us.

"This is not good, Master Ahrmin, not good at all. For the sake of the guild, we will leave Karl Cullinane alone. Let him be distracted by the ruling of his little empire; the guild can survive that, at least for his lifetime. We can survive him, Ahrmin."

Ahrmin didn't answer at first as he brought his fingers up to touch the ravages of the right side of his face.

Karl Cullinane was a very popular man, indeed. There had been a time, years and years before, when Ahrmin had watched this popular man, this gem of a human being, run through the passageway of a burning ship, while Ahrmin lay on the deck, writhing with the pain of his shattered jaw, his crushed fingers reaching for the bottle of healing draughts while the fire raged. . . .

Again, Yryn tapped his finger on the parchment. "There is more. I have been talking with the Wizards' Guild. They don't want to have anything to do with him—there is that damned sword involved, and that is . . . involved with Arta Myrdhyn. None of that guild want to involve themselves with Arta Myrdhyn; the last time that Grandmaster Lucius went up against Arta Myrdhyn, they turned the Forest of Elrood into the Waste of Elrood—do you want to see the Waste of Pandathaway? Do you want to leave that as a tribute to our time as masters of the guild?"

No, Ahrmin thought, *that's not at all what I want to leave behind. What I want to leave behind is Karl Cullinane's head.*

"The time may come, Ahrmin," Yryn said. "The time *may* come when we can take his head. But the time is not now. Not while he is where he is; not while his threat stays limited. As long as he stays within the confines of his paltry little empire, you will leave him alone. Completely alone. Understood?"

Ahrmin forced a hesitation. "Understood, Guildmaster. Masters, friends, and brothers," he said formally, "I obey the will of the council." He looked from face to face.

"I obey," he said.

Enough, he decided.

Enough waiting, enough patience—enough. For the past five years he hadn't even tried for Karl Cullinane's head, and there had only been a few furtive assassins sent out since the Bieme-Holtun war fiasco. He had hoped to regain the support of the council, but support or not, his patience would have to end.

There had to be an opportunity. Soon the waiting would be over, or Ahrmin would take matters into his own hands. Despite everything—despite the resistance of the other members of the council; despite the yearning of the craven Wizards' Guild to cower in the corner whenever the name of Arta Myrdhyn was mentioned—he *would* act. He would.

Still, it would have to be handled carefully. The proper bait would have to be selected, and the proper location, as well.

It couldn't happen while Cullinane was within Holtun-Bieme, of course; that left far too many ways for things to go wrong.

But there were other places in the world besides that tiny empire, other places with other charms.

How much, he wondered, would Grandmaster Lucius pay for the sword that killed wizards?

And how much for the head of the one person who could take it from where it lay?

And how much would Karl Cullinane risk for the ones he loved?

The answers were the same: everything, of course.

Still, an opportunity would have to be cultivated. It would all have to be done carefully. Rumors would have to be placed with consummate care, rumors that would have to be discredited in the appropriate quarters, only to be reinforced and believed elsewhere, to prepare the way to tempt Karl Cullinane away from his empire, away from Home.

No. Not to tempt him. To force him away.

I am cleverer than you are, Karl Cullinane. I will take the extra step. Plant the rumors, and wait. That was the key. The emperor would, someday, have to go for the sword. Perhaps he could be hurried along.

It would be tricky, but it could be done. Slowly, quietly, carefully.

It must be done. And it will be done.

One Year Before, in Wehnest:
Doria and Elmina

I'm worried about Karl, Doria thought.

"Doria, Doria," Elmina chided as she shook her head, sending the cowl of her robes falling back to her shoulders, revealing the stringy black hair that had been hidden beneath.

The fish-belly pallor of Elmina's skin would have been shocking under other circumstances, but here it was to be expected. It was almost reassuring, because it spoke of healing. Healing, even when the healing consisted only of stabilizing someone as badly wounded as their present patient, drained magical, physical, and even mental reserves; Elmina had just pushed all of hers as far as possible.

"Worry isn't for us, Doria. Only soothing. Only restoration. Only healing." Trembling with weakness, Elmina laid a soothing hand on the arm of their patient, an unwashed peasant who had been brought to the Hand temple in Wehnest, barely alive after being carried into town by the same ox cart that had accidentally been pulled over him, its ironclad wheels shattering an arm, crushing his ribcage, rupturing his spine.

Doria nodded. "Healing is for us," she agreed, then laid her hands on their patient.

The farmer wasn't in good shape, but he was alive, and the damage was repairable.

The first priority had been to prevent the screaming man's life from deserting him, and the second to quell his pain. Elmina had done both. The result left the man unconscious but safe, the pooled blood in his crushed chest refusing to either clot or flow from his body.

"Doria . . ."

"I know. Shhh, Elmina; be still now."

Doria licked her lips once, and reached back into her mind and soul for the spell. It wasn't as though she was speaking deliberately; she simply let the words depart from her as she began to chant the evanescent words of healing, letting the power flow gently with the airy syllables. And, as always, she was never totally certain if the warm glow surrounding the peasant was in the air, or her eyes, or her mind.

But, as always, it warmed her while it healed him.

The split and shattered pieces of bone welded themselves together, while torn muscle and snapped sinew flowed gently back into their proper places around the now-reassembled substructure, joined by nerves and blood vessels snaking their way in and assembling themselves.

The last was the blood itself. Crushed red blood cells and—worse, more difficult, more draining—shattered platelets reassembled themselves and then flowed through capillary walls, until they stood waiting, poised in place in veins and arteries, a column of soldiers waiting for the command to march to be given.

The command was given: The blood flowed; the healing continued until the horrid, deathly pallor left the man's face and his consciousness gradually returned to him,

"Very nicely done, Doria," Elmina said. She laid a finger across the farmer's dry, cracked lips, still flecked with dried blood and vomit. "Be still, friend. You are under the care of the Hand, and all will be well with you."

She turned to Doria.

"As it will be with you, sister, in one manner or another."

Doria nodded. What the Matriarch called her "feel for the way of things" was growing daily, and that feeling pointed to a confrontation. At least one.

And then there was the memory of the Matriarch speaking to Karl:

Never will the Hand aid you again, she had said. *Never will the Hand aid you again.*

"I understand." Elmina nodded. "But for now, we must . . ." She swallowed and swayed for a moment, then strengthened, her wan, almost transparent skin seemingly gaining thickness while it gained color. "For now," she said, her voice gaining force, "we must restore our powers. Both of us. And we will continue to do so, but perhaps someday, we will do so for different reasons, is it not so?"

Doria nodded. "It is so."

A Few Tendays Before, Just Outside of the Old
Warrens: Ahira and Walter Slovotsky

"I'm worried about Karl," Ahira said, leaning back in his rocking chair, squinting against the setting sun.

"You worry too much. Do more; worry less." Slovotsky glared as the dwarf eyed Karl's latest letter. Again.

Not that there wasn't enough to worry about.

For one thing, it had recently occurred to Ahira that Walter Slovotsky's daughter Janie was getting close to husband-high, and there wasn't even anyone of the right species around.

Ahira chuckled to himself. *I don't mind being a dwarf, but I wouldn't want my goddaughter to marry one.*

"You worry too much," the big man repeated, whittling at a piece of green pine as they sat on their benches at the entrance to the Endell warrens, waiting for the night to come on. "Particularly at the end of the day. I thought you were a dwarf, not a human. You're supposed to enjoy dusk."

"There's some truth in that, at least." Ahira nodded. Evening was the best time of the day, as the annoyances and labors of the day vanished into the oncoming night.

Or were supposed to, at any rate. That was the trouble with Slovotsky; while he tried to get along, he didn't have a dwarf's feeling for timing.

Not his fault.

> *Blood and bone are just clay; the world wears them down,*
> *With a moan and a grind, a grunt and a groan,*
> *A shudder, a quiver, a frown.*
> *So let the world go away, at the end of the day—*

—the old evenchant began; a simple reminder that night was a time for rest and sleep, and that the worries of tomorrow could well wait until tomorrow.

A simple idea, but dwarves were good at understanding simplicity. It came with the territory.

Timing was a part of that simplicity.

As the two friends sat chatting, the dwarves who lived in the so-called Old Warrens—although they were not the oldest warrens in Endell—were finishing their day, preparing to return to the warmth and safety of the warrens for the night.

Some astride small ponies and others afoot, they all made their way home to this entrance to the warrens, preparing for the onset of darkness. Some sweaty and dusty from the day's work in the King Maherrelen's fields, a rare few returning home with wagons laden with trade goods from the south—all managed to make the final or only leg of their journey so that they arrived at the entrance just before sunset, no later.

Dwarves had a talent, a gift, for timing, the way that humans excel at swimming. Dwarves didn't swim, of course. Dwarves couldn't even float.

Humans, after all, were only barely less dense than water, and barely able to float; dwarves' greater density of muscle and bone would make a dwarf sink like a stone.

That was a loss. James Michael Finnegan had always had plea-surable associations with swimming; supported in a flotation vest, the pool had been one of the few places his disloyal body couldn't betray him.

Swimming was one of the few things that Ahira missed from his days as a human. Perhaps the only thing. It was hard to think of another. But swimming...

Humans swim as well as they commit treachery and cruelty, Ahira thought, and then was suddenly ashamed of himself.

Some of his best friends were human, after all. Of all the people he loved, the ones he loved most dearly were humans: Walter, his wife Kirah, Janie—always special to him—and little Doria Andrea Slovotsky. If D.A. wasn't the cutest baby in the universe, then it was because Janie had just edged her out.

And then there was Karl Cullinane, who had brought him back, quite literally, from the dead—Karl was human, too. As had been Chak, and all the others....

And he had been human, once.

He had been the crippled James Michael Finnegan, once. Nev-ermore, thankfully, nevermore.

Humans weren't all bad, though. But still... dwarves were dif-ferent. As was where they lived, and how they lived.

Night was a dangerous time north of the Eren regions. One of the few things that the large, clumsy humans were good at was killing creatures they thought dangerous; dwarves preferred to avoid

dangers when they could, to fight when they must. A crusade—
be it the rabid imperialism of some of the Popes on the Other
Side or what Ahira's human half still felt was Karl Cullinane's
completely justified crusade on This Side—was something foreign
to dwarves.

Moderation came naturally to dwarves, but even that was
modified with judiciousness: moderation in moderation. Violence
was bad, of course, but still, one sometimes fought in self-defense.
The dwarven north was a cold land, with a short growing season;
sometimes it was necessary to fight for pay, as well. But only when
necessary.

Only when necessary.

"Time to go in," Ahira said.

With a groaning that suggested a much greater age than his less
than forty years, Walter Slovotsky got to his feet, and belted his
outer coat more tightly around himself.

"I am," he announced, "getting far too old for this."

"You are," Ahira said, "full of shit."

"True, true," Slovotsky said as they walked past the outer doors,
nodding genially down at the guards armed with their pikes and
hornbows. They passed into the warrens. "It's one of my many
charms."

"Right."

The floors and walls of the Old Warrens were worn smooth by
centuries of use; the floors in the Grand Concourse were repaved
with fresh flatrock every few decades, as the endless tramping of
innumerable dwarven feet could wear away even the hardest stone.

"You really worried about him?" Slovotsky asked as they turned
into the King's Tunnel, pausing only a moment to exchange a few
words with one of the king's courtiers, who listened respectfully,
then hurried away. King Maherrelen valued the services of both
of them, but particularly Slovotsky; there was only one Ag School–
trained person anywhere on This Side, and that caused Walter
Slovotsky to have almost as much value to a sometimes-hungry
Endell as Lou Riccetti had to Home.

"I am," Ahira said. "I am worried about him. You read his letter."

Ahira held back an urge to run for the cave entrance and shout
for someone to saddle a horse. The vision of himself climbing
aboard a pony and galloping away pulled him with a force almost
physical. Ahira didn't at all like the implications of Karl's suggestion

that he and Walter see if they could get some information in Pandathaway.

Both panic and Pandathaway are supposed to be history to me, he thought.

His second reflex, his contrary impulse, was to go to his rooms and dash off a letter—

> *Dear Karl,*
> *Not only no, but hell, no.*

—but even if that was what he finally decided to do, there was no point in hurrying with an answer. The letter from Karl was five, maybe six tendays old, and it would take that long for Ahira's response to get to Holtun-Bieme.

While there was a fast and effective postal service in Holtun-Bieme—often known as the Dragon Express due to its famous, if irregular, carrier—messages sent by trader took a long time to get from Biemestren to the Old Warrens. It would have been nice if Ellegon could have made his way this far north more often, but in order to do that, the dragon had to detour, to avoid flying over populated territory; what with his other obligations, they were lucky to see Ellegon once a year.

Dwarves understand timing, he thought.

Then he chuckled as he once again caught himself blaming his human half for the tendency to panic.

"He really might go for the sword," Ahira said, bringing a bitten thumbnail up to his mouth and chewing on it for a moment. "My info is the same as his; there've been rumors in Pandathaway that he's going to make a play for it."

Ahira shook his head. Could Karl really be halfwitted enough to announce an intention to try to get the sword? That couldn't possibly make sense; it'd be like a general sending a signal to the enemy saying, "Our army is coming through; please plant landmines here."

"So?"

"So . . ." Ahira shook his head. "You weren't there the last time. It's spooky. I don't like any of it."

"Magical." Slovotsky reached up and tinged a fingernail against an overhead glowsteel. "I've run into magical things before. As have we all."

"But you weren't *there.* I was. I don't like swords that tell their bearer to keep them, and I don't like swords that were made by that crazy bastard Arta Myrdhyn to kill wizards with, and I particularly don't like the fact that the breach between Pandathaway's Wizards' Guild and the Slavers' Guild is opening a chance for Karl to making a run down Melawei-way."

"Melawei-way? Yik."

The dwarf shrugged as he doffed his outer coat. He tapped the fresh hogshead in the corner, and tipped it to pour himself and Slovotsky each a cool pitcher of ale. While dwarf ale wasn't great, it was okay; you got used to the bitterness after a few years.

"I don't like the idea; you don't like the words." Ahira drained his pitcher and poured himself another.

"So?"

"So," Ahira said, pounding his fist against the tunnel wall, "what are we going to *do* about it?"

Slovotsky dropped into a chair and took a long pull at his ale. "We've chewed this over a hundred times before, and I still don't see more than a few choices."

"And they are?"

"Well, we could put our heads together on another letter and try to talk Karl out of whatever nonsense he's planning—which isn't going to work; he's as stubborn as you are—or we could just keep working on improving Maherrelen's yield and chewing over what we're going to do until we are too old to do anything, including chew our own food, or we could try for the sword ourselves or try something equally impossible, go charging in like a couple of bulls in a china shop. Or . . ."

"Or?"

"Or we could make sure that your godchildren and Kirah—"

"—your children and your wife—"

"—will be taken care of in case things go to hell, then get ourselves a team together and get back in business—nose around Pandathaway like Karl asked."

"I don't think we can." Ahira shook his head. "We don't have the money to hire and outfit a team."

"Wrong, short one. . . . You think Maherrelen's going to try to stop us from leaving?"

"No, of course not." Fealty and ownership are different concepts; dwarves made lousy slaves, and worse slave-owners. Doing anything that smacked of ownership would never occur to the king and would be dismissed more in puzzlement than in anger if someone else brought it up.

"You think he's going to let us go out and get killed?" Slovotsky raised an eyebrow.

Their Other Side knowledge made the two of them very valuable. The fact that both Home and Holtun-Bieme would extend both hospitality and trust—and, if necessary, succor—to anyone carrying a safe-conduct signed by either of them added to their value. Granted, absent the two of them, Home would not necessarily put an embargo on wootz sold to the dwarves, but it might not be so easy for someone without a letter of introduction from Slovotsky or Ahira to deal there.

And where else was Maherrelen going to get wootz besides Home?

Risk doing without wootz? No way—dwarven blades had long been among the best around, but wootz, Lou Riccetti's recreated raw Damascus steel, was the source of even finer weapons than had been possible before: lighter, suppler, stronger blades than This Side had ever seen.

"No, he doesn't want us to go out and get killed," Ahira said. "And he's not going to stop us. So?"

"So, I think we can count on our patron providing us with some help."

"Eh?"

"Well, I think our lives are worth a bit of insurance—the premium being a decent-sized team of dwarf warriors for our escort."

"That could work." Ahira nodded. "But you're dancing around the subject. Do you want to, or not?"

"You want it formal? Fine: I move we head Home with a load of blades, trade them in on a bigger load of wootz, and then head for Pandathaway, trading the wootz for less distinctive merchandise as we go. I further move that we nose around Pandathaway, find out what we can, and then make our way to Biemestren and talk to Karl. Your vote?"

"Mmm . . ." Ahira sipped his beer. "It has been a while since we've been back Home, and far too long since we've seen Andy and the boy."

"You giving in?"

Why Slovotsky needed Ahira to take the responsibility for their going back into harm's way was something that the dwarf didn't comprehend.

On the other hand, why *Ahira* needed *Slovotsky* to take responsibility for their sticking their faces back into the buzz saw was something the dwarf didn't understand, either.

Ahira nodded. "I'm giving in. Happy?"

"Yup." Slovotsky laughed. "Besides, I kind of miss Lou."

"You and Riccetti were never all that close."

"I didn't say I'm as fond of him as I am of you, little friend, just that I miss the Engineer. He is, in case you haven't worked it out, the most important of us all."

Ahira shook his head. Arta Myrdhyn didn't believe that; he'd made it clear that the most important one of all of them was Jason, the one who the sword was waiting for.

Slovotsky smiled. "And en route, I'm going to teach the dwarves that song that you hate so much."

"What song?"

"You know, the one that goes 'Heigh-ho, heigh-ho . . .'"

"Like hell you will."

"Like hell I won't."

"Like hell—"

"James?"

Ahira started. Walter almost never called him by his former name. "Yes, Walter?"

The big man stood and stretched. "I've got to tell you, I love my family and I like our life here, but—dammit, man . . ." Slovotsky shook his head and sighed.

"But you feel more alive now than you have in a long time, eh?"

"You too, huh?" Slovotsky raised an eyebrow. "Yeah."

"Not me, too—it may be necessary, but I don't like it. Just remember how much fun you thought it'd be later on, when you're dancing on the end of a spear."

Slovotsky smiled. "I'll try real hard."

"You would."

"You betcha. It'd be my last chance." Slovotsky drained his ale. "Now?"

"And now, shut up and have some more ale. Then let's go spend some time with your wife and my godchildren. Enjoy them while we're here—and let's get really drunk tonight. We're going to go back into training in the morning—right after we talk to the king."

"Training?"

"Training. We hit the road in a couple of tendays."

When the subject of going back in harm's way came up, Ahira had taken command before realizing it. He decided that he liked the feeling of being back in charge—even though he was only in charge of a party of two, as of now—instead of merely being an adviser, no matter how valued the counsel.

"Fair enough," Slovotsky said, with his usual Walter Slovotsky smile, the smile that asked, "Wasn't God clever to invent me?"— all the while making it clear that the question was purely and manifestly rhetorical.

"Always have to get the last word, don't you?"

"Yup." Slovotsky smiled. Again.

Only a Little While Before, in a House on Faculty Row: Arthur Simpson Deighton

"I'm worried about that boy," Arthur Simpson Deighton said, puffing on his pipe. "I am Arthur Simpson Deighton," he insisted to himself, "not Arta Myrdhyn. On This Side, I have to be. Please."

It wasn't just that the web of lies he'd used to sustain his Deighton persona were important to him, but his attachment to his Deighton-self was a too-light anchor in a sea of madness that grew worse slowly, inexorably. Once that madness had raged uncontrollably, a killing tempest. But for a long time the sea had been calm.

"The calm is deceptive, as it always was."

No matter how long the calm, it was only the calm at the eye of the storm. He had remained in the eye for ages, but it was only a chimera of tranquillity.

"Only an illusion."

There was nobody to hear him in the darkened room in the little house on Faculty Row; Deighton was, as had lately become commonplace for him, speaking to himself. Too much power use.

"Too much power use."

It wasn't always crazy for one to speak to oneself, of course, but a wizard had no business doing that, just as a gunpowder maker had no business smoking a cigarette while he ground his saltpeter and sulfur crystals. Words and symbols always had to be chosen carefully, to be impressed judiciously and certainly into the mind, the symbols and their power to be husbanded until the moment that their power was to be used.

Imagine a wizard moving his lips and muttering a flame spell as he impressed it into his mind: it would happen then and there, directed at nobody-knew-what.

For a wizard, talking to oneself was dangerous.

And foolish.

And, quite literally, insane.

Arthur Simpson Deighton was aware of the reasons for his talking to himself, but there wasn't anything he could do about it.

It could get worse.

It had been worse, away from the eye.

And it would be worse, if only for a short while. Only a short while, he hoped, fervently.

"Getting too old, Arta, that we are. 'Boy' indeed—he's almost forty years old, almost forty years he's lived through his own time. Not slow years like here."

Even so, it was hard to keep covering for the missing, and there were always fragile threads in the web of deception that had to be mended. School records were the easiest: Those could be fixed physically, with only a little power use necessary to rearrange a few molecules of ink or the magnetic alignment on a computer disk; less to gain the cooperation of a secretary who would then forget why, how, and even *that* she had allowed a philosophy professor access to records that he had no right to.

Worse were the parents and brothers and lovers and friends, all of whom had to be located and dealt with, before all hell broke loose. A suggestion to be planted *here*, a lie to be given substance *there* . . .

Eventually, the whole skein would unravel. But by then, the affair should be ended.

Just for a moment, he opened his mind to his gibbering enemy, to the insanity that lay on the Other Side.

Soon it ends, he thought.

Soon.

Please.

"But I'm still worried about the boy."

CHAPTER THREE:

Homecoming

To me, fair friend, you never can be old,
For as you were when first your eye I eyed,
Such seems your beauty still.

—William Shakespeare

"Honey, I'm home," Karl Cullinane called out as he bounded up the steps to the second floor—the residence floor—of Biemestren Castle, giving a smile and a nod in passing to the two maids who were sweeping the halls, making a special point to give a broader smile to the uglier of the two. It was a close call.

Why once he'd had an image of maids as being young and attractive was something he couldn't understand. He had yet to meet one who didn't sport at least a small mustache and a large potbelly, except for those who had a large mustache and at least a small potbelly.

Unfair, Karl, unfair, he thought. And definitely the sort of thing not to say aloud; Andy would call that a blatant example of male chauvinism.

Even if it was true.

He sprinted down the carpeting and turned into the hall that led to the outer room of their suite, stopped to hang his scabbarded sword on a peg by the door, and hopped first on one foot and then the other as he doffed his boots.

He looked at the sword for a moment, as it hung there in its plain leather and steel scabbard.

Sword ...

For the past couple of years, traders had been carrying rumors that there were people in Pandathaway who thought that Karl was someday going to go after Arta Myrdhyn's sword; that Karl had reconciled with the far-off Arta Myrdhyn, and intended to reclaim the magical artifact, left for centuries, waiting for his hand, his hand alone.

He smiled.

Good. For one thing, it wasn't true; the sword was waiting for Jason, not Karl.

Not my son, Deighton. You leave my son alone.

Still, the rumors had started. And that opened a world of possibilities.

Possibly that little bastard Ahrmin could be tricked into lying in wait, somewhere in Melawei, and if he was left to stew long enough, if the matter was handled carefully enough, Karl might be able to locate him, to trap the trapper, and end the threat to bring Jason into something that Arta Myrdhyn planned.

Perhaps someday he would make his way to Melawei, but not for the sword. Let Ahrmin set a trap there, with the sword as bait, perhaps. Karl would ignore the cheese and break the teeth of that trap.

Someday ... but in the meantime, there was work to do.

He lifted his hands and tugged at the amulet that hung from his neck by a leather thong. There was nothing to worry about. The amulet would have protected him as it signaled him that someone had tried to use magic to read his mind—there were only a few people who knew that Jason was the one who the sword was waiting for, and they would keep their mouths shut.

Ellegon knew, of course, but the dragon wouldn't tell.

Not my son, Deighton. You leave my son alone.

Karl had often thought about sending someone trusted into Pandathaway to snoop. The trouble was, the people he trusted were already too valuable in Holtun-Bieme; a paid agent might well want to collect from both sides, and Karl was absolutely certain that he didn't want Pandathaway to get any confirmation of his interest.

Possibly it was time to try to develop some less trustworthy, less valuable spies. People he wouldn't mind losing.

That wasn't acceptable, he decided. Using people as pawns wasn't something Karl Cullinane would choose to do; it was something he'd had to do all too often.

As far as Pandathaway went, maybe Slovotsky would pick up on Karl's hints and give it a try. Walter could probably spend half a day and a handful of coins and find out what the standing of Ahrmin was, how hot the Slavers' Guild still was to get its hands on Karl—was the present lull a function of a loss of interest, or were there plans brewing?

But there was no rush in trying to lure Ahrmin from Pandathaway; Karl couldn't leave now to go after him, even if there was an opportunity.

Best to let matters rest, for now. Let a couple more years pass before Karl went up against Ahrmin. It was important for Jason to get further along in his education; it was vital to calm down the bitterness between Holtun and Bieme and not let it break into war, or the Nyphs would try to lop off a piece of Bieme.

Enough worry for now. I deserve a bit of rest, at least for a day.

There had been a time when he had been able to insist on Karl's Day Off, and get it.

That was another country, he thought, *but at least the wench who insisted on it isn't dead. Pretty damn lively, as a matter of fact.*

Still, I just managed to piss on a spark of rebellion in Arondael and prevent it from turning into a blaze, so I am treating myself to a day off. Period.

Barefoot, luxuriating in the feel of the thick carpet, he walked into the bedroom that he shared with his wife, much to the disapproval of the house staff, who felt that royalty was supposed to act like royalty.

There was nobody there.

"Andy?" There was no sign of her, nothing except for a pile of clothes in the middle of the floor.

A chill washed across him. He dove across the bed, rolled across the floor to the weapons case, and came up with a flintlock pistol and a short stabbing sword.

As he checked to be sure the pan was charged—it was—and then cocked the pistol, he heard the hiss of distant water against stone.

Asshole. He almost laughed at himself, but he was afraid of how it might come out.

"Andy?" he called out, forcing a calm voice against the backbeat of the audible pounding of his heart. "That you?"

"No. It's Valerie Bertinelli," came the sarcastic reply. "Quick, come join me before my husband gets home."

He sighed both in great relief and mild self-disgust as he uncocked the pistol, then put the gun and blade away. He leaned his head against the bathroom door and chuckled under his breath as he shrugged out of the rest of his clothes and tossed them to the floor.

Not everything has to be a goddam emergency, after all. He took a deep breath and forced his idiot heart to stop pounding. Still, after all these years, he had to force his battle reflexes into the background. He raised his hands above his head and stretched broadly, feeling tense shoulder muscles hesitate, then hesitantly relax.

This is our home. It is not a battleground, he thought, repeating it to himself, like it was a mantra.

"Hi there," he said, as he swung the door open.

She shook her head as she stood in the shower, soap-slick and lovely, outlined against the murky glass window beyond. Even in her late thirties, there was only the slightest sagging of her breasts; her belly, thighs, and bottom were still as firm and supple as an adolescent girl's. Her nose held the slight bend that he had always loved, and the warm brown eyes were full of intelligence and life.

Then again, I'm prejudiced.

"Hi yourself," she said. "How's the hero business?"

"It's dirty work; pass the soap," he said, as he joined her in the shower.

To the best of his knowledge, their shower was the only such thing in the Middle Lands. Designed by Karl and built by the apprentices of the local master engineer, Ranella, it was one of the luxuries that Karl didn't like to share with others; the shower was *his.* He didn't feel selfish; apparently, it was an acquired taste. Jason, for example, far preferred the traditional bath.

The room above had been emptied, a large, sealed iron tank installed, and the appropriate plumbing built and connected. The hot-water tank was supplied by a pipe from the main cistern on the top floor of the castle, the flow controlled by a float-ball valve arrangement like the workings of an Other Side toilet—which was exactly where Karl had lifted the idea, although Ranella had played with it a bit—which kept the tank full. The water was heated by insulated copper coils that ran from the tank into the always-burning Franklin-style stove.

Mixed with cold water through another valve, the rig provided a controllable, if somewhat primitive and low-pressure, shower. The only trouble with the damn thing was that it tended to run out of hot water all too quickly, and was definitely more suited for a quick individual shower than a leisurely shared one; by the time he'd finished soaping himself thoroughly, the water was already starting to chill, even though it was now all coming from the hot-water tank; the heat output of the woodstove couldn't meet the demand.

"Hurry up a little, will you?" he said as Andy dawdled at rinsing the soap from her hair.

She glared at him, and then shrugged as she stepped out of the water and laid her hand on the now barely warm hot-water pipe. "I guess it is a bit tepid. Did you have a tough time in Arondael?"

"Tough?" He shook his head. "Not particularly. Just a bit nerve-wracking. Par game," he said, knowing that she would understand how he meant it.

The way Karl figured it, "par" was a reasonable job: the mission accomplished, no innocents seriously injured or killed. That nicely described his attempt at intimidating Arondael: He was certain no innocents had been killed, and he was willing to bet that the baron would stay intimidated.

"Well, maybe you deserve a treat—I'm going to go towel off, but first . . ." Her voice trailed off as her eyes grew vague; harsh words issued from between her lips, words that could only vanish on the ears and in the mind.

She held the thumb and forefinger of her right hand a couple of inches apart, the barely warm copper hot-water pipe between them. Sharp tongues of blue-hot fire leaped between her fingertips, instantly heating the copper pipe between her fingers to a dull red which quickly spread up the pipe and into the stone ceiling.

Her eyes opened as the spell ended, and she grabbed a small washcloth to protect her fingers as she closed the hot-water valve partway, opening the cold-water valve to prevent the now almost boiling water from scorching the two of them.

"Thanks," he said, pulling her close for a quick kiss.

She reached her arms around his waist and laid her head against his chest, her long wet hair tickling his belly as it dangled. "Too bad you've so much to do this afternoon, hero, or we could have ourselves a good time. A real good time."

"I've got a lot to do?" He raised an eyebrow as he cupped her bottom with both hands. "I didn't know that."

"You seem to, too damn often," she said, pushing him gently away. She padded off barefoot, toweling off her hair, adding perhaps a bit more hipswing than was absolutely necessary.

Karl watched her leave, enjoying the view, feeling vaguely guilty.

He quickly rinsed himself off in the hot water, and strained his mind as he thought, *Ellegon?*

What is it? came from far away; he could barely hear Ellegon's mental voice.

Then he remembered that the dragon was down at the knacker's, and he shuddered. Even if it was necessary, Karl didn't like the idea of knackers, and the thought of Ellegon dining on the leavings bothered Karl.

If you become a vegetarian, I may. Bets?

Karl shook his head, dismissing the subject. *Anything really pressing this afternoon?*

Mmm ... well, there's a trial—that poacher from Arondael. You did want to supervise it, and see how the boy handles it.

Does Thomen really need me? Or do you think he can solo on this one?

He can handle it—I told you, the poacher is guilty. Makes a nice backboard, eh?

Well ...

You will have to show up for sentencing tomorrow. If Thomen doesn't mess up and turn him loose today.

Okay; then tune me out for the afternoon.

Humph. Oversexed—

Enough.

Have a nice time. The dragon was suddenly gone from his mind.

He grabbed a towel and started to dry himself off as he called out, "Hey, Andy?"

"Yes?"

"Are you dressed yet?"

"No . . ."

"You in any real hurry to get dressed?"

"Well . . . no," she answered back, perhaps a bit too coquettishly. "Why?"

"I'm taking the afternoon off."

"Afternoon?"

"You said I deserved a treat, didn't you?"

"I did at that," she said. "Braggart. Afternoon, indeed."

He could hear her grin.

CHAPTER FOUR:

Home

When we are planning for posterity, we ought to remember that virtue is not hereditary.

—Thomas Paine

Walter saw the distant flash of a telescope several times that morning, which didn't surprise him: He'd seen an occasional rider paralleling their course for days; the nearer they got to Home, the more intense the scrutiny.

He nodded in silent approval and rode on, noticing with some pride that none of the others had caught it. The Home watchers were taking some pains to keep their attention inconspicuous.

Still, by the time Walter, Ahira, and their dwarvish escort reached the top of the ridge overlooking the valley that the elves called Varnath, Walter felt like he'd been thoroughly frisked.

A simple "Assume the position" would have sufficed, guys.

Not that Walter Slovotsky had anything against deviousness—in fact, he preferred it, all things being equal—but there was a time for a simple confrontation.

If it'd been his show . . .

Then again, it's not my show. Not anymore. Not even to the extent that it was when he was seconding Karl, back in the old days when they were on a raiding team together.

He didn't yearn for that time, not really. Food was eaten cold, then, for fear that the slavers would see a cooking fire; they had to sleep lightly, remembering the face of a man who hadn't. Those had been days of strain and nights wrenched in fear, all the time hoping, praying, that the next man doomed to fall to the ground, clutching at the crossbow bolt protruding from his mouth, *was* the next man, not Emma Slovotsky's baby boy.

No, he didn't miss the fighting.

But there had been a certain something to those days, something that the last years just hadn't had. Something hard to put a finger on.

Maybe it was that the heartbeats seemed stronger when you could hear each and every one, Walter decided. That was it.

And he cursed himself for an idiot. "There is an old Chinese curse, 'May you live in interesting times,'" he muttered to himself, before remembering that, after all, foolish consistency was the hobgoblin of little minds.

That made him feel better; Walter Slovotsky didn't want to risk the size of his mind by being unnecessarily consistent.

"There's also an old American saying," Ahira said. "Goes like this: 'People who talk to themselves are a bit loose between the eardrums.'"

Slovotsky dug his heels in a bit deeper and kicked his horse into a half-canter, smiling quietly to himself as the dwarves behind him cursed, spurring their own mounts. Dwarves and horses—even well-tempered ponies like Geveren and the rest of their escort were riding—were renowned for not getting along.

"You're a mean man, Walter Slovotsky," Ahira said, bouncing along on the back of his animal. He was the only dwarf to ride a full-sized horse, although he and his gray gelding didn't seem to like each other's company particularly well.

Then again, that was Ahira: He always seemed to pick a gray gelding that he didn't get along particularly well with. His swearing at his horse seemed almost as much a part of the dwarf as the clanking of the patched chainmail vest and the huge, double-bladed battleaxe strapped to his saddle.

Nothing ever remains quite the same; there had been a time when Ahira carried a smaller axe, strapping it across his absurdly broad chest. He had traded that axe in on a bigger one, one that was almost the size he was.

"Hey, Walter, doesn't that look like—" The dwarf's homely face creased in puzzlement, then broke into a broad smile. "It is! *Wheeee!*"

"Huh?"

"At the customs house—it is!" Swearing, the dwarf kicked his horse into a full canter.

The oversized log cabin that stood as the Home customs station was only a blur near the horizon to Slovotsky, but Ahira must have seen something. Clearly, it wasn't anything to worry about, or Ahira would have sounded some sort of alarm, but . . .

Slovotsky stood in the saddle and called out to the dwarf who was driving the flatbed wagon.

"Hey, Geveren," he said, putting the accent firmly on the first syllable of the dwarf's name, "I'm going to go catch up with Ahira. Take a *little* time, if you need to—"

"Just a *small* amount," Geveren said, a gap-toothed smile peeking through his beard. "Only a *short* while."

Slovotsky's short jokes didn't bother the dwarves; to them, they were the right height, and humans were stretched vertically, although not as badly as elves.

"—but you bring the rest in," Slovotsky finished. Then, remembering that none of these dwarves had ever been to Home before, he added, "And be prepared to put up with a thorough inspection at customs without taking offense—I don't want to hear about your giving the inspectors any trouble."

The dwarf smiled, nodded, and waved; Slovotsky spurred his horse after Ahira.

By the time Slovotsky's mare had gotten herself worked up to a full gallop, they were almost at the customs house. Ahira seemed to be wrestling with some human, while another, holding a flintlock carbine at the ready, looked on.

One hand on a pistol, Slovotsky brought the horse to a quick halt and vaulted out of the saddle, only to see that Ahira was hugging a full-sized human, a boy perhaps fifteen or so; tall and a bit gangly, he awkwardly patted the dwarf's back—

"Son of a bitch—Jason Cullinane!" Slovotsky dropped his hand away from the pistol's butt, noticing how the guard relaxed only microscopically, only lowering the hammer of his carbine when a strangely familiar metal rattling issued from the interior of the customs house.

A grizzled face leaned out and nodded. "Greetings, Walter Slovotsky and Ahira. You are welcome Home."

"Betcher ass," Slovotsky said, then switched back to Erendra. "That is, I thank you. It's good to be back."

The dwarf released the boy and turned to Walter. "Can you believe how much he's grown? Last time we saw him, he was tiny."

Slovotsky nodded. "Damn, but he wasn't much taller than this," he said, winking at Jason as he held his hand half a foot above Ahira's head.

"You'll pay for that, Slovotsky," the dwarf said, with patently false menace.

Jason walked over to Walter and held out a hand. "Hello, Uncle Walter," he said, perhaps a bit stiffly. The grip was firm, but it was clear that the boy was trying too hard. No problem—he was just growing faster up than outside, and probably faster outside than inside. It looked like he might easily end up as tall as his father; right now, his eyes were almost on Slovotsky's level.

Slovotsky shook his head. "A handshake is just not going to make it, kiddo." He seized Jason in a bear hug, sighing to himself when the boy's returning grip was only perfunctory.

"Damn, but it's good to see you, boy. How's everyone?" he asked as he let Jason go.

Jason smiled. "Just fine, as of a couple of tendays ago." He pursed his lips for a moment. "I'm sure that Mom and Dad would have wanted me to—"

"Sure, sure, and pass our best wishes along, when you see them. Which'll be when?"

Jason shrugged. "Another couple tendays. Ellegon's supposed to pick up some supplies here for Daven's team, and pick up Valeran—"

Slovotsky smiled. "Val's here? I haven't seen him since we gave your father the crown." *A good man to have around in a fight. Or just to drink with.*

Jason frowned. "Dad has him baby-sitting me," he said, making it evident that he didn't think he needed any watching. He brightened. "And teaching me swordsmanship, too. In any case, Ellegon's supposed to pick him and Bren and—"

"Bren Adahan? The Holtish baron?"

Jason whistled in irritation at being interrupted again. "Yes, *him.* Dad has him here, partly to be taught by Lou Riccetti, but mainly to keep an eye on me, like Valeran does." The boy tried to shrug away the notion that he needed watching over. "I don't have to put up with it for much longer. Then Ellegon will pick up Valeran and me on his way out; we're going to be his tenders while he makes a sweep to Ehvenor and then back Home. Now, what are you two doing here?"

Walter tried to smile disarmingly. "Whatsamatter, boyo, aren't you glad to see us?" he asked, trying to change the subject. Jason's was a hard question to answer honestly, and Walter had no intention of doing so.

Anything involving Walter and Ahira's plans to skulk around Pandathaway had to be handled on a need-to-know basis.

Jason didn't.

Walter had no intention of telling Jason that he and Ahira were going to pick up some trade goods to take to Pandathaway to sell while they were trying to dig up word of either what Ahrmin was up to or what Ahrmin thought Karl was up to; if a rumor of intended spying reached Pandathaway, the spies in question might be easily detected.

Which would be hard on the spies.

So Walter Slovotsky broadened his smile and spread his hands. "Just doing a little business, and checking up on Lou. I take it—"

He was interrupted by the same rattling from the customs house. He furrowed his brow, finally noticing the wires strung on poles that led from the building and down the hill and into the valley. "Son of a—"

"Telegraph." Ahira smiled. "He's got a telegraph." He looked over toward Slovotsky. "How's your Morse?"

Slovotsky shook his head. "I just barely was able to learn enough to pound my clumsy way to a beginner's license, and that's more than twenty years ago. You?"

"Not even that close." Ahira lifted his right hand, making it shake. "Remember? I couldn't make a dit different from a dah, much less get up to twenty words per minute."

"And a telegraph means electricity—coal, you think? Lou used to say that he thought there was a seam of coal up in the hills."

"Could be, could be." Ahira nodded. "I think we'd better have words with the Engineer; he's been keeping secrets."

Jason cocked his head to one side. "Excuse me?"

"Secrets, secrets," Ahira said. "I thought Lou was going to tell us about any major advances, and this telegraph is—"

"No, not that. You said that you couldn't learn Morse. It doesn't seem hard."

Ahira's face darkened; Walter stepped in. "You know how your Uncle Ahira used to be a human, on the Other Side?"

"Yes, yes," Jason said, tapping his foot impatiently.

"Well, as a human he had a dysfunction. It's called muscular dystrophy—his muscles didn't work right."

"Oh," the boy said, clearly indifferent.

The idea of a permanent disease wasn't something he could identify with, Walter realized; any member of the upper class could afford the services of a good healer, and even a clumsy Spidersect cleric could help someone compensate for disobedient muscle and nerve better than could possibly be done by the most competent physician on the other side.

Some injuries, granted, were permanent, or close to it; Tennetty's eyes, the missing fingers on Karl's left hand, scars from where the body had healed itself imperfectly without benefit of healing draughts.

But muscles not working right? It was foreign to the boy's limited experience. Lucky kid.

Slovotsky walked over to the shack and leaned in. "Please tell the Engineer that Walter Slovotsky and Ahira are here, bringing a load of dwarven blades, raw silver, and fourteen hefty appetites."

The man inside began beating a rapid tattoo on the telegraph key.

Walter Slovotsky threw his arm around Jason's shoulder. "So tell me, what's this bullshit I hear about your dad going after the sword?"

"I haven't heard anything about it," Jason said, his face reflecting what appeared to be only honest puzzlement. "And I'd like to. Now."

You're taking on something of your father's imperiousness, Jason me boyo, and I don't like that much. Before you get to sing the blues, you gotta pay the dues.

"Make it a bit later, okay?" he said, trying to put just a trace of sternness in his voice. "We've had a long trip."

Jason visibly considered it for a moment, then nodded. "Agreed, Uncle Walter."

Slovotsky smiled. "Now, get on your horse. I want the ten-cent tour of Home—by way of the bathhouse, and with special attention to the brewery. Seems there's been some changes of late."

"Brewery?" Ahira smiled. "Good idea. While you do that, I'm

going to head for Lou—is he in the cave?" he asked, raising his voice and turning to the guard in the customs house.

"Yes, Ahira; I'll alert him that you're coming."

"That won't be—"

"Easyway, warfday," Slovotsky said. "Ememberay ouyay aren'tway ayormay," he added in pig latin, knowing that it took most of a lifetime of English speaking to be able to follow deliberate fracturing of the language.

Jason smiled and nodded his agreement, but the guard was puzzled. Which was just the way Slovotsky wanted it; no need to embarrass his friend in front of strangers.

"Right," the dwarf said. "And please ask him to tap a keg; I haven't had Homemade beer for far too long."

Taking another pull at his third tankard of beer, Ahira nodded in approval, both at the brew—either his memory and taste buds were going, or it was a *lot* better than it had been back when Ahira was mayor—and at the noisy machine Riccetti was patting the side of.

The beer was awfully good, he decided. Not quite up to the level of Genesee Cream, but at least as good as St. Pauli Girl.

The machine was impressive, too. "An honest-to-God boiler and generator—Lou, you did good," Ahira said, shouting over the clangor of the machinery. The machine was hot and noisy, and Ahira really didn't understand the need for the odd-looking piston arrangement that had the huge generator humming, but it clearly worked.

Riccetti smiled briefly. "Thank you," he shouted back. "It seems to do the job."

Ahira looked the human over carefully as they stood near the warren holding boiler and generator, the heat from the machine beating against them like a wave, despite the cross-draft ventilation.

The years hadn't been kind to Lou Riccetti; his unhealthy-looking skinniness had only gotten worse, and his head was now completely bald. His face and hands were splotched and scarred, and he walked with absolutely no spring in his step. The marriage to an ex-slave that Karl and Chak had arranged had been a profound failure; Danni had left with a trader several years ago.

But there was an unselfconscious forcefulness in his manner, something that Ahira had never even seen traces of in the old days.

"The phrase, Ahira," Riccetti shouted, "is 'happy as a pig in shit.' Which I am. Hang on a moment; I have to do a bit of business."

He raised a hand and beckoned to the nearest of the engineers, a chunky man in his mid-twenties, who trotted over and bent his head near Riccetti's mouth.

"Bast, you remember Ahira?"

"Sure." The tall, broad-shouldered engineer stuck out a calloused hand; the grip was firm, for a human. "Good to see you again."

"Have him buy you a drink later; we've got a lot of work for now," Riccetti said, dismissing the formalities. "Now, send the word out that the telegraph is going down for the night, and then hook up the DC generator around dark—and have Daherrin post extra guards, all armed with signal rockets."

"Trouble?" Bast asked, clearly perfunctorily.

"No, but I'm getting skittish in my old age."

"Good." Bast nodded. "We going to run the hydroxy rig?"

"Right; I want a long run—all through the night and into tomorrow. So break down the compressor, clean it, then put it back together—and cofferdam around the bottles; I don't want anything else to break if they go this time."

"They shouldn't. I think the new valves will hold."

"We'll see."

"That we will." Bast nodded and walked off.

Riccetti beckoned to Ahira, and the two of them exited into another warren, the clatter of the generator fading in the distance.

"I take it you're suitably impressed?" At Ahira's nod, Riccetti went on: "A year or so ago, Karl asked me for some plans for a telegraph—he wants to set one up over there—and that led to all of this. I think we can give him a nice price on the whole package, now that we found that new seam of hematite."

The warrens were a bustle of activity; sights, sounds, and smells.

Riccetti guided him down a lefthand turn and into the residence section of the warrens, and past a guard into the Engineer's quarters. The room hadn't changed much, although Riccetti's sleeping area was now a real bed instead of a simple pallet.

Over in the corner, the telegraph rattled constantly.

Riccetti seemed to give it only a small portion of his attention; the news was probably not terribly important, Ahira decided, but he approved of the idea of keeping something going down the lines at all times. The mere fact of information traveling up and down the line was reassuring.

But there was something that the young engineer had said. . . .

"Hydroxy?" Ahira asked.

"Right—just elementary electrolysis. Pour a direct current through a tub of water, collect up the bubbles with a nice blown-glass rig, and then run the gasses through a compressor—"

"Electric motor?"

"Next year; right now, it's literally horsepowered. In any case, we squeeze the glass into brass bottles, and we've got bottled gasses."

"I could have guessed that."

"Eh?"

"If you put some gas in a bottle, it's bottled gas."

"All sorts of uses for that," Riccetti said. "You can get a very hot welding flame with hydrogen alone."

"I know; nice." Ahira nodded.

"Wait until next year—if we've got the valve problem solved. We may have electric lights—Aeia, of all people, pointed out how she could give night classes to farmers if we had decent lighting."

Aeia . . . Ahira smiled.

The first time he'd seen Aeia, she'd been a badly brutalized little girl who had been rescued by Karl, Walter, and Chak from a slaver; she was skinny, knobby-kneed, and homely.

The last time he'd seen her, she was lovely, almost ready to burst into her prime as a woman. He was willing to bet heavily that by now she was a treat for the eyes.

"How's she doing?"

"Good, but . . . I don't think we're going to have her around much longer." Riccetti shook his head. "It may not be long at all. Don't you believe that Bren Adahan is here just to help Valeran keep an eye on Jason. Or learn from me, despite his sincere smile. He's chasing her, and hard."

"You disapprove?"

"Not really." Riccetti sat silent for a moment before answering. "I just wonder about ulterior motives. Including my own; she's a hell of a schoolteacher."

"Good point." Being married to the emperor's daughter—even an adopted daughter—was hardly a bad political move for a conquered Holtish baron. Of course, marriage to Adahan would mean that Aeia would have to leave Home, and maybe Lou was just suspicious because he wasn't all that thrilled with that idea.

Ahira would have to talk to her. "And how are things political?"

"No problem." Riccetti shrugged. "I've been having Petros handle most of the local politics for me—and as far as Khoral goes, all I have to do is delay wootz shipments whenever he makes annexation noises. Only trouble's been with the raiders."

Ahira didn't like the sound of that. "Bad?"

Riccetti shrugged. "More of too much of a good thing. With the way that we've cut into the guild in the vicinity, it's hard to find caravans—some of the raiders are giving up on the life, taking up farming or mining." He shook his head. "Others drink too much. We had a murder earlier this year. Couple of Daven's men tried to extort some money out of a farmer, and killed him when he said no."

That sounded stupid; at Ahira's puzzled look, Riccetti shook his head. "No, I don't think they intended to; they were just trying to rough him up." He shrugged. "Didn't make much difference when they were dancing on the end of a rope." Riccetti took a long pull at his beer. "I can still see their faces, Ahira, still . . ." He slapped himself on the knee. "But we've got to—"

He cut himself off as the rattling of the telegraph took up a more insistent clamor. "That's my call; hang on a second." He walked over and tapped out a quick tattoo on the brass telegraph key.

At the clattering response, his face whitened. "*Shit.* Did you hear that?"

"I don't know Morse, Lou."

"Oh. Sorry." Riccetti shook his head. "We've got a messenger from Khoral. There's been a slaver raid in Therranj . . . numbers to follow—I think that's Artyn, rushing the elf along—three days ago. Major raid . . . they hit a baronial capitol hard, took treasure and slaves—elves and humans. Khoral's soliciting our help. We can keep the treasure; he just wants the raiders punished and the elves freed."

Riccetti nodded to himself. "The old elf is learning. He can afford to lose a few pounds of gold to us more than to let them get away with a raid."

Ahira bounced nervously in his chair. "And what does he use for soldiers? Marshmallows?"

Riccetti shook his head. "Most of his troops are on the Melhrood border, not dispersed along the west. He is anticipating trouble with Melhrood; he wasn't looking for an attack from the west—we've got a peace treaty with Therranj. You started the negotiations for it, remember?"

"Yeah, a treaty. Not a mutual assistance pact. Mmm . . . still, it is slavers and all. . . ."

"Exactly." Riccetti looked at Ahira. "The only difficulty is, what with a lot of Daherrin's people up in the mines, we're deficient in manpower."

Ahira snorted. Riccetti was sounding more and more like a bureaucrat. "You mean you don't have enough warriors handy."

Riccetti glared at him. "It'll take at least a couple of days to bring them out and get them all organized; we'll have to send runners, since we haven't strung the telegraph wire that far."

Ahira walked over to a sideboard and uncorked a bottle of Riccetti's Best, tilting it back for a long swallow. The fiery liquor burned its way down his throat. "Okay. What can you do?"

"Maybe I could spare a hundred warriors, but a lot of them would be fairly inexperienced."

"Unblooded. That's not good."

Riccetti jerked his thumb toward the telegraph. "I don't know the size of the raiding party, but it's not going to be any smaller than a hundred. I just hope it isn't a lot larger."

He paused expectantly.

Deep inside, the thought of violence still frightened Ahira as much as it always did, save for the times when his rare berserker rages washed such feelings away in a red flood.

But he just shrugged. "You could use an additional dozen or so? Thirteen blooded dwarves, plus Walter." If there was a better recon man than Walter Slovotsky, Ahira had never even heard legends of him.

Riccetti looked at him for a long moment. "I think so." He tapped a rapid message on the key, then turned back to Ahira. "I'm ordering horses, weapons, and supplies for a party of a hundred and twenty—half of the scouts are to be diverted to finding the raiding party. And a war council. Petros, Bast, Daherrin, Daherrin's second, you, me, Slovotsky. Hmm . . . I'll add Valeran, Bren, Jason, Aeia—"

"Why Jason? Why Aeia, for that matter?"

"She's got as good a head on her shoulders as anyone I know. And *he* is Karl's heir; he's got to find out how to do things like this."

"Then it's on?"

Riccetti shook his head and momentarily chewed on his lower lip. "All that's on is a war council." He tapped on the key again. "For the time being."

Walter Slovotsky held his peace through most of the discussion. Everyone was talking about whether they should send a raiding party, and Walter wasn't interested in arguing over closed cases. It was clear from the start that Lou was going to dispatch a raiding party after the slavers, but was letting everyone burn out his concerns while the team's equipment was being loaded.

Slovotsky was impressed. Riccetti was getting clever; it was a trick Lou had probably picked up from Karl, and one Karl had picked up from Walter.

The counterraid was a necessity, both political and financial. For one thing, local raiding-team pickings had been too thin for too long—Daherrin's team hadn't hit on a good slaver caravan for better than a year, and many of his men and dwarves had taken up mining or cropping to fill in. The thought of a nice slaver caravan, heavily laden with an elf baron's treasury, was irresistible.

It would have been nice if they'd had Ellegon to do a skyside recon, but the dragon wasn't due for several days, at a minimum.

Even that squared nicely with Karl's doctrine, which had always been to try to stage raids just before the dragon's arrival—Ellegon's arrival as the air cavalry had saved more lives than Walter could count.

Still, some kind of recon was necessary. Walter had a hunch who was going to get to do one, once the slavers were located. That didn't bother him, just as it wouldn't have bothered Paderewski to play a few arpeggios on a piano.

There was one thing that did. . . .

"Lou—is there any chance that this could be some sort of diversion, some sort of trick? Could the guild be trying to divert the Home Guard?"

"There's a theoretical possibility of almost everything." Riccetti considered it for a moment, then shook his head. "But it doesn't look that way."

Daherrin shook his head. "Doesn't matter. We got those cannons we been casting for Karl; there's about seventeen of them—"

"Sixteen," one of the junior engineers corrected. "The new one cracked under test this morning."

"Sixteen usable cannons," Riccetti said, picking up the train of thought as Daherrin acknowledged the correction with a smile and a nod, "ready to set up on the ridge. With grapeshot, we could hold off a terribly large force. There's been no word of any army marching on us; I don't think this is a decoy."

"Okay, it's not likely to be a diversion for an attack on Home." Walter shook his head. "Is it possible that they're trying to draw out a raiding team? Get us to chase them into an ambush?"

Daherrin shook his head, a merciless smile on his face. "You're always too tricky, Walter Slovotsky. So what if it is? If they try an' ambush us, we jump them, kill them, free the slaves, take the money."

"I still don't like it." Walter wasn't crazy about the dwarf's clumsy English, either, but he didn't mention that. Slurred words and bad grammar wouldn't get him killed. A trap very well could.

"I think we should go." Valeran toyed with a wine goblet. "Assume—"

"Excuse me, Valeran," Ahira said, "but I don't know why you think that you're going along. As I understand it, your job is to keep Jason intact, not go chasing after slavers."

Valeran looked at him coldly. "I think that is properly between me and my emperor. Or between me and the raiding-team leader."

"Ease up," Daherrin said, waving the matter away. "The boy'll be safe here; Valeran's in on the party if he wants it. You was saying, Val?"

"Valeran," the soldier corrected. "Suppose the slaver caravan *is* heading for a rendezvous with a much larger force—what are they going to do, hope that we arrive to attack them at the same time their reinforcements arrive? Prevent us from properly scouting ahead? Make us blindfold ourselves during the fight?"

Bren Adahan chuckled at that last. Sitting next to Aeia, Adahan had kept silent, his attention only occasionally distracted by Aeia. Which impressed Slovotsky; the man had good concentration.

As for me, little one, if you weren't Karl's adopted daughter, there'd be a bedtime story I'd be dying to tell you.

There was a certain exoticness to her barely slanted eyes, high cheekbones, and creamy smooth complexion, and while Walter Slovotsky loved his wife—Kirah was a swell girl—he'd never made more than a pretense of faithfulness; that just wasn't the way he was built. Her preference for tight clothing, both her shorts and gray knitted pullover, emphasized the changes he'd seen in her.

Still . . . no, best to skip it.

Bedding Karl's future wife had once come a heartbeat away from getting Walter killed; he wasn't interested in finding out if trying the same trick with his adopted daughter would do the same.

And maybe during a war council isn't the best time and place to figure out where and how and with whom I'm sleeping.

Then again, there was no time like the present to open negotiations, even if he wasn't sure if he wanted to bring them to the obvious conclusion.

He reached over and patted her bare knee in what could have been an avuncular way. "What do you think, little one?"

She covered his hand with her smaller one, a grin creeping across her face as Bren Adahan's easy smile turned into a glare. "I think, Walter, that all of you are going to go anyway, so the best thing to do is to figure out how to do it, rather than wasting time on whether."

"Right." Impressive girl. Not only did she have remarkable legs and what appeared to be a set of nicely firm breasts—but brains, too? Evidence of any skills of discretion would make Walter's decision easy. Of course, even then, she could ruin things by saying no. That happened to Walter, about one time in ten. His rare excursions away from Endell were usually successful in all respects.

"And a good point." Riccetti nodded and rose, speaking in rapid English. "Then I'm going to turn in; I've got a long night scheduled, and I don't see any reason to change things—except to get the cannons emplaced and manned, just in case. Aeia, Petros, Jason—you all have enough to do tomorrow without staying up for a planning session. Go to bed—you can say your farewells in the morning."

Wordlessly, Aeia smiled a general good night, rose, and left.

"Petros, you'll guest with me at the New House; Jason will fix up another room for you—it's far too cloudy tonight for you to ride home in the dark. Daherrin, you're planning on leading this yourself?"

The dwarf nodded, smiling broadly. "You betcha," he answered in English. "It's my kinda party, boss."

"Then leave me somebody good to act as chief master-at-arms while you're gone, and be sure we've posted extra guards. And watch yourself," he said, addressing them all. His brow furrowed, he turned to Jason, who was sitting quietly, listening intently. "Jason, I told you it was—"

"No." The boy bit his lip. Walter looked closely at the boy.

Uh-oh. Walter Slovotsky had seen that particular grim expression before, although not on Jason's face.

It was the look of someone about to do something that scared him shitless. Walter Slovotsky would have seen the expression more often if he ever carried a mirror into combat.

He wasn't surprised when Jason shook his head and raised his voice, each word echoing with the loud slap of a quiet step through a minefield.

"I'm going along," the boy said.

CHAPTER FIVE:
Judgment Day

It [is] more beneficial that many guilty persons should escape unpunished than one innocent person should suffer . . . because it is of more importance . . . that innocence should be protected than it is that guilt should be punished, for guilt and crimes are so frequent in the world that all of them cannot be punished, and many times they happen in such a manner that it is not of much consequence to the public whether they are punished or not. But when innocence itself is brought to the bar and condemned . . . the subject will exclaim, "it is immaterial to me whether I behave well or ill, for virtue itself is no security." And if such a sentiment as this should take place in the mind of the subject there would be an end to all security whatsoever.

—John Adams

*Good *morning*, your imperious majesticness,* sounded in his head. *It's time to get up.*

Go away, Karl Cullinane thought, pulling the vaguely musty blankets over his head, as he summoned up a mental image of himself holding Ellegon's saurian head under the water until the dragon gurgled. Goddam, goddam world, where the best blankets you could get smelled like horses had been using them.

As they often had, come to think of it.

*First of all, you couldn't do it, because I wouldn't let you.

Second of all, you wouldn't do it, because you love me, and third of all—*

"Third of all, that's imperial majesty, not imperious majesticness."

Out in the courtyard, flame roared skyward. *You say it your way, I'll say it mine.*

Go away. Just go away. I'll get up soon.

Fine.

So, go—

As long as "soon" means now.

"Leave me alone." Huddling in his blankets, Karl Cullinane tried to go back to sleep.

Being Prince of Bieme and Emperor of Bieme-Holtun wasn't, by and large, a whole lot of fun, but the job was supposed to carry with it some perquisites, and—according to Karl Cullinane—foremost among them was sleeping in late in the morning. He wasn't going to give that up. No way.

I always find it amazing, the stoicism with which the wealthy and powerful manage to bear their horrible burdens, and the deep resolve with which they refuse to have those burdens made more cumbersome.

Translation: I should stop bitching and get my lazy ass out of bed.

You have a keen eye for the obvious.

Even his morning-tasting mouth had to quirk itself into a smile. *I take it I needed that?*

That was my guess.

Part of the dragon's job, after all, was to yell *Cut the nonsense!* when Karl got out of line, even if Karl thought that the dragon was the one who was out of line this time.

But still, dammit, it was only fair.

After all, as rulers went, Karl Cullinane didn't demand all that much.

On the Other Side, the lowliest of French nobility had thought nothing of ordering their subjects flogged or killed for trifling offenses; of obliging peasants to stay up during spring nights, beating the surfaces of ponds with sticks and branches, frightening frogs to silence and thereby preventing the mating cries of frogs from interfering with Monsieur le Baron's sleep; or of taking advantage of the *droit du seigneur* or *lettres de cachet*, phrases that Karl didn't even translate mentally into English, not wishing to soil the language.

Hmm . . . come to think of it, the phrase "French nobility" was a contradiction in terms, as far as Karl was concerned. Not that the French were alone. *Lèse majesté*, no matter what it was called, was punishable by death in most countries.

Unlike Chinese and Japanese emperors—and many lords and princes on This Side, for that matter—Karl collected only this year's taxes this year, leaving next year's for next year.

Karl Cullinane didn't keep peasants up at night, and he didn't punish anyone outside the nobility for running off at the mouth. He neither seduced nor raped peasant girls; he didn't practice his skills with a lance by skewering boys.

He just wanted to sleep in.

That wasn't much to ask.

Well, life isn't fair, and you're going to have to get up. And that's the name of that tune, the dragon added. *Andrea and her escort have left to kill some rot in Bieme's Village; I've got to leave on a supply run; and you've got to finish your new letter to Lou and maybe the one to Walter and the dwarf before I leave.

*And remember, Thomen has that poacher to sentence this morning, and you really ought to supervise the sentencing—and *then* you have to hold court.*

I'll cancel it.

Sorry. You've got to see the ambassador from Khar. And I've got to grab some sky.

Goddam Khar. To hell with Nyphien. Fuck Pandathaway and—

And get up.

Right.

He swung his feet to the floor and rubbed his eyes for a moment before forcing himself to his feet and, naked, padding over to the mottled-glass window.

Down below, in the inner courtyard, several porters and soldiers were strapping Ellegon's cargo to his scaly back: various leather sacks, containing food, powder, shot, and comfort rations for Frandred's raiding team, which was prowling about the coastal areas, trying to grab a slaver caravan.

You'd better hurry up; I'm less than an hour from leaving. You go use the bathroom; I'll order up writing materials and breakfast.

He nodded; taking a silk robe from his nightstand and belting it around him, he walked down the hall to the garderobe.

When he returned to the bedroom suite, his pen, ink bottle, and lap desk were already in the window seat; he sat down and put his feet up.

He set his lap desk on his lap; it was a wedge-shaped box of wood, the lid hinged; inside were paper and other writing materials. He swung the lid open, pulled out the six or so pages he'd already written, and quickly scanned them.

He also had some Dragon Express messages for Home, including Master Ranella's notes on her latest innovation: an improved wash for guncotton, which seemed to bring the spontaneous-detonation problem under control.

And a couple of long letters for Jason. *I miss you terribly,* he thought. Maybe he should have kept the boy around.

No; Andy was right. Jason would get a better education at Home: Valeran teaching him the soldierly arts, Aeia working on language skills, Riccetti and the rest of the engineers teaching him what they knew—and without Jason having to labor under the burden of the security considerations that applied in Biemestren, where he couldn't take a step out of the castle without an armed guard.

Perhaps more important, it was best for Jason to spend as much time as possible being treated merely as someone important, rather than as the heir apparent to the silver crown of the Prince of Bieme, the Emperor of Holtun-Bieme.

Karl shook his head and forced himself to get back to work, as though it was something he didn't relish. There were just a couple of notes to be made to clarify Karl's rough sketches for his railroad—which might be the most important thing he ever did. A railroad was a catalyst for trade, almost literally.

He idly whistled a few bars from Gordon Lightfoot's "Steel Rail Blues." If he could tie Holtun and Bieme together with a railroad, and then expand the line into Nyphien and on to Khar and eventually Kiar, it would be a damn fine bit of work. In effect, Holtun-Bieme would conquer two or three other countries in his lifetime, without hurting anyone, without firing a shot, enriching both sides.

Not a bad way to win a war: never declare it, never fight it, never make anyone lose it. Cheaper transportation was a form of wealth; wealth would lead to better lives for the peasant class—better prices for grains, shorter hours, meat on the table every day instead of twice a tenday.

A chicken in every pot, eh? He could hear Ellegon's mental smile. Despite everything, despite the fact that humans had chained him in a cesspit for three centuries, Ellegon had learned to like humans.

Some of them.

There was a rap on the knocking board.

"C'mon in," he called, without looking up.

It was Tennetty, carrying his breakfast tray awkwardly; she was much more comfortable with a sword at her waist than with a breakfast tray.

She set it down less gently than he'd have preferred.

"Easy on the crockery, eh?"

"If I break it, I pay for it. Okay?"

The years hadn't treated her badly, but they hadn't left her alone, either. Her stringy hair had gone mostly gray, and her remaining eye had laugh wrinkles around it, but she still carried herself comfortably, easily, as she seated herself across the window seat from him, pouring herself a cup of herb tea first, and then handing him one. Not a bad trade: From the neck up, she looked older than her forty or so years; from the neck down, she was still strong and wiry.

"Since when are you sitting in for the upstairs maid?" he asked, reaching out an eating prong to spear a mouthful of ham. It was a bit too heavy on the salt, but nicely smoky; he washed it down with a swallow of tea, regretting it instantly when he realized how hot the damn tea was.

Not bothering to mask her amusement, she handed him an earthenware mug of water as she shrugged. "When the dragon called, I was down in the kitchen, hearing from U'len what an ungrateful wretch you are, how you don't finish what you start. And since we've got some business . . ."

He raised an eyebrow. "We do?"

"Yeah." She nodded. "I want to go with Ellegon again; be attendant this trip. Maybe spend some time in Home with the boy, teach him the right way to use a sword."

"I'd really like you around for the council meeting. Keep an eye on my back, eh?"

She shook her head. "I don't think so. With all the musclebound swordsmen you have cluttering this place, the only danger is that you might get glared at too hard."

He didn't like this. Having Tennetty watching his back was something he was used to; he'd miss her. Then again, if Tennetty was added to the group, Karl would have even less reason to worry about Jason. If Ellegon, Tennetty, Bren Adahan, and Valeran couldn't watch the boy, then things were in worse shape than Karl knew how to deal with.

What really bothered him was the usual: It was the difference between Tennetty and sane people; she *liked* violence, particularly when slavers were on the other end of the blade or gun.

He pursed his lips. "Getting twitchy again?" Tennetty didn't take to peace well; this wasn't the first time she'd made such a request.

"Yeah."

Or the first time he'd granted it. "Have a nice time, and say hello to everyone for me, okay? But easy on the load on the way back; I don't want to overtax the dragon."

"Thanks, boss." She smiled. "What would you think of coming along?"

He shook his head. "Sorry—too much to do. Besides, I'm slowing down. I don't want to be around when you go looking for trouble." He gave her his I'm-damn-serious look. "And I'd better not hear about your getting the boy into any danger; he's too young."

"That he is. But it's too bad," she said, picking up and corking his ink bottle, then setting it down gently on the windowsill.

"What are you doing?"

She shrugged. "Well, you said you were slowing *down*—"

In one smooth movement, she drew her beltknife with her right hand and lunged for him, the knife held properly, the point moving to cut him economically from just above the crotch to the sternum, one slash gutting him like a trout.

Reflexes took over; with his left foot, he kicked her hand away, then batted his pen and lap desk aside, while he used his right leg to kick himself out of the window seat, rolling away once, then bouncing to his feet.

She was still coming at him; he scooped up a throw rug and tossed it in her direction to slow her down enough for him to retrieve his sword from the swordstand.

He tossed the scabbard aside; Tennetty had already drawn her own sword, and moved to an *en garde* position, standing easily.

Slowly, she lowered the point of her sword and resheathed her dagger. "Slowing down, eh?"

He sighed as he lowered his own sword. "I wish you wouldn't do that. I really do."

"I wish *you* wouldn't give me any nonsense about slowing down. Had to show you better."

He knew better; she'd done it for her benefit, not for his. "Sorry, Ten, but I can't go. I've got to hold court, and then I'm going to ride back to Arondael and supervise the maneuvers." It was one thing to hold Arondael responsible for any violence; it was another thing to let that pot boil unattended.

She shook her head. "Night before last was the most fun I've had in what feels like years. Peace is too wearing on us blood-thirsty types. Including you," she said.

She just didn't get it. The fact was that Karl Cullinane really didn't like violence. He committed it, when necessary; he tried to be damn good at it; but he had no compunctions about avoiding it when possible.

He rubbed the fingers of his right hand over the stumps of the outer fingers of his left. Violence had costs; Karl Cullinane had been lucky to lose only three fingers. Tennetty had once lost an eye; Chak, Rahff, Aveneer, and all the others had died. Some quickly, some slowly—but they all were dead, dead, dead.

Mortality pressed down on Karl Cullinane like a corporeal weight. Again, he rubbed his stumps. If he'd been just a few inches to the left, out of the blast shadow, it might have been his head.

All he'd lost was fingers. . . .

Look at it this way—nobody can count better in base seven than you.

Thanks, Ellegon. "Some other time, okay? And you'd better leave me alone; I want to finish this letter in time."

She nodded; wordless, she sheathed her sword, turned, and left.

He gathered together the scattered writing materials, uncorked the ink bottle, dipped his pen, and got back to writing.

—as far as the survey goes, Lou, I only see three possibilities. Either:
   1) you're going to have to train a surveyor for me, or
   2) we're going to have to do it sloppy-and-dirty, or,
   3) you're going to have to give up, come here, and do
it yourself.
   You see a fourth?
   Personally, I'd rather have it be you, but Ranella—excuse

me: *Master* Ranella; she insists on it—would prefer that you train someone for her. That way, she'll have someone to teach her some of the advanced tricks of surveying; she can already manage a beam level.

Advice: Since you say that Petros—and tell the kid to keep his hands off my seed!—is capable of handling an election in your absence, come on along. Seems to me that a bit of air travel would be good for you.

But take your pick. And, if you do decide to go, don't publicize it ahead of time. You are *not* to leave Home announced; that'd just be asking for trouble.

Meanwhile, the new Furnael puddling operation is humming along, and I'm looking forward to finishing the Bessemer plant next year. Schedule still obtains: I want fast troop trains able to run from border to border within five years; full commercial use within ten—

—and that had better be it. I've got to polish off my letter to Slovotsky and the dwarf, and then go play emperor.

I guess I deserve it; I didn't have to decide to have all capital crimes tried in the capitol.

As always, old friend, you have

> All my best
> Karl Cullinane

Even in the old days, before Karl had taken over from the late, rarely lamented Prince Pirondael, trials in Bieme had been held in the courtroom, in, quite literally, the room where the prince held court.

Not that trials had happened often: court trials were exclusively for dispensation of high justice, for members of the nobility formally accused of crimes. The low justice was managed by the nobility, and that justice—such as it was—generally consisted of said noble ordering his armsmen to mete out a punishment, anything from a mild whipping to a dramatically painful execution, as an encouragement to others.

Karl shrugged as he walked into the courthouse, two of the four door guards taking up positions on either side of him as he walked down the corridor.

Things change, but they don't change enough. He'd been able to reduce the amounts and kinds of crimes, and to require that any trial for a capital offense take place at Biemestren, in the emperor's courtroom, but there were restrictions on how fast he could make changes.

He needed the cooperation of the Holtish barons, and that was a fact. The "Little Pittsburgh" steel plant in barony Furnael was only generating pig iron, and was a long way from paying for itself; it had been built with tax money, collected by those selfsame barons.

The Nyphien border *had* to be guarded by more than Tyrnael's troops; that meant a national army, and both the money and the men had to be provided by the barons.

And who would build the railroad? That would require manpower, and money. Tax money. Steel would have to be diverted from the mill—assuming that the Bessemer plant was on line by then—and a right-of-way would have to be partially seized, partially bought, and completely cleared.

The peasants, the rock on which any agrarian-based society rested, wouldn't provide the necessary wealth out of the goodness of their hearts—peasants were no more altruistic than anyone else—or because they loved the emperor. They would have to be compelled, and that meant enlisting the cooperation, if not the affections, of the ruling class.

He needed the barons, and that meant he had to be cautious in what he changed, in what he did.

Not that there were no changes, particularly in Holtun.

Military government gave him the excuse to make more sweeping alterations in society; and each Holtish baron knew that to rise up against the imperial governor meant immediate and savage retribution. Castle Keranahan was only a scattering of stones, and instead of banishing or killing off that barony's nobility, Karl had insisted that they remain as pensioners, and examples, at other castles in Holtun, under even less favorable circumstances than those of the relatives of the late Prince Pirondael. Of those, Karl had pensioned off some to outlying baronies; others he had simply banished.

Not so for the nobility of barony Keranahan.

Keranahan had had to be conquered; it had been necessary to make an example of the rebellious barony, else Holtun might have deteriorated into constant rebellion.

Perhaps it was unpleasant for, say, Lord Hilewan to be spending the rest of his life mucking out stables, but it was a lesson to the others.

Lessons were important.

As Karl Cullinane walked into the noisy courtroom, the bailiff rapped the hilt of his halberd smartly on the stone floor, and as if someone had yanked the speaker cord, all three hundred people in the room—jurors, defendants, complainants, and observers—fell silent.

Lord Kirling, a minor noble of barony Tyrnael, rose to his feet, his immediate half-bow perfectly correct, even if just a shade perfunctory. "Greetings, your highness."

None of the others rose; Karl had been able to get away with insisting that commoners were not to rise in the presence of the emperor; that was a duty imposed only on the nobility.

"Greetings, Lord Kirling. Greetings, all."

From his seat on the emperor's throne, Thomen, Baron Furnael, nodded, his hands folded away in his black robes; he did not rise. It was a fine point of etiquette, but one that the boy—boy, ha; Thomen was a full twenty years old—had picked up without it having to be specifically explained to him: Being a judge was, by imperial decree, exclusively a commoner's occupation, so if a member of the nobility was to sit the judge's bench, he did so under the fiction that he was a commoner.

Thomen accepted his role eagerly, often slipping a half-voiced article between his first and last names, sometimes referring to himself not as Thomen Furnael, but Thomen ip Furnael—Thomen of Furnael—or sometimes simply as Thomen ahv Restaveth—Thomen the Judge—as though he were a commoner, whose surname usually was, at least in the Middle Lands, a function of his place of residence or his occupation.

"Your honor," Karl Cullinane said, "a good morning to you."

"Highness," Thomen said, his slate-gray eyes impassive, missing nothing. "Good morning." His voice took on a ceremonial aspect. "I ask that you replace me here," he said, "so that I may sit and learn from you, and so that your greater wisdom may enlighten these proceedings."

Karl Cullinane shook his head, folding his arms across his chest. "If my wisdom were the greater in these matters, I would be the judge here, not you."

As the relatively new custom demanded, Thomen again indicated the throne minor. "Then I ask that you join me here, so that I might enlighten you," he said, with just the slightest twinkle in his eyes.

Karl half-bowed. "I thank you for the invitation. With your permission?"

At the boy's nod, Karl slowly walked to the dais, turning and seating himself on the lower throne before examining the room.

Over in the jury box, the dozen jurors' grimy faces were expressing puzzlement and shock; the implications of the five-year-old ritual often still had that effect. It was one thing to hear that their ruler customarily humbled himself before even a simulated commoner; it was another to see it.

Karl was planning for the future. The rule of a limited monarch was a step up from the rule of an unlimited one. The rule of law, even of good law, was by no means an ideal situation; it was merely possibly safer than the unfettered rule of individual men, and both safer and more stable than anarchy.

Anarchy. He muzzled an intolerant chuckle, thinking of how some of his college libertarian acquaintances would have handled things in his position. Their nonstate might have lasted longer than a tenday, although not much longer; it certainly would have turned bloody quickly. Then again, one of the self-centered bastards would have refused the crown in the first place, and let a bloody succession battle—in the midst of a bloodier war—decide the question.

Libertarian idiots figure the only blood of value courses through their own veins.

The sophistries of simpletons . . .

He shook his head and forced himself to pay attention to what was going on.

Thomen quickly dispensed with several local cases. With the jury's consent, he ordered a harnessmaker to redo a shoddy job on a horsecollar and fined a wineseller for improper disposal of trash; dismissed a smith's theft complaint against his cooper neighbor for lack of evidence, digressing to suggest that the two collectively keep track of the cooper's band stock; and finally sentenced a trembling peasant to time served plus an additional day in the castle's dungeon for public drunkenness.

Karl approved, although he might not have wanted to punish the peasant for drinking. Then again, he didn't particularly approve of drunken revelers caroling through the town while people were trying to sleep. Close call.

Then came the sentencing of the poacher.

The quick-eyed little man was brought out in chains, a huge armsman on either side half-carrying him.

Karl leaned over and whispered, "What are you going to do about him, Thomen? Put the fear of the gods into him?"

"No." The boy visibly suppressed a smile. "I'll put the fear of *me* into him. I follow through." He turned to the prisoner and raised his voice. "Vernim ip Tyrnael," Thomen said, "you have been found guilty of poaching deer on the private preserve of Listar, Lord Tyrnael. It has been determined by a jury of your equals that neither you nor your family suffered from excessive need; it has also been determined to my satisfaction that this was not the first time you have stolen from the baron."

Karl remembered hearing Ellegon's version of the case. Vernim was the nth in a line of small-plot farmers whose holding was outside of Myaryth, a small town in Tyrnael, right on the edges of Baron Tyrnael's personal preserve.

Tyrnael was a reasonable sort. He didn't mind a bit of rabbit hunting or pheasant snaring on his land—he even encouraged the first, to prevent the rabbits from overrunning his preserve. But deer were in short supply—and no wonder: Tyrnael's constable had literally unearthed evidence that Vernim's family had long been taking at least ten deer per year out of the preserve.

Nothing terribly surprising about it, but it had to be discouraged. The trouble was that, technically, poaching on baronial or princely land had long been punishable by death, and Tyrnael had—almost certainly deliberately—not asked Karl to waive the death penalty for Vernim.

Not a good situation.

Tyrnael was a solid ally, and Karl had no intention of slapping the baron in the face. In fact, Karl would have been tempted to close his eyes and let the baron execute Vernim, except that he had established that baronial courts could mete out the death penalty only for murder.

Tempted . . . it wasn't right to kill a man for poaching a few deer for his pot.

It just wasn't right. Karl was glad that Thomen had decided to frighten the man.

" . . . and the fact is, Vernim, that you deserve to end your days kicking on an impaling spear. But the emperor has outlawed that, and instituted the noose. Which is what I'm tempted to sentence you to."

Vernim should have been trembling, white-faced. But, defiantly, he threw back his shoulders, the look of a man past fear on his face. "May I speak now, *your honor?*" he asked, his voice dripping with sarcasm.

Shit. Karl looked over at Thomen. This wasn't the way it was supposed to go. Thomen had clearly intended to scare the peasant with the threat of death, and then to substitute some number of blows with the whip or tendays in the dungeon— enough to make the point that poaching was not going to be tolerated.

But—

"You have no right to judge me. What are you? Some kind of god? No; you're a man, just like I am." He started to turn his back on Thomen, but the guards yanked him back by the chains, a marionette on a string.

"Gag him," Karl said, forcing himself to keep calm while his mind raced.

There it was, the danger of being too damn clever. Thomen had frightened the poacher past fear, left him feeling that his fate was already sealed, that he had nothing to lose.

Helplessly, Thomen glanced at Karl, then recovered what was left of his composure. "You have, Vernim ip Tyrnael, eaten your last meat, poached or otherwise. You are sentenced to be thrown into the meanest cell in the dungeon of Biemestren Castle, there to be fed only on water until such time as you can conveniently be transported in a prisoner's cart to barony Tyrnael, there to be hanged by the neck until you are dead, to be buried in the ground, the ground salted."

He nodded at the bailiff, who rapped the hilt of his halberd again on the floor.

"Court," Thomen said, "is dismissed."

Karl nodded. It surely was.

Karl chased the armorer out of the armory and waved Thomen to a seat. "I can't spend much time on this, Thomen," he said, idly running his fingers across a rack of spears before taking a rebuilt flintlock down from the wall. "There's a lot to do today. But what the hell are we going to do about this?"

The trouble was that Vernim was right. The truth was that neither Karl Cullinane nor Thomen Furnael had any right to even threaten to kill a man for poaching. It was wrong. Maybe it was necessary, but it was wrong.

On the other hand, a ruler *had* to have it clearly established that he was the ruler, and to allow a convicted poacher to challenge his rule was just not tolerable. The magic of leadership, the *mana* of the leader, had to be preserved.

Thomen shrugged, his shoulders tight, barely moving, not as though he didn't care. Quite the opposite; it was as though the cares of the world weighed more heavily on his shoulders than they had any right to. His brother had had the same shrug.

"Only two possibilities, Karl, and I don't like either one." He chewed on his thumbnail for a moment. "I can trust Enrel, my bailiff—he's been with the family since before I was born. I'll have him weaken the floor of the prisoner cart, and instruct him to look the other way if Vernim tries to escape. With a bit of luck, he'll make it out of Holtun-Bieme, and he'll surely never come back."

Karl shook his head. That wouldn't do. "And what if, after Vermin breaks out, he picks up a sword and kills one of the armsmen guarding him? Or what if he gets away, and kills a farmer for his food or money?"

A hunted man was far more dangerous than a wounded wolf. Karl had been a hunted man more than once.

Thomen thought about it for a long while. "Maybe Kirling will ask for mercy for him? You can always give clemency."

"Possible, if unlikely." Karl nodded. "If I'm asked for mercy by Tyrnael or someone representing him. You can't tell Kirling to ask me, though—"

"No. It would look like you were the one who was asking."

"True. And if I'm not asked?"

Thomen Furnael drew himself up straight. "Then he'll have to hang. And it'll be my fault, Karl." He considered the matter soberly. "I miscalculated, and it will cost Vernim ip Tyrnael his life. It isn't *fair.*"

Karl Cullinane nodded. It wasn't fair, at that. But that was the way it was going to be. The way it had to be. "An expensive lesson, eh, Thomen?"

Thomen Furnael turned away, his shoulders shaking minutely. "Yes. It is. Karl . . . I never killed a man before."

It would have been one thing to kill in combat. Pumping adrenaline, raging fear, the relief of it's-him-and-not-me would have made it different . . . until later, until the long, interrupted nights when men with faces contorted in final agony stared back at you, clapped their hands to deathwounds that you had given them, never quite believing that it had finally happened to them.

It was quite another thing to order a man's death.

Ordering someone hanged for murder would have been easier, if not easy; an eye for an eye wasn't only an Other Side concept, after all. At nights, when you woke in a cold sweat, you could tell yourself that you had saved lives by ordering the murderer executed.

Karl had killed slavers in hot blood and cold. People who made others into property had to be stopped, and their example had to be fatally discouraged.

But ordering a man hanged for eating a deer? It wasn't right. It might be necessary, but it wasn't right. "You don't like the feeling much, do you?"

"No."

"So be it," Karl Cullinane whispered. That was how a death sentence was really passed: with a whispered resolve. "He dies. Think about how you can prevent it, next time."

"Karl, I hate this. I . . ."

"Good." Karl Cullinane drew himself up straight. "Keep it that way." He clapped his hand to Thomen's shoulders. "Keep it that way."

CHAPTER SIX:

"A Little Bird Told Me . . ."

The wise man in the storm prays God, not for safety from danger, but for deliverance from fear. It is the storm within which endangers him, not the storm without.
                                        —Ralph Waldo Emerson

It didn't look good, Walter Slovotsky decided, but maybe it didn't look too bad, either.

It was likely going to be goddam bloody.

But not yet. Squatting in their perch in the hastily manufactured blind in an old oak tree along the trail, Slovotsky patted Jason reassuringly on the arm while they both looked down at the progression of the slaver caravan below.

The slavers were moving both themselves and their cargo as quickly as possible, but it wasn't a rapid gait; the horses had to hold to the pace of the slowest of the neck-chained slaves—humans and elves of all ages and sexes—although the very youngest and weakest were carried by their companions.

Not a pretty sight; as he watched, one of the captives, a boy of perhaps eight, maybe nine years of age, tripped and fell, only to be dragged along for several feet by his neck chain until the rag-clad men in front of and in back of him could help him regain his feet. As he did, a horse-borne slaver's whip snaked out and caught him across the shoulders with a quiet *snap;* his scream trailed off into a whimper, punctuated by another yelp of pain when the slaver lashed him again and cursed at him to keep up. Crimson welts flared on the boy's shoulders.

Walter Slovotsky's fingernails clawed at the bark of the tree. Most of the time he let himself forget what this was all about. Most of the time he let things like a nine-year-old boy being whipped become only distant memories.

He didn't want reminders like this; the slaver with the whip would pay for that, would pay for reminding him.

The slaver was a big, blond man, with close-cropped hair, looking vaguely Germanic to Slovotsky's eyes. Probably from Osgrad. Slovotsky made a mental note to deal with him personally.

Walter nodded grimly to his companion in the tree. *Jason, me bucko, it seems that some of your father rubs off on us all.*

But not all of his father. Karl Cullinane probably would have dropped into the crowd of slavers and taken them all on, no matter what the odds, trusting on his extraordinary fighting ability and his even more extraordinary luck to carry him through.

Slovotsky held back a smile; Karl would probably have been right, at that. He probably would have chopped all of them into slaver pâté, only working up a good sweat.

That was the advantage of leading a charmed life.

Walter Slovotsky, on the other hand, was fully aware of his own mortality, and while he had the utmost faith in his own luck, he figured that it was best used as rarely as possible.

Besides, remember Slovotsky's law number nine, revised: Sometimes you can't do anything about something that sucks—until later.

Still, how to handle this one was hard to figure. At least it wasn't a trap, thank God; for once, his suspicions, if not quite groundless, had been proved wrong. Slavers trying to draw Home raiders into some sort of ambush wouldn't be driving themselves, their horses, and their chain of slaves this hard.

The slavers were on the run with their booty—both people and gold—trying to avoid a fight, not find one.

The trap hypothesis hadn't been likely, granted; slavers' minds wouldn't work that way. They wouldn't assume that a Therranj raid would draw Home raiders; besides, they hadn't been operating openly in the region, and wouldn't have the kind of support they'd need to make it a trap. The few communities between Therranj and Wehnest were far more attached to Homemade steel than to slaver-supplied slave labor—labor which could be liberated without warning.

If little ol' me isn't suspicious of a trap, it ain't a trap. And that's the name of that tune.

He nodded and smiled at Jason. *It's looking good, kid,* he thought.

Still, there were probably aspects of the slavers' marching order that could constitute a trap for the unwary.

But unwary isn't something I am. He pulled a piece of jerky out of his pouch and took a silent bite, offering the stick to Jason, who refused with a too-violent shake of his head.

The idea is to not move a whole lot, boyo. Still, not a huge danger; humans didn't tend to look up to spot danger.

Walter Slovotsky counted sixty-three slavers, with another ten or so probably resting in the wagons. The few ragged men helping to chivvy along the chain of the slaves were clearly the equivalent of trusties, and while Walter didn't have a whole lot of respect for that or for them, they didn't look like either a problem or a danger; they'd run, not fight.

The slavers, on the other hand, looked to be both a problem and a danger.

The horsemen riding point rode with an easy confidence, never turning to check behind them, manifestly trusting those at the rear to keep a lookout behind the group, while an advance party of five was about an hour and a mile ahead; it seemed that they sent back riders both to report an all's well and to switch off with decent regularity.

The classic Karl Cullinane method of taking on a caravan was out. Karl always liked to spook the slavers; a loud attack could get them running into a two-guns squad ambush that would cut the bastards to ribbons with minimum casualties to his raiders.

But the slick, professional way these folks were running their march suggested that the Slavers' Guild had been taking lessons in military tactics, and the importance of not letting oneself be stampeded into an ambush was something that they had likely worked out. That was too bad; Daherrin was a student of Karl's and wouldn't like another method.

Still, the news wasn't all bad, thank God.

Most importantly, there were no guns in evidence, and no sign of slaver powder. And while the slavers practically bristled with both crossbows and short Katharhd hornbows, there weren't any visible sign of longbowmen. Which was good. For reasonably close but not quite intimate combat, the longbow was the most dangerous projectile weapon available—when held by someone who could use it expertly, which was always the problem.

Hmmm . . . Walter wasn't surprised that this wasn't as large a group as they had been told about by Khoral's emissary; he'd more than half expected that. Reports of battles tended to grow in the telling, and the raid on a few Therranji towns had quickly grown.

Being off by a factor of two wasn't much; the last time Walter had heard about the time the legendary Karl Cullinane had killed Ohlmin and his slavers, Ohlmin had been the marshal of a force of a thousand slavers, and Karl had defeated them all by wielding the sword of Arta Myrdhyn.

Walter Slovotsky muffled a chuckle.

He'd been there, and it hadn't happened that way, not that way at all. At the final showdown, there had been precisely six slavers, and Walter had picked off four with his crossbow while Karl distracted them with an admittedly nice display of swordsmanship— and it was an ordinary saber that Karl had used that night, not the magical sword that they didn't even know about until long after.

Ohlmin hadn't been dispatched by the legendary single slash that clove him from head to crotch; in fact, he'd been a better swordsman than Karl, and although it was Karl who had killed the bastard, he'd done it with a half-dozen crude headsman's chops, while Ohlmin was clutching at the bolt Walter had fired into his groin.

—had *cleverly* fired into his groin, Slovotsky amended, chiding himself for his uncharacteristic and unintentional modesty.

It had been pretty damn clever, at that. As good a swordsman as Karl was, that murderous bastard Ohlmin was better, and would have carved the big man into bloody little chunks if Slovotsky hadn't distracted him by sinking a foot of iron-tipped wood into his crotch.

And if I'm so clever, he thought, *why didn't I mention to Lou the possibility—hell, the likelihood—that we didn't need as many men as he was willing to spare?*

The answer to that one was easy: While Lou might have wanted to keep the group as small as possible, from Walter's point of view there was no such thing as too many, and Walter didn't want to give Lou any excuse to cut down on the size of the raiding party. Port captains always liked to see ships in their ports; post commanders didn't like to see empty parade grounds.

Still, even a hundred warriors versus sixty wasn't going to make the job easy, not necessarily. Or bloodless, on their side.

Walter's maps were in his horse's saddlebags, and his horse was a couple of miles away; he didn't exactly remember this trail, but he knew that somewhere it fed into the major road toward Wehnest, and that could mean trouble. If the Home raiders didn't hit the slavers early enough, they'd have to do it in the cleared fields surrounding that town. Much better to jump the slavers in the woods; an ambush would be by far preferable. Something a bit complicated, maybe almost anything would be better than a meeting engagement on a farming road.

The last rider passed under their tree. Jason waited until he had passed out of sight, then turned to Walter.

"Unc—"

Slovotsky shot his arm out and clapped his hand over the boy's mouth. He put his lips next to Jason's ear. "Shut up, asshole," he whispered, barely any breath behind his words. "I'll tell you when you can make noise—if you understand, nod."

At Jason's nod, Slovotsky let go, not bothering to hide his irritation as he shook his head.

The boy pursed his lips as though to say something, but decided against it. Which was just as well.

Again, Slovotsky placed his lips next to the boy's ear. "A silence isn't over until I say it is," he whispered as quietly as he could. "Now just sit still."

After making sure that Jason was sitting still, Slovotsky leaned back against the rough trunk of the tree and closed his eyes, letting his mind drift. It was just a bit *too* neat; it would have been easy to drop to the trail and backtrack to the side trail where they had stashed the horses. Walter Slovotsky, always conscious of the fact that his own tendency was to do things the easy way, was by policy suspicious of too-easy solutions.

Policy aside this was a situation worthy of some suspicion: The slavers had put out an advance party; was it beyond possibility that they had a detachment batting cleanup? Not at all.

Five minutes of silence passed, and then ten. He nodded to himself and forced his eyes open, beckoning to the boy.

Hear that? Slovotsky mouthed, putting his hands behind his ears to pantomime listening carefully.

Jason wrinkled his brow as though to say, *Hear what?*

What is the strange thing that the dog did in the night, Watson? Slovotsky mouthed.

At the boy's puzzled look, Slovotsky was reminded again that these goddam kids had been brought up on This Side, with only traces of a proper cultural upbringing.

He put his lips next to Jason's ears. "We've been silent," he whispered, his voice pitched to carry no more than inches, "and we haven't been moving around; the forest noises should have returned by now."

But they haven't, the boy mouthed.

"Precisely my point, Watson." Slovotsky pointed down the trail in the direction from which the slaver party had come. "So keep your mouth shut and your eyes open—and on the trail."

Thank you, squirrels and birds. The animals were keeping watch for them. Since they were still quiet, their keener senses had picked up something. Possibly somebody else using this rarely used trading trail through the forest. . . .

In another ten minutes, he could hear the clatter of hooves along the trail; moments later, a party of seventeen sharp-eyed men rode underneath.

Make that a hundred to eighty-seven. Still, not the worst odds he'd ever run across.

As the riders disappeared around the bend, Walter turned to Jason. The lesson had made an impression on the boy. He didn't even breathe heavily as he watched the heavily armed troop ride slowly down the trail, and he didn't make a move to leave when the troop rode out of sight.

Walter Slovotsky mouthed, *See? I do know what I'm talking about,* then breathed on his nails and buffed them across his chest.

Still, if we can get the jump on them, it should be a piece of cake, Walter Slovotsky said to himself. Then a wanton burst of self-honesty forced him to respond: *Then why are you scared shitless, as usual?*

He shrugged off the question, and waited only a few more minutes before standing and stretching as the forest noises returned.

"Let's go get the horses, boyo—we've got some hard riding to do."

Jason hesitated. "Uncle Walter?"

"Yes?"

"How did you know?"

"Well . . ." Walter Slovotsky could have mentioned the forest's silence, but he wasn't sure he wanted to let the boy in on all the trade secrets. Not yet, anyway; right now, Jason's being impressed was more important—besides, the tone of admiration in Jason's voice was a definite and pleasant improvement over the previous disdain. "Elementary, my dear Cullinane, quite elementary—a little bird told me," he said, more or less truthfully.

"What?"

"Let's get moving; with a bit of luck, we can hook up with the team sometime tomorrow morning."

They were picked up by an outrider around noon, and Daherrin, upon the advice of Ahira, called a full midday halt in a nearby clearing. The horses were unsaddled and cooled, then brought down a side trail to a stream and watered, and then allowed to graze before being fed from the limited supplies of oats and barley.

Meanwhile, the raiding team ate a cold lunch of hard sausage and yet more of what was both the worst-smelling cheese that Walter Slovotsky had ever tasted and the worst-tasting cheese he had ever smelled, washed down with a bit of wine and quarts of cold stream water.

God, how he hated cold road food.

Most of the experienced warriors topped off lunch with a siesta; even after only a few days on the road, old habits were returning. You slept and you ate when you could—and as much as you could—because there might not be a chance later on.

Jilla, one of only two women with the team, lay stretched out under an improvised lean-to, snoring like a dwarf.

Aeia was the other woman, and while she wasn't really an experienced warrior, she had learned to sleep when possible. Napping, she huddled childlike under a blanket that Walter's fingers itched to pull up. Or simply to slip under and wake her for a quick *non*-nap.

Naughty, naughty, he chided himself, with no seriousness whatsoever. *I am* supposed *to think with an entirely different organ altogether.*

Meanwhile, the leadership and some of the newcomers were embroiled in a discussion. As was usual—the team's leadership had to plan while the opportunity presented itself; the tyros hadn't yet learned to get food and rest whenever the opportunity presented itself.

Understandably, the group consisted of Ahira, Daherrin, Bren Adahan, and Valeran as the seniors, and Jason and a fifteen-year-old named Samalyn from the juniors. What surprised Walter was how Daherrin actually listened to the young ones; Walter's own tendency was to tell them to shut up and listen.

Daherrin shook his massive head. "I don't like jumping 'em in the daytime." He tapped a stubby finger at his eye ridges. "Rather take advantage of darksight."

Ahira shook his head and spat. "There are only thirteen of the True People," he said in dwarvish. "Do you think we can kill all the slavers by ourselves?"

Jason Cullinane frowned. "Erendra or English," he half growled in the same language. "Your accent is too thick."

"Be still, Jason," Valeran said, trying on his *in loco parentis* role.

Bren Adahan hid a smile behind a hand. A human telling a dwarf that he didn't speak dwarvish right? He shook his head with clearly tolerant affection.

Daherrin nodded. "Jason is right."

Walter could have puked. First of all, Ahira had been part of the group since the beginning; if he figured that something needed to be said in dwarvish, then that was the way it was. A stripling boy had no business correcting him.

On the other hand, to Daherrin, Jason wasn't just a boy, not just an apprentice warrior and engineer; he was Karl Cullinane's son, and to Daherrin that meant a lot, perhaps too much.

Spoiled brat.

Daherrin frowned again. "I don't like not being able to jump them like normal. Could wait for 'em in a clearing, but then there's the problem of the advance riders—"

"Forget that." Ahira shook his head. "There could easily be worse. It's entirely possible that they've got somebody riding about a day ahead of them, doing a reconnaissance."

Slovotsky nodded. "If you don't mind me trying my hand at a bit of brilliance, I think I may have it."

He picked up a stick and drew a ragged line in the dirt. "Here's the main trail—they're about here, right now. Our road forks here, and we'll take this turn . . . figure that we can push ourselves fast enough to intercept them about here, a day outside of Wehnest.

This side trail leads off to a small farmholding; we can hide our main force a ways down it."

He picked up three stones and set them down in the dirt. "Here's their advance party. They ride past the trail, and get hit about . . . *here* by a quarter of our advance group—three, maybe four bowmen. They kill a few, maybe they just pin them down.

"Meanwhile, the other half of our advance group—maybe ten— hits them from the front, and forces them to dismount."

Daherrin smiled. "And then our main group hits them from the rear."

Valeran smiled too. "But that leaves their reserves."

Ahira turned to the grizzled warrior. "And why does that make you smile?"

"Because I know Walter Slovotsky." He turned to Slovotsky. "You have something clever saved for them."

"You betcha. Just as soon as the main body slips by the trail and the rest of you folks get to chasing after them, me and a couple others string rope across the trail, about head height. Then we duck back up the side trail and wait for the shit to hit the fan."

Bren Adahan nodded a reluctant approval. "When the shots ring out, the slaver reserves break into a gallop; some of them might even get their necks broken by the fall." He clearly didn't like the way Slovotsky had been looking at Aeia, but that didn't stop him from a blunt assessment of the plan, or the situation.

"Good man." Slovotsky nodded. "We pick off a few, maybe toss in a grenade or two—and then just pin the rest down. Once you're done with the main body of slavers, Daherrin, you split your main force in three: one part to stay with the slaves and mop up any straggling slavers, the second group to rush forward and join with the ones taking on the advance, and the last and most important group to pull my tender fat out of the fire. Assuming it needs pulling, that is."

Daherrin looked around to the group. "Sounds good, 'cept for the part about the grenades—you'll kill the horses, and we can get a good price for them in Wehnest." He sat still for several minutes, his eyes distant, his face impassive. "I can't think of any other improvements—anybody?"

A few ideas were brought up involving changing the proportions of the team to be sent with each group, but Daherrin allowed only minor adjustments. Finally, he rose to his feet and slapped his hands together. "Wake up, everyone. We ride."

✧   ✧   ✧

Unable to find a clearing as darkness fell, Daherrin ordered that they camp that night along the trail itself, then paired dwarf guards and human runners, and posted a set a mile away on each side of the main body of the party. Dwarves could see an approaching party perfectly adequately in this light; humans could carry back the news more rapidly.

In the chill of the dark, the leafy giants loomed darkly overhead, the light wind making them murmur both vague threats and unreliable benedictions into the night.

His gear and his weapons tucked under one arm, a lantern held aloft with the other, Walter Slovotsky walked a few hundred yards down the trail before slipping off into the woods. He didn't like sleeping in the company of a hundred others, and he far preferred not to have to tune out camp noises; much better for any strange noise or strange silence to waken him.

He hung his lamp on a projecting stub of a lower branch of a half-dead oak and cleared small plants from the mossy bed below before spreading a thin tarpaulin as a groundcloth, then covering that with two of his three blankets.

He chuckled to himself, remembering how he hadn't believed his scoutmaster's tip, way back when, about how it was more important to worry about insulation from the ground than from the air; the ground thieved warmth much more quickly than the air possibly could.

Walter Slovotsky had doubted the scoutmaster, of course, and when Walter's big brother Steven had soberly nodded and said that Mr. Garritty was telling the truth, Walter had been certain that he was being lied to.

He'd woken the next morning colder, and in more pain, than he would have thought possible.

He sighed as he stripped off his clothes and hung them over a branch before slipping under the third blanket. Sometimes those days seemed as if they had happened to another person. *I wonder how Steve's doing?* he thought, more conscious than he would have liked to concede that he hadn't thought of his brother in years. The two of them had been a study in contrasts; Steven was introverted and private where Walter was extroverted and—

A rustling of branches sent him reaching for his oilskin-wrapped pistol.

"Walter?" Aeia's voice whispered from the night. "Are you out there?"

In the back of his mind, he had been wondering when this would happen, not if.

"Over here," he whispered back, waving as a beam of light from her lantern caught him. She was dressed in a heavy cotton shift that fell to her calves. "I hope you don't mind," she said, as she seated herself on his blankets, "but I felt like talking."

"No, you didn't."

"Well . . ." She eyed him calmly. "Yes, I do. Before. Or do you want me to leave?"

"I don't believe in coincidences," Walter said, quickly blowing out the lantern—he didn't believe in getting caught, either. "Which leads me to believe that your adopted mother talks too much."

I hope you don't mind, but I felt like talking. Those had been exactly the words Andy had used, way back when, the night she had come to his cabin, the night that Karl had come within inches of killing him.

"Maybe." There was a rustle of cloth, and then she was warm in his arms. "Andrea once told me that the Other Side produced seven wonders, and that I was to keep my hands off one of them."

"Your dad?"

"Karl." She buried her face in his chest, her long, dark hair flowing over his chest and neck in a cool benediction. "I don't remember what the other ones were, except for you."

Her mouth was warm on his for a pleasant eternity, until they broke, leaving him half-breathless.

I may hate myself in the morning for this, but— "Don't take this the wrong way, but what about Bren?"

"I don't know that that's any of your concern," she said, her voice holding a decided edge.

Definitely Andy's daughter, he decided. And yet another blow for environment over heredity.

"I'm going to marry Bren. I'm even going to sleep with him, eventually," she said firmly, "once he's properly broken in. And don't worry, I can handle him. If he finds out. Which he won't."

I seem to have heard that before.

She pushed away from him slightly. "Or don't you want me?"

Then again, a gentleman doesn't keep a lady waiting. "Don't be silly." He pulled her toward him. "Don't be silly."

CHAPTER SEVEN:

A Walk in the Dark

A councilor should not sleep the whole night through, for he is a man to whom the populace is entrusted, and who has many responsibilities.

—Homer

The silence bore down on Karl Cullinane's shoulders as he stepped out onto his balcony and stared out into the night.

The night was dark and damp, the sky overcast, a west wind promising rain and cold. The darkness was relieved by no playful faerie lights; the only break in the curtain of black was the lights of the castle itself, and distant glows in a few stray windows in the town of Biemestren.

Why couldn't he sleep? The night was half gone, and it had been all he could do to rest for a few moments.

Was there something threatening out there? Had he suddenly developed some paranormal danger sense?

Nah.

Don't be silly, Karl.

There was nothing out there but dark. Nothing important at all.

There had been another time, when a young Karl Cullinane would have been out in the night, his mind on things of overriding importance, perhaps on hunting slavers, perhaps on other great deeds to be done ... perhaps on just being young.

Being young had been nice. But that was gone; the years had fled all too quickly.

That was it. The years went by too fast. Just too damn fast.

He closed the doors to the balcony and plopped down into his chair.

Maybe it was the baronial council meeting. Perhaps the time wasn't right, but he had called for the session, and it would have to be done sometime. Holts and Biemish would have to sit down at the same table and get used to the idea that this was one country now. And Nerahan deserved to own his own barony again. Still . . .

"Karl?" There was a rustling of cloth behind him; light flared as Andy used a piece of straw to bring fire from the fireplace to a lamp.

"Yeah. Just me." He tried for a light tone in his voice. "Who were you expecting? Go back to sleep."

Ignoring the halfhearted plea, she rose and came to him, her white, silken nightgown rippling in the wind.

"There was a time, old girl, when we both slept raw."

She smiled. "On the cold ground, with too few blankets between us and the ground." Her hand smoothed down her side, and then fluttered up to tug at his arm. "Come back in."

He shrugged. "Okay." He closed the doors to the balcony, reflexively slipping down the crossbar. "Just sit with me for a while."

"What is it?" Andy laid a gentle hand on his shoulder as he sat, scowling.

Karl shook his head. "I don't know. Nothing."

"Then will you please come to bed? Please?" She moved to the bed, pulled back the covers, and slipped between them. "You have a long day tomorrow."

"You get some sleep." He jerked his head toward the bed and took the lamp from her hands. "Just because I have a little insomnia doesn't mean you should stay up with me. Just give me a while. I've got some paperwork to do."

Ushering her back to bed, he padded across the carpet to his study, closing the twin doors quietly behind him. He set the lamp over his desk, then sat down and picked up a sheaf of papers, pretending to read.

The subject was important—it was a précis of the latest land-tax collection in barony Adahan—but, as usual, there wouldn't be any discrepancy he could catch. Minor stealing by tax collectors was the rule, not the exception. While, officially, embezzlement of tax money was a hanging offense, in fact petty tax theft wasn't frowned on, as long as the collectors didn't get too greedy; baronial tax collectors were paid poorly, and there was always the temptation to collect a bit more than the records showed a freefarmer owed.

But even double-entry bookkeeping couldn't catch that; it was the initial entry that was false, not subsequent reconciliations.

But he didn't care. It just didn't seem to matter.

He wished Ellegon were here. Karl could always trust the dragon to help clear his mind.

Damn. He reached up and tugged at the bellrope, twice—the nonemergency signal for a guard.

Boots thudded in the hall outside; the door swung open. "Yes, your majesty," the guard boomed, in a voice much larger than his slightly shorter than normal size warranted.

"Shh; not so loud." Karl turned in his chair. "And good evening, Nartham," he said. He would have known who it was just by the volume.

"I am at your service," the guard said, his voice rattling the night.

"Ta havath, Nartham," Karl said. *Easy, Nartham.* Why this guard always had to talk as though he were a half-deaf artillery sergeant on a parade ground was something Karl couldn't fathom. "My wife's sleeping in the next room, eh?"

"Sorry, sir," the guard said, at a barely reduced volume.

"The prisoner cart—did it leave this afternoon?"

"No, your majesty. Driver got here too late, I hear, and the bar—the *judge* told him to stay overnight. It should go out at first light."

Karl nodded a dismissal—"Thank you—"

—which Nartham didn't catch. "Is there anything else?"

"No." Karl shook his head. "Good night, Nartham."

"But—yes, sir."

As the door closed behind the guard, the twin doors to the bedroom swung open.

"Better talk about it," Andy said from the doorway, her arms crossed defensively over her chest.

"I thought you were going back to bed."

"No. You *told* me to go back to bed. There's a difference. Not that I was going to go back to sleep anyway, but Nartham's voice could wake up the dead. What is it? What's really bothering you?"

"Probably the trial." He shrugged again. "It doesn't make much of a difference. It's just that . . . Vernim. Idiotic bastard. If only he'd kept his mouth shut, if only he hadn't been too stupid to see that Thomen was only trying to scare him—"

She shook her head. "And that's what's bothering you? The poacher? Maybe I've gone a bit native, but so what? You declared an amnesty when you took the throne; all he and his family had to do was switch from poaching deer to snaring rabbits."

"But he didn't."

And it wasn't right.

But was that what was bothering him? He honestly couldn't say.

Didn't make sense. In Karl's time, he had had to put up with things a lot more raw than hanging a man who should have been, at worst, flogged.

He shook his head. "Something more's bothering me about this, and I can't figure out what it is."

Damn idiot thing, at that. A young Karl Cullinane always used to make fun of the California types who were always trying to "get in touch with their feelings" and similar nonsense. Get in touch with your feelings? Not know what you feel? Could anything be sillier?

Except when it happened to you. "Y'know, when I was younger, I wouldn't have put up with this."

Maybe that was it. Then again, maybe not.

"Put up with what?" She set her hip on the arm of his chair.

He reached over and stroked her knee. "I wouldn't have put up with not even hearing you get out of bed, that's what I wouldn't have put up with. I'm getting old," he said, glad that Tennetty wasn't here.

She shook her head and pushed his hand away, not falling for either distraction. "No. That's not it. You wouldn't have put up with a man being hanged for hunting for meat for his table, that's what's bothering you."

He shrugged again. So what? "I had to. There wasn't any choice."

She nodded. "So? You're going to let that bother you forever?"

He shook his head. "Not forever." He'd had to do worse in his time. He'd once marched a bunch of friends into enemy gunfire, and not regretted it for a moment, even though only he and Tennetty had survived.

No. His fists clenched. He had regretted it every moment.

Aveneer, Peill, Erek . . . he'd always miss redheaded Aveneer's booming voice, Peill's unrelieved but strangely reassuring frown, Erek's
expression of intense concentration—he'd always regret having
marched them into the cannon's mouth.

He'd always regret the action and the necessity, but not his
obedience to the necessity.

Some necessities were always to be regretted. Always; it was a
debt to the dead.

"Then what is it?" She smiled down at him. "You know, when
you were Thomen's age, you wouldn't have pouted over something
like this. You'd either have sprung the bastard, or let him hang
without worrying."

It wasn't so simple now. There were other things to be considered. On balance, it was better to let the idiot hang than to alienate
Tyrnael.

"You're right, though," he said. "When I was Thomen's age, I
wouldn't have put up with it."

"What would you have done?"

He shrugged. "I don't know. Maybe . . . I guess maybe I'd have
tried to spring him—'

No.

He looked over at her. "Did Thomen say anything to you?"

It hit her, too; she shivered. "No. But he wouldn't put me in
that awkward a position." She caught her lip between her teeth
for a moment. "I'm not sure that I'd have told you even if he had."

He rose to his feet. "We'll talk about *that* some other time." The
question was what to do now. The young baron would take
responsibility on his own shoulders. It was something that he had
learned from his late father, and that had been reinforced by his
emperor and mentor.

"Can you locate him for me?"

She nodded. "Unless he's protected—but are you sure you want
me to?" she asked as she stretched broadly. She gathered her long,
flowing hair up and with a few fingerstrokes almost magically
twisted it into a neat bun, securing it with a pair of ebony
hairprongs.

Are you sure you want me to?

That was the trouble. Technically, if Thomen was doing what
Karl half hoped he was, half prayed he wasn't, the boy was com-
mitting treason. . . .

Technically.

The job of a ruler, Karl Cullinane had once noted in his journal, *consists primarily of pissing on sparks.* This counted as a spark. "How quickly can you pin down where he is?"

"I haven't done any locating for a long time." She shook her head. "It'll take me a couple of hours to set up and work the spell."

That could work right. As long as Karl could leave before the prisoner cart did, he'd have the jump on Thomen.

But there were some preparations to be made, if he was going to get out quietly, or be reasonably certain of getting back safely.

Shrugging out of his nightrobe and dropping it to the floor, he padded across the carpet back to the bedroom. "Do it, then meet me at the stables."

As he reached for his clothes, he was smiling: There was something to *do.*

The engineer on duty at the desk outside of the underground armory was one of Karl's scribes, a thirtyish, somewhat overweight, dark-bearded man who, refreshingly, never seemed terribly impressed with the emperor. Engrossed in his scribblings, it took him a moment to look up as Karl walked down the hall.

He was clearly surprised to see Karl down here in the middle of the night, but managed to muzzle his curiosity.

"A good evening to you, sir," he said, as he put his steel pen back in the inkwell and took a moment to knead his hands together as he stood. "Anything I can help with?"

"No need, Jayar," Karl said, giving Master Engineer Ranella's wax seal across the keyhole a perfunctory look before breaking it with his fingernail. "Just get the lock for me. I'm going out for a bit of exercise around dawn, and I just want a few fresh pistols; I can handle that alone," Karl said, then thought better of it. "Mmm . . . better yet, let's do this assembly-line style—I'll charge, then you load and prime."

There was plenty of time, but there was also no sense in spending a lot of it playing around loading pistols.

"My pleasure." The engineer used the large key from his ring to open the door.

It took Jayar a moment to light the overhead lamp; the engineer carefully set the lamp back in its place before he took down three small wooden canisters; the chalk marks on the canisters labeled one as a portion of the latest batch of Ranella's gunpowder, the second as fine priming powder, the third, which rattled as Jayar hefted it, lead bullets.

They each took a brace of pistols from a rack on the wet stone walls and set the weapons down on a battered workbench over by the opposite wall.

"Aren't you a bit senior to be on the night shift?" Karl asked. After all, Jayar was a sufficiently high-ranking journeyman that Ranella had authorized him an individual signet ring; he was entitled to access the armory on his own authority.

"Tricky question." Jayar pursed his lips, and cocked his head to one side. Karl took a conical brass powder measure down from a hook, tapped out a healthy charge, loaded the first pistol, and after tamping the powder down, passed the tamping stick and weapon to Jayar.

"You and Ranella not getting along?" Karl asked.

"Well . . . careful of the pistol; that's a heavy load," Jayar said. "And in answer to your question, I'm technically too senior to draw it as a duty, but I make a real lousy Engineer of the Day." Jayar shrugged. "I get distracted too easily." He jerked his thumb toward the door and the table with the pen and paper. "Ranella would rather have me in charge when there's nobody else around to be in charge of."

"I haven't heard you complaining about it."

"You're not hearing me complain now, sir. It suits me." With the foot-long tamping stick, Jayar pushed some wadding into place, then carefully wrapped the ball in an oil patch and rammed it home, seating it firmly. "I like the night," he said, carefully tipping some priming powder into the pan before shutting it with a firm click. "It gives me a chance to get some writing done, without all the clatter of the day."

"Still working on the history, eh?"

The engineer shrugged. "Somebody's got to do it."

"Mmm? How far have you gotten?"

"Well . . ." The heavy-set man frowned. "Not nearly far enough. But farther than yesterday."

"In other words, I should mind my own business." Karl chuckled.

"I wouldn't have put it that way," the engineer said, setting the pistol down on the table, the barrel pointed toward the wall, away from the two of them. He picked up the next one. "I would have *thought* just that, mind, but I wouldn't have put it that way."

Karl chuckled. "When you're done, you will let me see it?"

"I'm not sure I want to." Jayar tilted his head to one side. "You might not like how I treat you."

"Then again," Karl said, putting just a touch of steel in his voice, "rank hath its privileges. You *will* let me see it, when you're done."

"Yes, sir. I'm ready for the next."

In just a few minutes, all four of the pistols were charged, each carefully loaded into Karl's holsters.

"Going to the stables, sir?" Jayar asked, as he locked the door behind them, reaching for the speaking tube with one hand while he picked up his sealing-wax candle with the other.

"Yes," Karl said, knowing what was coming next. He really didn't want anybody else in on this, but . . .

"Did you want anyone in particular for your guard, sir?"

"Garavar—and tell him all I need are him and his sons. And no rush. It's just a little thing—I'll be leaving at false dawn."

Garavar would keep his mouth shut, Karl hoped. After a few years, even an emperor learned to give up issuing orders that he knew would be disobeyed. It wasn't that it was considered improper for a ruler to go out at night sans escort; it was a matter of calculation. Even if Karl ordered no bodyguard, it was an open secret that he wouldn't order punishment for engineers and soldiers who insisted on accompanying him.

On the other hand, if he *was* killed on one of his nighttime jaunts, it was far less than clear that his successor—be it Jason or whichever baron managed to grab the throne—would be so merciful toward the then-late emperor's supporters, supporters who had let the emperor get himself killed.

With the possible losses being—at most—a slap on the wrist in one event versus a likely beheading on the other, the bet was an easy one.

"Yes, sir," Jayar said, pulling the tube close to his mouth. "Attention, attention," he shouted into the speaking mask, then put it to his ear until he heard a distant, muffled response. "Runner to General Garavar's quarters," he went on. "General Garavar and sons, repeat sons, report to royal stables for escort duty. No need to run; a sprint will do. Repeat and go."

He tossed Karl a quick salute and a friendly smile.

"In case it doesn't turn out to be just a little thing, sir," Jayar said, "it's been nice knowing you." He sobered. "And I mean that sincerely, sir. It has been a rare and distinct pleasure."

"It's mutual." Karl Cullinane forced a chuckle. "Take care of yourself."

The predawn light hung grayly over the dusty road as distant thunder sounded from the west.

Some riding in front of Karl and Andy, some riding behind, Garavar and his six sons kept their eyes on the horizon as they left Biemestren behind them and briskly cantered their horses away from the lightening sky. While the fiction of this merely being a pleasure ride was maintained orally, nobody believed it for a moment: Older hands tended to stay near swordhilts, while younger ones gravitated to pistol butts.

Even Garthe, the youngest. He was only fifteen, although large for his age, and could easily have been taken for several years older than he was—perhaps even to the mid-twenties. There seemed to be a tendency in the family to grow old quickly, then stop aging, although, Gashier, the oldest, actually looked older than his father; there were many more worry lines in Gashier's face. Way back when, Karl had guessed him to be the general's elder brother; Garavar didn't show his age.

Karl had speculated that it was partly genetic, partly repeated use of healing spells and draughts over the years—healing spells seemed to have mild rejuvenative effects in some individuals.

Maybe even in Karl himself. He ran his fingers through his hair. Maybe that was the trouble; he'd been out of combat for so long that he hadn't been even nicked in a number of years, although he exercised frequently and vigorously. Maybe he was slowing down?

I'd best not even think that loudly around Tennetty. He chuckled.

Danagar, riding at Karl's right side, scowled at the sound, then muffled it when he realized who he was glaring at.

"Ta havath, Danagar," Karl said. "We're just out riding for fun."

"Yes, sir," Danagar said, manifestly unconvinced.

The chill wind gusted harder as they approached a bend in the road. It was hard to see; while the rising sun was winning a temporary victory over the fog, the combination of fog and glare prevented him from seeing well.

"Garthe," Garavar called out, "ride ahead, scout, and report."

"Yes, Father," the boy said, giving a twitch to his reins.

"Wait," Karl said; Garthe subsided. "Andy?" Karl stood in his saddle and turned to his wife.

She shook her head. "I can't tell, now. He's in that direction," she said, pointing, "but it could be a mile, maybe three. Let me try something." She murmured a few harsh syllables. "No, he's just around the bend."

"Fine. Vanish and wait here."

She knew better than to argue with him; she closed her eyes and gripped at the air around her, speaking the harsh, foreign, evanescent words that could only be heard and forgotten, never remaining in the mind of either speaker or listener.

Silently, space itself spun into a solid fabric of mist and fog, swirling in a silent hurricane around Andy, as she sat astride her dappled mare, the mists spinning faster, faster, until they totally concealed her and her horse, and then, suddenly, as if someone had flicked a switch—

—she and the horse were gone.

"Andy?"

A familiar chuckle sounded out of the air. "No. It's Claude Rains," she said. "Get to work, hero. I'm fine."

Karl turned and kicked his horse into a canter.

"With me, not in front of me," he said, raising his voice. "Because we," he said, calling out, "and that means I, Karl Cullinane, prince and emperor, and my entire escort are going to be waiting around this bend for the prisoner cart to pass later this morning," he called out, "and we will all ride with it to Tyrnael, if necessary, to see that no mishaps befall it. If you catch my fucking drift."

There was a rustling from the woods. Garthe started for his pistol, but desisted at his father's emphatic shake of the head.

"We will wait here for it," Karl said. "And since I know the seven of us are alone, we won't have to worry about any sounds from the woods—they're just rabbits or something."

A voice called out from the mist and leaves. "I'm coming out, Karl."

In a moment, Thomen Furnael, dressed in a ragged farmer's tunic but with a sword belted around his waist, stood in front of him.

"He's not alone, sir," Gashier said. "I can hear two others, at least."

"Of course he's alone," Karl said. "The baron is just out for a pleasure ride, like ourselves. It wouldn't be old Hivar back there, would it?"

"Very good," Thomen said, his hands folded across his chest. "How did you know it was him?"

Karl swung a leg over the back of the horse and dropped to the ground, signaling at Garavar and the others to stay put. "Who else would you trust, boy? Hivar's been with your family since before I met your father. But you're wrong—he's not back there, and there aren't any other loyal family retainers back there, because you're out, alone, for a pleasure ride—and *you're going to finish your pleasure ride and hie your ass back to Biemestren.* Understood?"

It was the sort of fix that would have occurred to Karl at that age: dress up as highwaymen, free Vernim, and send him on his way. Simple, elegant.

The only thing wrong with it was that it wouldn't work. Too many people had seen how shocked Thomen was when Vernim spoke up during sentencing; Vernim had already demonstrated that he had a loud mouth—he would talk.

It wouldn't work, dammit.

"There's another possibility," Thomen said, his hand resting on the hilt of his sword. "We could settle it, you and I, your majesty."

"Make another move and you're a dead man, Danagar," Karl said, as he caught a motion out of the corner of his eye. He turned back to Thomen. "You think that you could take me? Truthfully?"

Some skill with the sword was something that Thomen had inherited from his father; blunt, brutal self-honesty was another. "No. I may not be good enough even to put a mark on you. But—"

"Then do you think that we'll all be better off if both you and Vernim die? Who benefits, Thomen, who benefits—" Staring the younger man straight in the eye, Karl Cullinane snapped a foot into Thomen's crotch; as Thomen gasped, clutched at himself, and crumpled, Karl gripped him and spun him around.

"Hivar, there's no need for a fight," he said, as he eased the groaning young baron to the ground. "He's not badly hurt."

There was a long pause, then a voice called out from the darkness. "He'd best not be."

"I told you, he isn't. He's not going to want to fork a horse for a while, but he isn't badly hurt." Karl beckoned to Garthe. "Take charge of the baron. Bind him—we'll release him after the cart has passed. He can ride home with us. I'll take responsibility for his safety, Hivar. My word."

"Very well," sounded from the fog. "And I?"

"You get out of here, old man," Karl said. "Because you were never here, and this never happened."

Garavar nodded in approval; Thomen, in pain, forced a question through his lips: "Why?"

"Don't ever threaten me, Thomen," he said. "It's impolite."

Because, Karl Cullinane thought, *hanging Vernim is my responsibility. You're not ready for it, not yet. You were ready to salve your conscience by letting me kill you; I'd rather salve your conscience more cheaply.*

I owe that to you, Thomen—and to your father and brother.

"Because I am the emperor," Karl Cullinane said. "And you'd better understand that, boy."

CHAPTER EIGHT:
The Best-Laid Plans . . .

I'm a hero with coward's legs. I'm a hero from the waist up.
—Spike Mulligan

Except for the weather, Walter Slovotsky's part of the attack went off like it was charmed.

Walter Slovotsky's commando—he insisted on the correct usage of the word; it referred to the group, not the members of the group—consisted of only ten; ten against the seventeen in the horseborne slaver reserves wasn't great odds.

But there were compensating factors. Lou had told him that Aeia was still just about the best shot in Home; Bren Adahan, while inexperienced with a pistol, was a better swordsman than Walter, and quite good with a crossbow—and, most important, an experienced warrior; he had been thoroughly blooded in the Holtun-Bieme war.

Six of the others were warriors that Daherrin had recommended, only two of them tyros, one of those serving as medic—which meant that in addition to his weapons, he carried bandages and the bottle of healing draughts.

Daherrin had suggested Jason as the tenth, but Walter had vetoed the suggestion: This was a tricky bit; much better to put Jason with the group that was going to hit the slaver scouts—that looked to be the relatively cushy job.

No, Jason wasn't his tenth. His tenth was Ahira. The two of them had been friends for half their lives, and partnered for much of that time. In or out of a fight, having Ahira around was to Slovotsky like having a concrete backboard when playing basketball: The ball would rebound, period.

Still, given that the goal was to end up with seventeen dead slavers and no-count-them-*no* dead Home soldiers, it was going to be touch-and-go. Their pistols should lower the odds some; the rope in his hands was going to even them even more.

As was the element of surprise.

Which was the reason that Walter was in tactical command, after all, and not Ahira.

Besides, Ahira was part of the tactical reserves. Way back when, when he was in ROTC, Walter Slovotsky had been told that it was always necessary to have a reserve; it was the only thing from his two-week military career that had benefited him.

A stray raindrop hit him square in the left eye, stinging as he rubbed at it.

The weather was not promising; it was hard to reload in the rain.

As before, there was no sign of the slaver reserves from down the road when the last of the main party vanished around the bend. Wind whispered down the trail, a further promise of the oncoming storm.

Walter crept around the bend and waited silently until they were far enough away so that he could be sure his low-voiced call to Aeia and Bren wouldn't possibly be heard.

Distant flashes of lightning and remote crashes of thunder sent chills racing down his neck.

"Okay, you two," he whispered, hefting a coil of braided-leather rope as he stepped onto the trail. "Let's get to it."

While the first spatter of raindrops touched the leaves overhead, Bren Adahan knelt next to a tree, easily lifting Aeia when she stepped into his cupped hands. Walter tossed her the end of the rope.

It only took a few seconds for her to make the rope fast to the tree; she dropped lightly to the trail, and she and Bren repeated the process on the other side.

"Gin," Walter said. "Now we just have to—"

Shots sounded from down the trail.

Too early!

Panic washed across him in an icy wave, as the rain intensified, hard drops spattering his chest. As he dove for the cover of the woods he heard a harsh voice whispering, "Everyone to his place, and hold your fire," and realized it was his own.

More gunshots sounded from down the road; distant *cracks* that had him reflexively reaching for the pistols in his belt, knives at his hip, the swordbelt that was slung over his left shoulder, the better to discard it.

He could see only four of his people; the other four, under Ahira, were farther down the trail, giving them two lines of fire.

If it worked.

The rain fell hard, icy sheets clawing down through the trees,

Hoofbeats thundered on the hard ground; the troop of slavers galloped down the path, four abreast.

His bare back against the rough bark of the tree, Walter reached across his waist and drew a pistol, cocking it as he brought it up to chest level, hoping, praying that the rain hadn't penetrated into the pan.

The first four slavers hit the rope almost simultaneously. The taut leather knocked them into the air as though they were bowling pins.

Except that bowling pins didn't have neckbones that cracked with a horrible snap. Bowling pins didn't fall to the ground twitching and screaming in a final agony.

Two of the horses stumbled and fell, one sending its rider tumbling, the other rolling and crushing the scream from its former rider.

Of the next four slavers, one was able to duck under, but a gunshot caught him in the shoulder, slamming him out of the saddle and to the ground. Walter Slovotsky stood, bringing his first pistol to bear on an advancing slaver, firing as the heavy-bearded man fell into his sights.

He must have overloaded the gun; it went off with a bang that shook Walter to the bone. He missed; he never did see where the bullet went.

But the flash of his pistol and the clamor of the gunshot had identified him as a target for the charging slavers, who were now reining their horses in, some with swords already unscabbarded, others with lances seated firmly against their hips, yet others with short hornbows brought up, arrows nocked.

The slaver he had fired at brought his lance down and spurred his horse toward Slovotsky.

It was strange, Walter thought as his fingers clawed for another pistol, the things you noticed at a time like this: mud splashing from the pounding hooves, the flaring of the horse's nostrils, a vein in the bearded man's throat pulsing once, twice, three times—

And then vanishing as a shotgun blast tore him from the saddle, turning the face into a bloody pulp and sending him tumbling in the rain to the wet ground.

Walter unholstered his remaining pistol, and cocked it. It had been perhaps ten seconds since the first of the slavers had hit the rope, and there were already eight down.

As he brought his pistol up, a flurry of gunfire knocked three more of the slavers from their saddles, including the one Slovotsky had been aiming at.

He switched targets, but missed; his bullet struck his intended target's horse in the neck as the animal reared.

The horse screamed.

Something whizzed past Walter's ear, stinging him as a new wetness touched his cheek.

Another slaver, this one a blond boy no older than Jason, reached with trembling fingers to pull his crossbow's string back, but Walter's fingers found the hilt of one of his knives, drew, and threw it, sending another one flying after it even as the first one *thunked* home.

And then, from behind the last of the slavers, Ahira stepped into the rain, a potlike steel helmet strapped to his head, new chainmail protecting his torso, the metal shirt dropping all the way to his knees.

His staff, freshly cut from a sapling, was easily three times his height; even though it was thicker than Walter Slovotsky's wrist, the dwarf held it easily in his huge hands.

With a guttural cry, Ahira swept the end of his oversized staff toward the nearest of the slavers, moving so quickly that the sapling visibly bent even before the end whipped around to bowl the slaver from his horse, the man broken like a discarded child's toy.

A bolt of lightning momentarily dazzled Slovotsky's eyes; as they began to clear he saw Ahira still wielding his oversized weapon as lightly and easily as a human would handle a wooden switch. The dwarf quickly batted five more from their saddles. Other Home warriors were upon the dazed or dead slavers in seconds, slitting their throats with an efficiency that chilled even Walter.

It had been less than half a minute since the trap had sprung, and there was only one slaver left alive and uninjured.

Slavery is an unjustifiable evil, at any time and in any place. But that does not mean that all slavers are cowards. The last one was a brave man: instead of trying to run, or cowering and waiting his fate, he vaulted from his saddle and with a muttered oath of defiance lunged at Ahira.

Ahira brought up his staff to parry, but his sandals slipped in the mud of the trail and he fell flat on his back, momentarily stunned, the pole falling from his hands.

The slaver lunged at the dwarf; the tip of his sword caught in Ahira's chainmail.

On his back, the dwarf tried to crab himself away, but the slaver turned only momentarily to parry the attack of one of Slovotsky's warriors, then went after Ahira, his sword weaving as it pursued the dwarf like a snake after a rabbit.

Walter Slovotsky had already snatched his own sword from its scabbard; at a full sprint, he barely paused, broken-field-style, to kick a dying slaver out of his way, and ran toward the dwarf and his opponent, hoping that he would make it in time, praying that Ahira could hold out just a few more seconds, just a few more.

"Hold your fire, everybody," Walter called out. Ahira and the slaver were too close; a mis-aimed shot could easily hit the dwarf instead of the slaver. And Ahira was trapped; he had crabbed himself backward into a tree, and had nowhere to go, no way to defend himself.

Walter dropped his sword and snatched at a throwing knife as the slaver brought back his own weapon for a final, fatal thrust.

Two shots rang out; the slaver's throat disappeared in an awful shower of blood and bone. As the body slipped to the mud, the slaver's head, its face miraculously almost whole, fell to the ground, all the while seemingly watching Walter with shocked, wide eyes.

A splash of muddy water covered the eyes.

Walter turned to see Aeia lower her second pistol. Her stringy hair, sopping from the rain, clung to her face and neck; she eyed him levelly as she pressed her free hand against her side. "I don't miss slavers," she said from between clenched teeth. "And I don't take chancy shots."

That was nonsense. Anyone could miss. But she hadn't missed, and that was what mattered.

Besides, there wasn't time for discussion, not now.

"Places, everyone," Walter Slovotsky said. "Gunmen, get under the tarpaulin and reload," he said, reaching for where he had dropped his own pistols and fumbling in his pouch for his powder horn. It still might work; they had set up a tarp as a fly, to give them a dry place to reload if the rain was too intense.

Which it was; he wiped the water from his eyes as he gathered up his own weapons, hoping that there were enough dry cloths under the tarp so that he could dry the weapons enough to reload.

"Jimmy, I want those trees *down*. Danerel, see to the injured animals; bind or put them out of their miser—"

In midword, it hit him.

Aeia was pressing her hand to her side. *No.*

He ran to her. She was sitting on the ground, leaning against the rough bark of a half-dead elm, staring blindly out into the rain, clumsy fingers clawing at her pouch, ignoring the pounding of the storm and the frightening dark wetness that spread across her hip, staining her shirt with her own blood.

"Aeia, please . . . let me," Bren Adahan said as he knelt next to her, but Walter shoved him away, sending the younger man tumbling.

It only occurred to him much later that he was acting like Karl would have—that monomaniac Cullinane could never concentrate on more than one thing at a time.

"Medic, dammit," he shouted, as he crouched beside her. "We need a goddamn medic here. We've got one down." He tore the pistol and powder horn from her hands and gripped both of her wrists in his left fist, ignoring her vague, distant protests.

"I decide what the priorities are here, understood?" he said, tugging at her shirt, trying to pull it up so that he could get at her wound. Wet, it resisted; it clung tightly to her skin.

Fastening both hands on her shirt, he ripped the cloth away, revealing the deep gash in her side. The hole went all the way through her, about kidney-height. Blood flowed evenly, a dark oozing. Trying to staunch the flow, he clapped a palm to her wound, then snatched it away as she screamed, her body writhing spasmodically.

"No," she said, struggling against his grip with a weakness that frightened him. "Later. Got to reload, or—" Her voice trailed off in a gurgle as a spasm sent a stream of bloody vomit pouring from her mouth, spattering him.

The runner arrived with the brass bottle of healing draughts; out of the corner of his eye Slovotsky saw Bren Adahan snatch it away and uncork it. Adahan splashed some on Aeia's wound, then forced the bottle between her lips, while Slovotsky held her still.

But another spasm splattered Walter's face with wasted healing draught and more sour vomit. Shaking his head to clear the vile fluid from his face, he tried to hold her still. Bren splashed more of the precious stuff on the outside of her wounds, and was only partly successful.

"Try it again—Aeia, you've got to drink this," Bren said.

"Can't—"

Walter Slovotsky called for his command voice:

"Do it, Aeia. *Now*," he said.

God, I sound like Karl, he thought, as she swallowed once, hard, and then went limp in his arms.

"No!" Bren Adahan shouted, a shrill half-scream, while Walter held her tightly against his chest, her cold, wet form horribly still.

No. Make it not so.

But—God and all the saints be praised!—the thumping wasn't just his own heart. It was hers, too.

"She's alive, Bren." Walter found himself smiling so hard he thought his face might split. "She's alive." Gripping her hands, he could feel her pulse. Thin and thready, but it was there. He fancied he could hear her heartbeat.

Somewhere off in the storm, Ahira was barking orders; a tree crashed to the ground. "Walter," the dwarf called, "we've got to set up."

Walter stood, Aeia in his arms. "Bren—take her away from the trail; I don't want her hurt any more."

Bren nodded grimly as he accepted her limp form, holding the girl easily, tenderly, leaving behind only a quick glare as he ducked his head and pushed away into the rain.

Clever, Slovotsky, very clever. You sure concealed that relationship well.

Walter Slovotsky had always prided himself on not being the kiss-and-tell type, but it never seemed to matter much; interested parties usually worked such things out.

To hell with it. He wiped sour vomit from his face and chest as he worked his way back to the trail, slogging through the now ankle-deep mud.

Save that for later.

"Save it for later, Walter," Ahira said, echoing his own thoughts.

The dwarf swung the woodaxe against the bole of another tree; chips the size of Slovotsky's fist flew off into the rain. "And reload, now."

Walter looked down at where he had dropped his pistols; they lay in the leaves, wet and muddy. It would take more than a few towels and a few minutes to dry them enough for reloading.

"No good; I'm going to have to substitute."

"Then *do* it."

Crossbow, that was the best bet—he could relieve one of the dead slavers of a weapon. The bastards always seemed to have good bows.

He walked over to where the still body of a slaver crossbowman lay on the ground, half covered by his dappled mare. Glassy-eyed, barely breathing, the animal whinnied in pain, its right foreleg badly broken, bloody shards of bone poking through the skin.

Dead slavers were something that didn't bother Slovotsky, not after all these years. But an animal in pain was something he could never get used to.

"Danerel?" he called out. "You find any healing draughts?"

The fat man nodded and pulled a small clay bottle from his pouch, tossing it to Slovotsky.

While healing draughts were precious, it wasn't possible to trust the slavers' potions—more than once, they had been booby-trapped; once he had watched one of his and Karl's team die a horrible death in front of their eyes. Four times, Walter had watched the same happen to a captured slaver, used as a test animal.

There weren't any test animals here. "Then again, Dobbin, I don't see that you're going to lose anything by my trying."

Walter uncorked the bottle and poured the thick liquid onto the horse's wound.

This time, the stuff was pure, the real thing: Skin and muscle reached out and drew bone into place, slashed flesh sealed up like a zipper. But the horse was still weak, still whinnying in pain. Internal injuries, probably.

Well, Slovotsky decided, laughing inside at his own hypocrisy, there could still be a slow-acting poison in this; best to use it on the animal and not himself.

He splashed the rest into the animal's mouth, then tossed the now-empty bottle aside.

The familiar miracle repeated itself: In less than a minute, the horse was on its feet. As he stooped to move the body of the slaver,

Walter took a moment to pat at its muzzle, resolving to take this mare as part of his share of the booty.

Half covered by the body of its former master, the slaver's crossbow was unbroken, surprisingly.

Cocking it, Walter took a quiver of bolts down from the horse's saddle and slipped one into the slot, nocking it into place. He hung the quiver from his belt and headed to the roadblock that Ahira had set up.

Three trees lay across the trail, their boles and branches making the way almost impassable. But over to the left, the brush on the side of the trail was thinned out, just enough. "Danerel—and you, yes, *you*—take positions over there. And restring the tripwire from that tree to that one. In case they crash through."

It had been only a few minutes since the start of the attack; retreating slavers should be due any moment. The only question in Slovotsky's mind was how long his commando could hold them without relief from the rest of the Home forces.

After all the anticipation, it was an anticlimax when only three slaver horsemen made it down the trail to the roadblock. Three bullets and two crossbow bolts were enough to bring them down.

"That was a pretty brace of shots from Aeia. I might have gotten myself badly nicked, otherwise," Ahira said, hefting one of the dead slavers' lances, then casually hurling it into what clearly was a corpse. The pole passed clear through the dead man.

"He was already dead," Walter Slovotsky said.

"So, no harm done. I take over from here, yes?" Ahira said, shaking his head to clear the rain from his eyes.

Walter nodded. "It's yours."

Fighting the exhaustion that threatened to drag him down into the wet darkness, Walter Slovotsky shook his head to try to clear it.

He shivered in the rain. Nothing that could be done about that, except maybe some internal heating. He fished a silver flask from his pouch, unscrewed the top, and tilted back a good mouthful of Riccetti's Best. The harsh corn liquor burned on the way down, then set up warming vibrations in his middle that pushed the chill away, if only a little.

He passed the bottle to Ahira. The dwarf took the barest taste—clearly doing that only out of politeness—before handing it back. "Good stuff. Now, put it away; we're not done for the day. Danerel, you finish with cleanup. Araven, go find Bren Adahan and Aeia, and tell them it's all over—and be careful, boy, keep calling their names as you go. You—what's your name?—Keevan, get Walter's and my horses; we're going to go hook up with the rest."

Ahira looked over at him in grim satisfaction, his open-palmed gesture taking in the corpses scattered across the ground, some almost lifelike, staring open-eyed at nothing, others, limbs missing and faces blasted into a horrid pulp, barely recognizable as human.

It all stank. Like a cesspool. In death, the slavers' sphincters had all relaxed, in the mindless reflex that tries to make all animals less tasty to their predators.

Ahira shook his head. "Remember when this bothered you?"

Walter Slovotsky swallowed twice, hard. "Nah," he said, forcing a smile that maybe even Ahira wouldn't have been able to tell from the real thing. "That was long ago, in a galaxy far, far away."

As always, the cleanup was tedious, but the familiarity of the routine was reassuring. The main assault under Daherrin had gone generally well, although not perfectly: The warrior who challenged Walter and Ahira on their way in said there had been many minor casualties among both Home warriors and ex-slaves, and, worse, two warrior deaths—Sereval and Hervan, two men that Walter knew only slightly—and almost a dozen slaves killed by stray shots and bolts.

It couldn't be helped. One of the many nasty facts of life is that innocence is no armor.

Even after a long layoff, Daherrin's team swung into their post-slaughter routine with practiced assurance, each one assuming his secondary role comfortably.

Warriors-turned-smiths chiseled through chains while warriors-turned-cooks sorted through the slavers' stores, handing out small pieces of jerky while several huge pots of stew were cooking, two men quickly butchering a killed horse for the pot. Others, now acting as medics, eyed all injuries skeptically, dispensing ointments and bandages liberally, doling out doses of healing draughts stingily. A detail dug graves for respectful burials for both Home warriors and dead slaves, while warrior-quartermasters stripped the slaver corpses and searched for personal effects.

Those with nothing else to do dragged the dead slavers off, away from the camp, to rot on the forest floor. Normal procedure was to leave the slavers' bodies where they fell, as an announcement and a warning. An exception had been made; because of the intermittent rain, Daherrin had decided—wisely, in Slovotsky's opinion—to make a rough camp here for the night, giving both warriors and former slaves a good rest before starting the long march Homeward in the morning.

Tarpaulins were pitched as lean-tos, sheltering some from the rain, which had slowed to a miserable drizzle, while others stood around the six cooking fires that defiantly shot flame out into the rain.

Getting close to half a thousand ex-slaves treated, fed, and bedded down for the night was a major operation, but Daherrin had it well in hand by the time Slovotsky and Ahira dismounted from their horses.

The dwarf issued a few quick orders to a lanky, teenaged horseman, then reached up and gave him a friendly slap on the leg. "Good. Be sure to run down the chart—and I want you to personally account for everyone on the team; we don't want anybody hurt and lost."

"Understood, Daherrin." The boy spurred his horse away.

"You have any casualties?" Daherrin asked.

"No problem. Aeia wounded, the wound treated," Ahira said. "Nothing else worth talking about."

"Looking good," Daherrin said, with a gap-toothed smile. "Don't like two dead, but it'll probably hold at that."

Walter shook his head. "What do you mean, probably? The guard said—"

"We don't have a report from the group that took on the outriders." The dwarf shrugged. "But not to worry—there were only two men in the slaver advance, and we had six waiting for 'em."

Hooves sending mud splashing into the air, Geveren's pony galloped up. Even before the horse had completely stopped, the battered dwarf had dismounted, stumbling on the muddy ground.

"Ahira, Walter Slovotsky," he said. "We have a problem."

"What—"

"Valeran is dead. And Jason Cullinane is gone." His expression grew grim. "When the shooting started, he ran. He took his horse and ran away."

CHAPTER NINE:

Jason Cullinane

I have saved myself; what do I care about that shield? Forget about it; I'll get another one that is just as good.
                                        —Archilochus

I'm going, too. The moment that the words were out of his mouth, Jason Cullinane had known that it was a terrible mistake.

But it had also been expected of him, required of him. Everything was expected of *his* son. By *him,* as well as everyone else.

Including Aeia and Valeran. Well, perhaps Aeia would have smiled tolerantly at him, even if he hadn't volunteered, but the old soldier, who didn't seem to approve of much that Jason Cullinane did or was, had responded to Jason's hasty words with a brief nod of approval, the highest praise that the old captain had ever deigned to confer on Jason.

It wasn't fair. It just wasn't fair. So what if other sixteen-year-olds were expected to use a sword, bow, or gun, to put themselves in the way of flying crossbow bolts and sharp steel edges—why did Jason have to be like everyone else? The others were all so stupid—didn't they know that swords could cut, that bolts could pierce too-weak flesh?

Didn't they know?

"Easy, boy," Valeran murmured as they crouched in the brush off the trail, waiting in the downpour for the slaver advance to ride by. "This is what Karl would call a 'piece of cake,'" he said, the English words awkward in his mouth.

Valeran's left hand patted the crossbow that the old captain rested easily on his knee. "Just a bit of simple, basic butchery. It will be bloody, but easy—we've practiced and discussed it enough, eh?"

"Yes, Valeran," Jason whispered back, grateful that he had to whisper, knowing that if he tried to use his voice, it would break.

It should have been easy.

Their horses were hidden farther down the trail, all well hitched; it was six from Home against the two advance riders, with a simple plan, one that should have been foolproof. If the main part of the attack had already started—if they heard gunshots from down the trail—they were free to take their pistols from their oilskin wrappings and use them. Otherwise they were restricted to crossbows and swords—and the throttle loop that Jason's old friend Mikyn, crouching in a crooked limb of an old oak, had waiting as a surprise for the slavers.

It should have been easy.

Down the trail, hooves beat against mud in a loud, rapid tattoo.

"Get ready," Valeran said.

The two horsemen rode down the path, the second trailing a full twenty yards behind the first, clearly to minimize being splattered by flying mud.

Gently, like a strand of spider's web floating to earth, Mikyn's noose dropped from the cover of the rain—

—and settled around the suddenly outflung arm of the trailing horseman.

The slaver's reflexes were superb: With a shrill cry, he fastened a gloved fist around the cord and pulled, hard. Mikyn, unprepared, fell from the tree, landing hard on his side in the mud.

This wasn't what was supposed to happen.

It should have been easy.

The other slaver, hearing the cry, wheeled his horse around, fingers clawing for a weapon.

This wasn't what was supposed to happen.

Valeran rose to his full height, bringing his crossbow up.

"Shoot the one in front!" he called out, taking aim at the slaver who had pulled Mikyn down, and who now, his sword held out and down, was bearing down on the stunned boy. But doing that necessarily forced the old soldier to ignore the other slaver.

This wasn't what was supposed to happen.

The slaver drew and threw a knife.

Time lost its forward motion, and froze into an awful moment:

—Valeran, his strong fingers curled around the crossbow trigger, leading the slaver carefully, knowing that this was his only chance at the grizzled man bearing down on Mikyn—

—a flickering of steel as a throwing knife tumbled end over end through the air—

—Jason, his arm reaching out as of its own volition, trying to shout a warning to his teacher and mentor, to the man who had been more of a father than *he* could ever be—

He had to warn Valeran. He had to. But time was frozen for him, too; he was part of the scene, frozen into the same icy slice of time, not merely an observer.

This wasn't what was supposed to happen.

And then it all resolved:

—The horseman bearing down on Mikyn looked puzzled as his sword tumbled from nerveless fingers, clumsy hands reaching up to feel at the crossbow bolt buried feather-deep in his chest.

—Two other bolts sprouted from the other slaver; yet another grew from the neck of his now-rearing horse.

—And Valeran slumped back to the ground, a wood-handled throwing knife buried hilt-deep in the bloody mess that had been his right eye.

This wasn't what was supposed to happen.

It should have been easy.

Jason ran. And kept on running.

CHAPTER TEN:

Decisions

Three may keep a secret, if two are dead.
                                    —Benjamin Franklin

"We don't have much time," Ahira said, staring out into the night. The rain had faded to a drizzle, but it was enough to mask Jason's trail. Just a couple of miles farther, the forest opened on the cleared land of the holdings outside of Wehnest; he could go in any direction.

Go after him now? Riding down a forest trail at night was a fine way for horses and people to lose eyes; maybe once they broke through into cleared land they might be able to make some safe progress.

But cleared land was miles away. It might as well be light-years.

Ahira didn't like it at all.

Why did humans have to make a bad situation worse? The dwarf shrugged. It was typical.

"He might turn back," Aeia said, taking another mouthful of stew. "I doubt it, but he might. Stubbornness runs in the family," she said, a little proudly.

Bren Adahan shrugged, the flames of the cooking fire dancing in his eyes. He ran dirty fingers through his sandy hair. "I don't see what the problem is. As Mikyn tells it, Jason . . . left after the matter was decided; it wasn't cowardice—"

"Says you." Walter Slovotsky shook his head. "And says me, for that matter. All it looks like is squeamishness. But what if it looks like cowardice to him?"

Trust Walter to put his finger right on the problem.

Adahan didn't understand; he shrugged again. "So? We find him and explain otherwise. It's not uncommon to panic, one's first time in a fight."

"Tell that to the boy," Ahira said. *Please tell that to the boy.*

"Very well; I'll go after him," Bren Adahan said, spreading his hands. "But, again, I do not see the problem. We can send easily half a hundred men to find him, persuade him to come back, even force him if they have to."

Aeia's eyes flashed at that. "Force my brother?"

"Never mind that, Aeia. Think again, Bren Adahan," Daherrin said. "Think again."

"Excuse me?"

"He's telling you to think it through," Aeia said. She spoke slowly, patiently, as though explaining something obvious to a half-witted child. "Jason isn't just my little brother; he's also Karl Cullinane's son—don't you think that any member of the Slavers' Guild would give his right leg to have his hands on the emperor's son?" She swallowed more stew. "It's got to be done fast. We don't have much time until the word gets out."

That was true. Word of Jason's desertion had quickly spread among the Home warriors—and probably the ex-slaves. Gossip travels at around the speed of sound, even though it feels like the speed of light. Those Therranji heading back to Therranj would quickly spread the story; even those going Home would soon pass the news throughout the valley, and from there to an outbound trader.

Within weeks, word would be out: Jason Cullinane was traveling. Alone, unprotected.

When the news reached that bastard Ahrmin, would he try to kidnap the boy to use as a lever to pry Karl out of Holtun-Bieme? Or would he just torture the boy to death, and use that to draw Karl out to where he could be killed?

Did it matter?

Ahira shook his head. It didn't look good at all.

"Got to find him before it's generally known," Daherrin said. He shook his head. "Don't like this much at all; this sorta thing is not my job." He called to his second, "Three or four days until we should be seeing the dragon?"

"Four," the answer came back. "If he makes it Home on time, and if we get to the rendezvous on time."

"Ellegon! That's the solution," Bren Adahan said eagerly. "Couldn't Ellegon find him?"

"Sure." Walter Slovotsky poked a stick into the fire, then pulled it out and considered the glowing ember at its tip. "If they're close enough, Ellegon can read him—the two of them have been around each other since before Jason was born; Ellegon can read him from a greater distance than he can Karl, even. But that's not much; the dragon's got to be reasonably close." Walter shrugged. "Jason can cover a lot of ground in four, five days. Ellegon doesn't dare get too close to towns; he's too liable to get shot out of the sky."

Ahira nodded. "Let's assume he's going to at least stop off in Wehnest. Maybe we can catch up with him there—we'll bring in some of the slavers' gear, and play merchant as a cover."

Aeia set her bowl down. "Fine with me."

Bren and Walter both spoke up. "You are not going," they said in unison.

"Really. How interesting." Aeia tilted her head as she looked over at Ahira; it was one of Andrea's gestures. "Do you think I'm not going?"

Ahira didn't like it, but he knew as well as anyone that he didn't have the authority to stop her. Besides, it was a family affair.

"Aeia," Walter said, "you're not going. And that ends that discussion."

She stared off into the dark for a moment. "Have you ever heard my father talk about threats, Uncle Walter?"

Walter frowned.

"He says," she went on, "that if you make them strong enough, and mean them sincerely enough, you almost never have to follow through. So . . ." She eyed him levelly. "If you're going to try to keep me out of this, then you'd better find three or four big men to chain me down, because he's *my* little brother, and I'm *not* being left behind," she said, one hand on the butt of her pistol. "And they'd damn well better not want to live, because when I get unchained, I'll kill them. Dead."

Despite himself, Ahira grinned. He looked over at Walter. "She's going."

"I worked it out."

Ahira laughed. "Aeia, I think you've spent too much time around Tennetty. Hmmm . . . who else do we want?"

Bren Adahan stirred at the ashes. "I'll come. I already said I would."

Hardly surprising, considering that Aeia was coming.

"You're in." Ahira nodded. "But we'd better leave it at that: Aeia, Bren Adahan, Walter, and me. Any more, and the size of our group will draw attention. Can't have a whole troop of dwarves marching into Wehnest."

Walter Slovotsky grinned. "I don't know. It might be kind of fun to see Geveren and the others marching in, singing, 'Heigh-ho, heigh-ho.' Could draw a lot of attention."

"Shh," Daherrin considered the flames for a moment. "What do we tell the dragon?"

"Simple," Walter said. "The usual rendezvous south of Wehnest still where it used to be?"

"No," Daherrin said, then visibly reconsidered. "Well, yeah, if you're thinking of the one we used to use when you were seconding Karl—we just moved it back last year. It's the clearing, just 'bout three days out. Where we first ran into slaver powder, back when *he* was running the team."

"Right. So we'll meet Ellegon there."

Daherrin spat into the fire, a sizzling glob that vanished in a hiss of steam. "That wasn't what I meant. Ellegon isn't going to be happy about losing the boy—what do I tell him?"

"You just tell him the truth," Ahira said. "The truth. The truth, the whole truth, and nothing but the truth. With a bit of luck, the truth will be that Jason, Aeia, Bren, Walter, and I are heading back toward Home."

"Without luck?"

Ahira picked up a log that was half as thick as his arm. It was a bit long for the fire; he gripped it firmly and snapped it in two. He turned to the others and looked over the faces, shining in the firelight.

"Without luck, we're all dead."

CHAPTER ELEVEN:

Jason, Alone

What is left when honor is lost?

—Publilius Syrus

By the time dawn broke, Jason was sure of four things: first, that he'd been a coward to run; second, that there was no way he could go back; third, that he was hungry; and fourth, that he was tired.

As dawn broke redly across the cornfields, the weariness beat down on him like the rain had; a dull, metallic morning taste clung to his teeth.

But it just didn't seem to matter. Still, he pulled a piece of jerky from his saddlebags and let the leather-hard meat soften in his mouth before chewing.

"See," he explained to the brown gelding that his father had named Libertarian, for reasons he wouldn't explain, "I'm not just anybody else. I'm supposed to be special." He mumbled around the mouthful of jerky. "Supposed to be special." He was leading his horse, as he had been doing for most of the night; it was one of the lessons from *him* that had apparently sunk in; *he* had always said that cruelty to animals was unforgivable.

But what could he do? Jason considered his situation, turning it over once again in his mind. He had a bit of money in his bags, his swords, pistol, and rifle, his horse and saddle, and the clothes on his back.

And that was all.

What would Valeran have done?

Valeran. He let the reins fall from his fingers, fell to his knees in the mud, and wept. What would Valeran have done? Valeran wouldn't have had to do anything; he wouldn't have run like a coward in the first place; he would have stood his ground.

Jason never knew how long he cried, but when he stopped, he was kneeling in the mud on the road, his horse waiting patiently.

He got to his feet and rubbed at his eyes.

There was something Uncle Lou had once said, something about how if you don't know how to solve all of a problem, try solving a piece of it and working from there. He called it "getting a man on base," whatever that meant.

But it made sense. *May as well give it a try,* he decided. Ahead was Wehnest. If he wasn't going to turn around and go back—

"I can't," he said. "I *can't* go back."

—well, then he'd have to either stay there, go through the fields, or go forward. He'd walked the horse long enough; he picked up the reins and swung himself to the saddle, nudging the gelding into a slow walk.

He patted at the rifle in its saddle boot. Clearly he'd have to do something about the guns; they identified him as from Home. Home warriors weren't popular everywhere; there were always some who wanted to try to earn guild rewards. While concealing his pistols was easy, he knew he should throw the rifle away, but Jason had studied smithing under Nehera; the barrel alone represented hours upon hours of hard work, and it would be wrong to just toss that away.

Besides, it might be handy to have a gun.

And, besides, he thought, almost choking on the tears welling up, it was a memento of Home.

He didn't deserve it, but he'd keep it anyway.

Down the road, at the bottom of a gentle dip, a circle of low grasses surrounding an ancient oak interrupted the cornfield, its leaves arching over a well. He wasn't sure whether the well had been dug specifically for travelers and their animals or if it had formerly served a habitation, but it had been maintained: the bucket was made of new ash, and the rope was both sturdy and neatly coiled.

He watered his horse first, then set it to grazing.

Jason stripped to the buff and brought up another bucketful, giving his clothes a brief washing, wringing his tunic and leggings as vigorously as he could, spreading his clothes in the sun to dry.

He brought up another bucketful, and dumped it over his head before he could lose his nerve.

It was colder than anything he had ever felt before; by the time he had sluiced the mud from his skin, his teeth were chattering.

He dried himself awkwardly with his sleeping blanket, then spread it out and stretched himself out on its damp surface to dry.

He sat up with a jerk, for a moment wondering where he was, then remembering.

The sun was high above the fields now, and his clothes and blanket almost dry. He was still hungry.

He quickly dressed and stood over his gear, rubbing his eyes, then knelt to rub his rifle down with an oily cloth from his bags before wrapping it in his blanket and tying the blanket shut. Well, it was hidden in a manner of speaking, but what it looked like was a rifle wrapped in a blanket.

Not good enough, he decided as he untied the package.

Jason took a couple of quills from his fletching kit, tied them to a small stick, and stuck the stick down the barrel of the rifle. Taking his bowie from his belt, he cut a few stalks of corn, stripped off the immature ears and fed them to his horse, then set the stalks down next to his rifle and wrapped the whole bundle in the blanket.

Now, that looked a bit better.

To the casual observer, it could easily seem to be a bow and some arrow stock.

He stood, grinning widely, then caught himself.

Cowards had no right to smile. He would never smile again, he decided as he wrapped his pistols in oilcloth and hid them in his saddlebags.

But, still, Riccetti had been right, as usual: Solving even a little, unimportant problem did make the day seem a little brighter, life seem a little better.

Hitching at his swordbelt, he swung to Libertarian's saddle and gave the horse's reins a firm twitch.

Wehnest wasn't like Home, or even like the smaller-sized towns in Holtun-Bieme. Home houses were wood-frame dwellings and log cabins, built with pine. Both Holtun and Bieme had long favored stone as a building material, although the ramshackle huts that tended to be built up against permanent structures could be anything, but were usually of half-timber construction, wattle-and-daub buildings: oak-framed shacks with walls made of woven mats of wicker, sealed—to the extent that they *were* sealed—with mud.

Here, everything except the lord's keep in the distance was wattle-and-daub, with all of wattle-and-daub's questionable benefits.

Half-timber houses were as drafty as the worst of stone construction, their walls were home to vermin of all descriptions, and—as if that weren't bad enough—they were incredibly easy to burn. Which was why *he* had outlawed any new half-timber construction in Holtun-Bieme.

And which also might have explained the guard station on the road. Far off in the distance, Jason could see the lord's guard station, a stone gatehouse around the outer wall of the houses immediately surrounding the lord's castle.

But Metreyll had long been at peace, and the settlement had overflowed the stone surrounding the castle at the heart of the city; the dirt road was watched by only a ramshackle half-timber building that was more shack than anything else, the shack watched over by two lazy-eyed guards.

Jason waited with simulated patience while the two guards waved a farmer and his ox cart along.

He dismounted at a nod.

"Your business in Wehnest, lad?" the older of the two said. The frown on his lined face was of almost infinite weariness, and both his breastplate and helmet were rusted through in several places: a worn man, wearing worn armor. Not much life left in either.

"Just traveling through. And I'm older than I look," Jason said as gruffly as he could, ruining the effect when his voice cracked.

The other guard snickered. "And where from? As if we didn't know."

"Excuse me?" Jason's hand dropped to his swordhilt. The younger guard was as fast as he was; his sword was halfway from its scabbard when the old soldier raised a hand.

"Ta havath, Artum, ta havath," the old man said wearily, then turned back to Jason. "It happens all the time, boy; nothing unusual—and, usually, the rejected head here rather than back to the elves. The lords of Home didn't need your sword, eh?"

Jason wasn't sure what the other was getting at, but playing along looked right. "If you say so." *Back to the elves*—that had to mean Therranj. It sounded as though the old soldier had mistaken him for a Therranji human.

The old one nodded. "Thought so. Ten years back, I tried to sign up myself. Looked to be good pay. They didn't want me."

The younger one—Artum—snickered. "You never were much with a sword, Habel."

Habel drew himself up straight, and for just a second, Jason could see a trace of the strength that he must have had in his youth.

"It wasn't my sword that was the problem, boy," he said quietly, his voice almost a whisper.

Sometimes all a warrior has is his dignity and pride; for a moment Habel's ancient pride threatened to flare into a present fire.

But the moment passed, leaving Jason almost choked with rage. Not at Habel, and not at the other soldier—Jason was furious with himself. At least Habel had some pride; perhaps, once upon a time, Habel hadn't run, hadn't proclaimed himself a coward.

"Artum . . ." The old man leaned back against the wall of the guard shack and sighed. "That damned dragon of theirs stared into my soul, and pronounced me unfit."

Ellegon. *His* son didn't have any close friends, except for two: Valeran and the dragon. And Valeran was dead; Ellegon would look into Jason's heart, see the coward, and recoil in disgust.

Jason had never felt so alone.

"Which village are you from?" the younger guard asked.

"Is that important?"

"I say—"

"Artum." Habel looked at him for a long moment. "No, probably not," he said, becoming suddenly businesslike. With a rough hunk of chalk, he made a mark on the wall of the guard shack. "By nightfall, you are to be out of Metreyll or registered with an armsman—you'll need to either be hired, or show enough coin to persuade him that you're not going to have to steal to eat."

"I'll be gone before dark," Jason said, sounding more sure than he felt. Where do you go when your life is over?

"Very well, but if you're after work, Falikos the rancher is hiring drovers. Pay is shit-poor, but I hear the food is good."

"Thank you; I may look into that."

"No thanks necessary; it's my job. Now be gone."

The first thing to do was to find a place to stay; while Jason didn't particularly want to show all of his money—how would someone of his age and appearance have come by so much?—surely he could show enough to establish some means of support. The idea of hiring on as a drover didn't have any appeal. Still, he had to do something about getting his horse fed and rested, and himself occupied.

Where do you go to give up?

Karl Cullinane had smiled and asked Mother that, once, when she was frustrated with the inability of an apprentice to handle Other Side numbering. Her answer had been to swear at him and redouble her efforts. There wasn't anyplace to go to give up.

He couldn't stay here long. They'd be after him, lying to him that everything was all right, that it was okay for *his* son to be a coward—a filthy coward.

The worst of it was that Ellegon might find him. He couldn't face the dragon, or *him*, not ever again, not until . . .

. . . until what?

That was the problem; he didn't have an answer to that.

A few days. That was all he needed. Just a few days to settle his thoughts and try to figure out what to do next.

He found accommodations at Vator the hostler's, where he gave his name as Taren, a common name throughout the Eren regions.

The fat, bald man, after giving Jason's gear a thorough eyeing, insisted on rather more than Jason thought was standard for boarding his horse, but after Jason gave him a hand reshoeing a recalcitrant mule, he changed his mind and offered board and sleeping space in the hayloft above the stables in return for a day's work; he also agreed to report Jason as employed.

It seemed a fair deal; Jason nodded and got to work.

The work was hard, but, even dog-tired as he was, he couldn't sleep that night.

Part of it was the insects that infested the straw; by midnight, he was bitten in half a thousand places. He couldn't use the few healing draughts in his saddlebag; those had to be saved for emergencies.

Which he was likely to run into.

There was, after all, a way out. If he could do something, something so important, so brave, that his cowardice would pale by comparison, that would make up for it, at least somewhat.

Rubbing at yet another bite, he curled himself up in the straw.

A coward didn't have to stay a coward, not forever.

My father proved himself when he killed your father, Ahrmin. You're mine.

He noticed that he was crying again, that he had been silently weeping for so long that his eyes ached.

I'll work it out, somehow, he decided. The point was that the decision had been made: He'd prove himself, somehow.

And this time, he swore to himself, *I won't run away.*

There were only two questions: how could he . . .

. . . and *could* he?

Jason didn't know. There wouldn't be many chances; would he freeze? *No.* No, he wouldn't freeze.

That was the only answer he had: He just wouldn't freeze up again. That was all.

What was left a man who had lost his honor?

There was only one thing: resolve. For the time being, that would have to be enough.

He dropped off to a tentative sleep that was made only of icy nightmare.

CHAPTER TWELVE:

An Acquaintance Renewed

Old friends are best.

—John Selden

Walter Slovotsky smiled genially at the old soldier. "So you think he was just passing through?"

The old man nodded. "That's what he said, yesterday. Did seem to be in a rush. What's your interest? You around when them Home snobs rejected him?"

Whatever the old man meant didn't matter, and he seemed to be expecting agreement; Slovotsky nodded, and thumb-flicked him the copper coin that had been enough to attract the soldier's interest but not so much as to excite suspicions.

"Just curious." Slovotsky shrugged. "I knew him when he was younger; thought I might offer him some work."

"If I see him, who should I say is looking for him?"

"Warrel," he said, picking the common Erendra name that was closest to his own, his usual phony name. "Warrel ip Therranj."

As the old soldier knowingly nudged his partner, Slovotsky kicked his horse into a slow walk. Maybe the others were having better luck. Or worse.

At least he had some information. That was something.

Wehnest was much the way he remembered it: a scattering of buildings and streets randomly radiating from the walled castle at the center; a crude painting by an incompetent artist, colored only in brown and gray.

It was a market day, though, and the markets were busy, although not as busy as he remembered them. Perhaps because the main trading and feed grains were not ready for harvest, he could spot only two or three traders.

Still, there was a brisk business in horseflesh; it seemed that another cattle drive for Pandathaway was in the works.

Could Jason have signed up for something like that? Surely the boy wouldn't be so stupid.

There was one thing that made Walter smile, although he carefully kept the smile inside: Over in the markets, the slave pens that once had overflowed with enslaved humanity were empty. There was still slave owning and slave trading in Wehnest, but it was a much smaller affair than it had been, and prices had gone through the ceiling.

The rest of the merchants didn't seem to be suffering, though. Ahead, in front of a half-sunken storefront, a meatseller had half a dozen fist-sized hunks of delightful-smelling mutton turning on a spit over a carefully sized fire.

Suckered me in, Slovotsky thought, dismounting and holding up a Pandathaway half-copper and pointing with three fingers to three of the servings.

The seller held up a single finger; Slovotsky started to return his coin to his purse, allowing the merchant to stop him by holding up a two-finger V. Slovotsky nodded and smiled, flipping the coin into the air, drawing a knife, and hacking off the two biggest chunks from the spit before the merchant could catch it.

When the merchant opened his mouth to protest, Slovotsky carefully set an irritated expression on his face, sticking one of the pieces of meat on the tip of his knife and offering it back to the man, allowing just the trace of flare of his nostrils.

The merchant thought about it for a moment, decided that it wasn't worth the trouble, and planted a professional grin on his own face, waving Slovotsky along.

Not bad at all, Walter Slovotsky thought, wolfing down the first piece, taking his time with the second.

"Nicely done," floated across the noisy crowd to his ears. "I think I taught you part of that."

He turned to look at the stall across the way; it was marked with the sign of the Healing Hand—

—and the voice had been in English.

Doria. He snatched at his horse's reins and headed for the stall, pausing for only a moment to tie the reins to a hitching post.

Some people age poorly, some gracefully. Doria hadn't aged at all; almost two decades had swirled around her, leaving her untouched. Beneath her white robes, her body was unbent by the years; as she laid a hand on his shoulder, her sleeve fell away, revealing a firm young arm.

He swept her up in his arms for too short a moment, and then pushed her slightly away.

"God, Doria, you look good."

Her face had long lost any look of childhood, but time had etched no lines, the weight of years had created no sag. She could, perhaps, have been as young as twenty, except for the eyes.

The eyes. They bothered him. It wasn't just that her irises were yellow; it was that they seemed to see too much.

Doria gripped his shoulder with a surprising strength. "It's good to see you, too." She led him through the stall and into the coolness of the small, dark room beyond.

There was another Hand cleric inside, a sharp-eyed little woman whom Walter instantly and instinctively disliked. She turned and left without a word.

Doria waved Walter to a seat. "You seemed surprised to see me."

Words failed him. "I didn't think they'd ever let you leave. Or . . ."

She smiled gently. "Or what? Or you'd have come to take me away from all that?" The smile widened as her hand gripped his. "Even if I'd gone with you, what would your wife have said? It's okay, Walter. I've been well. And fulfilled." The corners of her mouth turned up. "As I see you have been," she said, her smile turning it into a double entendre.

"Yeah. Just last night."

"Careful." She waved a finger. "But you are irrepressible, you know."

"It's one of my many charms."

Her face fell; she cocked her head as though listening to a distant voice. "Walter, we will have to make this short; a rancher has hired me as a healer, to accompany a cattle drive to Pandathaway."

"Pandathaway?" They were probably all still wanted there.

She dismissed his concern with a wave. "I'm of the Hand, Walter. There's no danger, although I must leave soon—" Distress clouded her face, and her fingers flew to his temple. Her fingertips rested gently in his hair, unmoving, while an almost electric charge seemed to emanate from them.

"Karl's son!"

"Yes, I—"

"Shh." She closed her eyes momentarily, then reopened them. "This way was faster."

She was silent for a long minute, her eyes focused on some far-distant point. "I see."

This new competence was going to take some getting used to, Walter decided.

Then he decided to get used to it now, and save himself the trouble of having to do it later.

"Can you do anything?"

She shook her head. "None of the Hand will, Walter. I doubt if I could, even if it was permitted; it would take skills greater than mine to pierce the spell around Jason's amulet. The Mother could, if she would. . . ."

"But she won't."

"Can't. None of the Hand can help you. Believe me. There's a geas on all of us." She bit her lip, momentarily bringing up her hand, touching a fingernail to her nose in a gesture he remembered from long ago. "It's just because I'm only *mainly* Doria of the Healing Hand that I can help you—"

"Doria, I—"

She held up a hand. "Please, old friend. I can only do a little. Please. Ahira is still much more James Michael Finnegan than I am Doria Perlstein."

"There's nothing you can do?"

She licked her lips once, twice, then shook her head. "If I broke the geas, perhaps—if I could. But that would leave me with the spells in my head, at best. No—" She shuddered all over.

Again, he put his arms around her and held her close. This time, he didn't let go quickly.

"I missed you," he whispered. Until now, he hadn't realized how very much he missed her.

They had been lovers, long ago. No, that was putting it too solemnly: They had enjoyed each other, in and out of bed; Walter thoroughly, Doria in the limited way that was all she allowed herself.

But that was long ago.

Now, as he held her, there was a warmth, but no passion.

Warmth would be enough.

Snaking her arms around him, she laid her head on his chest. "There is only one thing I can do. . . ."

"Yes?"

"I can wish you well." She looked up at him, her face wet. "It's not much. . . ."

Walter had always been kind to Doria; one of the things he had always liked about her was that behind the mask she showed to the world, she was so fragile that he *had* to treat her gently.

"It's plenty, Doria." He pressed his lips to her hair. "It's more than enough."

Nodding, she pushed him away. "But you have to go. If you can find him between here and your rendezvous with Ellegon and Tennetty, this all can still be saved. If not . . ."

It was as though a curtain descended over her face; suddenly there was no expression in Doria's face.

No, that wasn't true, on both counts: It wasn't Doria's face, not anymore; and there was an expression, but it was a distant, icy one, no trace of humanity in the chiseled cheekbones, in the thin lips, in the camera-eyes.

"Doria?" He reached for her, but her hands blocked him easily.

"*Walter Slovotsky,*" she said in a voice that he had never wanted to hear again, "*you must go now. There is nothing you can do for your friend here.*"

It was the airy but powerful voice of the Matriarch of the Healing Hand, only barely diminished in strength as it issued from Doria's lips.

"*You must go now,*" she repeated.

"But—"

"*Now.*"

For just a moment, Doria peered out through the fleshy mask. "Please, Walter, go."

And then she was gone, as the Matriarch reclaimed her. "*Go. Or need I compel you?*"

A snarl forced itself to his lips. But he didn't do anything. There was nothing he could do.

"I'll leave," he said, addressing his friend, ignoring the Matriarch, who had appropriated her body. "Doria, be well." He touched his fingers to his lips and then brought them to hers. "Farewell, old friend," he said. "Until we meet again. And we *will* meet again."

He turned and left, without a glance back.

At sunset, he met the others at the filthy inn where they had taken a small room for the night. The walls and floor were covered with roaches, and he could hear the skittering of rats in the walls. They could have afforded better accommodations—an inn that charged enough so that the owner could afford hiring a Spidersect cleric to use a death spell on the vermin but conspicuous consumption would not have been in accord with their cover as merchants.

He was the last one to make it to their room. Ahira was stretched out on his bedding, his eyes half closed, while Aeia and Bren Adahan were going over a map of the town that they had scratched into the dirt floor.

"Hi, all," Walter Slovotsky said, pleased to note that his voice came out more casual than he felt. "Any luck?"

Aeia shook her head. "No. And we've covered the whole town, as far as I can tell. How about you?"

Ahira had caught something in his voice. "What is it? Jason?"

Walter shook his head. "No sign. But I did see Doria."

The dwarf hid his surprise well. "How is she?" he asked, perhaps a little too casually.

"Okay." Walter shrugged. "She doesn't seem to be hurting. And I don't think any of us ought to go back and see her—it seems she's been reassigned, and . . . we'll talk about it later." It didn't seem right to discuss Doria in front of these kids; this was a matter for the original group, and maybe not even all of them.

Ahira nodded. "Agreed. You didn't find any sign of him?"

"I found the guard he talked to on his way into town. From what he said, my best guess is that Jason's left." Slovotsky shrugged. "I move we hit the Aeryk road in the morning. If he's gone that way, we can probably catch him before we rendezvous with Ellegon."

"I agree if we don't take the Aeryk road," Bren Adahan said, "we have to pass up the rendezvous. It doesn't make sense to me to do that without good reason."

"Aeia?"

"I don't know." She shrugged her shoulders. Despite everything, Walter noticed and enjoyed how the motion was echoed under her shirt. Not that he was going to do anything but look tonight. Forgetting for the moment about the Adahan problem, a vermin-infested room didn't leave a lot of opportunity for romance.

"Walter and Bren make sense, but . . ." She shook her head. "I just don't know."

Slovotsky turned to Ahira. "It's up to you."

"I want your best guess."

The main trading road was the Aeryk road, but there were dozens of other, smaller byways Jason could have taken. Hell, he could have gone north, or even be holed up, hiding in Wehnest, or heading off across the Waste toward the Hand tabernacle.

"Spending another day in Wehnest and trying to dig up some more info might work, too." He shrugged. "Could be he talked to somebody."

Bren Adahan shook his head. "That doesn't make any sense—"

"Shut up," Slovotsky said. "It's not your call."

They couldn't take all the possible paths. The dwarf's desire to go see Doria might as well have been carved into his forehead; the obvious decision was to stay around for another day, just one more day, and then try to double-time toward the rendezvous.

But Ahira just pursed his lips. "We leave for Aeryk first thing in the morning. Now get some sleep. All of you." He looked knowingly at Walter, as though to say, *You don't know me as well as you think you do.*

The others probably didn't understand when Walter answered back, "Yes, I do, Jimmy."

CHAPTER THIRTEEN:

A Rumor of War

I must study politics and war that my sons may have liberty
to study mathematics and philosophy. My sons ought to study
mathematics and philosophy, geography, natural history,
naval architecture, navigation, commerce and agriculture, in
order to give their children a right to study painting, poetry,
music, architecture, statuary, tapestry and porcelain.

—John Adams

Astride his mare on the crest of the hill, Karl Cullinane looked
down over the carnage below.

It had been Kernat village, a small community in barony Tyrnael,
insignificant to the general economy of either barony empire except
for, in some years, a minor surplus of grains, and occasionally of
meat animals. Nobody of any importance had ever been born there,
as far as anyone knew; the closest Kernat came to a local hero was
a corporal in Karl's House Guard.

It had been an unimportant little place, except to the people
who lived there.

Who *had* lived there . . . nobody lived here anymore.

"Andy, I don't need you for this."

Her brown gelding pawed the ground as she shook her head.
"Yes you do." Her fingers twisted in the reins, knuckles white in
the leather straps.

Nobody lived here anymore.

It wasn't a village now.

Now, it was a charnel house. Bodies littered the streets, some gaping in surprise that death had finally overtaken them, some without faces with which to gape.

Below, a crow pecked at the eyeholes of what once had been a teenaged girl; a soldier shooed it away with the haft of his spear, then swore in remote irritation as a crossbowman raised his weapon and shot the crow out of the air, the bird twitching while it shit and bled and died on the dirt road.

Karl sympathized with both of them—this was horribly wrong—but it wasn't going to be fixed by killing the scavengers. It wasn't going to be fixed at all; there is no medicine for a life that has fled, no healing of a rotting body, lying in the dirt, stinking in the sun.

There had been no wounded; all who had not been fleet of foot and well endowed with luck had been put to the sword. There had been some looting, but not much. There could not have been much; Kernat village simply hadn't had much wealth to loot.

Nothing moved in the streets except Baron Tyrnael's soldiers, who were busy clearing the town, checking through the rubble of the stone houses and the smoking ash of the half-timber ones for either enemies or survivors.

But there were none; the raiders had long since gone.

Karl swallowed as he turned to Listar, Baron Tyrnael. "They took captives?"

"Yes." The baron nodded his head slowly, then rubbed at his tired eyes and unshaved cheeks. He clearly hadn't shaved in days; he probably hadn't slept, either. "Not many. Perhaps ten. Given slave prices these days, it would justify the raid. Perhaps. They were thorough," he said, a funereal calm in his words. "A runner tells me that there's a messenger from Lord Pugeer waiting me at home. Offering me his protection, do you think?"

"No, I don't think so." Karl shook his head, and he dismounted, handing his reins to one of his soldiers.

As he did, Danagar, who was commanding the House Guard bodyguard detail, nodded to his escort and issued a few monosyllabic commands.

The forty pairs of riflemen and gunner's mates spread out, the riflemen with weapons at half-cock, each mate holding a loaded replacement piece, ready to either switch and reload or, if necessary, draw sword and protect the gunner while *he* reloaded.

It was a matter of discipline, not necessity; the killers were long since gone.

Andrea gestured with her right hand, an awkward motion that spoke more of magic than anything else. "I can smell the power."

He nodded. The fact that there were no escapees clinched it— even a large force of raiders couldn't have killed or rounded up everyone. No, there had been a wizard involved, locating villagers who hid in bushes or in their homes, perhaps putting some to sleep, to be chained or slaughtered.

"Any idea how much?"

She shrugged. "One or two, in my league or close to it. At least."

"Stay here."

"Karl—"

"Shut up and stay here." Karl started to walk toward the town, grateful that the wind was at his back.

Tyrnael walked beside him. "You don't think he's going to offer cooperation."

"Too crude. No, Baron, that's not what he's going to say." Karl shook his head. "He's probably going to tell you that a village in Nyphien, too, has been hit by raiders, and he's surely going to suggest some coordinated patrols between your people and Pugeer's, so that raiders can't slip between the cracks again."

The awful thing of it was that it might even be true. Maybe it wasn't Lord Pugeer trying to spread his influence into barony Tyrnael.

There were many with possible motives for this. It could be Pandathaway, trying to drive a wedge between Karl and one of his more important barons, working on bringing Karl's throne down; or Khar, trying to create trouble between Nyphien and the empire, the better to slice off a piece of Nyphien.

Or it could have been Deighton, for that matter.

Why Deighton? Because of the magic? No. There were other wizards besides Deighton. The trouble was, despite some suspicions, Karl wasn't sure what Deighton's motivations were, when it came down to it; without knowing what ends Arta Myrdhyn sought, Karl couldn't possibly swear as to what means might suit those ends.

"You ordered a pursuit?"

Tyrnael paused for a moment before answering. "Yes, sire. Only to the border. They found sign of the raiders, but they didn't go past the river." He didn't add that it had been pointless, that barony

Tyrnael and Holtun-Bieme ended at the Jerun River, only a day's ride away, and that with their lead, there was no question but that the raiders were long since gone, escaped into Nyphien.

The only clue would be in the enslaved Biemish citizens—if they knew anything, if they could be recovered. Doing it quickly didn't seem likely; the raid was three days old, and the raiders were long since gone.

Tyrnael dropped to one knee and knelt beside what had been a stocky peasant; now it was just a body stinking in the sun, pinned to the ground by a spear. The baron took a long look at the man's face, then shook his head as he rose.

"You knew him?"

"Name of Hen'l." The baron nodded. "I know all my people, sire." He pulled himself up straight. "We'll need some reinforcements for when I retaliate."

The calm was purely a pose, Karl decided. All that the baron wanted to do was punish whoever was responsible—and if whoever that was wasn't handy, the nearest Nyphs would do.

It even made sense, in a way. Lord Pugeer should be told, in no uncertain terms, that it was *his* responsibility to see that no attacks on Holtun-Bieme occurred across the frontier; imperial forces couldn't patrol both sides of the border, so the Nyphs would have to take their side of it.

Basic Orde Wingate strategy: When Brigadier Wingate was advising the pre-Israel Palmach, Arab terrorist strikes were always met by retaliation against the nearest Arab village—care being taken to inflict the maximum property damage, leaving villagers alive to learn that allowing one's village to be a terrorist staging area was unwise.

It might be necessary to try that here. But . . . not yet.

"We'll see," Karl said. "We'll have to decide what we're going to do, first."

"At least you'll move some troops toward the border."

Karl shook his head. "Nothing for now."

Although the baron made no movement, not the slightest motion toward his sword, for a moment Karl thought that Tyrnael was going to draw on him. They had sparred many times—Tyrnael was, technically, a better swordsman than Karl, and utterly unbothered about the possibility of humiliating his emperor—but that had always been for sport and practice, never serious.

But the moment passed.

"Trust me," Karl said. "I'll do what's necessary. First we have to find out what that is."

"Yes, sire." Tyrnael didn't sound convinced.

Karl raised his voice. "Danagar."

The captain wasn't far from his side. "Yes, sir?"

"You're relieved of guard duty. Turn over your guns and command to your second."

Danagar's face was studiously blank. "Yes, sir."

Good man; he knew how to take an unpleasant order. "Tonight, I want you to take as many men you need and sneak over the border into Nyphien, in disguise—you pick the disguise. I'll need to know everything you can find out about this, as quickly as possible. The baronial council is in twelve days; I'll want you there, with a report, then."

"Yes, sir."

Tyrnael watched Danagar's retreating back. "I doubt if he'll have time to find out much. I've long had spies in Nyphien, but there's been no report of troop movements."

"Which perhaps means that Pugeer isn't behind this. We shall see, Baron."

Tyrnael didn't answer.

Karl raised his hands and placed his palms on the baron's shoulders. He looked him straight in the eye. "Look at me, Listar," Karl said, dialing for his most sincere expression.

As his acting teacher had long ago said, actual sincerity didn't excuse you from appearing sincere. "I will do what's necessary. They won't be unavenged."

"Agreed, Karl," the baron said. "They won't be unavenged."

CHAPTER FOURTEEN:
"Before dark . . ."

All is flux; nothing stays still.

—Heraclitus

Vator the hostler was silent that morning as he banged on the wooden ladder that led up to the loft, bringing Jason his breakfast of fresh brown bread and raw onion. While Jason ate his sketchy meal, he and Vator turned the animals out into the yard.

Then Vator left, mumbling something about some business with the smith down the street, after setting him to mucking out the stalls.

Jason was left to his own devices; the fat man was simply too busy to supervise him. His pasty-faced wife and three ragged children were no help, as they spent their day just outside of town, working the few acres that provided Vator with grain and vegetables for both animals and table.

He had always said that a bit of hard work was good for the soul; Jason couldn't see it. But a lot of what his father did didn't make much sense to Jason. While he liked horses and all, there really didn't seem to be a whole lot of value or knowledge to be gained from being up to your calves in horseshit, the smell combining with a nauseating breakfast—such as it was—to set you gagging.

Didn't make much sense at all.

A lot of things didn't make much sense.

His fists clenched around the handle of the spadelike manure fork, as an image welled up of Valeran falling away, blood fountaining around the knife stuck hilt-deep in his right eyesocket . . .

No. Make it go away.

He hadn't slept well; he had had nightmares all night. That wasn't new; he'd always had nightmares, as far back as he could remember. Too many nights brought visions of himself wading through pools of blood and gore, accompanied by friendly faces who would turn suddenly vicious, huge fangs growing from their jaws, drool falling from the corners of their mouths only to hiss and steam on the ground below.

Usually, *he* was gone, off raiding in Jason's early years, off governing in the later ones. So Jason's screams would wake his mother. She would come to him, shake him gently awake, and hold him tightly, a smile always on her face, as though dispelling his nightmares was a great joy.

If that failed, she would mutter a few quick words that could only be forgotten, and her fingers would quirk into awkward and powerful contortions, as she beckoned lights from the darkness, whirling blinking motes of ruby, emerald, and actinic blue through a dance of reassurance and comfort.

Sometimes, if the dreams persisted—and when she was in residence; often she was in Home while he was in Biemestren, or vice versa—Aeia would spend the night holding him, until he decided that he had grown too old for that.

Twice that he could remember, Karl Cullinane had been home during the worst of Jason's nightmares. Both times, he sat next to Jason's bed, sometimes allowing himself to nod off, but holding his hand through the night.

Lately, Valeran had been the one to be wakened by his cries.

The old warrior had a different method; he'd brew a strong pot of herb tea, and tell Jason stories of the old days, some of things he had seen, others of things he had only heard of: about battles during the Katharhdn wars, of the conquest of Holtun after his father had taken the crown, stories about Ch'akresarkandyn, the Katharhd who had given his life in a battle over slaver powder. Jason remembered Chak, of course—and would smile tolerantly when Valeran would talk of him as a little man. Little, hah! Chak had been a gentle giant.

Jason would always listen intently, asking for stories by name.

Tell me How-Tennetty-Lost-Her-Eye, he would say. Or Daven-and-the-Slaver, or How-*He*-Killed-Ohlmin. That last was his favorite; it was about how *he* and Uncle Walter had killed the hundred slavers who had hurt Mother.

Valeran would never spare the details: the high-pitched screams of wounded horses, the sulfurous stink of gunpowder that somehow was worse when the shots were being fired for real, the rotting-garbage smell of a wound that festered when there was no healer or healing draughts to be found.

And when the sun came up in the morning, his mind buzzing with battles and bullets, swords and slaughter, Jason would make his way to his bed and fall into a dreamless sleep, waking refreshed, his inner demons stilled for a time.

It was Valeran's way of holding his hand, but there was nobody to hold his hand now. He rubbed the backs of his fists against his aching eyes.

"Taren," Vator said, the hostler's voice strangely low.

It took a moment for Jason to remember that this was the name he was using. "Yes?" He turned to see the fat man silhouetted in the open stable door, standing nervously, tentatively, as though ready to run at any moment.

"I was just at the smith's. He says that there are people looking for you."

Jason shook his head. "Couldn't be me."

"The description was exact," Vator said. "The smith thinks he recognized him—he thinks he's one of those Home people. About this tall, dark hair, eyes look a little slanted, easy smile."

Uncle Walter. Jason quelled the urge to run.

"There's more. There is a Pandathaway guild slaver in town; the smith sold him the information that Home is looking for you—he figured that if Home wants to find you, so would the guild." Vator licked his lips and shook his head. "I can't have any trouble here. You're going to have to go."

Jason was already heading for where his rifle and other gear were buried in the straw; by the time he had it all tied down for travel, Vator had Libertarian saddled. He filled a canvas bag with oats, and another one with corn, and lashed those tightly, expertly to the saddle.

"I'm not a brave man, Taren," the hostler said. "I can't help you. I'm sorry."

You feel like a coward, Vator? Well, there was one thing one coward could offer another: forgiveness. "You've nothing to be sorry for. I'd best be on my way to the Hand tabernacle, where I was going in the first place," he said, hoping that the words didn't sound as clumsy in Vator's ears as they did in his own. Still, if someone did ask Vator where Jason was headed, best he had a false destination.

"Be well, Vator." They briefly clasped hands.

Jason rose to the saddle and without a further word kicked Libertarian into a fast walk, heading for the west road. Let Vator see that he was leaving town in the direction of the road to the Tabernacle; let others see, too, and be able to verify the hostler's story, if it came to that.

Where would he go, though?

There seemed to be only one choice: the cattle drive.

But what if they wouldn't take him on?

He shrugged to himself. Then he'd be no worse off than he was now. Better—he'd be farther away.

He spurred his horse into a trot as he considered the provisions problem. What with circling around, it might take him a couple of days to catch up, but by allowing plenty of time for grazing, he had enough food for his horse for at least that amount of time. He could probably hunt something for himself to eat, if need be.

It was only hours later, when he stopped to make camp for the night, that he discovered that the oat bag contained another, smaller canvas bag, and that bag contained enough onions, jerked beef, smoked chicken, and dried carrots to feed Jason for days, easily—

—plus one piece of battered Wehnest silver, and a scratched note that said only, in sloppy Erendra printing, "Be well. —Vator."

He wept as he tossed the note into his campfire.

Falikos the rancher was a rapier-slim man, with dark brown, almost black eyes that bore into Jason's. "I can always use more help, though I don't know as I *need* another drover," he said. "Although there may well be land pirates between here and Pandathaway—" He cut himself off with a shrug, then turned in the saddle to shout a few rapid commands to the drover sitting in the high seat of the cook wagon.

Jason had seen larger herds of cattle—even after the ravages of the Consolidation War, barony Adahan had many more beasts on the baron's personal lands alone—but never on the move.

Why did cattle have to stink more when they were moving?

The wind changed momentarily, blowing the dust toward the rear of the herd, where Jason was engaged in trying to persuade the rancher to take him on. But for only a moment; it changed again, picking up as it blew the dust away instead of trying to bury it in his eyes.

A tall, rangy man, his rapier bound to his saddle in fast-drawing position, looked Jason over carefully, no trace of friendliness in either his expression or his voice. "And it could be, Falikos, that this one is a spy for a band of land pirates?"

The rancher spat. "So? Don't be more of an idiot than necessary, Kyreen. Couldn't we find that out quickly—just like we did with all the rest of you?"

Before Jason could sort that out, and before Kyreen could answer with more than a scowl, the rancher went on, rubbing his chin contemplatively. "What I'm concerned with is how good he is—" He turned to Jason. "—how good *you* are with that bow of yours. And sword, for that matter. Let's see. . . ." He looked across the plain. "There isn't a decent target within range. Hills don't make good targets for bows," he added with a halfhearted chuckle. "But—"

Bow? The trouble was that there wasn't a bow in Jason's bundle; it contained his rifle.

His mind raced, trying to invent a distraction.

Kyreen came to his rescue. "Damn the bow. I want to see how good he is with a sword." He pulled his horse up and dropped lightly to the ground, unstrapping his rapier from the saddle, holding it easily in his hand.

He saluted Falikos with the scabbarded weapon. "With your permission, sir."

"A bit of sparring is fine." Falikos nodded as he dismounted. "A nick or two is acceptable—but no serious injuries, understood? I don't want to have to have any serious healing done. Cuts into the profits." He put two fingers in his mouth and whistled, giving three sharp blasts, then raising his hand over his head and clenching it into a fist.

The drover driving the last of the three boxy wagons raised himself in his seat, then acknowledged the signal with a wave and brought his six-mule team and wagon to a halt, setting the brake, then vaulting to the ground before going around to the rear of the wagon. He opened the door and held out his hand to help a white-robed woman down to the ground. She pulled back her cowl and tossed her head, her long blond hair shining in the sun, then watched him levelly with her yellow-irised eyes.

Over toward the rear of the herd, two other horsemen wheeled their horses around and trotted them over.

"Well?" Falikos said, looking up at him. "What are you waiting for?"

Jason swallowed heavily as he dismounted. He'd faced a variety of opponents with practice swords, of course. And he hadn't done too badly, generally, but that was always against friendly opponents. Tennetty liked bruising him, and Bren Adahan always tried for a disarm—but all of that was for practice and fun, not for real.

The only time he had really been in a fight, he had run like the coward he was.

But this isn't real, he said to himself. *It's just practice.* He drew both of his swords, first taking the long saber in his right hand, then drawing the bowie with his left.

Jason wasn't a wizard with weapons, not like *him. He* seemed to be able to use any weapon with little to no practice; when questioned, he said it "came with the territory," whatever that meant. While Tennetty had made Jason reasonably competent with a single blade, Valeran had taught him to fight two-swords style, and Jason was best at that, although he substituted a Nehera-made bowie for the usually shorter dagger.

He worked his shoulders under his tunic, debating whether or not to shed it and gain the added freedom of movement, deciding to keep it for the extra protection.

As the cleric and her guide walked up, Kyreen took up a fighting stance; his sword held out in front of him, gripped firmly but easily, weight on the balls of his feet, face impassive, eyes fixed firmly on Jason.

His concentration was impressive; Jason could almost see the way the taller man dismissed the rest of the universe, ignoring everything except Jason and whatever could apply to the sparring.

For a moment, it was almost as though Valeran was there beside him.

Take three breaths, and let them out slowly, he could almost hear the old warrior say. *Forget about what happens if you lose; just concentrate on what you are doing.* That was important; the task at hand required Jason's full attention, and worrying about getting hurt was only a distraction.

Now, let him come to you. Easy. Remember there is no such thing as practice on defense, ever.

That was important. Jason could remember a horrible blading he'd once received, when he'd thrown up his wooden practice blade and surrendered. Valeran had been furious; it was the only time that the old man had ever screamed at him, and one of very few times when he had laid hands on Jason.

His light rapier whistling through the air, Kyreen moved in. He tried a tentative lunge which Jason parried easily, beating aside the blade with his heavier saber, not falling for the obvious trap of turning his body toward Kyreen in order to use his bowie.

That was the danger of fighting two-swords style: the temptation to overuse the dagger. Too often, that required turning your body to squarely face your opponent, exposing your torso to a direct attack. Much better to keep it turned at a forty-five-degree angle away from your opponent, bringing the right arm and its long sword out, the other held back as a reserve, waiting to parry the blade if a lunge would bring the other's weapon close enough, or—better—to fall chest to chest, and plant the dagger in the enemy as you pushed him away.

Of course, it had always been a game for Jason; even now, it wasn't quite serious. Kyreen intended to humiliate him, perhaps nick him, not kill him.

So why is my heart pounding so loud? He tried a tentative high-line attack, but Kyreen beat his sword aside, leaving Jason open from ankles to throat.

The other was barely too slow in taking advantage of the opening; as he lunged, Jason was able to turn and bring his dagger around, catching the rapier's blade with the dagger's guard, levering the rapier to one side as he braced himself for the impact of Kyreen's body.

The bigger man crashed into him, chest to chest, but Jason was set, even though his swordarm was blocked by Kyreen's free arm.

Jason's training had been for fighting, not style; Valeran had not drilled Jason in the niceties of parlor fencing.

As the two broke apart, Jason snapped his instep into Kyreen's groin.

The taller man's breath *whooshed* out of him; as he dropped his sword and clapped his hands to his crotch, Jason dropped to the ground, bracing himself on his left foot and the fist holding the dagger as he kicked out his right leg and swept Kyreen's legs out from underneath him.

Jason got lightly to his feet and lightly tapped the moaning Kyreen with his saber. "My point, sir," he said.

Falikos was laughing, thoroughly amused. "Very pretty, Taren. Very pretty indeed. I wouldn't have thought Kyreen would be handled so easily. You are hired."

"I was just lucky," Jason said, scabbarding his weapons, then reaching over to offer Kyreen his hand.

It all happened fast: Kyreen accepted the proffered hand, then kicked Jason in one knee while drawing his beltknife with the other.

He brought the knife up, stabbing.

Jason tried to twist away, but the tip of the blade slashed into his left thigh.

Kyreen brought his arm up for another stab.

The white-robed cleric was just a blur as she dove between the two of them, but Kyreen's arm was already moving, bringing the knife down at her chest.

With a metallic *ting!* the blade bounced off her robes.

She muttered a quick, guttural phrase, and made a squeezing motion with a thumb and index finger; Kyreen recoiled as though he had been shocked, the knife falling from nerveless fingers.

White-hot pain shooting up his leg, Jason clutched at his thigh. Nothing had ever hurt so much. He wanted to black out, to fall away into the dark haze clouding his vision, but the pain kept drawing him back.

The woman laid a gentle hand on his leg, then froze. "I can't heal this one," she said.

"Doria," Falikos said, "what is it?"

She shook her head. "It's a Hand matter. But I can't heal him. Do you have any Spidersect healing draughts? Or Eareven?"

Still sitting astride his horse, he shook his head. "Do you think I am a rich man, woman? Then there's nothing you can do for him?"

"First aid," she said in English, then switched back to Erendra. "That'll have to do."

The pain washed up and over him in a red wave that drowned all else.

He awoke in painful darkness, and instinctively reached for his weapons, but his fingers couldn't find them. There was a light, but his eyes couldn't focus on it. He was lying on a flat wooden surface, his thigh still throbbing horribly.

Every heartbeat was echoed with agony; he groaned.

"Ahh . . ." The distant spark flared into light, and the white-robed healer knelt next to him. "You're awake, I see. How are you?"

He tried to raise himself on his elbows, then thought better of it. "I'm okay," he answered, in English. "Doria."

"Ahh." She smiled. "Good. You know who I am, Jason. I obviously know who you are. Where you are is in my wagon, where you're going to be spending the next couple of days, until you heal up enough to ride." She considered him for a moment. "You do have the Spidersect draughts in your bags, but don't use them; Falikos would want to know what a drover was doing with enough money to afford those."

He was naked underneath the thin blanket. "Who . . . ?"

She shrugged. "Me—you soiled your clothes, and what with all the blood . . ." She shrugged again. "We were able to salvage your tunic and your boots, and that was about all." She pressed a hard object into his hand. "And this. I couldn't figure out the spell—then, on a hunch, I tried locating it. It's a nice shield against being found."

She bit her lip. "It was out of your . . . field for a while. It's not likely, but it's not impossible that you were located—if your mother was looking for you at just the right time, which I doubt." She barely smiled. "I was never all that fond of Andrea's timing." She raised a hand to forestall his questions. "Your gear is under the bed. Your horse is taken care of. And, Jason, while I can't use my magic to help you, I can do one thing for you. . . ."

The throbbing grew more intense. "Yes?"

"I can be your friend. I think you need one."

He didn't know why, but that started the tears flowing, a torrent that didn't cease until a deep, dark sleep claimed him.

CHAPTER FIFTEEN:
"I Like Jason . . ."

Come not between the dragon and his wrath.
—William Shakespeare

Leathery wings flapped, suddenly, jerkily. Whether in irritation or frustration, Walter Slovotsky couldn't say.

Tennetty's remaining eye flashed in the firelight, her hand never off the hilt of her sword. Walter Slovotsky kept out of lunging distance; at the moment, Tennetty's temper wasn't fully under control.

Not that it ever was.

"You lost him." She seemed to sway for a moment, then straightened. It couldn't have been emotion—other than loyalty toward Karl Cullinane and cruelty toward anyone who got in her way, Tennetty didn't have emotions. "You lost him."

Sit, Tennetty. You haven't rested since the rendezvous with Daherrin's team; you've been three days without sleep. You must get some rest.

"I'll rest when I'm ready!"

But she accepted a hot mug of tea from Aeia, anyway.

Ahira shrugged as he received a bag from Bren Adahan, who was up on the dragon's back, unloading cargo. "I can't see that now's the time to discuss this." The dwarf set the bag down on the ground and reached for another. "Now is the time for Ellegon to take off and find—"

140

No, the dragon said, tilting his huge bulk slightly to make it easier for Bren Adahan to climb over to where the next bag was tied down. *I can't. Daven's team is trapped in a mountain passage in Khar, and they need food and ammunition. I have endangered them more than enough by diverting here. Another few moments, and then I *have* to turn around and start back toward Biemestren to pick up the supplies, so I can get them to Daven.*

"And then?" Aeia asked.

That's up to Karl. While I'm in Biemestren, I will fill Karl in on all of this. He will decide what's to be done now that it's quickly becoming known that Jason Cullinane is without protection.

Quickly? How could that be? And how could Ellegon know—?

Daherrin. Some of his team were in Wehnest after you, escorting those of the ex-slaves who asked to be brought there. Some of them talked. Rumor has it that Jason was on his way to the Hand tabernacle, but I doubt that; it sounds like a planted story.

Shit. This was getting worse and worse.

"So?" Aeia cocked her head to one side. "Who do you want to take as your loader? Me?"

Slovotsky wasn't going to volunteer for that.

Understandable. I wouldn't want to face Karl if I'd lost his son, either, Ellegon responded privately. *Better find him.*

Slovotsky opened his mouth to protest, shut it. If Ellegon didn't see it—

"No!" Tennetty's eruption interrupted. "I can carry the news to Karl just as well as you can."

It wasn't, Walter decided, that she liked bringing bad news to Karl; it was more that she saw it as her responsibility.

Aeia shook her head. "You're barely holding on to consciousness; Ellegon says you haven't slept in three days. It's me or nobody. My choice."

Bren Adahan didn't like that. "Why is it your choice?"

Because this is a Cullinane family matter, and she's a Cullinane. I suggest you stay here, Aeia. I can give the news to Karl. He'll want to know that you're continuing the search.

"Very well. Tell him we will," Aeia said.

Walter Slovotsky didn't like that note in her voice. It didn't really belong to Aeia, it belonged to Karl Cullinane. The last time Walter had heard that idiot tone in Karl's voice, it had been before Karl had sent him to sneak into Biemestren castle and almost get his balls cut off.

The lashings on the last of the bags fell free, the leather sack after it. Bren Adahan leaped to the ground, Ahira half-catching him.

Then farewell, the dragon said. *Find him, please. He's far too young and stupid to be off by himself.*

Walter snickered.

All humans are too young and stupid.

Even Karl? Slovotsky asked.

I am prejudiced there.

"Ellegon?" Ahira asked. "Can't you just do some sort of spiral search? Try to find Jason."

There's no time. Daven needs to be resupplied, desperately. The dragon flapped his wings and leaped high into the air; his mental voice went distant.

Jason, I'm sorry, but I just don't have time.

A huge wet drop struck Walter Slovotsky's hand. He looked up at the dark shape vanishing into the clear night sky.

As the dawn barely began to threaten the darkness, Walter Slovotsky, wrapped in his blankets, sitting on a flat stone keeping watch, poked a stick into the ashes of the night's fire, debating whether or not to relight it. He was also debating whether or not to stand up and move around before or after the cold stone froze his ass solid, even through three thicknesses of blanket.

That's the way it was when you're on watch, he decided. Decisions came in two varieties: the really important ones, where you had no time to think and had to react instantly, and the relatively trivial ones, whose major purpose was to give you something to think about while there was nothing important to do.

God, I hate being on watch, he thought, then tried to estimate how many times he'd thought that before, until he gave up doing that and tried to estimate how many times he'd tried to estimate . . . and then let the whole silly fancy drop.

That was the way it was, on watch. Idle thoughts.

Well . . . there was no particular reason why they shouldn't be where they were, but there was also, as always, an argument against a daytime fire, which would announce their presence for miles.

As far as standing up went, he'd be miserable whether or not he stood. He huddled deeper in the blankets.

Around the remains of the fire, all but one of the others slept quietly. Aeia looked very young and very vulnerable. Bren Adahan, lying facedown, huddled deeply in his own blankets, only his sandy hair visible. Ahira snored loudly, while Tennetty was gone. She had set up some sort of hammock high in the trees, adhering to the principle that setting a guard was fine, but having one of the party separate was better.

Not that that would do much good if they were jumped.

Walter shrugged, as he closed his eyes and strained his ears for sound. Nothing but the wind through the trees, a distant, mocking call of a crow, and the dwarf's damn snoring.

He thought about waking Ahira for the dwarf's turn at watch, but decided against it. They were probably going to have an argument, and Walter wanted to put that off.

Good luck, the dragon had wished them.

Good luck, indeed. It would take more than that.

If only the dragon could have stayed to search, it would have all been different.

Yeah. And if dogs had thumbs, they could vote Democratic in Chicago.

The big lizard was right, though: He was needed in Holtun-Bieme. But the dragon had missed a point or two. He was too used to mindreading to spend the effort figuring out what people would do.

Such as Karl's next move, which was obvious.

Like a mother bird leading a prowling cat away from her babies by offering herself as bait, Karl would distract the hunters on Jason's tail by offering himself.

Where would Karl go?

Where else?

Given that Ahrmin probably had spies all throughout Holtun-Bieme, news would probably reach Pandathaway damn quickly that Karl Cullinane was on his way to Melawei.

News wouldn't be the only thing that would reach Pandathaway. Ellegon had missed another point—Home searchers were surely out hunting by now, and they could find Jason as easily as Walter's group; Walter's group wouldn't make much difference. They were only five, after all; they could better be used spiking the guns of the slavers, so to speak.

Over in his blankets, Ahira stirred momentarily. Then, perhaps moved by some internal alarm, he silently opened his eyes, glared at the new day, and rose, drawing his clothes about him as he walked into the forest to relieve himself.

When the dwarf returned, he dug into a pack and pulled out a carrot, cleaning it somewhat by rubbing it against a rock. "Get some sleep; it's my watch, no?"

"Yes, but . . . but I want to talk to you about what we do now."

Walter started to marshal his arguments: the fact that a large Home party was certainly now scouring the countryside for Jason, while Karl was going to be riding into the cannon's mouth alone; the notion that a party of five wouldn't make much of a difference in the former effort, but might well make a big difference as Karl's unknown hole card—

—but the dwarf stopped him by raising a gnarled palm.

"I know how your mind works. And I agree," Ahira said chewing on a carrot. "But we've got to put in at least a few days looking for the boy. If we find him, then we can try to beat Karl to Ehvenor, and stop *him.*"

"And if we don't find Jason in, say, a week?"

"I like Jason, and I wish him well. But . . ."

"But?"

The dwarf's face was grim. "Then we head into Pandathaway to slow down the dogs."

"And then?"

"Then we go after Karl anyway."

CHAPTER SIXTEEN:
The Council of Barons

I agree with you that there is a natural aristocracy among men . . . the grounds of this are virtue and talents.
—Thomas Jefferson

"Ladies and gentlemen, be seated."

I'm going to have to do it myself, Karl Cullinane thought as he stood on the dark spot on the red carpet in the great hall of Castle Biemestren. This wasn't the sort of thing he could leave to anyone else.

The only question was how to maneuver the barons into supporting him. He couldn't tell them what he planned since he didn't know yet.

Force did have its place. The carpet was blood-red; the black spot was long-dried blood. The first time that Karl had called his barons together, Baron Derahan of Holtun had called him out, challenging him, man to man.

A brave act, really; by making it personal, binding his barony to loyalty to Karl if Karl defeated him, Derahan had made the challenge tempting.

Tennetty had advised against it, as she stood behind the baron, one hand gripping his hair, the other holding a dagger at the side of his throat, fully prepared to economically slice through a jugular and kick him on his way.

There was no tradition of the prince being subject to such, of course. Holtun's Prince Uldren, like Bieme's Pirondael, had been a fat man, barely able to wheeze his form upright. A twelve-year-old boy could have danced around either and killed either with a pin.

But Karl had just told her to let him go, then nodded at the baron. When Tennetty cut Derahan's hands loose, Karl had simply dragged him across the room, pushed him away, tossed Derahan a sword, and then batted the baron's sword out of his hand and hacked his head off.

Karl nodded at Terumel, the new Baron Derahan, sitting next to the military governor of his barony. Terumel returned Karl's gaze levelly as Karl deliberately stood on the spot where he had killed Terumel's father.

Karl faced the table where the barons sat, the Biemish ones with a senior adviser or majordomo, the Holtish with their military governors. There was one exception to that latter. Vilmar, Baron Nerahan, sat conspicuously alone, the seat to his immediate right conspicuously empty.

The Holt had a sharp-nosed face and a bristly mustache; he always reminded Karl both of a weasel and that appearances could be deceiving—while the little baron looked like somebody had called Central Casting for a stool pigeon, he was a self-disciplined man, resolutely fair, always more concerned with gaining his barony the most benefit out of the Consolidation, never with evening old scores.

Ellegon had mindprobed the little man more thoroughly than usual, and had been impressed with both his intelligence and his resolve.

Karl itched to kill the bastard for some of the things he had done during the Holtun-Bieme War . . . but that would have violated the amnesty.

He smiled genially at Nerahan.

Just give me an excuse, Nerahan. Just a little excuse, and I'll kill you with my own two hands.

Sometimes, life really sucked. Nerahan had been a goddam Boy Scout ever since the war, never coming close to giving Karl an excuse to take his head. He never would; not only did the baron know what his future held if he turned against Karl, but events had persuaded him that the new ways were the better. He was a brutal man, but a flexible one.

Behind Nerahan, General Kevalun stood quietly, looking more like one of Nerahan's retainers than the military governor of that barony. And a younger retainer, at that—his short blond hair hadn't receded with age, and his face was almost baby-smooth. Kevalun looked perhaps twenty-five, too young to be a general, but he was actually the father of a sixteen-year-old girl.

"To begin," Karl Cullinane said, as he took his seat at the head of the table, General Garavar at his left, Thomen Furnael in the seat of honor at his right, "I want to make the obvious announcement: Effective immediately, the military governor of barony Nerahan is relieved of his duties and reassigned to the House Guard." Karl nodded to Kevalun. "General, I thank you for your services on behalf of all of Holtun-Bieme. You have done a splendid job."

There were nods from around the table, mainly from the military governors of other baronies and from several of the Biemish barons. The only Holt to join in was Nerahan. "If," he said, raising a finger to emphasize the word as he repeated it, "*if* the emperor is ever . . . inclined to dispense with your services, General, I'll have work for you."

At least for public consumption, Kevalun took it as intended. "I thank you, Baron." He bowed toward the baron—the first time he had ever done so.

Karl smiled. "Dismissed, Kevalun. See Garavar later about your new assignment." He deliberately kept his eyes away from the far end of the table, where Baron and Baroness Keranahan sat, the military governor of their barony sitting between them.

Kevalun's new assignment was going to be barony Irulahan, where General Caem'l was alternating between almost Prussian repression and Marshall Plan flaccidity. Karl had no objection to hanging people for fomenting rebellion, but it made less sense to lynch suspected robbers assaulting his tax collectors than to hang the lords who gave them protection. Noble necks snapped with more effect.

Still, there was no need to embarrass Caem'l in front of the others; he would be allowed to retire with dignity. Or with what dignity was possible when a man was being relieved for manifest incompetence, which wasn't all that much.

Kevalun stood up even straighter, his eyes fixed on infinity. "Yes, Emperor."

He spun on his heel and stalked out of the hall, barely limping at all on his bad leg.

"I don't know, Karl," Ranella said, sitting next to fat Lord Harven of Adahan barony, "but I think Adahan's about ready to be turned loose, if you can get the baron to do his job, instead of . . . being educated at Home." The master engineer cocked her head to one side. "Or let Harven be regent. He can handle it, Karl."

To Ranella, he was always Karl. To Ranella, it was much more important that they were both Home engineers—she a master, he classified as a senior journeyman—than that he was the emperor and she a barony's governor.

At least that was what she affected. Maybe she just liked to be able to first-name an emperor.

Seated at the far end of the table, Andy-Andy shook her head. "It seems to me that that is not properly a matter for this council," she said. "If the emperor requires the advice of this body, he can ask for it."

She kept her face grim; Karl nodded his agreement. He didn't want to rush into liberating the Holts. Nerahan's new freedom was going to make the Biemish nervous enough. Best to let them see how that went before freeing another Holtish barony.

"No, Ranella," he said as he shook his head. "I see no need to rush forward and remove military government—we'll see how Nerahan does, first."

The Holtish barons were good poker players; not a face creased into a smile. Thomen Furnael's frown even deepened.

Damn Ranella, anyway. She was good at what she did, but only at what she did. Getting the Adahan mines and the Furnael steel plant into operation was going well, but Karl was often thankful that the influx of labor, money, and goods for the two projects kept barony Adahan well pacified; Ranella couldn't have handled an uprising, and another governor couldn't have handled the building of the plants so well.

Part of it was that she was a woman. With the exceptions of clerics and wizards, women were expected to breed children, not practice formal crafts and professions.

There was a payoff: The few women who did manage to succeed against such expectations tended to be pure cream of the crop. Tennetty was a good example. While Tennetty was a vicious, sometimes sadistic killer, it wasn't her naked brutality that had made her able to run squads on Karl's raiding teams; it was the general acknowledgment that her combat judgment was as good as there was.

Plus, of course, Karl's sponsorship. That counted for a lot.

Similarly, Riccetti had always been very openly impressed with Ranella's intelligence, and while the years had put wrinkles around her eyes and an unbecoming potbelly on her torso, her mind had only sharpened—but as a tool for building, not governing.

"We'll discuss your administration of the barony tomorrow, Ranella. You're to stay over tonight; the barony can get by on its own for an extra day."

"Whatever you say, Karl." Ranella shrugged. "And—"

"*Governor*," Dowager Baroness Beralyn of Furnael put in, "if I can address his majesty properly, so ought you." There was a slight emphasis on the personal pronoun; Karl decided to let it slide. He had always had a problem trying to keep Beralyn in line; she blamed him for the death of Rahff.

That makes two of us, Beralyn. He swallowed, hard. In Karl Cullinane's time, many, many good men had died fighting on the right side of their just cause, but the way that Rahff had died in his arms was always freshly painful.

Tyrnael snorted in disgust. "This is—" He caught himself and swallowed. He shook his head, then raised a palm in apology. "I'm sorry, but there are babies lying dead on the ground in my barony and you are arguing over forms of *address*?"

Arondael looked at Karl, then, at Karl's nod, spoke. "I am in agreement with Baron Tyrnael. We're faced with responding to an attack; let's not be distracted by minor issues of address and of who governs where."

Getting out those last words was clearly difficult for the slim man; the freeing of Nerahan's barony bothered him. During the Holtun-Bieme war, in an attempt to bull Arondael into sending a detachment out of his besieged castle, Nerahan had begun catapulting prisoners over the wall and into the courtyard.

The prisoners had included Arondael's son, his son's wife, and three of their children. War brings out the ugliest in men. All were dead long before they hit the ground; all—*all*—had been, within earshot of the castle walls, repeatedly raped by Nerahan's men, at Nerahan's orders.

Arondael's eyes searched the table for support, finding some, which didn't surprise Karl. "We have to show the Nyphs that we won't be attacked without fighting back," he went on.

Thomen Furnael's young face was grave beyond his years as he leaned back in his chair and folded his hands over his belly. "Baron, what if it wasn't the Nyphs who attacked us?"

"So? What if it wasn't?" The older man dismissed it. "There's no way of knowing for sure. Say it wasn't; assume it wasn't. How can they know that we know that for sure?"

Andy-Andy's chuckle sounded forced. "I think you lost me on that, Baron Tyrnael."

"Baron Tyrnael? If I may?" Nerahan raised an eyebrow. At Tyrnael's surprised nod, Nerahan went on. "The problem is this: Assume that the raid was actually executed by non-Nyphien forces. Nevertheless, for all we can know, it *might* well have been done by the Nyphs.

"The Nyphs know that. Now, if they discover that they can raid into Hol—into the empire without retaliation, won't that encourage them? Regardless of whether or not they did so this time, won't they see it as weakness?"

Tyrnael grunted an assent. "Exactly. Better for the Nyphs to know that if *anyone* crosses into Bieme to kill and enslave our people there will be a reprisal. Let the bastards guard our border from their side, instead of sending raiders across, or," he went on, the scorn heavy in his voice, "*forgetting* to stop them."

Everybody started talking after that, although the Biemish barons carried most of the conversation.

Karl sat back in his chair and let the argument flow undirected, Tyrnael and Nerahan urging immediate retaliation, Arondael and Ranella counseling accepting the official Nyph explanation.

The trouble with Nerahan's argument was that it made sense. It was much better, as a general principle, to force your neighbor to keep his own country from being a source of raids into yours than it was to try to patrol a border. That last was doomed to frequent failure.

Better an educational combination pursuit/reprisal raid à la Black Jack Pershing or Ariel Sharon than some Jimmy Carter–style loud talk while carrying only a small stick that you were frightened to use.

But that was only a generality. Every case was different: Pershing had known he was chasing Pancho Villa; Sharon had always had good intelligence as to where the PLO was hiding.

With Danagar yet to return from Nyphien—and that, all by itself, didn't bode well—Karl still didn't know who was responsible, and he didn't know where whoever was responsible was.

Better to find out who was responsible, and punish him or them.

While it probably didn't make much of a difference to a *Realpolitik*-oriented baron, Karl shrugged to admit that he had this fetish about trying to restrict punishment to the guilty. One of the troubles with war was that innocents died, but at least you should try to limit the damage to innocents on the other side.

Still, as a matter of state policy, if the Nyphs allowed their rulers to strike into Holtun-Bieme, it was proper to hold them collectively to account.

But what if it was Ahrmin? What if it was the Slavers' Guild, trying to trigger an empire-Nyphien war the way it had the Holtun-Bieme war?

He needed some time. Ellegon could be back any day. Maybe the dragon could do some good—but probably not. If the raid had been instigated by Pugeer, he would hardly have informed his envoy.

Karl would have to confront Pugeer. In person, with Ellegon at his side to read the Nyph's mind.

And if Pugeer was responsible?

He could practically hear Walter Slovotsky. *If you insist on juggling knives, you're going to get cut.*

If Pugeer was responsible, he was dead.

He turned to Thomen Furnael. "You've been quiet, Thomen. I need your thoughts."

"I doubt that. I might not keep quiet with them."

He knows!

Karl kept his face somber as the boy eyed him coldly.

"I think this is all premature," Thomen went on. "It's not enough to guess, not when we can know. I say we should wait for Danagar." He seemed about to say something more, but stopped himself. "Wait until we know."

"You have nothing to say with regard to my point?" Nerahan asked airily. "You don't find it relevant, Baron?"

"If—*if* we can discover for certain that it wasn't the Nyphs who are responsible, then we can let them know that. It would be insane to hold people to account for something that they're not responsible for." He turned back to Karl. "You asked my opinion. That is it."

Karl nodded. "And a sound opinion it is. Tyrnael, Thomen, please stay. The rest of you are dismissed."

He caught Andy's eye. "All of you." He didn't want her around for this.

CHAPTER SEVENTEEN:

Cowboy

The absence of romance in my history will, I fear, detract somewhat from its interest.

—Thucydides

"Down in the valley," Jason Cullinane sang as he rode night herd, looking out on the sea of cattle.

He kept singing as he decided, not for the first time, that there was something he would have to ask his father—if he ever was able to face him.

In the meantime, he kept singing. A few hundred yards away, he could hear, although just barely, the slow dirge that Ceenan kept up for the benefit of the idiot cows around him.

"Down in the valley . . ." Jason sang. He had a lousy singing voice, but the cattle didn't seem to mind.

Whether or not it was true, Falikos had the belief, common among drovers, that singing to the cattle would help prevent them from stampeding. During the day, while the beasts were moving, a stampede was merely unfortunate; it could scatter cows far and wide, but almost always in the direction of their march.

At night, a stampede could be deadly. A sudden sound could send the nervous, stupid creatures in any direction, trampling anyone who was insufficiently vigilant or inadequately lucky.

Maybe the singing did help keep them calm. There was nobody else within earshot; he sang a slow, mournful tune he had half learned from his father, improvising the lyrics that he couldn't quite remember—

> "*Down in the valley, the valley so low,*
> *Hang your head low, cows, hang your head low.*
> *They'll chop you for burgers,*
> *Or make you a stew,*
> *And if I live to be a hundred,*
> *I'll never smell anything worse than you. . . ."*

—and adding an editorial comment or two as, under a canopy of twinkling stars and slowly pulsing faerie lights, Falikos' herd mooed and shuffled and stank into the night.

It was almost enough to turn you into a vegetarian, Jason decided. Although Father had said that vegetarianism had some problems: It tended to make you vote for peace-at-any-price candidates, whatever that meant.

Off in the distance, a few hundred of the stupid beasts away, Jason could see another of the night riders spur his horse and gallop off after some dumb stray.

Jason wasn't impressed with the intelligence of the beasts, such as it was. Even what little there was worked at cross-purposes.

Take their homing instincts. Jason seemed to spend half his time chasing cows and calves. If the two were separated, some idiot instinct forced both dumb animals to head back to the very spot where they had last seen each other—no matter how far the herd had moved in the interim. All of the drovers were constantly looping back to find and speed along pairs of cows and calves.

A west wind brought the odor to his nostrils yet again. Every other smell he'd ever smelled was something he had gotten used to. But not this stink.

He brought his gloved hands up to rub at his itching nose, then gripped at the bridge of his nose, as though that could reduce the pain he felt elsewhere.

He felt absolutely lousy. His eyes burned from lack of sleep. His lower back ached with the pain of having spent the last half day in the saddle—the only moments out of it when he had to relieve himself. And even that had just made things worse: The unending hours in the saddle, combined with the indigestible lumps of fetid mush that Falikos' cook had the unmitigated gall to call food, had given him a case of hemorrhoids that forced him to put a soft blanket between his butt and the saddle.

It was easier on the horses, at least. They couldn't be worked too hard, or they'd just lie down and die. Like all the other drovers, Jason cycled through five or six of the ponies throughout the day, resting the others. Libertarian, while a great riding horse, didn't work cattle; the gelding was getting an easy trip to Pandathaway.

He jerked hard on the reins; the stubborn roan moved reluctantly to the right, refusing to break into a canter as Jason headed back toward where the spare ponies were hobbled for the night.

Why the drovers couldn't be treated as well as the horses was one thing that Jason wondered as he dismounted and moved his saddle from the tired roan to a weary bay gelding.

The other thing was about his father. Karl Cullinane had told Jason that when *he* was a boy, he had often dreamed of being a cowboy; it seemed to him to be a romantic kind of life.

While he was trying to get the halter settled around the bay's head, the animal stepped on his foot, sending him tumbling to the ground, pain shooting up his leg.

He had to be silent in his agony; a shout could send the cattle into hysterical flight in any direction.

As he—slowly, painfully—got to his feet to try again, he wondered, for the thousandth time: What kind of idiot thought that this was romantic?

CHAPTER EIGHTEEN:
After the Council of Barons

Political power grows out of the barrel of a gun.
                                        —Mao Tse-tung

When the rest had left, Karl led Tyrnael and Thomen up the back stairs and into his private office, the one that connected to his and Andy's bedroom. He brought a dusty bottle of Riccetti's Best down from the shelves, uncorked it, and poured each of three mottled-green whiskey glasses half full.

"What are we going to do?" Tyrnael asked.

"It's simple." Karl waved them both to a seat and braced himself against the wall. "Tell him, Thomen. You worked it out."

The boy—no, it wasn't fair to call him a boy—Thomen Furnael sipped his whiskey, smiling over the rim of the glass. "We are beginning to think too much alike, aren't we?"

"I don't think like either of you." Tyrnael downed his whiskey and shook his head in irritation. "I don't understand what's going on."

While Karl poured Tyrnael a second glass, Thomen sipped at his. "True. Two things are happening. For one, do you remember that poacher that you hanged?"

"Of course."

"Well, I tried to turn him loose—but Karl figured out what I was trying to do and stopped me."

Karl had to admire the way that Tyrnael merely said, "Oh?"

"The reason he was able to stop me was that he figured out what I was going to do, and took the next step. I am about to do the same thing, in reverse: Karl is thinking of trying to take on Pugeer in person, have Ellegon sort through his mind and find out if he was behind the Kernat raid, and if he was guilty, kill him. Correct?"

"Correct." Karl nodded. "Like I said, we think too much—"

"*Then you're a damn fool.*" Thomen Furnael threw his glass against the wall. It shattered, spraying glass and whiskey around the room.

Footsteps thundered in the hall outside; three guards, pistols drawn and cocked, rushed into the room.

"Majesty—"

Thomen didn't move. "It's nothing, soldiers," he said, sitting absolutely still, his hands folded across his lap.

The soldiers' faces were studiously blank.

"Dismissed," Karl said coldly. "Get out of here."

When the door closed behind them, Karl spun on the younger man. "What was that about?"

"That was to get your attention. I would have preferred to kick you in the balls to get your attention, but I don't think I could."

"And now that you've got my attention?"

"You're not going to do it." The younger man stood and walked to the window, tapping his signet ring against the glass. "Karl, if you even think about trying it, I'm going to break security and this window and shout so loudly about what you're planning that you won't believe it."

He turned back to Karl. "You had to stop me quietly; I may have to stop you noisily."

"You—"

"I don't like the odds, and I'm not going to let you play the game. Think it through, Karl," Thomen said, slowly moving to the sideboard to pick up a fresh glass. "May I?" he asked, hefting the whiskey bottle.

"If you're going to drink it this time."

"Fine. —What if it *is* Ahrmin, Karl? Don't you think he's noticed that you do things yourself? Even after all this time, the extent you like to stick your hand in the way of the knife manages to surprise most of us, but he's been studying you for years—and he's been on to you ever since he set up the siege at Furnael Castle, back during the war. That was intended to catch you. You like to be out in front of things; you always have.

"Just in case anyone might have thought that you had outgrown it, you ran that raid on Arondael's castle a few tendays ago. If it is Ahrmin behind all this, you'll find yourself breaking into the castle, and then—"

"And then the trap gets sprung. If it is a trap."

"Exactly."

"Your suggestion, then?"

Thomen drained the glass as he returned to his chair, taking the bottle with him. "I don't like the odds; we have to know." He poured himself another glass.

Tyrnael looked from one to the other. "So? We let matters rest where they are?"

Thomen shook his head. "No. We investigate; we send out spies, we move troops into position—"

"Can't that set off a war between us and the Nyphs?" Tyrnael cocked his head to one side. "Wouldn't we be better striking first?"

"We are better off *not* striking at all, if the Nyphs aren't guilty." Thomen, Baron Furnael, shook his head. "You'll have to gamble, just like the rest of us. His majesty will have to brace Pugeer's ambassador, and get him to understand that there's going to be a reprisal only if Nyphien was responsible."

"If they are?" Tyrnael asked dubiously.

"Baron, when I was a boy, my father sent my mother and me away from the war. To safety, he thought. We were seized by slavers and sold off."

For a moment, Karl could almost see Thomen's father standing there, as Thomen gripped the glass with white-knuckled fingers. "I am not going to talk about that time, Baron," Thomen said quietly, the words paced like metronome beats. "It was not pleasant. Not for my mother; not for myself."

Setting his glass and bottle down on the floor, Thomen Furnael drew his beltknife and balanced it on his palm. "I swear, Baron, that we are going to do our best to find out who did to your people what was done to me, and when we do, they are going to die."

The young baron slid the knife back into its sheath. "If we can capture any, you and I are going to work the choke nooses ourselves, and watch them dance in the air while they beg for another breath. Unless you want in on that, your majesty."

Karl Cullinane smiled. "When you get older, Thomen, you'll learn that it doesn't matter who does it."

Thomen's anger at him was still manifest, but the young baron had dismissed it as irrelevant. Karl had to admire him; while he hadn't forgiven Karl for stopping him, this was a matter of state policy, and personal feelings couldn't be allowed to enter into it.

A simple application of reasoning, really—the emperor planned to risk himself, but the emperor couldn't be risked. Nor, for that matter, could he afford to strangle a baron with his own two hands to shut him up, passingly tempting as that seemed.

So: "Okay, Thomen, we'll do it your way." Karl Cullinane drained his own whiskey, looked longingly at the bottle, then shook his head. Too much work to do. "First thing is we work out how many troops we're sending into Tyrnael. I'll want to get Nerahan in on this"—he tugged on the bell rope, twice—"since he seems to understand cannon better than the rest of you."

"Cannon?"

Karl Cullinane seated himself at his desk and pulled out paper, reaching for a map of the border area. "Cannon." He spread the map out on the floor and pulled out a box of gaming pieces. "If we're taking on the Nyphs, we're going to be able to blast them into little, bloody pieces." The door opened. "Nartham. Good— I want Garavar and Nerahan here, now."

Karl Cullinane rubbed at tired eyes and looked from Nerahan to Garavar to Thomen to Tyrnael. "Anybody got anything else?"

Kneeling at the northern edge of the map, General Garavar leaned forward. "I can't see any major improvement," he said, tapping at the map, "unless you want to move this battery from here to here."

"I don't like it." Tyrnael shook his head. "Not close enough to the border. We can't move cannons quickly; I'll want them to be as close as possible to the troops."

Which made sense, both for defensive and offensive purposes.

"Hmm . . ." Nerahan raised a finger to his lips and then touched it down to the map. "*There.* There's a good road down the side of the hill, and it seems to make sense to me to keep the guns as high as possible."

Karl looked over it again, trying to decide. "It could work either way. If it rains, those roads are going to turn to mud, and we're not going to be able to get the guns down from there for days."

"I disagree. Respectfully, always respectfully." Nerahan shook his head. "It doesn't matter. We only need to move them in order to attack, and we attack at our convenience, not theirs."

"Good point. Garavar, who do you want in tactical command? Gashier?"

"No. Too hotheaded," the general said. "Kevalun."

"I was going to give him—"

Karl. A distant voice sounded in his head. *Karl, we've got trouble.*

He jerked upright. "Ellegon!" *What is it?*

He's probably not hurt, but Jason's missing.

What? Tell me—

We're not going to be able to do anything about it tonight. I will be landing in the courtyard in just a minute. Meet me.

"On my way."

CHAPTER NINETEEN:

Decisions

Not every man was born with a silver spoon in his mouth.
—Miguel de Cervantes

There had been a time, long ago, Karl Cullinane decided, when he could allow himself the occasional trace of panic in his voice.

That time was long gone.

"Andy?" the big man asked, his voice steady and level as he stared out into the night. "What are we going to do?"

In the courtyard below, Ellegon dipped his massive head as the dragon dined on the bloody hindquarter of a sheep while a dozen men swarmed over him, strapping down leather bags filled with supplies for Daven's team, trapped in Khar.

"Maybe the others have found him by now." Andy gripped his hand, hard. Karl could feel her pulse, going like a triphammer.

Karl Cullinane put his arm around her and pulled her close. "I'll do what can be done," he whispered. "I swear it."

Andrea could be right. Maybe Tennetty and the others have caught up with him. Steam hissed from between Ellegon's teeth; the dragon daintily dipped his head to take another mouthful of the sheep. Or, rather, what had been the sheep; there wasn't much left.

Karl shook his head. Maybe Jason was safe, and maybe not. But he wasn't going to assume anything. If it worked out that way, fine;

160

certainly, Tennetty and Ahira could track Jason down, given enough time, absent sufficient competition.

If they had enough time.

"Very well," Karl Cullinane whispered. "So be it." Cullinane turned slowly to the old general. "Garavar—can you help Andrea handle things while I'm gone?"

The old soldier nodded slowly. "The military side of it. Not the political. Even at that, I'll need Kevalun as my deputy. Or Danagar." Garavar looked at Karl reproachfully.

"I understand." Karl nodded. "Danagar is overdue from Nyphien, and you're not sending out parties after him. But it is different, dammit. Danagar is a professional soldier; Jason's just a boy. Garavar, you understand why I have to treat this differently."

"No." Garavar's face was rock-still. "But I accept it."

"You'll need me," Thomen Furnael said. "To help keep the nobility in line. If you insist on doing this."

Karl nodded. "Right. Thank you, Thomen. You're a good—"

"*No.* This doesn't change anything between us, Emperor. The empire needs stability right now, and if you're going to run out—"

Andy plucked at Thomen's sleeve. "He has to. Your father would have understood."

"My father would *not* have understood." White-lipped, Thomen snatched his arm away and drew himself up straight. "He sent Rahff into danger, knowing that the chances of his coming out alive were small. He sent my mother and me away, and let us be clapped into slavers' chains. But he *never* left his barony behind. He never abandoned his people, his duties." His voice softened as he turned to Karl. "He understood what came first; he understood his responsibilities. Better than I do, perhaps; certainly better than you seem to, Emperor."

"Good point." Karl nodded. "And well taken. But I'm still going, Thomen."

Andrea went to Karl and gripped his hand. "I'm going with you. Maybe I can find him."

Karl shook his head. Not while Jason was wearing his amulet, she couldn't. *And I don't think I'm going to get out of this one, Lady.* "Besides, I'm not going after him. I'm going after the sword."

"What?"

It was a necessity. The others could track Jason better than Karl could. Karl's presence as one of the searchers wouldn't make a difference.

This might. The only way for Karl to get the heat off Jason's neck was to put it on his own. The only quarry more interesting to the guild hunters than Karl's son would be Karl himself.

"As long as I wear this," he said, tugging idly at the amulet around his neck, "Ahrmin can't locate me. As long as I wear this. . . ."

He brought up his other hand and, holding the thong between thumb and forefinger of each hand, pulled at it; it parted as though it had been made of wet paper.

"Now," he said, his voice almost a whisper, "they can find me. I'll take a few men, ride to Ehvenor, and take ship out of there. Ellegon, I want you to stop off and relay the story as you make your rounds. Let everyone know that Karl Cullinane is going for the sword."

The dragon gave a mental shrug. *Hardly necessary, even without that. News travels by the shortest possible route. But I will.* The dragon's flame roared skyward, cleaving the night. *After I resupply Daven, where do I go? Search? Or join up with you?*

"Neither. You are going to be needed here, to pick the brains of the Nyphs and find out who was behind the massacre. And then there's Daven's team. More supplies are probably going to have to be ferried to them." He looked out into the night. "You and I have taken on many responsibilities, old friend."

I understand.

He turned to the rest. "Is there anything else that has to be done before I—?"

"*No.*" Thomen Furnael stepped in front of the emperor. "Karl, you can't do this. I understand why you want to, but you can't. Your first responsibility is to the empire, not to Jason. And you—"

Karl laid a hand on his arm. "He's my son, Thomen. I have to." He turned to face them all. "I'll be leaving in the morning. Garavar, pick out a party of five to accompany me—one of them a junior engineer—and have my supplies packed before you go to sleep. Thomen, I'll want you and Harven to ride with me to the border—we'll have time to go over some details."

Ellegon nodded. *I hit the sky, now. Yes?*

For a moment, a smile peeked through Cullinane's stony

expression. "You're not going to take me aside and try to talk me out of this?"

I may be a young dragon, Ellegon said, as he shook his massive head. *But I've gotten older and wiser in the time I've known you,* the dragon said, the light tone of his mental voice manifestly false. *I won't waste my time. Or yours. Go take your wife to bed, Karl. It may well be your last time.*

It might, at that.

Karl was tempted to blame Walter or Ahira, or Valeran. But that wasn't right. If—*if*—Valeran had been wrong to take the boy on the raid, Valeran had paid for his error. Besides, Karl didn't blame him. Or Walter or Ahira. Jason would have had to go through this, sometime.

Hell, he didn't even blame Jason; it must have been hard on the boy, and it wasn't right to expect a sixteen-year-old to make the right decision. Once he'd run, turning back would have been very hard. There were some things that couldn't be turned back from.

Take care of yourself, Karl, Ellegon said. *Walter and Ahira will find him. And when he's safe, we'll send someone after you.*

"I'll be okay. Just make sure that the hounds go my way." He pulled Andrea to him, and, ignoring all the others in the room, held her tightly.

We will. Craning his neck upward toward the balcony where Karl and Andrea stood, Ellegon's eyes searched his deeply, as the mental voice softened. *Karl, just between you and me, do you think you'll get out of this?*

"Of course," he said, smiling. "Haven't I always?"

I hope so, he thought. *But I don't know.*

It all depended. Which way would Ahrmin and his hunters jump? And could Karl stay a jump ahead of him?

Guess we'll all find out, the hard way.

I guess so.

Ellegon? In case I don't make it back, will you watch over her?

Of course, Karl. Karl?

Yes, Ellegon?

In case you don't make it back, thank you. I'll always remember. A relayed image flashed through Karl's mind: a younger version of himself, waist-deep in sewage, reaching up to cut through a strand of the golden cable that held the dragon down. *I'll remember everything.*

Karl smiled. *Don't go maudlin on me. The last thing we need around here is ten tons of maudlin dragon.* "Andy . . ."

She held him tightly. "I know. In the morning?"

"In the morning." Taking her hand, he gave a sketchy salute to the others. "Good night all, and farewell."

"Good night, your majesty."

Goodbye, Karl.

Flame roared, as the dragon leaped skyward.

CHAPTER TWENTY:

Pandathaway

Our swords shall play the orator for us.
—Christopher Marlowe

As they reached the top of the last hill, Jason gasped; he clutched the wagon's reins tighter and gave a slight, unconscious hitch to them, as though to speed up the team.

"Don't be silly," Doria said, with a chuckle. "We'll get there soon enough. It is pretty, though."

Between rolling hills and the blue Cirric sparkling in the sun, the city of Pandathaway stood, white and gold, dancing in the sun. The streets were broad and even, some curving to help cup the harbor, others cutting across evenly, regularly. There were small parks scattered all over the city, squares of green checkering the field of white and gold.

Doria extended an arm. "That's the library, there—and over there is the Coliseum, where your father beat Ohlmin."

"Shh." Why did she have to talk so loosely? What if somebody overheard?

Behind him, hooves clattered on the road, as Falikos eased up alongside the wagon.

Doria patted Jason's knee. "Taren," she said, in a normal voice, "I do have my skills; trust me. Oh, and—greetings, Falikos." She eyed the setting late-afternoon sun carefully. "Are you going to try for the stockyards before dark?"

Falikos shook his head. "No. We might be able to get all the beasts in, but I've found that some always manage to disappear when we try to count them in the dark. We'll make camp just outside the walls, and move the herd in the morning. Speaking of which, Taren, what are your plans?"

Why, Falikos, I'm going to prove that I'm not a coward by assassinating Ahrmin.

"I'm not sure, sir." He shrugged. "I'm open to anything."

Doria spoke up. "If you're good with a sword, I've heard that there's money to be made in the Coliseum."

"If you're some kind of Karl Cullinane," Falikos said, with a chuckle. "It's supposed to be a hard way to make a living. But probably worth a try, at that."

Some kind of Karl Cullinane.

Jason swallowed, hard. "And your plans, sir?"

"After I sell the stock I'll take ship out of here; that's all I can say." Falikos shrugged. "I've been thinking about making a run up north and buying a load of blades, or south to Ehvenor and seeing what the faerie are trading—I will have to spend a few days and a few coins in a trader's tavern to pick up the gossip. What with all that I'll be carrying, Kyreen and Dyren will be staying with me, although I'll need even more of a bodyguard; I'm sorry that I can't ask you."

"Oh?"

"I haven't known you long enough. Too much of a risk." Falikos dug into his saddlebags and pulled out a small leather sack. "Speaking of which, here are your wages, as agreed—I threw in a little extra for the scar. I won't need you tonight; you can enter Pandathaway when you please. Doria? I don't believe I owe you any more, do I?"

The cleric shook her head. "No—there hasn't been cause for extra charges, Falikos."

"Then I'll bid you both farewell." He leaned over and pointed. "The entry station is—"

"I've been in Pandathaway before, Falikos," Doria said, her voice holding a decided edge.

The cattleman nodded. "Then be well." He wheeled his horse around and kicked it into a canter.

"Let's go, Jason," she said. "I want to check in tonight."

Jason turned to see that Libertarian was still hitched to the rear of the wagon; seeing that the gelding was still trotting easily along, he gave a sharp whistle and flicked both sets of reins.

"Nice of him to pay us off today," he said. It really was; Falikos could have made him guard the camp that night, waiting for the next day and the entry of the herd into Pandathaway.

"Nonsense. Don't be so gullible." Doria shook her head. "You've led a sheltered life. There's a tax on entry into Pandathaway— sometimes they charge warriors, sometimes not. Now, Falikos doesn't have to gamble; if we were still with the herd, Falikos would have had to pay it. Nothing I can do about it, either; Elmina negotiated with Falikos, not me. But enough of that."

She eyed him carefully. "Any idea about what you're going to do now?"

He shrugged. "I should be able to find some sort of work. Or take a chance in the Coliseum," he lied. First step was to find a place to load his weapons; second step was to find out where Ahrmin was; and then the last. To kill Ahrmin.

You killed my Uncle Chak, bastard.

But would Jason run again?

Not again. No.

Doria didn't say anything for a long time. Then: "Think it through, Jason. Don't you think your father sent assassins after Ahrmin?"

Jason shook his head. "No. *He* wouldn't do anything like that."

"Jason, grow up." Doria chuckled. "You'd be surprised what your dad would do. But I agree, for once: I don't think he would have sent good men after Ahrmin, because he'd know that Ahrmin is going to have at least as much security around him in Pandathaway as Karl does in Biemestren or Home. Swordsmen, bowmen, magic—he's going to be fully protected."

"*What?*" It hit him: she knew he was after Ahrmin. "You knew I was going to—"

She shrugged. "It's obvious. You feel you have to prove some- thing. You have to go out and slay the biggest dragon you can find."

At his puzzled look, she chuckled and shook her head. "Sorry— Other Side metaphor. The point is, though, that you're acting just like your father used to: You fix your mind on one thing, and forget everything else. Not good, Jason. Not good at all. You've got to think this through; this will require some patience, not just crashing into a situation the way," she said with a warm smile, "your father always does."

She had known what he was up to. She had known, and she had kept the fact that she knew from him. The fact that she was right—that he did have to do this carefully—didn't make any difference. The fact that she'd misled him did.

"Move over," he said. "You're blocking the door."

"No. I want to talk about it."

"Go talk with yourself."

He gathered the reins together and handed them to her, vaulting from the wagon's bench and recovering in time to swing himself up, and in through the back door.

"Jason," she called out, "what do you think you are doing?"

He threw his things into his saddlebags and retrieved his disguised rifle. "What does it look like?"

"You're not leaving. Listen to me. It can end here. Here's where you can turn around, and head back to Home. By the time you get there—"

"No."

"Then at least stay with me for the night. We'll drop off the horses and cart at the Hand Residence; I'll go find us a room somewhere and we can talk about it." She muttered a few quick words and hung the reins in the air, rising from the bench and crawling into the wagon.

Doria drew herself up straight. "I swear, Jason, you put all that down and agree to stay with me tonight, or I'll Compel you." She turned halfway away from him, almost into a fighting stance. "I swear it."

"You can't." He sneered. "You can't help me, remember?"

"I could." Doria smiled thinly. "Once. The spells are in my head, boy. My . . . standing wouldn't be forfeit until I used the spell, until I actually helped you."

"This isn't help."

"*I* say it is. Now, do I have your word?"

"Go ahead, Doria. Try it. Then what'll you be? A nothing, a nobody—how would you get by?"

She shook her head sadly. "I don't know. But I swear, unless you give me your word, *now*, that you'll stay with me tonight and hear me out, I'll Compel you."

"Doria, you're bluffing."

"Am I now?" She swallowed, once, twice. "Very well." Her eyes went vague.

She wasn't bluffing,

"Wait! No—don't." The words tumbled out. "Agreed, Doria. Agreed, dammit. I'll stay with you tonight and talk to you."

"That's *listen* to me."

"Agreed. Whatever you say. Just don't. Please."

She lowered her hands, all menace gone from her manner. "Good. Now, let's get ourselves ready to go through customs, okay?"

Her voice was light and steady, but her forehead was covered with sweat, and her hands shook until she clasped them together.

The inspection proved to be even more *pro forma* than Jason had suspected; the elf asked them their business in Pandathaway, charged Doria a silver piece for entry, and waved their wagon through the gate, into the city of Pandathaway itself.

Just then, the wind changed, and blew the stench of the city toward him: Pandathaway smelled like a well-used outhouse. Like Biemestren on a hot day, only worse.

Doria's nose wrinkled, too; she brought up a finger and rubbed at it. "It wasn't this bad last time. But we won't notice it after a while."

Thankfully, the wind changed again. There was a row of stables down the street to their right; Jason turned the wagon, the wheels rattling on the cobblestones.

"First thing is to find a stable," he said.

"No, Jason, we've got to find a place for us to stay tonight. We can leave the team with my sisters."

"Not my horse, though. We take care of Libby, first."

"Mmm . . . agreed."

That was one thing that both Valeran and *he* had always insisted on: You fed and watered your animals before taking care of yourself.

They left his horse and too much of his pay as a deposit for Libertarian's care with the third hostler they tried, a bored dwarf whose prices were merely highway robbery.

And then they went into the markets.

It was all new to him, but somehow it was all very familiar. It took him a while to figure out what it reminded him of.

Back when he was just a baby, back before they had made the move from Home to Biemestren, Mother used to occasionally cook, giving U'len the night off. She always made the same thing, a dish she called *paella.* When she brought it to the table, Father always went into the same little speech about how it was a damn strange thing for a good Greek girl to make as her specialty, which always puzzled him, because he knew that Mother and Father came from a country called America.

She would always laugh at that, and the stern lines in both of their faces would soften. It didn't bother Jason, being left out of their private joke, their own little world that contained just the two of them. It warmed him.

Besides, he liked *paella.*

It was always different, but the general theme was that of saffron rice cooked in chicken broth and a whole variety of spices, surrounding a rainbow of things that had all been cooked together: little cubes of chicken, beef, and lamb, all of which had been carefully browned until their outer crust was a dark brown, almost black; tiny wild onions; headless freshwater prawns and the huge mussels from the Seven Streams; strips of slow-cured ham; and tiny little peppers, always hiding so that they could make your eyes tear when you bit into one accidentally.

He had always loved *paella,* and perhaps not just for the taste. Maybe it was the fact that Mother was doing something for him, for once; perhaps it was just that the idea of mixing different kinds of things excited him.

The Pandathaway markets were like *paella:* a collection of sights and sounds and smells, some of which weren't things that he would have thought would go together . . .but they did, nonetheless.

The walls near the markets were plastered with broadsides proclaiming the virtue of some wares for those who could read, and the air was filled with the cries of loud-voiced merchants for those who couldn't.

One of the broadsides caught Jason's eye. *Are You a Swordsman or Bowman with Great Skill and Greater Ambition?* it asked.

He nodded for a moment as the press of the crowd swept them by the poster. He wasn't at all bad with a sword, and he did have a great ambition: to kill Ahrmin. But he doubted that that was what the broadside was all about.

"What about my horse?" he asked.

"What about your horse? He—it—should be fine where it is."

"No. After. After I . . . do it. I may have to get out of Pandathaway quickly."

"True. In which case you'll either have reclaimed your horse first, or you'll find another way out of town and just leave the horse behind." Cocking her head to one side, she eyed him quizzically. "Or do you really think that the hostler will let a valuable beast starve to death rather than decide that it's been abandoned?"

"Good point." Still, the idea of abandoning the animal rankled. But she was right. As usual.

Doria guided him down through the markets, past basketweavers and cobblers, coopers with freshly made barrels bleaching in the sun, and one baker's stall where the scent of fresh bread momentarily threatened to overpower the miasma of stale donkey urine and rotting dung.

She stopped for a moment by a sandalmaker, a shrunken little man with tired eyes and a graying ponytail, and bargained hard for a pair of sandals to replace the riding boots that had Jason's feet sweating, then insisted that the sandalmaker shorten the anklestraps on the spot when they were too loose, threatening to leave him with blisters.

Shortening the straps took about a fifth as long as the argument.

The next stop was at a Spidersect stall, of all places, where a fat, greasy-bearded, black-robed cleric muzzled his puzzlement at Doria's presence long enough for Jason to purchase a small pot of unguent that the fat man swore would take all the sting out of Jason's saddle sores. Checking to make sure of the wax-and-cork seal, Jason tucked it in next to his boots in his backpack.

They walked on.

Ahead, a dwarf armorer worked at a portable forge, beneath a sign that proclaimed, in awkward Erendra phonetics, that he sold genuine Nehera bowies. His list of posted prices looked reasonable, but Jason didn't stop. For one thing, he didn't need any blades. He had a good sword at the left side of his belt and a bowie at his right—and both of them had actually been made by Nehera; Jason knew full well that this blacksmith was selling only weak imitations.

But pointing that out wouldn't accomplish anything except drawing attention to himself.

Another copy of the broadside he had seen before caught his eye.

Are You a Swordsman or Bowman with Great Skill and Greater Ambition? it still wanted to know.

Possibly, he decided.

Over by a fountain, a flute player and a dancer were setting up; he sitting down crosslegged on his straw mat, she stripping off layers of clothes, leaving behind little besides a few silks and beads. While most of her face was hidden by a silken veil, the rest looked interesting. She started to move in time to the flutist's hesitant runs, then stopped as the crowd gathered.

He started to move toward where the show was obviously going to be, but Doria caught his arm.

Her look held only disappointment. "Look again," she said.

This time, Jason saw the black iron collar, almost hidden by the silks, and was more than a little disgusted with himself.

"Sort of an owned dancing prostitute," Doria said. "She'll get the men worked up, and then take them on, one by one," she said, in a flat expressionless voice. She shook her head, as though to say that there was nothing that he could do, so there was no shame in doing nothing.

"We go left here," she said.

The Hand Residence stood out on the street like a clean spot on a well-used napkin; the other two-story stone buildings on the narrow street sagged with age, the cracks in the stone mortared in places, all crumbling around the edges.

The Hand Residence, though, looked new, the corners of the building sharp as razors, the granite blocks clean enough to suggest that dirt was intimidated away. Jason pulled up the horses, set the brake, and gathered his gear together, while Doria climbed down from the wagon.

"I'll just be a short while. I have your word that you will be here when I come out, Jason." She raised an eyebrow.

"You do."

Doria looked at him for a long moment, then eased herself down to the street and walked in through the Residence's archway, without a glance behind.

She disappeared into the dark of the building.

Now was his chance to disappear, but . . .

But he wouldn't. He wouldn't let her talk him out of anything, but he'd given his word.

I may be a coward, but I don't have to be a liar, too,

Jason chuckled to himself. *Idiot.* He noticed another copy of that same broadside on the wall beside him, and glanced at it.

Great Risk   Great Pay

**Are You a Swordsman or Bowman with Great Skill
and Greater Ambition?**
AHRMIN, Master Slaver
is hiring WARRIORS
for an expedition past Faerie.
Apply immediately at the Slavers' Guildhall.
TRAINING in the ART of GUNNERY will be
provided.

*   *   *

A Cook, Armorer, Cobbler, and Smith are also needed.
Great Pay   Great Risk

Past Faerie? That meant Melawei. The slavers raided into Melawei
all the time, but they didn't hire mercenaries to help them. They'd
only do that if there was something more dangerous than a bunch
of Mel—

No.

Father was going after the sword, and Ahrmin was going after
him.

He snatched the broadside down from the wall and dashed for
the arching door. "Doria!"

Two slim women emerged from the shadows, barring his way.
"You may not enter the Residence, Jason Cullinane," the nearest
one said.

"*Doria!*" he shouted again.

But there was no answer.

"I have to see her—"

"You may not enter."

Neither of them was close to his size; he tried to push past them
as gently as possible, but one of them caught his left wrist with
her slim hand, the long, delicate fingers wrapping themselves tightly
around his wrist.

He should have been able to break the grip with a twitch of
his arm, but as the woman muttered words that could only be
uttered and forgotten, her grip tightened, and then tightened some
more, until his bones threatened to break.

Time froze as Jason's free hand fastened on the hilt of his bowie, and he started to draw his knife.

"Ta havath," Doria's clear contralto proclaimed, shattering the moment. "What is it, Jason?" she asked, separating him from the others, rubbing at his wrist with strong fingers that seemed to ease the pain magically, even if he knew that was impossible.

"Read this."

Doria's face went ashen. "Past Faerie. It—"

"It has to mean what we think it does," Jason said. "These are going up all over the city."

"It must be," Doria said, as she turned to the other two Hand women. Their fingers met and clasped for a moment, before she turned back to Jason.

"The word is out," she said. "Karl is making an overland try for the sword, and Ahrmin plans to beat him by sea." She gripped his arm, with far more strength than she had any right to. "He's painted a target on his back, and Ahrmin is setting sail to put a cluster of arrows in the bullseye."

Jason nodded. "How soon?"

"I don't know. But we had best find out."

"That we had."

The night passed slowly, as they lay on their blankets in the single room they had rented. The night was hot and muggy; sweat ran down Jason's forehead and into his eyes as he sat at the window, looking out into the street.

He rubbed his stinging eyes. He couldn't sleep; it was just too hot. He uncorked a jug of water and tilted it back. The water was blood temperature; it quelled his thirst without giving him any satisfaction at all.

"I don't know, Doria—what can we do?"

Getting an opportunity to kill Ahrmin was out, now; the slaver was due to leave in only a couple of days, and he'd certainly be unusually careful until he left, his suspicious mind open to the possibility of an attack.

Of course, Jason could sign on with Ahrmin . . . possibly.

But what good would that do?

Doria muttered a few harsh words that could only be forgotten. Jason turned to see a fat, dark-haired woman of about fifty, who reminded him of U'len.

"I picked it from your mind," Doria said. "U'len looks like a cook. I . . ." Her voice trailed off into a gurgle, as she staggered back against the wall and slipped to the floor, one outstretched arm fluttering at him to keep his distance.

I can't help you," she said, her form shimmering, waves of shadow washing across her bulk. The voice wasn't hers, not really, it was richer, deeper, older, more powerful.

"No," she said in her own voice. "I *can* do what—"

"*No. I can't—*"

"Yes. I can take on a form that will protect me. I can go where I please, and I can disguise myself for my own protection. For my own protection, I can disguise myself."

She clenched her fists tightly, leaning back into shadow as dark sweat beaded on her forehead.

Jason picked up a cloth, uncorked the water jug to wet it, and went to wipe her forehead.

"No. Keep your distance. My burden. Price to . . . pay for challenging the Mother."

He pushed aside the vague fingers and daubed at her face. "Easy, Doria. Easy."

The cloth came away dark with blood.

Doria held up a hand. "Don't come closer. You'll only make it worse."

His gorge rose; he fell to his hands and knees and vomited until he was bent over double, his belly wracked with pain from the dry heaves.

"Jason . . . I'll be okay. Jason. *Jason.*"

He waved her away as he tried to get his churning belly under control. He had to; he just had to. If they were going to sign up with Ahrmin tomorrow, he'd have to be in command of himself.

"I'll . . . be okay, too," he said. "And call me Taren. Even when we're alone."

CHAPTER TWENTY-ONE:

Ahrmin

In a well-governed country, poverty is something to be ashamed of. In a badly governed country, wealth is something to be ashamed of.

—Kung-Fu-Tze

His heart thrumming a steady backbeat, Jason slowly advanced in the line outside the Slavers' Guildhall.

He wasn't impressed with the others in line with him; they were a dirty bunch of swordsmen.

But he couldn't really look down on them. Maybe they weren't cowards.

"Where you from, boy?" the man in front of him asked, probably just to make conversation.

Jason ignored him. The man took a too-long moment deciding whether or not to take offense, decided against it and then struck up a conversation with the man in front of him.

Doria had warned Jason about getting involved in idle chatter. It wasn't a deliberate interrogation he had to worry about—he knew enough about the fictitious Taren ip Therranj to answer questions—but an accidental slip.

It was a deceptively pretty building, or set of buildings: four connected three-storied structures of glistening white marble, surrounding an interior courtyard. Each of the linked buildings was supported by a pair of high fluted columns, guarding an entry arch.

He had seen the spreading branches of an ancient oak through an archway. It looked gorgeous, rising cleanly into the sky.

But the facade faded at the edges. A pair of rag-clad Mel women, the younger about Jason's age, the other perhaps a decade older, were on their hands and knees a short way down the corridor to Jason's left, scrubbing the floor under the watchful eye of a half-tunic-clad boy, of about fifteen or so, who, every now and then, snapped his many-stranded whip to draw their attention to missed spots, real or not.

Jason wasn't sure what the purpose of it all was, or if the boy was merely being cruel to no purpose. Blood was trickling down the back of the younger of the two women, staining the marble, causing the slaver to redouble his efforts.

Jason turned his face away, but the sound persisted.

The line in front of him slowly shrank. Over the background noise of whip cracks and stifled screams, the guard at the door looked into the room beyond and nodded.

The grizzled soldier in front of him had been gone only a few moments when the guard nodded at Jason.

"Next. Taren ip Therranj."

Jason followed the guard's gesture into the outer room, where a skinny, cringing man knelt in front of him with a damp rag.

"To wash your feet," the guard explained, as the slave began scrubbing at Jason's sandals and feet. "Must mind the carpeting, even in the Stranger's Room."

The soap felt slimy between his toes. Jason forced himself not to let the disgust he felt show in his face.

"Lift your arms," the guard said, patting Jason down thoroughly, checking even the contents of Jason's purse, and, after a quick explanatory gesture, even checking to be sure that there was nothing in Jason's scabbard other than his sword.

"Nice blade," the guard said, slipping Jason's saber back into its scabbard and handing it to Jason. "You can keep that; I'll need the beltknife."

Jason handed over his bowie. He wasn't worried that the Nehera markings on sword or bowie would expose him; smiths all over were trying to copy the dwarf smith's striations, even if they couldn't get quite the same strength and sharpness from their own inferior steel or quite the same edge from imported Home wootz.

"And now," the guard said, knocking a staccato tattoo against the oaken door, "they should be ready for you."

He wasn't sure what he had expected, but this wasn't it.

The room was about as he'd thought it would be: high ceiling above, plush crimson carpet below, the pile tickling his ankles. One wall was windowed, the glass—far clearer, less mottled than the best that Home and Holtun-Bieme could boast of—revealed a huge oak that stood in the courtyard between the buildings that made up the guildhall.

The other wall was covered with a faded tapestry. Or perhaps it wasn't really a tapestry; the endless scenes of buxom young women in iron collars and chains kneeling before muscular, whip-bearing men seemed to repeat in some sort of odd progression— it could have been some sort of complex print.

The two guards to either side of the large padded chair impressed Jason. Even the slightly smaller one was larger than Father; they were armored from greaves to helmet; each man held a short fighting spear easily, comfortably.

Jason wasn't surprised that Ahrmin would have a bodyguard— under these circumstances, it would otherwise have been too easy for Karl to send an assassin into Ahrmin's presence.

Between the two, sitting comfortably in the chair, was a small man in a dark slaver's robe.

He was repulsive, of course. What Jason could see of the side of his face that the slaver turned away was an awful brown mass; the right side of his cheek was gone, revealing gapped, yellowing teeth and burned gums. A claw of a right hand was almost con-cealed in the folds of his robes.

Jason had expected something more than a crippled little man in a chair. From all that he had heard about Ahrmin—from *him,* from Tennetty, from Valeran, from Mother—Jason had expected an aura, an atmosphere of evil to surround him.

There was nothing of the sort. "Taren ip Therranj?" Ahrmin asked, consulting a sheet of paper in his lap. "Swordsman, it says."

Jason nodded. "I am."

"Good. You're willing to take a risk for good pay?"

"Yes."

Ahrmin nodded, turning to the guard on his left. "Fenrius, I like the looks of this one."

"Your pardon, Master Ahrmin," the big man said, "but our manifest is only halfway full, and the day is no longer young. We need to hire a cook, and at least another—"

"Yes, yes, it's just that I used to be a swordsman, when I was younger. I like to talk to the type." He gestured to Jason. "Show me something."

"I fight two-swords-style. The guard outside took my second."

"Pretend. Please. And we do not have all day, as Fenrius quite properly pointed out."

Jason reached across his waist and drew his saber with his right hand, pretending to draw his bowie with his left.

He tried to repeat his battle with Kyreen, with a few minor improvements: Jason parried an imaginary lunge, but the fact that there was no blade to beat aside put him off. Still, he feigned a high-line attack with his saber, binding his imaginary opponent's blade and slipping in until they were chest to chest.

This time, he did it right: He blocked his opponent's imaginary dagger with his sword arm, switching grips on the imaginary bowie and bringing it almost straight up.

If there had been a real opponent, Jason would have opened his side from hip to ribcage.

Out of the corner of his eye, Jason saw Fenrius and the other guard change positions slightly. In his mock swordfight, Jason had edged a bit closer to Ahrmin, and the slaver's guards had moved to block any possible attack.

They couldn't suspect him, could they? No, he decided, not specifically; they were just being careful on general principles.

Jason raised his sword in a casual salute to Ahrmin. *You're a dead man. Not now, it seems, but soon.*

"Quite nice," Ahrmin said, nodding in response to Jason's salute. "Quite nice indeed. You move smoothly; I'll be interested to see how you do with a gun." He looked over at Fenrius. "Which ship should we put him on?"

The big man turned toward Jason, like a cannon being rotated on its wheels. "We will be taking two ships. Master Ahrmin will be on the *Flail;* most of the inexperienced gunners and instructors will be on the *Scourge.* Which would you prefer?"

Well, there clearly was one wrong answer. Jason shrugged. "It sounds like the *Scourge* would make more sense, for training purposes. But you haven't told me the important information."

"Which is?" Fenrius raised an eyebrow.

"Which one has the better food?"

Ahrmin laughed thinly. "My ship. But we'll put you on the other. You're a clever man, Taren, and I don't like having clever men too near me." He waved a dismissal. "We sail at sunrise tomorrow. That is all."

CHAPTER TWENTY-TWO:

Return to Pandathaway

Every once in a while, I wake up and realize where I am and what I'm doing, and then it occurs to me: Stash and Emma Slovotsky's baby boy is an asshole.

—Walter Slovotsky

Walter Slovotsky had wanted to stay in the Inn of Quiet Repose, but Ahira had overruled him: granted, they hadn't been in Pandathaway for years, but Tommallo might recognize them.

Still, they would have to make up their minds and make their arrangements soon; it was late afternoon, and the sun sat only about ten degrees above the horizon.

He stretched his arms as he sat on the passenger's side of the flatbed wagon, then continued the motion to grab the muslin sack of jerky behind the bench seat. After serving himself, he offered the bag around; everyone else declined, except for Tennetty.

"Still think it'd be worth a try."

It had been years and years since they'd first come through Pandathaway, but Walter could still remember the meal they'd had in the inn. Wonderful, wonderful food.

"We'll try another inn," the dwarf said, bouncing up and down on the back of his pony. "Nearer the docks. We'll want to sell our cargo, as long as we're here. But I don't want to take any chances on being made. Understood?"

Bren Adahan twitched his reins. "What's the difference? There's no price on your head."

"Not specifically," the dwarf admitted. "But the Slavers' Guild still has a reward out for Home warriors. I think we qualify, so we'll keep a low profile."

"Right," Tennetty said, sitting next to him, as she drove their flatbed wagon. She flicked the switch at the left drayhorse; the animal lowered its head and slogged on. "That's my vote."

Walter had to repress a chuckle at the way she kept a lock of hair in front of the right side of her face, concealing her glass eye; she looked sort of like Veronica Lake.

A wiry, scarred, completely unpretty Veronica Lake, who could as easily slit your throat as look at you.

Her level look at him said it all: *I don't like you much, either.*

"I didn't think it was a voting matter," Aeia said, with a sly smile. "Isn't this supposed to be a led party?"

"Shut up," Walter explained, returning her smile with interest.

Things had settled down to a relatively stable set of relationships. Whatever Aeia had said to Bren Adahan while Walter had been off in Holtun-Bieme was working: As long as Walter didn't rub Adahan's nose in what he and Aeia were doing, Adahan seemed resolved to ignore it.

Bren Adahan's brow wrinkled for a moment; his face brightened. "Let me make the arrangements for housing; I have an idea."

Ahira nodded, bouncing up and down on the back of his pony. "Sure. Meet us in Dolphin Plaza. It's down by the docks."

"If you can't meet us there, try at the steps of the Great Library," Walter put in. It wasn't impossible that that place had been torn down or something; best to allow for an alternative.

Adahan spurred his horse. Aeia, after a glance toward and a nod from the dwarf, went after him. Walter Slovotsky approved; she made a good brake on Adahan. Or anyone else, for that matter.

Tennetty chuckled ruefully. "Like a couple of puppies, them two." She eyed Walter speculatively. "She any good?"

"None of your business."

"Hey, Walter, ta havath." Tennetty shrugged. "I like them young, too."

"Boys or girls?" he asked, then immediately regretted it as her face clouded over. But he couldn't resist adding, "Careful, careful,

Tennetty—you're in disguise, remember. Slitting the throat of a robust fellow like myself might draw some attention."

"I won't always be in disguise."

"*Enough,* the two of you," the dwarf said, shaking his head. Then: "Damn you, ease up," as his gray gelding half-reared, spooked by a something small and furry that scampered across the filthy street.

"Fine," Tennetty whispered. "We'll settle up for this some other time. When I clear it with Karl."

"If."

"When."

Walter didn't understand Tennetty. As devoted as she was to Karl Cullinane, the notion of the big man riding into the jaws of a trap didn't bother her. It was as though Karl was a force of nature, not merely a very tough man.

The dwarf squinted at a broadside, pasted against the building ahead. "Does that—*shit.*"

Great Risk   Great Pay

Are You a Swordsman or Bowman with Great Skill and Greater Ambition?

AHRMIN, Master Slaver
is hiring WARRIORS
for an expedition past Faerie.
Apply immediately at the Slavers' Guildhall.
TRAINING in the ART of GUNNERY will be
provided.

*   *   *

A Cook, Armorer, Cobbler, and Smith are also needed.

Great Pay   Great Risk

Walter vaulted from the wagon and studied the paper for a long moment. Too fast, this was all happening too damn fast. There must have been some spies in Holtun-Bieme, spies ready to drop their cover and gallop away. Probably even some sort of pony-express-style relay; otherwise the news couldn't have gotten here so quickly.

A tall man, wearing the steel helmet and the center-ridged breastplate of Pandathaway's police force, walked up to where Walter and the dwarf stood.

"Interested?"

It took Walter a millisecond to slip into character: "Of course I am," he said, hitching at his swordbelt.

"You're too late," the guardsman said. "They left two days ago. Are you any good with that sword?"

Walter drew himself up straight. "Sir, I am Warrel of Horelt village. *The* Warrel of Horelt village."

The guard shrugged—"Never heard of you"—and walked away.

As soon as the soldier was out of sight, Ahira threw back his head and laughed. "*The* Warrel of Horelt village?" Ahira asked. "Really? Not *the* Warrel of Horelt village?"

Even Tennetty grinned. "And I thought you were just a useless piece of meat."

Walter Slovotsky shrugged. "Well, now that he's put me down, he's going to forget about me: I'm just some local champion who's come to Pandathaway to show off."

Tennetty nodded. "Clever. Very clever. What do we do now?"

This screwed things up profoundly. They could switch gears and go searching for Jason, but the Home searchers could handle that.

The important point was that any chance of delaying or sabotaging the slaver hunters was gone with Ahrmin and his hunters. Unless, of course, they gave chase.

Walter shrugged. "Guess we've got to find a fast ship that's heading for Melawei."

"Whether they know it yet or not," Tennetty said, eyeing the edge of a knife that Walter hadn't seen her draw, hadn't known she had.

The dwarf eyed the setting sun. "Well, we're not going to get out of here today. Let's go find the kids."

Aeia and Bren Adahan were waiting for them in Dolphin Square.

Walter sighed. Some things seemed to improve with age. Some things *were* improved with age. And some were just fucked with until all their charm was gone.

The Dolphin Fountain was one of the last.

Years before, the center of the fountain had consisted of a gorgeous pair of marble dolphins, spouting water into both the breeze and the fountain. The dark-veined white marble, carved simply and elegantly, had glistened in the sunlight; stray traces of mist had refreshed him as he'd watched the smiling statues that were more dolphins frozen in midleap than cold stone.

In the interim, some soulless criminal had gilded the statues; some unfeeling murderer of beauty had covered the innocent marble with gold leaf. It was probably the same boob of a sculptor with no fire in his veins who had carved miniatures of the dolphins into the edge of the fountain itself, in an awkward bas-relief that looked like a school of hopping minnows.

The fountain was a caricature of its former self. It was almost enough to make Walter cry.

"Have you ever seen anything like this?" Aeia asked, smiling up at him. "Isn't it gorgeous?"

"No, I haven't," Walter said, keeping his voice flat and level. "It's unique."

"I have arranged lodging for us," Bren Adahan said. "A suite of rooms in the Inn of Quiet Repose."

"I thought I told you no on that." Ahira shook his head. "Tommallo knows us."

Bren Adahan looked insufferably pleased with himself. "It's been years and years; Tommallo sold the inn long ago. I said I was the son of Vertum the hostler, and that I wanted the same suite of rooms that he rented, ten years ago; the owner shrugged to admit that there's nobody in the inn who was there ten years ago. So you get what you want, Walter Slovotsky," he said, turning to Walter. "You owe me one."

The Inn of Quiet Repose wasn't as Walter had remembered it, either. Maybe it was that the colors in the tapestries had faded over the years; perhaps the food wasn't prepared with the same care that fat, jolly Tommallo had lavished. The meals were filling, but the beef was overdone and stringy; the beetle-paste was cloyingly sweet; the chotte tasted like it had been marinated in stale lard instead of fried in fresh butter.

The rug in their rooms was worn through in spots, and the chipped marble beneath was cold on his feet.

Well, it cost less than it had last time. And at least the bathwater was hot.

Toweling himself off, Walter walked into the common room, where Ahira and Tennetty were stretched out on the floor, talking while they worked on Tennetty's slave outfit. The ragged tunic drew attention to her long, skinny legs, drawing it away from the collar and manacles with their solid-appearing lock that she actually could remove in less than a second. The hasp of the padlock at her neck was actually the handle of a small Nehera-made knife; the body of the lock was its sheath.

"Where're the kids?"

Ahira jerked his head toward the door. "I sent them out to have a look around—see what fast ships are docked, and where they're headed. We'll want something speedy, and planning a bit of a run— say, at least as far as Lundesport."

"If we're going to ijack-hay it, it'll have to be something fairly small, too. We can't ride herd on a whole lot of crew."

"True. Get some sleep—we've got a long day tomorrow."

When they made love that night, it finally hit him, and not just as an intellectual proposition: Someday it would be over between the two of them. Not that night, but someday soon. After Melawei—assuming that they could hire or hijack a ship and get to Melawei—it would have to end.

Aeia's and his relationship was unnatural. You just couldn't go on having sex without consequences, not with someone you cared about.

Something would have to change.

Idiot. Something always changes.

He was homesick, he decided. Even with Aeia lying here, warm in his arms, he missed Kirah. Ridiculous. She didn't have Aeia's intellect or complexity, but there was something . . . comfortable, reliable about the old girl. Old girl, hah . . . she'd kept her looks. But she did have some funny ideas about Walter; she saw him as some sort of knight in shining armor, a kind of miniature Karl Cullinane.

Ridiculous.

Even more, he missed Janie. Damn, but she was a good kid.

She reminded him of himself; they were two of a kind, Walter and his elder daughter: totally without restraint, without conscience, substituting prudence, when necessary. Janie understood her father; she'd probably understand this.

It would be a shame for Janie and D.A. to grow up without a father.

Have to be some changes made, he decided. Not that Walter

Slovotsky was going to be the faithful type, but it was time for some changes. Time to grow up a bit.

"Aeia . . ." He stroked a hand down her smooth flank, then brought it up to cup her breast.

"Shh," she said. "I know." In the dark he could see her smile glisten. "But don't count on the timing. I might leave you before you leave me."

"Very funny."

"Isn't it, though?" There was a distant hint of hysterical laughter in her voice.

"So why are we both crying?"

She didn't answer. She just held him, her face wet against his chest, while he held her, his face wet against her hair.

CHAPTER TWENTY-THREE:
"Not Twice . . ."

*Go sir, gallop, and don't forget that the world was made in
six days. You can ask me for anything you like, except time.*
                                    —Napoleon Bonaparte

The area around the Pandathaway docks was neither as crowded
nor as fast-moving as Walter Slovotsky remembered. The first time
they had entered the harbor, Avair Ganness and the rest of them
had been forced to wait while the elf running the guideboat found
them a place among the dozens and dozens of ships there. Silkies
at the waterline had nudged the *Ganness' Pride* into its berth, while
Ganness' pigtail twitched in irritation and worry; he'd babied that
boat of his.

The water had been clean, sparkling in the sunlight; the docks
had seemed more burnished than weathered by wind and water.

Now, the morning sun shone down a sludge pipe dumping a
slow trickle of raw sewage into the harbor, while foul green algae
lapped at the pilings. Over at the far dock, the single working
guideboat leisurely dragged a schooner into its berth, both boats
propelled by polemen in the guideboat, not enslaved silkies.

The dwarf nodded. "Put another one in the plus column."

"Right."

"Daven's raid, I think? Or was it Frandred's?" Aeia asked. "I
don't remember, for sure. I don't like either of them." She shivered
visibly.

"Daven, as I recall," Ahira said. "A strike that close to Pandathaway itself was too much for Frandred. He's not clever enough."

"Let's go," Tennetty whispered.

Slovotsky lightly tugged at the leash leading to the chain around Tennetty's neck.

"Harder, asshole," she hissed at him. "If you blow our cover, we're dead meat."

"Right. Just don't blame me later," he said. One of the seamen loading the boat—it looked like a junk, in both senses, Walter decided—glanced at them, then frowned, turned away, and turned back.

"Shit," Walter said. "Tennetty—sorry. *That will be enough talk from you, Ettlenna,*" he said, backhanding her across the face, leaving blood at the corner of her mouth.

Tennetty whimpered.

She did a good whimper.

A very good whimper.

Slovotsky would have commented on what a good whimper she did if he didn't remember that she did a *great* eviscerate.

"I've found three possibilities," Bren Adahan said. "Only three, and none of them heading as far as Ehvenor."

Slovotsky frowned. While it was clearly a slow time in the Pandathaway harbor, there had to be at least six ships sufficiently fast for their needs.

Bren Adahan caught his expression and shook his head. "You're not thinking it through, Walter Slovotsky. We need a single- or double-masted boat, or it'll take too much crew to run it. And it's got to be large enough for us and the horses to fit on." His face grew grim. "I am *not* selling Seabiscuit; the emperor gave her to me."

Ahira nodded. "Besides, we may need horses in Mela—*whoa.*"

"Melawhoa?"

"Take a look at that big one, over there. The square-rigged job. Look at who's running it."

Slovotsky looked. Sure, it was large, at least by local standards; except for a broad-beamed, three-masted ship on the far dock, it clearly was the biggest boat around. Supervised by a shaven-headed man who was clearly either the captain or somebody awfully senior aboard the ship, a gang of at least a dozen men were working a winch-and-crane setup, unloading a net filled with canvas sacks.

"Yeah. So?"

"Use your eyes, man."

"I am using my eyes. They're just not seeing anything."

What he saw was a square-rigged ship that clearly needed a crew of at least a dozen to sail: Unlike the way a lateen-rigged boat was sailed, it would be necessary to send seamen into the rigging to trim the sails. Granted, the design gave the ship a lot of useful deck space and allowed it to move a lot of cargo in the hold, but running it called for a large, well-trained crew operating under the guidance of someone who knew the Cirric and his ship, not a scared captain operating with a cocked pistol stuck in his ear.

"I still don't see anything useful," Walter said, shrugging.

Bren Adahan nodded. "I have to agree with Walter Slovotsky. This wasn't one of the ships I think we ought to consider."

"Aeia, Tennetty," the dwarf said. "Take a good look at the boat. See him?"

"No; and the boat doesn't look fam—oh." Aeia chuckled. "Him."

"Yup."

Tennetty snickered out of the corner of her mouth. "He shaved his head. And he's done a lot with the ship since we saw it last— switched the masts, added on the raised poopdeck. All in disguise, eh?"

"All in disguise. Follow me," the dwarf said, leading them toward the ship.

When the captain saw them, his dark face turned almost white; he staggered and clutched at the rail, only to miss and fall overboard, splashing into the filthy water below, sputtering out curses as he shinnied up one of the pilings to the pier.

Under the coating of black-green slime, the captain's face was pale.

Walter Slovotsky grinned down at Avair Ganness. He turned to the others. "I do believe we have ourselves a ride."

Avair Ganness toweled at himself vigorously, while a pair of deckhands working in tandem dumped bucket after bucket of water over his head. They were all gathered at the stern of the boat, just aft of the wheel. Over on the raised poopdeck, a rack of marlinspikes was partnered with a rack of bolts for the twin arrow-engines. The smooth wood was hot beneath his feet as

Walter Slovotsky slipped out of his boots. Somebody had once warned him about losing his footing on shipboard.

"Itches, it does, as well as stink. I can remember when you could drink harbor water; now, I don't like even having *Fortune's Son*'s hull in this water."

Ahira didn't let him dodge the question. "Moving quickly back to the subject, Captain Gan—"

Ganness hissed. "Crenneth. Voren Crenneth. Don't use the other name. I'm no more loved around here than you are. I have no wish to be a main feature in a Coliseum execution; they have gotten no prettier over the years."

Walter Slovotsky shrugged. "The real issue is how soon you can hoist anchor and set sail for Melawei. You know why."

"I know why; I have been hearing the news." The captain finished toweling himself off and stepped into a pair of blousy sailor's trousers, shivering in the wind.

"Try some of this," Slovotsky said, pulling a flask of Riccetti's Best from his bag and taking a healthy swig before passing it to Ganness.

The captain eyed the flask suspiciously.

Aeia frowned, snatched it away from him, drank some, and handed it back. "There. Now if you drink it, all three of us are poisoned. If it's poisoned, which it isn't."

"You weren't so forward with your elders when you were younger, girl." Ganness eyed her sourly, and drank, his eyes opening in possibly affected surprise. "Quite good." He was silent for moment. "You don't dare reveal who I am, any more than I'd try to expose you."

Things got suddenly quiet on the deck; without making a threatening motion, most of Ganness' eighteen-man crew had managed to work their way to the stern, perhaps answering a silent signal. The temperature on the deck suddenly seemed about twenty degrees colder.

Walter Slovotsky started to open his mouth, but Bren Adahan raised a hand.

"This one is mine," Adahan said. "I'll handle it."

Aeia raised an eyebrow; Tennetty looked at Walter and gave a half-nod, which he relayed to the dwarf.

Ahira spoke up. "Go ahead."

Adahan turned to face Ganness. "I understand your position,

Captain . . . Crenneth. The . . . one whose name we're not going to mention here has always spoken highly of you, and many times has told me that he felt bad that you lost two ships on account of him. But you understand our needs, and how very serious and resolved we must be on this matter."

Ganness eyed Tennetty, Ahira, and Slovotsky, who tried his best to look quietly threatening. Aeia's right hand didn't stray far from her bag, with its loaded pistol.

"I see," Ganness said.

"We don't ask for charity," Adahan went on. "We have a load of wootz to trade for passage. Also, you know there are places where a safe-conduct signed by Ahira or by Walter Slovotsky is of value. But, in return, we need your help. We need to get to Melawei."

"Not just that." Aeia shook her head. "We need to be snuck into Melawei—there'll probably be a slaver ship guarding the usual channels. Of course, perhaps you're not the seaman Karl used to say you were."

Ganness chuckled. "Yes, I have charted more of the coast of Melawei than most I know; if anyone can find a tricky route through the offshore islands, it's I. No, I am not enough of a fool to fall for cheap flattery."

"Captain, Captain," Aeia said, turning up the wattage on her smile, "it may be flattery, but it's not cheap. Or insincere."

Ganness looked like he was teetering on the edge; Slovotsky forced a laugh.

"No need to be so nervous, Captain; you're acting like . . ." He paused to snort derisively. "Like we don't have a plan."

"Ahh . . . right you are." Ganness smiled, and relaxed. "You'd hardly be without a plan. Well . . ."

"Well?"

"You have wootz, you say? I could do well in Sciforth with some good Home wootz. How much do you have?"

"Ahh, now that we know what we all are," Ahira murmured in English, "it's time to haggle over the price." He switched to Erendra. "Step over to our wagon, and let me show you our wares."

As the two of them walked away, Slovotsky turned to Bren Adahan. "Often? With all the blood on Karl's hands, I can't imagine him often getting bent out of shape over a boat or two."

"True enough." Adahan grinned. "I'm sure he is upset about it, though; it's just that he didn't mention it."

"Liar," Aeia said, grinning.

"Terrible, Bren, terrible. Telling such falsehoods."

Tennetty muttered a curse under her breath; Aeia turned to her.

"What is it?"

"Is there any way we can speed things up? I know you all have a great need to congratulate yourselves on how damn clever you all are, but I'm standing here on the pier with everything hanging out in this slave outfit, and I'm getting pretty tired of it."

Her hands were shaking; Slovotsky decided that she'd been expecting the confrontation with Ganness to turn into a fight, and her body hadn't yet caught up with the fact that there wasn't going to be one.

Adahan cocked his head to one side. "And this *plan* of yours? What is it?"

"I'll let you know when I think it up."

Over by the wagon, Avair Ganness had a sword balanced on his palms; he spoke a few words, then passed the weapon to Ahira.

"Well," Slovotsky said, "if we're up to swearing on swords, it looks like we got a deal; let's get loaded."

"Hmmm . . . let's get packed, instead," Aeia said, with a girlish giggle.

The water hissed quietly against the hull as they sailed under a dark but cloudless nighttime sky. Between the sky and the stars, faerie lights winked down, pulsing slowly, gently.

Above Slovotsky's head, a full set of sails snapped and crackled in the light breeze; the deck heeled over more sharply than he would have expected on such a large ship. *Fortune's Son* was making good time.

He was getting sleepy, though; best to go down to the cabin and sleep. But it would have been handy if Adahan had taken this opportunity to catch up with him—

"Alone, Walter Slovotsky?" Bren Adahan said, from behind him causing Walter to start. "Getting old, it seems. The legendary Walter Slovotsky couldn't be snuck up upon, as I recall."

"I was expecting you," Slovotsky said, smiling. "I've been through this before. Lots of times, going back to my school days."

"Oh?"

"Yeah. This is where you try to persuade me to leave Aeia alone."

Adahan nodded, his face a little sad. "And are we all so predictable to you, Walter Slovotsky?"

"Yeah. You remind me a bit of Karl."

"I thank you."

"Don't put on airs, man; I said 'a bit.' He once braced me over her mother. On Ganness' ship, as a matter of fact."

Adahan was similar to Karl, in a lot of ways. Which is why Slovotsky had taken certain precautions, like the loaded pistol at his hip, and the rope tied to the spar halfway up the mast. If necessary, Slovotsky could play Errol Flynn and swing away from the younger man, raising a cry as he did. Not exactly the way Captain Peter Blood would have done it, but it had that same kind of style.

"You're too damn arrogant, Walter Slovotsky. You assume, because I was raised on This Side, that I'm a simple barbarian without thought or care. Or language." Bren Adahan scratched at himself. "Aiea Bren woman. Walter leave Bren woman alone." Bren Adahan smiled sadly. "It's not like that, although it is simple: I want her badly, Walter Slovotsky, but I want her to be happy, even more. Think about it," he said, resting white knuckles on the rail. "Perhaps we're not so different, after all. —You'd best not hurt her, Walter Slovotsky. You'd best not hurt her."

You really care for her, don't you? Or you maybe really want everyone to believe that you do, when what you're really after is marrying an emperor's adopted daughter.

Quite possibly, both. Almost certainly both; if Adahan was simply an opportunist, Ellegon would probably have taken him out of the picture, one way or another. Besides, most people weren't simple.

He missed Kirah, he decided. She was simple. Not stupid, mind; just simple. The opposite of complex. There was something to be said for simplicity.

"I wouldn't hurt her," Slovotsky said. "Intentionally."

"You won't hurt her," Bren Adahan said. "Twice."

CHAPTER TWENTY-FOUR:

Ehvenor

I know a bank whereon the wild thyme blows,
Where oxlips and the nodding violet grows
Quite over-canopied with luscious woodbine,
With sweet musk-roses, and with eglantine:
There sleeps Titania some time of the night,
Lulled in these flowers with dances and light,
And there the snake throws her enameled skin,
Weed wide enough to wrap a fairy in.

—William Shakespeare

Under a dome of stars, mocked by the pulsing faerie lights, Karl Cullinane rode with his three companions down into Ehvenor, his sheathed sword bound across his saddle, his right hand never straying far from the butt of the short-barreled single-shot shotgun in his rifle boot.

Kethol, the broad-shouldered redheaded warrior riding at Karl's left, worked his pistol loose in its holster. It was just a nervous habit; the shoulder holster didn't need to be primed to release its cargo. "'Ware the crazies," he said quietly. "They're not after a reward, more'n likely. But they're dangerous, just the same."

"Tell me something I don't know," Pirojil said. He rubbed a blunt finger against his heavy brows. He was a remarkably ugly man, his flat nose splayed to one side from some long-ago fight.

Karl could understand why Pirojil hadn't bothered to have the nose taken care of. It wouldn't have helped.

Pirojil visibly winced every now and then. He'd taken an arrow in the thigh during the ambush outside of Tinkir that had killed Aren and Ferdom, and the scant portion of healing draughts that Kethol had doled out hadn't quite been enough to bring him back to health; a steady regimen of riding and walking hadn't allowed the wound enough time to heal. But Pirojil pushed on, bringing up the rear, he tugged at the ropes of their two packhorses, keeping the animals and the party's supplies close.

"Movement, off to the left," Durine said. A treetrunk of a man, he rode with his reins held daintily in his hamlike left fist, his massive right hand holding his shotgun easily, as though he didn't notice the weight.

"Just a rabbit," Pirojil said. "Ta havath, eh?"

The Cirric glistened in the starlight, small waves lapping the shore. As the company rode down toward Ehvenor, Karl could see only two large ships docked there, although a wide-bellied sloop seemed to be putting in.

Between the road and the water, Ehvenor stood, waiting.

Ehvenor. The sole outpost of Faerie in the Eren regions. Off in the distance, the faerie embassy, woven of light and mist, glimmered in the night, its brightness refusing to dispel the darkness surrounding it. It was almost cylindrical, almost three, four stories high. Almost, almost, almost—always almost; it was hard to look at; the building seemed to change before his eyes, to mold itself into another form ever so slightly different from what had been the moment before, but the change so slight and subtle that Karl couldn't put his finger on just what it was.

"Want me to go on ahead, sir?" Kethol asked. He was no Walter Slovotsky, but he did a good recon.

"No. Just keep alert." Best not to go separately; the Ehvenor crazies sometimes ran in packs. And who cared that a warrior could take down a dozen of the filthy creatures before they brought him down? The idea was to avoid the crazies, not to kill them. "And let's keep quiet."

Kethol nodded, transferred his reins from his right hand to his left so that he could draw his blackened saber, holding it easily in his hand.

The main road into the city led past a row of ramshackle houses, none of them issuing any light at all. Perfect cover for another ambush, for someone else after the guild reward on Karl's head.

Karl didn't like the looks of it; he nodded at Kethol, who led them down a side alley.

The alley twisted and turned through the dark, dung-laden streets, past the hovels of Ehvenor. Occasionally they could see dim faces peering out through windows or shutters, only to disappear instantly when Durine brought his shotgun into line, or at the whisk of Kethol's steel cleaving the cold night air.

The plan was to go down to the pier and make a rude camp until morning, when—they hoped—passage to Melawei could be procured. They carried with them twenty coins of good Pandathaway gold and ten fine Nehera-made swords, both the gold and steel distributed among the party; leaving it all on the packhorses could leave them in trouble if they were separated from the animals.

There were also a few surprises in the horse's pouches. This Side wasn't used to explosives yet, and the twenty or so pounds of guncotton on the rear horse might come in very handy.

Not that it would make much of a difference, not in the long run, Karl thought, wishing that he could take his amulet out of his saddlebags and put it on again.

But he couldn't. It had to be known that Karl Cullinane—

With no warning, a dim shape rushed out of the shadows and leaped on Kethol, dragging the warrior down from his saddle before he could begin to bring his sword into play. It clawed at the man, uttering a satisfied, low growl.

Instantly, Karl was off his own horse, his drawn saber in his hand. Firing a gun at whatever had jumped Kethol was out of the question; he'd be as likely to kill his own man as whatever it was.

Durine's animal reared, while the huge man looked desperately for a target for his shotgun.

Karl couldn't exactly make out the form of whatever it was that was clawing at Kethol, but he could find parts that he knew *weren't* his warrior; Karl stabbed into the dark mass, and felt his blade slice through flesh and cut into bone.

With a hideous, liquid scream, the form went into a spasm, arms and legs twitching and then falling still as the body went limp, the body voiding itself of its waste in the final reflex of all animals.

Karl kicked the stinking mass away from Kethol, and then immediately ducked to one side to make himself a bad target for the next attack.

But there wasn't any.

Pirojil spoke up. "I don't see anything."

"Me, neither," Durine put in. "Nothing."

Kethol got slowly to his feet; he looked okay, if a bit shaken.

"Light, Pirojil," Karl said.

As Pirojil pulled a glowsteel from his tunic, horribly bright blue light flared in the alleyway, sending a watching rat scurrying for cover. But there was nothing else there, nothing except the rag-clad, half-starved body of the man Karl had killed.

As he got painfully to his feet, Kethol used the toe of his boot to turn the crazy over, after stabbing the corpse a couple of times with his own sword, just to be on the safe side.

That's all it was, just a crazy. It happened in Ehvenor. Spending too much time around faerie was very bad for some humans, turning them violently, self-destructively insane. It didn't affect many—perhaps no more than one in five hundred, perhaps less—but that was enough.

Above, the faerie lights pulsed more brightly, echoing Karl's pulse.

Walk this way. Come to me.

Kethol muttered a startled cry. Durine brought up his shotgun. Pirojil spun his horse around.

Walk this way. Come to me. The voice was directionless, and quiet.

Karl started. "Who is it? Pirojil—douse the light."

Walk this way. Come to me. As Pirojil tucked his glowsteel away, the faerie lights hovered over the alley, pulsing even more intensely, the speed of the pulsations become an urgent staccato. Strangely, though, they didn't make the alley any brighter.

Walk this way. Come to me.

Karl retrieved his amulet from his saddlebag and slipped the thong over his head. It should provide some protection from whoever it was that was—

Walk this way. Come to me. The faerie lights descended to line up over the alley, a path in the air that wound toward the faerie embassy.

Embassy is such a silly word. "Finger" is better. Walk this way. Come to me.

"Are you for me or against me?" Not that he could trust an affirmative answer, but perhaps a negative one would make his decision easy.

No. Walk this way. Come to me.

He decided not to, and was turning to tell the others that they were moving out when the universe twisted.

When it untwisted again, they were all standing in front of the faerie embassy, squinting at the uncertain shapes.

"What do we do now, sir?" Kethol asked.

Durine's beefy face was sweat-sheened in the harsh white light; he raised a flipper of a hand to his forehead to wipe away beading sweat. "I don't want to go inside."

Distant memories returned to Karl, of himself ordering the others to follow him, and of them following the path of light to the embassy.

But the memories were flat, emotionless, unconvincing.

True. I warped things. I can do that in Faerie. I find it convenient.

"But this isn't Faerie."

That's a matter of opinion, in Ehvenor. My opinion differs, Karl Cullinane. In Ehvenor, in Faerie, my opinion is what matters. It's my opinion that you and I are—

The world twisted yet again, and he was alone in the glow. It wasn't exactly a room, he decided. More of a place.

—in the same place.

While it didn't look like it, it felt like nothing so much as the room where he'd last encountered Deighton. Or Arta Myrdhyn, or whatever name was really his.

"Both are, actually," a nearby voice said.

"Deighton?"

"Is *his* name. Oh, you think I'm him? Hardly." The voice took on color and tone. "He is human, of a sort."

"And you're not?"

"Good guess, Karl Cullinane."

"Who are you?"

"My name? Oh, anything will do." There was a distant chuckle that became distinctly feminine. "Titania might be best, all things considered. If you can do that. Or even if you can't."

"Queen of the faeries?"

"Quite."

He forced himself to speak calmly. "I take it you're not after the guild reward."

Another chuckle. "You take it correctly."

She appeared in a blink: an immensely ugly, remarkably fat woman, reclining on a tattered purple couch. She played with a gilt tassel on her shiny red silk vest with one hand, while another reached out to grab the greasy leg of mutton lying on the mist next to the couch. She took a hefty bite. "Or would you prefer another form? It's not important. I'll change the rule a little for you." The immense fat woman stretched broadly on her side. The leg of mutton disappeared.

He must have blinked, because he didn't see the change. And while the couch was the same, as she finished her stretch, she was different, and so beautiful that he had trouble swallowing; her high, firm breasts threatened to rupture the mist that barely contained them as it swept down her torso, leaving her long, lovely legs completely bare.

"Is this better, Karl Cullinane?" she asked in a warm contralto. She propped her chin on the palm of one hand and eyed him levelly. The face said that no worry had ever crossed her mind; it was smooth, the high cheekbones touched with pink. Alien eyes stared at him unblinkingly from beneath long lashes. Ruby lips parted for a momentary grin, revealing sparkling white teeth, and a tongue that momentarily peeked out, then hid.

"Do you like what you see?" She rose and stood in front of him, the mist clinging to her like something live, swirling about its tight confines.

She was beautiful, like a combination of all that was supposed to be lovely in a woman, but the effect was chilling. It wasn't real; it was only for display.

You've got a staple in your navel, lady.

A real woman's breasts moved and sagged with gravity; when standing, a real woman didn't float above the ground to point the toes of both feet in order to emphasize the curve of her legs. Flesh was soft and real, not a sterile illusion.

He closed his eyes as longing for Andy cut into him. *God, Lady, I miss you.*

"I'm sorry, Karl Cullinane," Titania said. "I don't mean to tease you. I just wanted to meet you and maybe send you on your way.

Think of it as an idle impulse." She laughed, her laughter distant silver bells. "I—we? they?—I have many idle impulses. Like this."

He opened his eyes again, and Andy-Andy stood in front of him, dressed only in a silken robe. She shook her head, sending her hair flying.

"Andy?" Karl Cullinane didn't question his fortune; he took a step toward her.

"No," she said, in Titania's voice. She shook her head and stood back, the features melting. "And it seems I've hurt you again. You humans are so . . . delicate, aren't you? Is this better?"

Again, he must have blinked; she had become some sort of compromise between Andy and the beautiful woman she had been moments before: Andy, but without the wear that the years had laid upon her; no bend in the nose, no laugh lines around the eyes, none of the scattered gray hairs.

Andy. He missed her so much. They had been together ever since the Hand tabernacle, and in that time he had never had another woman. It wasn't that there hadn't been opportunities, it wasn't that he hadn't been tempted, it was something very simple: She could chase away the darkness, if only for a while.

And this creature had the gall to mock her form. He let a distant coldness sweep over him. "That will be enough of that, faerie."

"It wasn't mockery. Maybe this would be best," Titania said, the voice now issuing from a dark patch in a mass of mist. "I do have something to show you."

"Why?"

"Because I'm bored, and you're entertaining. Be nice to me and I might even have an offer to make you."

The air in front of him shimmered, and then solidified into an aerial view of a shoreline. The viewpoint had to be at least a thousand feet up; Karl couldn't make out any of the individuals below, although he could see a dozen or so Mel outriggers on the sands below, and a two-masted ship of some sort bobbing in the waves offshore.

"Ahrmin," Titania said, "is there. Waiting for you. You've now distracted him sufficiently. Were your son wandering loose around Pandathaway, he would remain safe; the guild's attention is elsewhere."

And I get to be elsewhere. That was good, if true; things were going according to plan. "Why are you showing me this?"

"This was beginning to bore me; you didn't have a chance."

He kept his voice slow and steady. "You think this is all a game, Lady?"

"Don't be silly; threatening me is nothing better than absurd. Your sword can't cut mist.

"Besides, I didn't mean it that way. What I mean is that by the time you and your friends arrive, the slavers will have you. One ship is out at sea to cut off escape that way; the populace of village Eriksen has been driven away. Most of them.

"Karl Cullinane, if you wait for a ship heading toward Melawei, by the time you get there, the trap will have already been laid out. Ahrmin will simply take you, either dead or alive. I offer you two choices. Turn around here, and ride back. Or . . ."

"Or?"

"Or I will weave mist and light and air, make you a boat, and send that boat to Melawei. Just you and a few knapsacks, no more." She laughed again. "You will arrive stark naked."

"Why?" He didn't understand any of this. It was as though she was playing with him. But why?

"Amusement. Don't look for deep motivations, Karl Cullinane. You will find none in me. All I offer you is a little chance to escape alive, but more chance to save those you care for." The mist grew firmer. "Choose."

"Why?"

"Why do I help you? Beyond the fact that I'm bored and you're fun?" The mist swirled. "If you need a reason—your kind always needs these reasons, don't you?—then think that I'm doing it because the guild is of Pandathaway, and Pandathaway is human magic, while I am faerie magic. The two are not the same, nor particularly friendly."

That wasn't news. "But why help me?"

"Reasons, reasons, reasons. You want a reason? Because I owe it to Arta Myrdhyn for all the amusement he and you have provided me."

Anger rose. "I take no favors from Arta Myrdhyn. And I'm not going to abandon my men."

"As to your second point, they will think that you ordered them home. As to your first, it is not a favor from Arta Myrdhyn. It is the gamble of a powerful and weary creature to prolong a game she finds entertaining. Even if you, Karl Cullinane, are now beginning to bore me."

The world twisted, again, and all of the gear that Kethol, Pirojil, Durine, and he had brought was in front of him.

"Choose."

He pointed to his sword, to the bag of explosives, to the ...

"Enough. I see your method. Very well." Again, the world twisted.

Karl Cullinane found himself stark naked beside the Ehvenor dock, the pile of goods he would have selected in front of him.

Beside the dock ... he was on a five-meter-square platform woven of light, mist, and air. It was solid, but not persuasively so; it stretched and gave, threatening at any moment to give way beneath his feet.

Soundlessly, the raft pulled away from the pier, accelerating smoothly, evenly as it passed into the bay.

Even in the darkness, he could see three figures on the shore, spurring their horses toward the dock, calling to him. Kethol, Pirojil, and Durine.

He lifted his arm and waved a goodbye as the accelerating raft left the docks far behind.

"Better see to your gear, Karl Cullinane. You'll be in Melawei by morning. Farewell." The voice went convincingly silent.

"Fuck," he said. "What have I gotten myself into now?"

Mmmm ... perhaps it was just as well. Karl didn't need the others to draw Ahrmin away from chasing Jason. In fact, he had already drawn Ahrmin away.

Now it was time to make the distraction permanent.

There is a notion, he had said, many times, *called the last run. The idea is this: None of our lives are taken cheaply.*

He swallowed three times, hard. *None of our lives are taken cheaply.*

Hell, he even had an outside chance to survive. Whatever the slavers were looking for, it wasn't going to be Karl Cullinane arriving on a faerie raft. They'd probably be expecting him to arrive on dragonback. But if Ahrmin's spies knew that Ellegon couldn't leave the Middle Lands now—or if Ahrmin had helped to arrange events so that Ellegon was needed in Holtun-Bieme or to resupply Daven's team—the slavers would be expecting him by some overland route or, more likely, via ship.

But if they were following his path, via magic, they'd see that he was moving, even if they couldn't triangulate on his exact location.

His hand fell to his knapsack and brought out his amulet. He could even put it on and sneak up on them.

No. Not yet, he decided. It was important to keep the slavers chasing him, not giving up on a wild goose chase. He would put the amulet on when he reached Melawei, not before. If Ahrmin couldn't locate Karl, he'd assume that Karl had backed off, and might divert his men and his attention toward finding Jason.

He clutched the amulet tightly, then shrugged his shoulders and tucked it back in his pouch.

What next?

Better check the gear, he decided.

His sword and his Nehera-made bowie were both fine. He eyed the Damascus striations on the knife.

The knife had never been blooded. That was about to change.

His four pistols were laid out in a row next to his rifle and shotgun, his repair kit and powder horns beside them.

He stooped to check the contents of the next two knapsacks. Yes, the fifty cylinders of foot-long steel tubing, each containing a hefty charge of guncotton, were still intact, each bomb in a tightly sealed tube of pig intestine for waterproofing—like a steel sausage. They looked fine, as did the blasting caps in their separate bag.

A role of fusing and a firekit completed his sapper's bag.

It finally hit him: He was scared as all hell, but *he was looking forward to this.*

The young Karl Cullinane, the one who had vomited in horror after killing those men outside of Lundeyll, was gone. Slaughter had become second nature to him; he'd missed it since the war had ended.

His only regrets involved the people he was leaving behind. It had been too long.

And what does that make me?

He didn't care, he decided, as he stretched out on the too-soft surface of the raft and willed himself to sleep.

He was never sure how many hours later the raft beached itself on the Melawei shore; until the harsh grinding of sand underneath the craft woke him, he had been sleeping. Sleeping soundly, for the first time since he'd left Biemestren.

As it pushed itself ashore, the half-solid raft, woven by faerie out of mist, light, and air, suddenly became mist, light, and air; with a deep sigh it vanished underneath him, leaving him lying upon the wet sand, only half awake.

Even sleepy, warrior's reflexes took over. In an instant, he had scooped up his gear and dashed for the treeline, his ears straining for the sound of a cry or gunshot.

But there was nothing. Only the lapping of waves on the sand, the whisper of wind through the trees, and a distant mocking call of a crow.

Nothing.

He peered out onto the beach. It was empty.

There was no sign of habitation; he was between villages, or beyond the Mel range of settlement.

The first was more likely, he decided.

Dawn was still some time away; the sky was barely beginning to brighten in the east.

He couldn't tell where he was, but a bit of exploring would see to that. The first thing was to find a place to cache what gear he wouldn't need for a quiet stalk, and the second was to hide out for the day.

Night was the time to stalk.

He slipped the thong of his amulet over his head. For now, he would hole up in the woods, but he would have to find a more permanent place eventually.

Where to hide?

Of course! There was only one place, and he had been a fool for not thinking of it sooner.

"Now you see me, now you don't," he whispered, "but I'll see you."

He cursed himself silently for talking aloud. *Asshole.* It wasn't time for gestures; it was time to get to work.

He took a piece of hard cheese from his knapsack and wolfed it, then washed it down with a quick swallow of water from his canteen.

His smile was that of a stalking tiger.

CHAPTER TWENTY-FIVE:

"Ta Havath, Jason"

*But patience, cousin, and shuffle the cards, till our hand is a
stronger one.*

— Sir Walter Scott

Slaver rifle slung over one shoulder, Jason Cullinane walked along
the beach in the early-morning light, following Hervian, the leader
of the five-man squad. As far as he could see, the sand, beaten
down by last night's rain, was unmarked save for their own foot-
prints and the deep hoofprints of the two horses that had been
ridden out to relieve the distant watch at dawn.

"Just as well," Hervian said. "I don't see no sign of 'em. We'll
have a good hunt-down for later. Maybe get your wick dipped for
you, boy, if you can earn it," he said with a genial, gap-toothed
smile. "For a good bowman, you make a sorry gunner, Taren."

Pelius, a lanky, spade-bearded fellow, chuckled at that. "True,
true. I don't think you're going to enjoy much of those Mel girls.
Then again, if you need it, you could try the cook, although meat
that old is too tough and stringy for me."

The villagers had long since scattered; undoubtedly they were
back in the hills someplace, waiting until the slavers left.

Ahrmin had made no attempt to sneak up on Eriksen village;
he had merely sailed the ships along the coast, letting the Mel run
and hide. This wasn't a slaving raid, after all; the purpose was to
set up to capture or kill *him,* not procure hard-to-train Mel as

slaves. A confrontation might have necessitated using some of their hard-purchased magical defenses against Clan Eriksen's wizards— the only magical facilities the slavers had with them, as no guild wizard had been willing to risk going up against the possible combination of Karl Cullinane and Arta Myrdhyn's sword.

It was easiest to chase the Mel away, although Ahrmin and the first party had managed to seize a dozen or so; the men had been killed when they proved too intractable for immediate taming, the seven women had been impressed into service in a hut that was used as a bordello by the slavers, a treat to be withheld for poor performance of duty.

Jason had chosen to be a dreadful shot with the slaver rifle; while he couldn't do anything about the screams at night, at least he didn't have to participate.

He was more than vaguely sickened by his inaction. But what was he supposed to do? Take on more than a hundred men all by himself?

It wasn't fair. It was already too great a demand of an already overexacting universe that he kill Ahrmin to prove himself and save his father from getting killed; adding the additional require- ment that he rescue some Mel he didn't even know or kill off two companies of slavers was just ridiculous.

He wouldn't do it; he didn't feel obligated to try. Not really.

Several bowshots offshore, *Scourge* bobbed lazily in the waves. *Flail* was somewhere over the horizon, waiting to locate Karl Cullinane's ship if he came that way, or to prevent its escape if it managed to slip into Melawei—assuming he could find some- one foolish enough to grant him passage to Melawei. The scuttle- butt was that he'd try the overland route; if so, there was going to be at least another tenday until he stepped into Ahrmin's trap. Ahrmin had announced yesterday that Karl Cullinane was defi- nitely on his way toward here, and that everyone ought to keep alert for him.

Plenty of time, Jason thought.

All he needed was a chance. Just let him get close to Ahrmin with either a loaded gun or bow, and he'd finish that problem.

The chance hadn't come, yet. On the trip out, Jason and Doria had been on the *Scourge,* while Ahrmin had traveled ahead on the *Flail,* a faster, less-broad-beamed sloop, the same ship now lying off the coast to the west, waiting to drop off a horseman on shore to report that Karl had been spotted, or receive a signal from shore to reinforce the Pandathaway forces in Eriksen village.

I'll get him, Father, he thought.

The timing would have to be right. He'd have to find the opportunity sometime before his father arrived, and it would have to allow for an opportunity to get Doria out. Jason felt responsible for her, and was more than a little aware that she felt responsible for him. His woodsmanship was good; given a knife and bow, Jason could feed the both of them off the land on the trip overland.

"Deep thoughts, eh, lad?" Vikat said. The well-muscled blond fellow was only a year or so older than Jason, but, as a junior journeyman of the Slavers' Guild, he outranked all the rest in the squad, save only Hervian, the senior journeyman slaver. "Taren, Taren, whether you're going to join the guild or no, you're going to have to learn to concentrate on the task at hand."

Hervian chuckled again. "Fine one to talk, guild brother. I remember when you gelded that Salke for Lord Lund." He gave Jason a friendly nudge. "His hand was shaking so hard that instead of just cutting off the bugger's balls, he sliced all the way through—"

"Shut your festering gob, *guild brother,*" Vikat hissed. "Will you mock me in front of outsiders?"

Hervian gestured an obviously insincere apology, and fell silent, only to furrow his brow. "We haven't walked so far that we've neared the watch post, have we?"

Jason followed his gaze. The hoofmarks, instead of hugging the waterline, led up across forty meters or so of sand toward the treeline.

One of the mercenaries started to break into a trot.

"Carefully, now." Unslinging his rifle, Hervian stopped him with a gesture. "Slow and steady, now, we'll take it slow and steady. Check your loads, all."

The five men crept toward the treeline, Jason taking up a position a bit to the right and front, separating himself from others, just in case. They found the horses hitched, a short way into the woods. The two animals, stripped of saddle and all gear except for an improvised rope halter, were idly chewing on some ferns around the base of an old oak.

"Look, over there," Jason said.

Off in the distance, Jason thought he could make out a shape, but it wasn't *him*.

Hervian pushed past him. "No."

Faces pale, almost yellow in death, both slavers hung upside down by one heel from an overhanging branch, their arms outstretched toward the ground as though raised. Each man had been neatly slitted under the chin, unmarked save for that.

Flies buzzed around their wounds, and around the clotted blood marking the sands beneath them.

"Cut them down, Taren," Hervian said, his voice quavering. "Cut them down."

Jason swarmed up the tree, then steadied himself on a limb, drawing and reaching out his bowie, neatly slicing through first one rope, then another, the riflemen below easing the bodies to the ground.

Jason dropped lightly to the trail as Vikat snatched at a piece of parchment that had been tied to a nearby tree.

The young slaver's hands trembled as he read; wordless, he handed it to Hervian, who read it and handed it to Jason.

In steady Erendra script, the brown letters said, "I understand that you want to see me, Ahrmin. I wait for you."

It was unsigned.

Despite his rising gorge, Jason almost smiled. The dead slavers were all the signature that Father needed.

"Karl Cullinane," Hervian said. "He's here sooner than expected. Are you enough of a horseman to bring the news back to camp, Taren? For Master Ahrmin's eyes only, on my authority as a journeyman guildsman, understood?"

"Understood."

Doria was busy at work next to the big stewpot on the lee side of camp when Jason rode up.

In a strange sort of way, the hag illusion was starting to wear a bit thin. It wasn't that pieces of Doria were poking through, or anything like that. On the contrary, her illusion of Enna, the old, ragged, overweight cook, was too unchanging: Enna's wrinkled skin didn't redden or darken under the sun, her sparse, dirty gray hair neither grew longer nor lighter, the ragged sack she wore as a dress didn't become more ragged or fall apart.

He didn't like it. There wasn't time to talk to her, though; he had to report to Ahrmin.

"Cook!" he shouted out imperiously as he dismounted and tossed her the reins. "You will take care of the horse." As he passed the reins, their fingers touched momentarily; it was as though invisible sparks passed between them.

Her eyes didn't widen, but she nodded slightly, then shook her head. "Patience, boy, patience," she whispered. "There's nothing we can do to help him. Not yet."

"We can—"

"We can wait. If we were to leave food out for him, he'd be sure that it's poisoned. Just watch and wait, and make sure when you're on night guard that he can't sneak up on you without seeing you first, understood?"

She was right. Jason would have to find some opportunity to shoot Ahrmin before Karl was captured, but that opportunity was not now.

It would have to be watched for, waited for.

She raised her voice. "Since when is it my task to feed and water the horses? Prepare them for the stew-pot, perhaps, but—"

"Enough," he said, addressing both her and two guards in front of the long lodge that Ahrmin had appropriated for himself. "I have news for Master Ahrmin, for him and him alone," he said, stripping off his weapons and pouch, removing only the parchment note that had been found on the bodies. "I must see him now."

Ahrmin was seated on a high-backed chair in the dark of the lodge, his face cast into shadow. He seemed to like the darkness, rarely venturing out into daylight, sleeping most of the day, sometimes walking the sands at night, his two huge bodyguards never far from his side.

They were there now. It wasn't that Jason was distrusted, but Ahrmin was cautious as a matter of policy; he never saw anyone alone.

There were two other men in the room, both short-bearded, dark-haired: Chutfale and Chuzet. Brothers from Lundeyll, they were renowned as a tracker-hunter team. Chutfale was said to be able to follow anyone, anywhere; Chuzet was by far the best crossbowman that Jason had ever seen.

"So," Ahrmin said, his voice distant. "He is here. I'd thought as much."

He lifted his hand, examining a glass sphere filled with a slimy yellow liquid. In it a dismembered finger floated, aimlessly. "But he is again protected. From this. But not from you, not from me."

Hefting the now-useless sphere in the palm of his hand, Ahrmin turned to the brothers. "Find him. Bring him to me; alive if you can, dead if you must. Take what help you need. But find him." Ahrmin turned to Jason. "You may go."

CHAPTER TWENTY-SIX:
The Butcher

Ek som tyme it is craft to seme fle
Fro thyng whych in effect men hunte faste.
—Geoffrey Chaucer

Reach out the arms. Wait. Pull up the legs. Pause. Push slowly, slide. Rest.

This was one of the times when Karl Cullinane envied Walter Slovotsky. Karl tried hard, but creeping through the night silently didn't come naturally to him.

Reach out the arms. Wait. Pull up the legs. Pause. Push slowly, slide. Rest.

It didn't matter. It couldn't be permitted to matter. Acquired skill and unrelenting effort would have to serve him where natural inclination couldn't.

Flat on his belly, the cold sand sticking to his damp body from face to toes, he crept along the edge of the treeline, the woods at his right, the beach, and beyond it the Cirric, at his left.

Careful. Slow and careful does it.

This called for stealth, not strength.

Reach out the arms. Wait. Pull up the legs. Pause. Push slowly, slide. Rest.

Ahead in the dark, two nervous slavers stared off into the night, their backs to a campfire. Karl crept a bit closer.

From the safety of his cache and refuges, he had watched the beach throughout the day to see if the slavers had set up watchmen to watch the watchmen. That would be their next step, but they hadn't taken it yet.

They probably have as little respect for my skulking abilities as I do, he thought.

Unarmed save for his bowie, he moved closer, moving with exquisite slowness, arms moving glacially forward before he transferred his weight to his hands and then pulled up his legs to push himself across the sand slowly, tediously, deliberately. He froze in place, and repeated the process.

Reach out the arms. Wait. Pull up the legs. Pause. Push slowly, slide. Rest.

He had to make his game plan work. The slavers would assume, at first, that they could hunt him down during the day, and would keep their watchmen out during the night.

But after a few were found dead, with no clue as to Karl Cullinane's hiding place, they'd set watchmen to guard the watchmen. That would be their next step, along with setting booby traps. Probably some sort of tiger pit, punji sticks on the bottom. Perhaps some kind of deadfall.

He'd have to keep alert, to keep a watchful eye, in order to beat that.

And after that, when that failed—*if* that failed—the slavers would huddle together at night, pulling in all of their men into one camp, hoping to chase Karl down during the day.

That would be Karl's chance.

Reach out the arms. Wait. Pull up the legs. Pause. Push. Slowly slide. Rest.

Right now, the odds were just weighted too heavily against him. If he'd had a dozen men, he might have been able to launch a dozen simultaneous attacks, but he didn't. It was just him. Which meant that he would have to get the enemy all together one night, then attack with his stash of guncotton bombs, and blow them all to hell. Even a successful attack wouldn't kill all of them, but it might cut the odds against him down to a manageable level.

Possibly, with the slavers weakened, the Mel might even come down from the hills and counterattack, and even aid Karl in setting up an ambush for any arriving slaver reserves.

But that was for later.

For now:

Reach out the arms. Wait. Pull up the legs, pause. Push slowly, slide. Rest.

First he'd have to scare the slavers into collecting in one place, and then he'd have to take it from there.

Until they all gathered in the killing zone, he couldn't use any of his stash of guncotton bombs; it was vital not to get the slavers thinking about the dangers of huddling together; vital to get them worrying about the dangers of *not* huddling together.

Reach out the arms. Wait. Pull up the legs. Pause. Push slowly, slide. Rest.

He froze in place as a stray sound from the forest sent the two watchmen into sudden motion, the larger of the two men bringing his slaver rifle up while the other hefted his sword.

He didn't move for at least fifteen minutes, until the watchmen had sat down and relaxed, until their eyes had glazed over again.

And even then he slipped the index finger of his right hand to his left wrist and carefully counted a thousand pulsebeats before he resumed his slow progress.

Reach out the arms. Wait. Pull up the legs. Pause. Push slowly. Slide. Rest.

The trouble with his plan, of course, was that it probably wouldn't work. The odds were all too great that he'd be brought down on one of the nightly raids, or that the slavers would dig a trap that he wouldn't see in time.

Well, the plan was a long shot, but at least it held some chance. Besides, he did have an intelligence source that the slavers didn't know about.

He hoped.

Reach out the arms. Wait. Pull up the legs. Pause. Push slowly, slide. Rest.

After two hours of slow, diligent creeping, he was barely ten yards behind the nearest of the two slavers.

Two hours setting it up, and it took all of thirty seconds to finish.

He slid his arm back to draw his bowie—*slowly, Karl, slowly*—and like a cat setting itself up to spring, dug into the soft dirt with his bare toes, gaining purchase.

Karl Cullinane took a deep breath and launched himself at the farther of the two slavers, barely breaking stride in his headlong flight to send the nearer one sprawling with a well-aimed kick.

There was a horrid scream from behind him, while the slaver in front of him flung out an arm to block the downward descent of Karl's bowie.

Karl turned his lunge into a tackle, grappling with the man momentarily until he found an opening to set the tip of his bowie between two ribs. Karl shoved the knife, the warm fountain of sweet-smelling blood wetting his arm to the shoulder as he continued the motion to push the dying slaver away.

One down—

Karl Cullinane rolled to his feet and turned to face the other.

—No, two down; the other man was screaming in agony as he clawed at his smoking face; Karl's kick had sent him face-first into the fire.

The slaver dropped to his knees, pawing blindly for something as his cries alerted everyone for miles to Karl's location.

Karl's first inclination was to grab his bowie and get going, but he decided that he could spare another second to make this even more memorable for the slavers.

First things first: He kicked the slaver rifles away from the screaming man's outflung hands. Even a blind man could find a gun and shoot someone by accident.

But what was this man pawing around the ground for?

Of course. There was probably a bottle of healing draughts in the bag by the fire.

Karl swept up the bag and threw it deep into the forest.

"No." He kicked the slaver back into the fire, and the man's hysterical screams grew even louder, thoroughly piercing the night.

Ignoring the shrieks, Karl retrieved his bowie from the body of the dead slaver, and after slipping it into its scabbard and quickly thonging it into place, he dashed for the water, turning his headlong rush into a clean dive when the water rose to his knees.

The water cut the sound off as though a switch had been thrown, but still the burned man's screams followed him all the way throughout the long swim to his hiding place.

As Karl Cullinane pulled himself up, wet and exhausted, onto the flat stones of the cavern of the sword, he swore he could still smell the ghastly reek of burning flesh and hair, and the awful cries of the dying man.

He stripped off his clothes quickly, wrung them, then spread them on the cold stones before drying himself off with a Mel blanket and hanging that up.

The smell didn't leave him. There had been a time, long ago, when a younger Karl Cullinane, the same smell in his nostrils, had fallen to his hands and knees on a dusty road, vomiting until he thought he'd puke up a lung.

But that was long ago. Karl Cullinane spread dry blankets on the cold stone, stretched out, and closed his eyes, pillowing his damp head on an outflung arm.

He was unconscious in seconds.

The next night, he bagged only one; the night after, three.

Karl Cullinane slept very well each night, like a mountain lion who had gorged on a fresh kill.

CHAPTER TWENTY-SEVEN:
The Hunters

The dead don't die. They look on and help.
　　　　　　　　　　　—D. H. Lawrence

The cavern of the sword was empty, save for a naked, shivering Karl Cullinane and the shining sword.

The sword . . .

Clutched in fingers of light, the sword of Arta Myrdhyn hung in the air above a roughly hewn stone altar.

There was no sound, save for his own breathing, the wet slap of his footsteps on the cold stone, and the fast, even thrum-thrum-thrum of his own heart.

Karl Cullinane had never felt so alone.

The sword looked the same as it had years before, probably the same as it had for century after century: a two-handed broadsword with cord-wound hilt and thick brass quillons, its surface shimmering in the ghostly light, unblemished save for the spidery shapes that crept across the blade, forming letters and then vanishing.

Take me, the letters spelled out. *Give me to Jason.*

"Like hell," he said.

He crouched for a moment, huddling in the Mel blanket. Under the rough blanket, he was still wet and naked except for his amulet, shivering from the cold; the cavern, hidden inside a close-offshore island, was accessible only by the underwater passage.

Across the blade, spidery letters again played.

Take me, they said. *I wait for your son.*

"Not as far as I'm concerned," he said. This was what this was all about, at least according to Arta Myrdhyn: a sword that protected its bearer against even the strongest of magical spells; a sword made for killing wizards.

Arta Myrdhyn's way of preparing to strike at Wizards Grandmaster Lucius, his ancient enemy.

Not with my son, you don't.

Jason would find his own destiny; Karl's son would not become a pawn in Deighton's game.

Karl Cullinane forced a chuckle, the laugh sounding thin even in his own ears. Make a play for the sword, indeed. Hah. It wasn't the sword that had brought him to Melawei; it wasn't the sword that had brought him to the hidden offshore caverns. But he did have to see it again; he couldn't have come all this way without seeing that it still stood here.

No, what Karl Cullinane had come here for was in the outer room: his edge against the slavers.

Ahrmin had taken Eriksen village, chasing the Eriksens back into the hills. It was understandable: That was the area of Melawei where Karl had defeated him before; Ahrmin would want to avenge himself on the land and villagers, as well as Karl Cullinane.

But there was something else near that village.

You made a huge mistake, bastard, he thought as he walked into the outer room. *You picked the wrong spot to lie in wait for me.*

Glowing crystals were scattered across the walls and ceiling of the outer chamber; captured starlight played across the mottled far wall. Karl knew that if he'd had the genes to work magic, the dim markings on the wall would have resolved themselves into sharp-edged runes, the words of spells that could be impressed on the mind of a user of magic, to be saved, hoarded in the mind, spilled out as needed.

But he didn't; it was only a dirty wall to him. It wouldn't have been to Andy, but . . .

But she wasn't here.

She wasn't here. He'd likely never see her again. What would he give to hold her in his arms again? What *wouldn't* he give?

Easy, Karl. We've got work to do. He forced his mind back to the task at hand, and decided that it had been too long since he had last eaten, although he didn't feel hungry. Killing took away his appetite.

At least, it used to; it used to be that he felt sick to his stomach both before and after a kill. Lately, over the past few days, he had returned from his forays ravenous.

He wasn't hungry now, but, still, the body-as-machine had to be taken care of, if only for a short while longer. Karl Cullinane left the cavern of the sword and walked back through the roughly hewn tunnel to the outer chamber where he had left his gear.

His tunic, breechclout, and leggings were spread out on the cold stone, drying as well as they could. He squatted for a moment, feeling at his clothes. His? Well, close enough; the slavers he'd relieved of them wouldn't have any further use for them. They were all still wet from last night, as were half the stack of blanketlike towels that the Mel had left in the cave, for the convenience of their clan wizards.

He shrugged. He'd be in for worse than damp clothes before the night was over.

Ignoring the two big sacks containing guncotton sticks and the small one with the detonators, he dug into the fourth one for a hunk of dried beef, and bit off a piece while he examined the near wall.

What appeared to be a picture window looked down on the nighttime sea.

Waves roiled beneath flickering stars, while a distant darkness covered the horizon. To the west, south, and east, other offshore islands lay, some only tiny rocky outcroppings sporting a tree or two, some large ones only technically islands, just barely separated from the shoreline by passages too narrow for any craft save a Mel dugout canoe. A bird flitted across his field of view; it was gone before Karl could make out what kind it was.

Off in the distance, a slaver ship lay, floating freely at anchor. That would make a juicy target, but not for tonight. The slavers were starting to pull in their outlying posts, but the process wasn't finished.

There was an old Vietcong trick Karl planned to try tonight, which should speed things along, another turn of the screw: He'd cut off tonight's victims' genitals, and leave them stuck in the corpses' mouths. He'd thought about doing so for days, and had decided to wait on it. Mutilating bodies didn't bother him, not at all. He had put off doing it to give himself something else to add to the pressure on the slavers.

He turned back to the window. It wasn't really a picture window, of course; the cavern was at sea level, but the view looked down from a height. The Eye, the sphere, which transferred the image to the glass, was on the island's heights, waiting.

For this.

Karl ran his fingers over the glass; in dizzying counterpoint, the view spun until the beach filled the window. Karl would have given a lot to be able to move the Eye out and over the forest to do a more complete remote recon—village Eriksen was hidden by the trees—but even without that, it was a powerful tool.

Besides, he liked it; the Eye and window suited him.

It was magic-as-technology—do *this* with *this,* and *this* happens, see? There was something far more satisfying about a device that he could see work, emotionally preferable to even something as useful, as important, as the amulet that protected him from being located.

He moved his fingers again, then examined the glass closely until he could see a distant fire that was at least a mile down the beach. It was the spot where, just a few nights before, he had killed the two watchmen, leaving one burning.

Right now, all it was was a vague glow, so he lightly touched his index finger to the flicker, and pressed down while the flicker grew, zooming in, the watchfire growing on the screen until he could see the two slavers sitting in front of it, one tending a head-sized piece of meat on a spit, the other scanning the water and forest. The view was flat, as though he was looking through a telephoto lens.

That didn't bother him. The trouble was that it looked far too easy. By now, the slavers would be trying to trap him; there would be a backup.

"So, let's find the backup."

It took him five hard minutes of scanning to find it: another pair of slavers, hidden in a blind built into a nearby tree, visible only momentarily when the more skittish one would shift position.

He still didn't like it, though. Ahrmin was clever; there was probably a second backup, at least, but a half hour of intense scrutiny, making minuscule motions to barely move the Eye, didn't reveal it.

Karl Cullinane sighed. He probably wasn't going to be able to hit that target. Not tonight. There had to be backups, or booby traps on the approaches to such a tempting target; until he could figure out exactly what the slavers were up to, he'd have to give this target a pass. The next step *had* to be to persuade the slavers to pull their men in close, defensively. Pull all the outlying guards into one camp, and huddle together there.

So that Karl Cullinane could blow them to bits with guncotton bombs. He smiled. Just a little more, he thought. Just a few more deaths, and the slavers would gather together for him. And then, boom. Cut them down to size, then cut them to pieces.

Back to work.

Maybe he could spot the traps here. It would be nice to take apart a three-level trap; that would mean killing at least five slavers. Not a bad night's work at all. If he could do it.

He spun the view and looked westward down the beach, scanning slowly until a motion caught his eye. He zoomed in, yet again, and spotted three dark figures moving single-file along the treeline.

Not a bad job of skulking, he decided. The slavers wouldn't be visible except from the sea, and except for their own ship, there were no ships in evidence—even a keen observer wouldn't have been able to spot them from the island, not without the Eye.

Too bad—for them—that the slavers didn't know about the Eye.

Wait. He shook his head.

That hadn't looked right. There was something about the walk of one of them.

He zoomed in closer, but they were gone; they had probably ducked back into the trees. He scanned the Eye farther down the beach, and saw two others, trailing the first three by about a hundred meters. The hunting team's backup, probably, looking for traces of him, wisely figuring that Karl wasn't going to be skulking inside the forest itself at night, for the same reason that the slavers weren't: Only a few dozen meters inside the forest, the overgrowth of leaves blocked out all light.

But . . . that didn't make sense. Maybe they would put out one man as a Judas goat—Ahrmin seemed to have little concern for his men; likely most were hired mercenaries and not guild slavers— but not three, not with two following. To justify using three men as bait, there would have to be a much larger party waiting to spring the trap.

Granted, the two following looked to be fairly tough: two large men, one half crouching as he followed their trail, the other holding two loaded crossbows.

But still. It didn't make sense at all. Unless . . .

Karl spun the view again, leaving the two hunters while he searched for their quarry.

He found them. Three figures, hiding in darkness. Not hiding well enough.

The three came to a spot where a wide trail led away into the trees. The right move would have been to go into the forest, and cross the trail under cover.

Even Karl knew that; Walter Slovotsky had taught him.

You didn't cross open spaces, not if you didn't have to.

They crossed the open space.

"No!" His heart pounded in his chest as he zoomed in tight on their faces, his fingers automatically making the minor corrections to keep them in view.

It was Aeia, Tennetty, and Bren Adahan. What were they doing here?

Getting themselves killed, in just a few minutes, if Karl didn't do something.

Wait a minute, he thought, and then smiled. If they were here, that meant that Jason had been found; they'd still be looking for the boy, otherwise. This had to mean that they'd found the boy; they were here to pull Karl's head out of the noose.

He knew how Atlas felt after his shrug.

Change of plans, Ahrmin, Karl thought. "I, Karl Cullinane, hereby cancel my last run, and promise to get my butt out of here in one piece, if at all possible."

He would take another try at Ahrmin, and soon, but with better odds than were offered here and now.

Now, to rescue his rescuers. . . .

He ran to his gear and pulled out his bowie, then went into one of the leather sacks and produced a dozen guncotton sticks, each carefully sealed for water-tightness. He dug into the small bag for sealed packets of detonators, igniters, and fuses, putting all of the retrieved explosives and equipment in a canvas rucksack. His guns, powder, and sword were cached in the woods with his boots; he hadn't wanted to expose his guns to the water, and, once having tried swimming with a sword, had no intention of swimming with it and other gear.

His clothes were still wet, but dark clothes would provide more cover in the night than his bare skin. On top of the explosive, he set a brass flask of healing draughts. Just in case.

No. He shook his head. He couldn't afford to take the bombs, because he couldn't afford to use the bombs. If he did use explosives on the hunters, it would only call attention to this area—and while the offshore island probably could stand a casual search, it probably couldn't take a more thorough one. There was a crack in the outer chamber that let in air and, during the day, a bit of light. A thorough search might involve someone putting his eye to the crack, and seeing the crystals inside.

Worse, any use of the bombs might suggest to Ahrmin what Karl's game plan was; the slavers would spread out to several smaller camps, and wait Karl out.

But what if he needed the bombs?

Shit. If I need the bombs, I'm dead anyway. He set the canvas sack down. Best not to take it.

There was something wrong. It felt suddenly colder in the chamber. But only physically; inside, he was warmed.

For a moment, he wasn't alone anymore.

He closed his eyes, and they were there. Maybe. He was never sure if it was real or just his subconscious sounding an alarm in a way it knew would get his attention, but it was as though the three of them were there, with him: Fialt, Rahff, and Chak.

He opened his eyes, and they were gone; but when he closed them again, he could almost see them; their presence was almost palpable.

Saturnine, slow-speaking Fialt, who didn't want to be a warrior, but had died on an Ehvenor dock, distracting assassins for a priceless second. Karl knew the price of that second; it had been Fialt's life.

As Karl squeezed his eyes tightly shut, he could almost see Fialt shaking his head no.

Young Rahff, his face a mirror to his soul, never able to resist asking why—like his brother Thomen, but even more so. He'd died here, in Melawei, protecting Aeia, here on the goddam Melawei sands, his belly sliced open, gutted like a trout.

Karl could almost feel Rahff looking up at him, a puzzled frown on his young face that would never grow old.

And short Chak, an easy grin always on his dark face. Chak, who had spent too much of his life protecting Karl's back, making sure it didn't start sprouting knives. Chak had died outside of Kiar, blown to pieces in an explosion of slaver powder, protecting the myth of the invincibility of Home forces.

It was as though Chak was there, cocking his head to one side.

Leaving the bombs behind doesn't make sense, kemo sabe, he seemed to say. *Since when do we count on getting out of anything alive?* There was a distant chuckle. *If you need them, you need them. Take any weapon you can carry.*

Karl Cullinane opened his eyes.

There was nobody there. But there was.

Take the bombs, Karl.

Karl squeezed his eyes shut once more, and then nodded as he opened them to stoop for two of the packets, packed them in a small leather pouch, then tied that tightly to his left shoulder. It was less than a tenth of his stock, but that would surely be enough for now; with any kind of luck at all he wouldn't even need it.

He patted his bowie for a moment, then shook his head. He was going to have to make a run from the sea, and take out the two of them before they could react. It was a chancy gambit, at best. Better to have more than fourteen inches of steel to use.

He dashed back to the cavern of the sword.

It still hung in the air, the spidery letters playing across the surface. *Take me,* they said.

He fastened his fingers around the grip. It was blood-warm, alive.

"No promises, Deighton," he said. "No deals. But I'd like to borrow this, for a while. With no obligation." He tightened his fingers around the hilt and pulled.

The sword didn't give.

Take me for your son, the letters said.

"No." He pulled once more, hard. But the sword was anchored tightly in the air.

"Fuck you, asshole," Karl Cullinane said.

He dropped his hand from the hilt and ran from the cavern of the sword of Arta Myrdhyn and into the outer chamber. He paused a moment before the pool leading to the underwater tunnel that was the only exit from the caverns. Karl Cullinane didn't believe in ghosts. It must have been just his subconscious acting up, trying to prevent him from making a mistake.

Still, it wouldn't hurt. He hefted the canvas bag.

"Fialt, Rahff . . ." He choked for a moment, "Chak. My friends. Thank you. For everything." He raised his bowie in a quick salute, then slipped it back into its sheath, thonged it into place, took a deep breath, and dove.

He broke surface on the seaward side, quickly crossed the rocks, and resubmerged on the landward side of the island to keep the island between him and the offshore slaver ship.

Good. If only he could keep the island between him and any possible observers, he might be able to take out the hunters without drawing any undue attention.

Tennetty's group was more than a hundred yards to his left as he crept up on the shoreline; the two slavers were too intent on them to notice Karl Cullinane silently rise from the water and bear down on them. The only sound he made was the whisking of his bare feet on the sand, and that was covered by the lapping of waves on the shore.

The slavers crept on silently, the leader in his curious half-crouch, the bowman lagging behind.

Unstrapping the package and setting his packet of explosives gently on the sand, Karl Cullinane drew his bowie and closed in on them.

Perhaps he was breathing too loudly, perhaps an unconscious growl forced itself from between his lips, perhaps his heart was beating too hard; he was never quite sure why, but when he was only about six feet behind the bowman, the slaver gave a gasp and turned, bringing his bow up.

Karl Cullinane took a broken-field half-step to one side and launched himself toward the bowman, just as the bowman fired.

The bolt burned against the left side of Karl's ribcage; he knocked the weapon aside, the slaver losing the other bow as the two of them rolled around on the sand.

The slaver clawed for Karl's eyes with one hand; he tried to block the downward thrust of Karl's knife with the other, fingers straining to grip Karl's wrist.

Fingers snapped as Karl Cullinane stabbed downward, once, twice, three times into the slaver's chest, then jerked his knife from the enemy and rolled free, coming to his feet to rush at the other.

The other man stood silently wide-eyed, his mouth working as though he was trying to say something. But only a harsh moan and a trickle of dark blood escaped his lips as his spastic hands pulled at the knife that projected from his throat.

Knife? The slaver fell to his knees.

Another knife *thunked* home, this time into the slaver's chest.

"Tennetty, Aeia, Bren, freeze," Walter Slovotsky hissed from behind Karl. "It seems that we found him."

Karl turned to see three people: Slovotsky, Ahira, and someone he didn't re—no, by God! it was Avair Ganness!—emerging from the trees.

"O ye of little faith," Slovotsky said, his smile unforced. "You think I'd send them out without giving them an escort?"

As Karl stripped off his bloody tunic and examined the six-inch-long shallow gash on his side, Ahira hauled the bodies past the treeline, the others gathered around him.

"Bad?" Ahira asked, dropping to his knees, scrubbing at his arms with handfuls of sand.

"I'll live." It hurt like hell, but it wasn't deep. Certainly not bad enough to waste any of his precious supply of healing draughts; he let Tennetty apply a bandage and tie it in place, then he took a brief moment to exchange hugs with Aeia and Ahira and hand-clasps with Bren, Tennetty, and Ganness before turning to Slovotsky.

"Is he back in Biemestren or with you?" Karl asked.

"Who?" Slovotsky's brow furrowed. "Oh, Jason. Well, I hope he's back in Holtun-Bieme, or Home. —Now, let's get the hell out of here. We've got Ganness' ship hidden in a cove about—"

"You *hope*?"

It was instantly clear.

Slovotsky had gone independent on him.

Again.

Once more.

As goddam usual.

Blindly, Karl swung a fist at Slovotsky's face, but the smaller man wasn't there when the blow should have arrived; Slovotsky ducked to one side, raising both palms.

"Easy, Karl. Just take it easy," Walter Slovotsky said.

"You were supposed to go after *him*," Karl said. "I can take care of myself."

Stepping between the two of them, Ahira shook his head. "Save it, Karl. Now, is this gear what I think it is?"

"Don't change the subject. You deserted my boy."

"Karl," Ahira said, "Jason's not the one who's really in danger. You are."

"That's your opinion."

"Karl." Ahira took a deep breath. "We don't have time for this. You'd better get your temper under control right now; we can argue later. We all decided that you would probably need our help more than he would. Walter's right; let's get out of here. I don't like the odds. We've bought Jason as much time as we're going to, by now. He's probably hooked up with some Home warr—"

"No." Karl shook his head. "You get going; I'm going to finish this."

He wasn't done here; the disappointment was like a physical blow. From the moment he'd seen Tennetty, Aeia, and Bren skulking along the beach, Karl had been sure that he was finished here, that he could leave Melawei and Ahrmin behind, and go back to Andrea.

Back to Andy. . . .

But not now.

To his left, Tennetty stood motionless, her arms folded across her chest. "You're not going to finish this alone. Not alone."

"Father," Aeia said formally, "I won't leave you, either." She took his hand. "I won't."

Bren Adahan reached out for her arm, "Compromise. We'll compromise."

"Compromise," Ahira said judiciously. "Makes sense."

Tennetty frowned. "I don't like it. Let's make sure we finish the bastard here."

Slovotsky snickered. "With these odds? Are you tired of living? I don't mind a hit and run, but let's not just put our heads on the block."

"I think we ought to leave," Ganness said. "I don't even know why I'm here."

Karl raised an eyebrow as he looked at Walter. Come to think of it, why *was* Ganness here?

Ahira snorted. "We wanted to make sure that the ship was still there when we got back. So, since nobody else aboard knows these waters enough to guide it out safely, we, er . . ."

"We took the keys," Slovotsky finished. "But how about it, Karl? A nice compromise, instead of a goddam *Götterdämmerung?*" Slovotsky cocked his head to one side. "An old time hit-and-run?" He gestured at Karl's packet of explosives. "We have enough there to put a hole in their ship while we make a run for it."

"We've got better than that." Karl smiled and nodded, which wasn't a good idea; he realized that he must have lost more blood than he'd thought. His head spun as he clapped his hand to the gash in his left side; he leaned against Tennetty to steady himself. "A lot more than this. We use it all, then we run. Okay?"

Slovotsky nodded. "Deal."

Karl turned to the dwarf. "You or me?"

Ahira didn't have to think about it. "You know the lay of the land better than I do. Take it."

"Fine." It all clicked into place. The trouble had not been that there were too many slavers, just that there had been too few of Karl.

Now, that had changed. Even if they couldn't wipe out all the slavers, they could do a lot of damage, and then get the hell out.

"Aeia, Bren, Walter, and Ganness—I want you to swim out to the cave and get the rest of the explosives. Bren and Aeia, you swim over to the slaver ship, set the charges, and get ready to blow it— and be sure to—"

Aeia held up a hand. "Yes, Karl. Make sure to swim away fast after we strike the igniters. And I won't," she added with an impish smile, "forget not to breathe underwater."

"Right. Walter and Ganness, you bring back what they don't need."

"I like it." Tennetty smiled. "An old-fashioned Karl Cullinane-style ambush?"

Slovotsky smiled too. "Just like Mother used to bake."

Karl nodded. Just like in the old raiding days. Dammit, those days had been too long gone; it was good to remember them properly. "Right. We'll set up a bomb attack from the far side of the camp, drive them down the path toward the sea, blow the hell out of them on the path, and then run like hell." He turned to the dwarf. "I'll want you and Walter to take the far side—"

"We throw out the first ball?" Slovotsky asked.

"Right. Then use the rest of your bombs to take out as many as you can—but you'd better make fast tracks back to the ship, because your bomb will be the signal for Aeia and Bren to light their detonators, and that'll start all the rest of the fun."

It would also stir up the slavers in the outlying watchposts, but that couldn't be helped; they'd have to get to Ganness' ship and get out before the slavers caught up with them.

The dwarf nodded. "Makes sense to me."

"Tennetty?"

"I know." She nodded as she hefted her rifle. "Ahrmin. If I can get him in my sights. Then I get back to the ship. I'm not as fast in the dark as Slovotsky is; I'd better get going."

"No." Karl wanted Ahrmin dead, but Tennetty didn't have the dwarf's darksight, and she didn't have Slovotsky's recon skills—and, besides, he needed her here. "I need someone to watch my back. Ganness isn't going to be enough."

She opened her mouth to protest, then stopped herself and gave a grim smile. "Yes, Karl."

It was amazing: He felt young again; a weight that he hadn't realized he'd been carrying was dropping from his shoulders. "Let's get to it, people. Walter, the entrance to the cavern—"

"—is exactly where it was the last time you told me about the cavern." Slovotsky was stripping off his boots and shrugging out of his clothes as he spoke; he was stark naked in seconds. "Aeia, Bren, Ganness—let's go. We'd better get this show on the road before that patrol's officially missing."

Walter's group headed into the water; the four silently swam away toward the island.

Karl turned to the dwarf. "Looks like it's just the three of us for a moment. Ten, you keep your eyes on the trail. Ahira, you want to keep watch to the east, or to the west?"

Ahira shrugged. "Dealer's choice." He clasped Karl's hand, hard, with one hand, while he hefted his axe with the other. "It *has* been too long."

It felt like hours, but it couldn't have been much more than half an hour later when Slovotsky and Ganness returned, pushing the floating sacks.

With Ahira and Tennetty watching for possible slaver patrols, Karl waded thigh-deep into the water and helped Ganness and Slovotsky drag the explosives up on the beach and back up to the treeline, then helped Walter and Ahira assemble a dozen sticks, detonators, and igniters into a dozen bombs.

The big man and the dwarf disappeared into the night.

Tennetty sighed.

"Save it for later," Karl said. "And keep an eye open." He turned to the captain. "As far as assembling the bombs goes, it's you and me, Captain Ganness," Karl said.

"Captain Crenn—" Ganness caught himself, and gave an almost Gallic shrug. "Ahh . . . it makes no difference, I suppose."

Karl looked over the path. He mainly had to go by a memory of what it looked like in the daytime, but there was a little dogleg about thirty yards in; that would be a fine place for the ambush, when the slavers were sent charging down the path.

But first things first.

"Ganness, were you watching when I assembled the bombs for Walter and Ahira?"

"I could do it," Tennetty put in.

"Shut up. Just keep your eyes open. Ganness?"

Ganness spat. "No. I've been too busy trembling to watch, if you must know."

"Do what I do. It's not difficult." He beckoned to Ganness. "First, you take a stick of explosive, carefully—easy, easy; this stuff would just as soon blow up on you as not—and stick one of these metal things in the end. That's a detonator. Then this thing that looks like a match—I mean, then this other thing. You stick that in the other end."

The mixture on the end of the fuse was mainly gunpowder; the detonators were fulminate of mercury; the explosive itself was guncotton, nitrocellulose. Karl had first used these bombs against slaver cannons, but he had avoided making more since the end of the Holtun-Bieme war. Until Ranella's new wash had gotten rid of impurities in the guncotton—if indeed it had—the stuff had been too unstable to leave around for long.

The British had fooled around with guncotton too early; deadly explosions had forced them back to black powder for years and years. Better to have to make the transition only once.

Ganness spat on his palms, rubbed them nervously together, and knelt next to Karl. He reached out his hands, then drew them back. "*No.*" The captain rose, shaking his head. "No. A man has to say no sometime. I won't do it, I *won't* do it. This kind of magic frightens me, Karl Cullinane, and I won't have any part in it." Ganness folded his arms over his chest.

"You're not thinking of abandoning us, are you?" Karl said in a low, cold voice, forcing a grim smile to his face. It was intended to chill the blood.

It worked. Even in the starlight, Ganness visibly paled. "No, no," the captain protested. "But I don't want to touch that. That's all."

Karl shrugged. "Then you keep watch to the west. While I finish."

While Ganness kept watch, Karl assembled the bombs. He was only halfway done when Tennetty spoke up.

"Karl, I heard—"

Something whizzed by Karl's ear.

Tennetty's word turned into a harsh scream as she looked down at the crossbow bolt projecting from her belly; drooling blood, she fell writhing to the sands.

A harsh voice whispered, "Ta havath, Karl Cullinane. If you move, you die."

Two large men stepped out of the darkness. Each carried a slung rifle and an unslung crossbow, the nearer reloading his with a fresh bolt.

Avair Ganness turned toward Karl, his face even paler than before. "I was looking, Karl Cullinane, but—"

"Silence," one of the men hissed. "Karl Cullinane, step away from there, and set that device on the sands, then stand back. Or you may fight us and die here and now. It doesn't matter." He spared his companion a brief grin. "We've *gotten* him, Chuzet."

"Just be careful. Do what he says now, Karl Cullinane. Or die now." The slaver gave a half-shrug. It didn't matter to him.

"Let me get some healing draughts into her, first," Karl said. "The bottle is in the bag over there."

Tennetty was almost motionless, her eyes staring glassily up at him. But even in the starlight he could see the pulse beat in her neck.

"No. I'll put her out of her misery, if you like. But put the device down now, or die now."

Play for time, he thought. There wasn't anything else to do; these two looked like they knew what they were doing.

Karl took three slow steps away from the explosive and then crouched to set the bomb gingerly down on the sand in front of him.

"Now, Chutfale? May I?"

"Now. Stand up and move away from there, Karl Cullinane."

Chuzet pulled a horn from his pouch, brought it to his lips, and blew. The horn shrilled a pure note into the night.

The clear, pure sound chilled Karl Cullinane quite thoroughly.

CHAPTER TWENTY-EIGHT:
The Cutting Edge

I begin to regard the death and mangling of a couple of thousand men as a small affair, a kind of morning dash—and it may be well that we become so hardened.
—William Tecumseh Sherman

The blast of the horn shattered Jason's light sleep.

He hadn't wanted to sleep, but there wasn't anything else to do until some opportunity to do something constructive presented itself.

Hervian's squad was billeted with the rest of the company in one of the larger Mel feasting lodges; even so, it was cramped. The arch-framed building was really meant to serve as a place for an extended family of perhaps fifty to cook, eat, and drink in close quarters; there was barely enough room for the hundred-plus sleeping places. If a quarter of the company wasn't always on duty, it would have been like being back on shipboard, but at least they hadn't gone to some sort of hot-bed system here.

It also stank. Of shit, piss, sweat, and fear.

His campaign of terror was having an effect; the mercenaries huddled together like a bunch of sheep on a cold night.

The horn sounded again, as Jason sat upright with a start, the almost motionless snoring bodies around him transforming into a flurry of motion.

"The horn! They got him—"

"Just give me my gun. It may be a false alarm—"

"—or it could be some trick by that murdering pig."

"Don't start counting your bonus money until—"

"Get yer foot off my scabbard, you pocked bastard, or I'll feed you your balls—"

A lantern flared, bright, at the entrance to the lodge.

The loud basso voice of Ahod Channar, the company's commander, boomed through the noise. "Silence, everyone," the slaver shouted, punctuating his words with a thump of his staff against the entrance arch. "We have all heard the horn. It may mean that we are finished here, or it may mean that things are just starting. I want everyone up and awake. I want the weapons loaded, and all outside right now; we'll wait for information and orders before doing anything else."

Pelius, who had apparently slept fully dressed, hefted his rifle and leaned over toward Jason, who was busy strapping on his swordbelt. "Which means that we're as disorganized as usual," he whispered. "I bet we don't get fed until morning."

Pelius had the usual mercenary's primary and continuing concern: his stomach. The tall, lanky man always seemed to feel he was at least two meals behind.

To give credit to Channar, Jason had noticed his preoccupation with getting his men fed at frequent intervals. Jason suspected that Ahrmin didn't care any more for the bellies of his hired mercenaries than for their necks; quite probably all there was of the cripple's plan was to let Karl hack the hired hands to bits until Ahrmin's hunters got lucky and brought their man down.

"I bet we don't get fed until morning," Pelius repeated. "What do you think?"

"I don't know," Jason said, cursing himself as his voice trembled, then realizing that a demonstration of fear wasn't going to blow his cover; he was *supposed* to be scared.

"How about ammo and food?" a voice cried out. "I've only got the one flask—"

"Silence, I said!" Ahod Channar considered it for a moment. "Kakkum—take your squad, go to the armory, and retrieve an additional basic load for each man. As for food . . . Hervian, since your squad has been so damn talkative, you can help the cook build up the fire and bring food to the company."

✦   ✦   ✦

Parts of the forest had been canopied over too thoroughly for even Walter Slovotsky's extraordinary—for a human—night vision to cope with, but Ahira's darksight was able to pierce the gloom, leading him down paths that Slovotsky could barely feel.

Even under these limited circumstances, for Ahira to be better than he was like somebody else fitting better into his clothes, or exciting Kirah more in bed than he could.

Walter Slovotsky was amused at how much he found that he really didn't like the feeling. On a night skulk, he was supposed to be unequaled, much less unsurpassed. He shook his head. *Oh, what fools these mortals be,* he thought, *including me.* He could almost have laughed; Walter was always his own best audience.

As the trees thinned, the path lightened ahead of them, black touched with gray.

Indicating with a touch that Ahira should lag behind, Slovotsky took the lead. Now, this was definitely his kind of thing. It wouldn't be possible to move through the underbrush without making a sound, but the paths were a different matter. The slavers would post a guard on all even theoretically possible approaches to the camp, even a too-dark path.

Where was the guard? That was the question. And were there many backups? Karl's little war of nerves with the slavers would have them all on edge.

Walter Slovotsky crept forward, looking and listening.

A single clear note sounded through the night. There were a few seconds of silence, and then it sounded again.

Up ahead, rough voices talked in hushed tones.

"You heard the horn. It's supposed to mean that they have him. We'd better get back to camp—"

"We can stay here on guard until we're relieved, or Ahrmin will feed us our fingers. And that isn't a figure of speech. Now shut up."

Karl captured? Maybe that's what the horn was supposed to mean, and maybe it meant something entirely different. Ahira's fingers touched his wrist; Walter knelt so the dwarf could whisper to him.

Ahira's breath was warm on his ear. "I think we continue. You?"

Slovotsky didn't like any of this. But following through with their part of the plan had to make sense, and God help them all if Bren and Aeia, or Karl, Tennetty, and Ganness, weren't able to do their jobs.

"Yeah," Slovotsky whispered. He pulled a pair of garrotes from his pouch, handing one to Ahira, hefting the other himself. "We continue."

Maybe his feeding you your fingers isn't a figure of speech, but neither is "I'll choke you to death."

The camp was a maze of activity, save for Ahrmin's tent and the brothel cabin. Those two were quiet, the slaves apparently secured, only a single guard outside. And he, like everyone else, was watching the approaches to the village, not worrying about his charges.

Next to Jason, by the now-roaring cookfire, Hervian shook his head, his face sweaty in the light of the built-up cooking fire. "I don't see how we can serve stew," he said, looking at the big iron pot. "We'd have to collect all the bowls, spoon it out, then see that the bowls got back to their owners."

It was a different kind of organization than Home used, more primitive, less efficient. On a Home raiding team, there would be warriors responsible for cooking and serving food and seeing that bowls and eating utensils were gathered up and washed. Here, although there was a central cooking fire and a hired cook, serving was a bit of every-man-for-himself.

"Then it will have to be bread and ham," Doria said, her face dry, unsweaty. She gestured at the rough stone oven. "The bread's in there; you can hand it out." She looked from one to the other. "Taren, you can help me cut the ham," she said, lifting a lantern and walking into the darkness of the small hut that was the camp's larder.

"You, too, Vikat," Hervian said, loading lanky Pelius' arms with the hot, round, flat loaves of brown bread. "Help the two of them."

Vikat led the way inside.

Hanging from ropes suspended from an arching bamboo framing member were a dozen hams, as well as long brown ropes of braided strips of jerked beef.

One of the hams had been carved almost to the bone. Doria took up a butcher's knife and seemed to consider it for a moment before moving to the next one and scraping at the green mold that encased it.

"Hurry up, old woman," Vikat said. "We don't have all night—fighting could break out at any time."

Doria raised a finger to her lips as she glanced toward the doorway, and then nodded at Jason. "Then give me a hand. *Now.*"

Now? he thought.

She nodded. "Definitely now."

But . . . he set his rifle down and approached Vikat from the rear.

Walter Slovotsky had once shown him the grip, and Valeran had vouched for its usefulness; Jason snaked his left arm around the slaver's throat and locked his right arm against the back of Vikat's neck, squeezing before Vikat could utter a sound, only relaxing his grip well after he'd slid the other to the ground, although Vikat went limp almost instantly.

Jason used a strand of rawhide to tie Vikat's thumbs tightly together behind his back while Doria gagged him.

"He could choke on that," Jason whispered.

"So?" Doria looked at him from an impassive, flat face. "When Ahrmin leaves his lodge, he's going to cross the doorway. Just hope that that's soon, before somebody notices that the boy here is missing."

"But—" But what? But Vikat, like Hervian, had treated Jason well? Did that matter? Didn't that have to matter?

He looked down at the form of the man he had spent days on patrol with, eating with, even laughing with. Vikat was sort of a friend; Jason couldn't just slaughter him like a pig.

"You can object to killing slavers after you've been raped by one, little boy," Doria said, her voice, although pitched low, sharp and clear. "No. After a dozen have taken their turns on you."

He turned.

The guise of an overweight old woman was gone; Doria stood next to him in her white robes. There was a majestic quality in her bearing as she drew herself up straight; it was the carriage of someone who proudly endured pressure beyond what she had thought she could.

"Doria—"

"Come here." She knelt next to a pile of rags in the corner of the tent and produced Jason's rifle, pistol, and the leather pouch containing his powder horn and other shooting supplies. "Quickly now, load. You won't have a second chance, and you're not going to be as accurate with a slaver rifle."

Across the cooking fire from the larder, Felius, the larger of Ahrmin's blocky bodyguards, was standing in front of the large lodge, his rifle held in front of him, shadows flickering across his face in the firelight.

As he tipped a measured load down the rifle's barrel and then tamped it down, Jason realized with a shock that it had been only a few minutes since the alarm had sounded. Ahrmin was probably still gathering his wits, deciding what kind of patrol to send out to bring in the hunters' catch.

Or, probably, deciding if it was a Karl Cullinane trap.

He might well have caught the hunters, Jason realized as he wrapped a ball in a hastily cut spit patch, then rammed it home, reflexively replacing his ramrod in its slot underneath the rifle. If he did, he might well force one to give the success signal, and decoy some slavers into a trap before running and striking again later.

Please, Father, let it be so.

If not, everything rested on Jason's shoulders. Those shoulders had already proved far too weak.

Jason primed the pan, then snapped it shut and turned to load his pistols, going by touch, his eyes on the compound beyond.

Ahrmin's other bodyguard emerged from the lodge, a horn held in his hands. He blew a staccato question into the night, and was immediately answered by three pure, clear notes.

The man raised his fist and shook it over his head as he shouted in triumph, "We have him! We have him!"

Ahrmin emerged from his cabin and stepped into the firelight.

Before, Jason had been surprised at how innocuous Ahrmin had seemed: a crippled little man, huddling in his slaver's robes.

Now, he seemed to gain bulk and strength as he drew himself up straight in the firelight and turned to face the company.

Lit by the raging central campfire, his face was demonic; his single eye seemed to burn with an inner fire.

"Brothers, friends, and companions," Ahrmin called out, his voice carrying farther, more powerfully than it had any right to. "We have triumphed. That is Chuzet's horn, and the note is too clear, too calm, the signal coming too quickly for me to believe that he is acting under threat. We will send out—"

"Now!" Doria hissed. "Shoot him now!"

Only one pistol was loaded; Jason cocked it and set it on the ground, then took up his rifle, momentarily running his hand down the smooth stock. He put his thumb on the brass hammer and pulled it back, cocking the piece.

Jason brought the rifle up and caught Ahrmin in his sights.

The crippled slaver seemed to wrap himself in power as Jason stood there, a darkness creeping in from the edges of his vision as the world seemed narrowed to just Ahrmin.

Half supported by his bodyguard, Ahrmin turned the remains of the right side of his face toward Jason.

"Now, Jason," Doria hissed.

All sound was gone. All sight, except for that face. It would have to be a head shot. Jason would have to kill Ahrmin with a single shot, before anyone could get healing draughts to him.

Ahrmin was dead. The warrant was signed and sealed. All Jason had to do was pull back on the trigger.

But his index finger wouldn't move. It was the same thing that had happened in the forests outside of Wehnest: Time lost its forward motion, and froze.

Except that this time, the frozen time was wrapped only around Jason; the rest of the universe seemed to move faster, robbing him of his chance. As he crouched there, unmoving, Ahrmin finished his oration and began to move away.

I can't do it.

His finger wouldn't move. His father's life depended on killing Ahrmin now, but something had robbed Jason of his will.

Jason swallowed, hard.

There was a rustling at the door, and Hervian stepped inside. "What's going—" He caught himself as he spotted Vikat's bound form, motionless in the corner.

Hervian reached for his sword, all the while shouting, "Traitors! Assassins in the larder!"

No. Not this time. I won't fail.

"Not this time."

Jason Cullinane gritted his jaw tightly, and he bent time to his will. As though he had seconds, minutes, hours, in which to shoot, Jason carefully, slowly, gently squeezed the trigger, keeping Ahrmin in his sights.

The hammer fell, snapping sparks into the night. There was a bang that he felt more than heard, and a cloud of acrid smoke.

Ahrmin's head exploded. Brains splattered onto his bodyguard's chest, white curds among the red.

It felt like he was moving in slow motion as Jason Cullinane dropped his rifle and tried to roll away from Hervian's lunge, sure that he wouldn't make it.

When the second note sounded, Walter Slovotsky and Ahira were standing over the bodies of the guards, trying to decide what to do. Walter couldn't see the camp, and trying to creep closer was not only not part of the plan, it was almost certain suicide.

Only one thing made any kind of sense: start the attack, then get the hell back to the beach and see if they could be of some sort of use.

Slovotsky laid their dozen bombs on the ground in front of him. The brightness that showed where the camp was was just too far away for him to reach.

"I don't have that good a pitching arm."

The dwarf smiled, his white teeth shining in the darkness. "You light 'em, I'll throw them."

Slovotsky struck the tip of one of the igniters, and as it sputtered into flame, laid the stick firmly in the dwarf's palm.

Ahira threw it sputtering off into the night.

The night exploded into fire and screams.

"Next."

Jason rolled to one side, the tip of Hervian's sword taking him high in the left arm.

The pain was dazzling, but his right hand seemed to have a mind of its own; it clawed at the pistol on the ground, bringing it up, the thumb pulling the hammer back, the finger curling around the trigger, jerking, as the world outside the hut exploded into a horrid din and orange fire.

He never knew where the shot went, except that it must have gone wide, but the edge of the muzzle blast must have caught Hervian in the eyes; the slaver screamed, dropped his sword, and clapped his hands to his face.

Jason dropped his pistol, and scooping up Hervian's sword, clumsily set the point against the slaver's chest and rammed it hilt-deep before pushing the dying slaver to one side.

Another explosion sounded outside the hut, this one turning the cooking fire into a shower of sparks, fire, and stone, some of which pierced the flimsy sides of the hut.

A stone *tinged* off Doria's robes, knocking her down; what felt like a horse's kick caught Jason in the side. Two ribs broke with an awful snap. He tried to get to his feet, but pieces of bone in his chest moved as if of their own volition, in sharp, horrid counterpoint to the torment of the gash in his left arm.

Grabbing his good arm, Doria helped him to his feet and pulled him from the hut.

Another explosion rocked the camp. Some men tried to hide from the bombs, while others fired their guns off into the night, trying to shoot whoever was attacking them.

"We've got to get down to the beach," Doria said. "Now."

Leaning on Doria, Jason Cullinane limped off into the night.

When the first explosion roared, somewhere far off in the night, Karl Cullinane moved. Like a soccer player picking up a ball after practice, Karl used his toes to scoop the bomb at his feet into the air, then caught it, rolling away, striking the igniter on his belt as he did, then throwing the bomb, immediately realizing that his adrenaline rush had betrayed him; he'd thrown it too far.

He rolled to his feet and reached for his bowie.

The first crossbow bolt caught him in the right shoulder, sending his knife falling from nerveless fingers; the second slammed into his right thigh, knocking his leg out from underneath him, slamming him to the sand.

Karl Cullinane tried to breathe, but couldn't. He couldn't even force his feet under him.

I will not die on my knees.

As the slavers went for cover, the bomb went off behind them—too far behind them—shattering the night into fire, barely knocking them off their feet.

From the corner of his eye, Karl could see that Ganness, too, was down, must have been stunned.

The sky behind Karl lit up as the charges Aeia and Bren had placed aboard the slaver ship went off.

Good kids. The rest is mine.

Ignoring the agony from the crossbow bolts in his shoulder and thigh, Karl crawled to the nearest slaver, falling over on his side as he fastened his hand on the man's throat.

His good hand. His left hand, which only had a thumb and forefinger left. His right side was useless; this would have to be enough. He squeezed, hard, harder, letting the universe narrow to his thumb, his forefinger, and the slaver's throat.

Cartilage and flesh tore wetly between his finger and thumb; the slaver died with an awful liquid gurgling.

Beyond the offshore island, yet another pair of explosions rocked the night.

The other man rose, a dagger gleaming brightly in the starlight, but fell back as a gunshot rang out, shattering his face into a bloody pulp.

Karl turned his head. Half propped up by Ganness, Tennetty was holding an open bottle of healing draughts in one hand, a smoking pistol in the other. She dropped the pistol, groaning as she fastened two trembling hands around the crossbow bolt that projected from her side.

She screamed as she jerked at the crossbow bolt in her side. The bottle fell from her fingers, spilling too much of the precious stuff into the sands before she could snatch it up.

She then took another swig of the healing draughts, then pulled again. This time, the bolt came free, its wooden shaft dark with her blood.

Tennetty crabbed herself over to Karl and forced the bottle between his lips with one hand while she fastened the other on the fletching of the bolt in his shoulder.

White-hot fire shot through him as she pulled the crossbow bolt from his flesh, and then yanked three times, three separate, awful spasms of agony, to pull the other from his thigh.

The sickly-sweet liquid dulled the pain, bringing strength back to his vague limbs, letting him breathe again, pushing away the darkness at the edges of his vision.

Tennetty smiled weakly, while Ganness vomited on the sands.

"Stop congratulating yourself," Karl said, as he lay on the sand, gasping for breath. He felt at the wound in his shoulder and at the one in his thigh. Not good. Both wounds had closed, but that was all. There just wasn't enough left of the healing draughts to bring him back to full health, to finish the healing process. His wounds were closed, but he was dead tired, barely able to move.

The hole in Tennetty's side was a bit better, maybe, but not much.

"Reload," he gasped. "Reload." Aiea and Bren would be back on the beach in a few minutes, and they'd need cover.

❖   ❖   ❖

"Bad news, Jimmy—very bad." Slovotsky shook his head. "They've reformed and they're heading out the wrong way."

"Wrong way?" Ahira hefted his axe. "The other path? Shit."

Slovotsky nodded. Things were quickly going to hell. Karl was busy preparing an ambush on the path that led most directly down to the beach, but Ahrmin, or whoever was in charge, was leading the slavers down another path toward the beach.

It would bring them down to the beach west of where the others were.

Which wasn't all bad, in and of itself. Karl and the rest would be between the slavers and Ganness' ship. But the plan had been to blow up the slavers while they were crowded together on a trail. Karl didn't have sufficient explosives or manpower to stop more than a hundred slavers advancing in the open; the slavers would spread out and fight a rifle duel from a distance. A duel that they would win, eventually.

Ahira nodded. "Let's get back down to the beach."

As he led Slovotsky down the path, Slovotsky caught a flash of white in the night at a momentary break in the trees overhead.

A slaver limped along, supported by a woman in white robes.

Walter reached for a knife, only to let his hand drop. It wasn't a slaver.

"Jason, Doria," he breathed.

They turned about, Jason moving away from Doria to draw his sword, his eyes widening when he saw who it was.

The boy was badly hurt, Walter realized, as he took over the task of supporting him, while the dwarf and the cleric embraced silently.

There was little that could be done. The bottle of healing draughts was back at the beach with Karl; Walter had only a tiny flask of the precious stuff in his pouch.

He drew the flask, pulled the cork, and tilted it between Jason's lips. "Let's move it, people. We got troubles."

CHAPTER TWENTY-NINE:
Profession

Being a hero is about the shortest-lived profession on earth.
—Will Rogers

They gathered around the bombs, more than slightly the worse for wear, although Walter Slovotsky and Ahira were only out of breath. Karl's and Tennetty's wounds were closed, but by no means fully healed; Karl's right shoulder was a constant deep ache, and his right leg refused to support him.

Bren Adahan and Aeia were winded, gasping on the sands like fish out of water. Ganness seemed stunned, still white-faced from his bout of vomiting.

Doria seemed physically fine, but she was almost silent, barely able to speak.

Karl gripped Jason's hand. Jason was the worst. While healing draughts and pressure bandages had stopped the bone-deep gash in Jason's arm from bleeding, the boy's ribs were badly broken, and the pieces had shifted during their half-run, half-stagger to the beach. Jason screamed every time anyone tried to move him.

"You'll have to carry the boy," Karl said to Ahira. "Careful, now."

Slovotsky nodded. "Bren—go cut Karl a staff; we're going to have to hobble ourselves out of here."

Bren Adahan drew his knife and moved away in the dark.

"Not a boy, Father," Jason shot back, clenching his teeth as he spaced out the words evenly. "I killed Ahrmin."

"You sure?" Walter Slovotsky said.

Doria turned a sweat-shiny face toward Slovotsky. "He shot his fucking head off."

Karl forced a smile. "Not a boy." He let go of Jason, and accepted the stick that Bren had cut for him to use as a cane.

Ahira helped Karl to his feet. He could barely move at a slow walk, and this was a situation that called for running. He didn't like it at all.

Best to get moving and worry later about how much he didn't like it.

"Let's get out of here, people," he said. "Ahira, you carry Jason; Walter, you and I will bring up the rear, slow down any pursuit."

Slovotsky nodded. "Right. And—"

A single shot rang out.

Karl had never seen Walter Slovotsky move faster. Diving, Slovotsky drew and threw a knife at something in the darkness, then completed his dive to snatch up one of Karl's pistols, brought it up and cocked it, and pulled the trigger.

It spat fire into the darkness.

Two men screamed.

"Everybody down," Karl said as he let himself fall to the sand.

He snatched up a bomb, struck its fuse to sputtering life with his thumbnail, and threw it in the direction that Slovotsky had fired. The slaver or slavers had missed once; even if they were injured, it wasn't safe to assume that they would miss again.

"Cover your eyes," he said, throwing an arm over his own face.

The bomb went off with a flat *crump* that drowned out the slavers' screams. Hot sand spattered him.

"Okay, people," Walter Slovotsky said. "We've drawn about enough attention to ourselves." Walter smiled down at Karl as he offered a hand. "Nice toss, Karl. Now, let's get out of—"

"*No!*" Aeia screamed. "Jason . . ."

Karl crabbed himself around.

Jason was still stretched out on the sand, but now he clutched at his belly, where the dark blood flowed freely. The slaver's shot hadn't missed.

Oh God. *No.* Not Jason.

"Healing draughts. We have to—"

"We don't have any," Tennetty said, her tone flat, her words evenly spaced.

"Help." Jason's face was contorted into an almost inhuman mask. "It hurts so *much.*"

"No." Karl held his son to him; he could feel Jason's fast-pounding heartbeat getting weaker. "Please God, no."

Doria's voice was calm and level.

"Let go of him, Karl," she said, her words evenly spaced, distant. "Let go of him."

Gentle fingers that were far stronger than they had any right to be pried Karl's arms away from the boy.

"You must let go of him,"

She stretched Jason's form out on the cold sands; the boy's body was limp, perhaps unconscious, perhaps already dead.

No. Not dead. Please not dead. Not Jason.

Logically, it didn't matter whether or not he was dead yet. If he wasn't dead already, he would be in just minutes, his life's blood dripping away into Melawei sands. Just like Rahff.

"No! There's got to be something we can do besides give up on—"

"Shh." Ahira's grip was strong on Karl's good shoulder. "Be quiet, Karl. Don't interfere."

"I will heal him." Doria's fists were trembling in front of her face, her jaw clamped tightly as she stood over Jason's prostrate form.

Her forehead beaded with cold sweat, her breath came in short gasps as she flailed her arms at something nobody else could see, her body tightened as she matched her strength against her invisible adversary's.

"I will," she said. "I will do as *I* will, not as you would have me. I belong to me, not to you. I belong to *me!*"

Bands of force became almost palpable, tightening around Doria, first dragging her arms down to her sides, then slowly driving her to her knees, forcing her head down.

You will obey me, daughter, a distant voice seemed to say in a whisper, a harsh whisper that could shatter rocks.

"No."

Doria weakened; she pulled her hood around her head, and, almost vanishing into her robes, began to jerk spasmodically. But she did not give up. She struggled on.

Just when it seemed that the battle would not be won, could not be won, the forces restraining Doria snapped, gone to where a burst soap bubble goes.

Doria's strength tore through the darkness, and the evanescent words of healing poured from her mouth in a rapid torrent.

The words flowed into Jason; the wound in his belly expelled a flattened hunk of metal before sealing itself behind the bullet. Ribs snaked under his skin, freezing into their proper places. Beneath the bandage on his shoulder, skin and muscle twisted and shifted.

Doria staggered away from the boy; if Ahira hadn't reached out a supporting arm, she would have fallen.

Karl reached out a hand as Jason's eyes flickered, then opened. He lived.

My son lives. Karl gave Jason's arm a quick squeeze, then called to Ahira and Walter.

"You'll have to carry him. Now. Leave me some of your guns, and get the hell out of here, all of you. The slavers will be along any minute." He propped himself up against the base of a tree. "I'll hold them off."

It was a logical necessity. His leg wouldn't support him; the best he could do with the staff Bren had cut him would have been a slow hobble. With slavers closing in on them, the others needed more of a head start than they had. It wasn't only necessary to get to Ganness' ship; they also had to get it moving, to get it at least far enough offshore that the slavers wouldn't be able to swarm aboard, overwhelming them by sheer numbers.

And they had to get going now, before the other slaver ship could arrive in the morning, and be told that someone had snuck a ship by. This attack, and the healing of Jason, had eaten up time they couldn't afford. They had to go.

Now.

"The others can go." Tennetty clasped her hand to her side. "I won't leave you."

There wasn't time. Somebody had to stay and slow the slavers down. Only one. Two wouldn't do any better.

He looked her straight in the eye. "It's an order. Or are you going to betray me by staying?"

There were shouts and cries from down the beach. Off in the night, the slavers had made it to the sand. Only a matter of time until they headed this way; only a matter of time until they were all caught.

Karl looked from Bren Adahan to Aeia, to Walter, Tennetty,

Doria, Ahira, and the still-woozy Jason, staggering until the dwarf swept him up in his arms. Doria had saved his life; she hadn't been able to bring him back to full strength, not after the injuries the boy had suffered.

Wordless, Aeia knelt beside Karl and kissed him on the forehead, then rose.

But nobody moved. "We don't have time for long goodbyes," Karl said. "Get going. And know that I love you all."

Tennetty thought it over for a long second. "Yes, Karl." Tennetty laid the last of the rifles near him. "I'll take the powder," she said. "I don't think they'll give you a chance to reload."

"Right. Good luck."

"Karl," she said, dry-eyed, only a little tremor at the edge of her voice. "Is there anything you want me to tell Andrea?"

"She already knows it. Move."

"Be well." Her hand still clapped over her own wound, forced herself to her feet. "You all heard the man. Let's move out, people. And now means now."

Aeia started to say something, but Karl shook his head. "We don't have time, girl. Just go. Run for it. Get her out of here, Bren."

Bren Adahan threw Karl a brief salute, then caught Aeia's hand and dragged her away. She only resisted for a few feet, then broke into a sprint, her shoulders shaking.

"I said *now*," Tennetty first kicked Ganness into a trot, then shoved Slovotsky into motion, while Ahira, holding Jason in his arms, took off in a dead run.

"Just a moment. I'll catch up with you," Doria said, her voice cracking.

"He said to move it," Tennetty snapped. "So you move it."

"It's okay, Ten," Karl said. "Get going. Get them home."

"Understood, Karl." Tennetty nodded once, and staggered off after the others, her pounding feet sending sand flying into the air.

Doria laid a hand on his arm and looked into his eyes. "I have something for you," she said. She gripped his arm more tightly. "It's not much, but it's all I have left. The Mother took all the rest. I can't heal you, Karl, but I can sustain you. Just a little longer."

The wind whispered a distant message, a vague threat.

"Oh? That's not what you left me this for?" She addressed the air. "I don't care; we take care of our own, old woman. We take care of our own."

Staring into Karl's face, she laid her hands on his shoulders and began to mutter harsh syllables, words that could only be heard and forgotten.

It was strange. Weren't Doria's eyes yellow on This Side? And wasn't her face gaunter here? The eyes seemed dark; the face seemed to soften.

Where her fingers touched him, strength flowed into him like an electric current.

His wounds still ached; as he tried to get his right leg underneath him, it still refused to support him. But the pain in his leg and side were somehow distant; all fatigue was gone.

"It will . . . sustain you longer than they'll think possible, Karl," Doria Perlstein said. She was twenty again, a bit chubby, her eyes brown now. The Hand cleric was gone. "I hope. It's not enough, but it's all I can do—"

"Get out of here, Doria."

"Goodbye." She turned and ran off after the others.

God, he felt strong.

He looked down at what he had. Six rifles, and thirty or so assembled bombs, plus three pistols. He crabbed himself over to the pistols and gathered them all together, then tucked one into his belt.

He waited.

He didn't have long. There was a distant shout as three men came into view.

Rolling over into a prone firing position, Karl cocked the nearest rifle, put it to his shoulder, took aim and pulled the trigger; at the crack of the rifle all three of the slavers fell. It took him half a moment to realize that at least two of them had taken cover; his single shot couldn't have knocked down all three.

I knew I was good, but I didn't think I was that good.

He laughed out loud, letting them hear it. "Come on, you bastards. I'm waiting for you." He thought about ducking back toward the treeline, but decided against it. It would be too hard to haul the rifles along with him, and he was going to need all of them. As well as the bombs.

He hefted one of the bombs. Probably best to use a bomb next. Shake them up a bit.

Maybe there was another way to shake them up. Maybe he could make them think they were up against more than one lone man.

"Chak, Rahff, Fialt," he shouted, "the next one of the bastards is mine. Hold your fire."

Another man crept around the bend, his rifle held out in front of him as though it was some sort of magical shield. Karl disabused him of that notion with a misthrown bomb that sent sand flying into the air, and the man flying for cover.

"Dammit, Chak," he shouted, "I wanted that one. I had him in my sights until you threw the bomb."

Maybe he could hold out long enough. Maybe. Give the others just a few minutes to get going, and then perhaps Karl could crawl into the woods, dig himself into some sort of cover, and hide out.

"Ease back out of the line of fire, Rahff. You'll kill more of them if they can't see you."

But first he had to give the others enough of a head start. The slavers wouldn't be long in coming. Not long at all.

Another man poked his head out from around the bend, and Karl let him fire off a shot before taking aim with his next rifle. He let the man creep a bit forward, and then potted him neatly.

"Nice shooting, Fialt. We'll kill them all by dawn."

Just a bit more time, that was all.

He waited patiently for several minutes. What was keeping them?

Maybe it's just as well I didn't go through such a long goodbye scene. A few more minutes of this and I'm getting my butt out of here, if at all possible.

He didn't look forward to holing up while he healed, and then trying the overland route back to the Middle Lands, but he'd been through worse. Probably he had sufficient supplies in the cave of the sword, and he could swim out there even without the use of one leg.

He smiled as he forced himself to a sitting position and pulled two more of the rifles onto his lap, cocking one and bringing it up to his shoulder. Just a few more slavers, a few more minutes, and—

Pain exploded in his back; he tumbled to the ground, his body gone from the chest down.

From behind—idiot! They had sent somebody to creep around him. The other slavers had just been trying to slow him down.

There was blood in his mouth. Salty, it seemed to warm him.

The world began to grow gray around the edges. The dark shapes gathered around him.

"Careful with him. He's still dangerous."

"He's nothing. I'll take him."

Got to—

His distant, clumsy thumb and forefinger worked hard between his belly and the sand, pried a pistol from his belt, and cocked it.

But he couldn't turn over. The world was just too far away; his arm was just too weak.

"Careful, I said. Turn him over and make sure he doesn't have another weapon. Then bind him."

Rough fingers pulled at his shoulder, adding just enough to what remained of his fast-fading strength to let him get his pistol out from underneath him.

Grayness spreading across his body, Karl Cullinane—

"He has a gun! Stop him!"

—pointed it at the stack of guncotton bombs, each with its own detonator.

"Andy . . ." he said, then decided that he didn't have the time for fancy last words.

He pulled the trigger once, hard.

CHAPTER THIRTY:
The Heir Apparent

Once we have a war there is only one thing to do.
It must be won. For defeat brings worse things than
any that can ever happen in war.

—Ernest Hemingway

When the final explosion sounded, and the distant fires lit up the sky, Ahira and Slovotsky had already loaded all of the others into the launch that lay half grounded on the sandy beach.

Walter Slovotsky closed his eyes for a moment. *Dammit, Karl.*

"Move it, you two," Tennetty commanded. "Get in the boat."

In the launch, Aeia buried her face in her hands, while Bren Adahan put an arm around her.

Doria, this strange, new-old Doria who now looked like the Other Side girl who had crossed over with them, wept openly as she supported Jason Cullinane's half-conscious form. Ganness only paused for a moment, then resumed passing out the oars.

Ahira's fingers closed on the gunwale tightly, so tightly that wood cracked and split beneath his hands.

Only Tennetty appeared unmoved, her face rigid, her eyes flat and lifeless. "We don't have time. Get in."

Summoning up a bravado he most certainly did not feel, Walter turned toward the dwarf. "Shit. We can't allow it. Can we?"

"Hell, no." Ahira smiled and shrugged. "And we won't. Besides, I hate boats."

Tennetty started to rise from her seat in the rear of the launch, but as Walter and Ahira pushed the boat out into the water, she sat back down. "What do you two think you're doing?"

"It should be obvious." The dwarf's chuckle probably didn't sound forced to the others' ears, but Walter knew him better. "We're staying," Ahira said. "If Karl survived, we'll find him and we'll get him out, no matter what it takes."

Walter blew a quick kiss to Aeia. "I know this is going to sound strange, but I want you to watch out for Kirah and my daughters—have Ellegon bring them to you, as soon as he can leave Holtun-Bieme."

Setting your mistress to take care of your wife and kids was peculiar, but that, in and of itself, appealed to him. Besides, it meant that Janie and D.A. would spend the next while in Home and Biemestren. Jason stood to inherit the crown; he might like the way his childhood playmate had filled out as she had grown up, and that might work out well for Janie. Worth a shot.

"No," Jason croaked out. His arm shaking as he tried to prop himself up on his elbow, he slipped back to Doria's lap. "No more sacrifices. Not now. Tennetty, stop them."

"Yes, Jason." One hand still holding her side, Tennetty drew a pistol and pointed it halfway between the two of them. "I won't have you waste his death." She motioned with the pistol. "Get in."

"Don't point a gun at someone you aren't willing to kill," Walter said, crossing his fingers and hoping that she wasn't, or if she was, she'd explain it rather than demonstrate it. "And we're not talking sacrifice. We can hide better than any two other people. Trust me."

"Jason?" She turned to the boy.

"No. Don't let them get killed, too."

Tennetty looked Walter Slovotsky in the eye. "I haven't made a habit of disobeying Cullinane orders."

Walter stared back at her. "Until now. It's necessary."

Ahira nodded. "It is, Tennetty."

She was silent for a long moment. Then: "It had fucking well better be." Tennetty uncocked her pistol and tucked it into her belt. "Push us off, then."

"No." Again, Jason tried to raise himself up, but failed.

Tennetty gripped the boy's hand. "Sorry, Jason. This once, we'll do it someone else's way. Bren, Aeia, Ganness, out oars," she said, using her free arm to wrestle her own oar up and set it into the crude wooden oarlock. "You two, push us off."

"But what is the point?" Ganness shrilled.

"The point is nobody is going back to Pandathaway to brag about having killed Karl Cullinane," Ahira said, fastening strong fingers on the gunwale. "Even if they have killed him. Now, get out of here. If we get out of this, we'll see you someday." Wading waist-deep into the cold water, the dwarf gave the launch a tremendous shove that hurled it away from the shore; the shock of the release sent the dwarf falling face-first in the water.

Walter Slovotsky quickly waded to his side and helped him get to his feet.

The oars were set in the water; Ganness calling cadence, the launch began to make its rough way away from the beach, toward the offshore island beyond which Ganness' ship was anchored.

As they returned to the beach, sputtering, coughing, Ahira turned around and waved a farewell to those in the boat. He couldn't say anything, not still half choking on the water.

Or maybe the water he'd swallowed was just an excuse, Slovotsky decided. Maybe the dwarf didn't trust himself to speak right now.

But somebody had to say it.

"Jason?" Walter called out.

Doria helped him up to a sitting position.

"Walter . . ." He worked his mouth, then shut it. Jason Cullinane shook his head. "Good luck."

"Like your father said, we don't have time for long goodbyes. Just remember this: You're inheriting something more than a crown. Understood?"

Jason Cullinane's tear-streaked face was grim. "Understood."

EPILOGUE:
Requiem

Let no one honor me with tears, nor celebrate my funeral rites with weeping.

—Quintus Ennius

A Few Tendays Later, in Biemestren

The cool, clear voice of Ellegon sounded through Biemestren: *I have found them at the border, and we come. With sad news.*

They all came out to see, waiting not in the throne room, but in the courtyard, beneath the window of what had been Karl's study.

They gathered—the rulers Andrea Cullinane, Listar, Baron Tyrnael, and Thomen, Baron Furnael; the warriors Garavar, Garthe, Pirojil, Durine, and Kethol, plus a full troop of the House Guard; Master Engineer Ranella with Journeyman Aravam and Bibuz and a dozen apprentices; fat U'len, the castle's head cook, with her assistants Jimuth and Kozat; maids and scribes, coopers and blacksmiths and stablemen—they gathered, waiting.

Above, a distant black spot in the sky grew slowly, then took shape and form as the dragon descended, leathery wings beating the air in a relentless fury.

We come.

Dust flew into the air as the dragon stooped in for a landing. By the time eyes had begun to clear, Bren Adahan had unstrapped himself and vaulted to the ground, reaching up to help Aeia down, then Tennetty, Jason, and finally Doria.

"Doria!" Andrea Cullinane's eyes widened. "Is it really you?"

The blond girl nodded, while Jason and Aeia ran to Andrea.

Thomen Furnael eyed him levelly, his face grim. Bren shook his head.

"He's dead," Andrea Cullinane said, her eyes searching his for some hope as she held her son and adopted daughter to her.

I can't offer you the hope you need, Lady, Bren thought, holding his face impassive.

On the trip home, he thought he had gotten used to the idea of Karl Cullinane being dead. But he hadn't, not really. Not until now, not until he had to inform Andrea that she was a widow.

They stood still for a moment, none able to give word to what everyone in the courtyard knew.

But for just a moment. Slowly, as though the motion was an immense effort, Jason Cullinane nodded. "Yes."

"He's dead, Andrea," Tennetty said.

It still seemed impossible. Bren had heard tales of the outlaw Karl Cullinane as a boy; when he had first met the giant, Bren had been only a little younger than Jason now was. Karl Cullinane had towered over his life.

Ellegon's mental voice was slow and even.

You are certain, he said. It was no question; it was a statement.

Andrea nodded, slowly, her face holding no trace of pain, displaying no emotion whatsoever.

Doesn't it matter to her?

She will not hold up her grief for your inspection, human, the dragon said, looming above him, eyes the size of dinner plates staring back at him. *And neither will I. It is a family matter.*

Jason pried himself from his mother's arms, his eyes dry and clear.

He stood easily, resting his hands on his belt. "We have some things that must be handled immediately," he said as he turned to Thomen. "I may be my father's heir, but I have no business ruling Holtun-Bieme. Not now; maybe not ever. The crown stays where it is. You will continue to help my mother rule."

"Jason!" Andrea drew back, shocked. "You've just—"

"I may have just returned home, but there are matters that must be handled now, Mother." The boy drew himself up straighter, his face holding no trace *of* passion, or of compassion. "Bren will help you rule, too. He's one of you—"

"*Damn you.*" Bren Adahan shook his head. "Damn you, Jason Cullinane."

The boy looked like he had been slapped. "What?"

Tennetty stiffened, her eyes narrowing slightly, her stare softening only fractionally when Aeia laid a gentle hand on her arm.

"You, your father, and that arrogant bastard Walter Slovotsky have always been the same," Bren said, letting the long-repressed fury flow. "You think that you're the only ones who care, you think that you Other Side people are the only ones that . . ." Words failed him; he flailed an arm helplessly. " . . . that all this matters to. You had better understand me, Jason Cullinane: There are others of us in this, too. You think Aeia doesn't care? Do you think she isn't a part of it?"

Aiea smiled at him, cocking her head to one side. For more than the thousandth time it occurred to him that there was nothing Bren Adahan had or could have that couldn't be bought by one of those smiles.

" . . . or Garavar?"

The old general nodded grimly, briefly clasping a strong hand to Jason's shoulder.

" . . . or the rest of the warriors? Do you think they aren't part of it?"

Feet shuffled on the dirt, while grim faces stared levelly. Standing side by side, Pirojil, Dunne, and Kethol faced Jason, each raising a hand in a sketchy salute, huge Durine adding an encouraging smile.

" . . . or Ranella?"

The master engineer raised inkstained fingers in a brief acknowledgment, then returned to her private thoughts after her lips briefly moved: *I'll build you your railroad, Karl, I promise.*

" . . . or Thomen?"

Thomen, Baron Furnael, the son of the man who had had Bren's father killed, the great-grandson of the man who had kidnapped and raped Bren's great-grandmother, extended a hand to Bren Adahan and clasped it firmly.

"Or even that crazy one-eyed attack bitch of yours?"

Tennetty smiled at that.

"If you think this revolution your father began is the property of the Cullinane family," Bren went on, "you're wrong. It belongs to everyone. We're all in this together; we each have our parts. Fine: Thomen will help your mother rule Holtun-Bieme; that's what he's good at. Agreed, I'll help; I'll do what I can. Of course, Garavar will command troops, while Pirojil and Durine will fight; Ranella and Lou Riccetti will build; U'len will cook. Ellegon, Aeia, Doria— we all do our parts. But so will you, Jason Cullinane. You'll do two things for the rest of us."

"And those are?"

He wanted to say: *You'll tell your sister to marry me.* But he wouldn't say that. Partly it was a matter of pride. Besides, it wouldn't make a difference. Aeia was just as stubborn as the rest of her family.

"First, you'll work like a dog trying to learn everything you need to, so you can do your part, whatever that is. I don't think you know, yet; I surely don't."

"Agreed," Jason Cullinane said. His voice, while no louder, somehow seemed to gain depth and power. "And second?"

"Second, you'll accept that the rest of us are part of it, too," Bren Adahan said quietly, each word dropping into the silence. "Each in our own way; each and every one of us."

There was a little something of his father in his eyes as Jason nodded and looked from face to face, finding something there that he had not seen before.

And there was more than a little of his father in his voice as he folded his arms across his chest, nodded slowly, and said, "Your terms are agreed to, Bren Adahan."

His mother took Jason's hand. "Then come in and rest. There is much to do tomorrow."

"No." Gently, he pulled away from her. "No," he said. "There is much to do today. Today." His face was emotionless, but his eyes were wet. "Tennetty."

"Right here."

"My swordsmanship needs work. While it's still light." Tears ran down a stern, unmoving face. "There is much work to do, and the day isn't over. Let's get to it."

"Quite right," Tennetty said, with a shrug and a smile. "Walk this way," she said, walking twenty steps away and then drawing her sword, mirroring Jason.

While steel rang on steel, the words seemed to echo: *There is much work to do, and the day isn't over.*

The crowd dispersed until only Bren Adahan, Thomen Furnael, Doria Perlstein, and the two Cullinane women were left with the dragon.

Could that not have waited? Ellegon looked down at Bren. *You leave him little time for private mourning.*

Perhaps. Bren nodded his head. *But I'm not sure he has much time. He is Karl's heir.*

As are we all. The fire burns more brightly each year, doesn't it?

I don't understand.

Of course you do.

Great wings folded tightly against his side, the dragon lowered his saurian head, turning toward Andrea. *I . . . am so sorry, Andrea. I loved him, too.*

Clumsily, her face and her tears buried in her daughter's hair, she reached up to pat a thick scale. "He's dead, Ellegon."

Doria reached out an awkward arm, and Andrea included the younger-seeming woman in her embrace.

At the sound of steel on steel, the dragon looked over at Jason Cullinane and Tennetty, their swords flashing in the daylight. Jason parried a high-line attack, stopped his own lunge just short of Tennetty's torso, then backed up a few feet, saluting before taking an *en garde* position once again.

Slowly, the majestic head turned to look down at Thomen Furnael, Aeia Cullinane, and finally at Bren Adahan.

Ellegon stretched his neck, the huge head moving slowly from side to side, the eyes, each easily the size of a dinner plate, staring unblinkingly.

Andrea, the flame burns more brightly, year by year. You say that Karl is dead? Ellegon unfurled his wings, braced himself against the smooth stones, then leaped into the air. Flame roared into the clear blue sky.

My dear, dear Andrea, that is entirely a matter of opinion.

In a House on Faculty Row

Even a sight that spans worlds can be blurred by tears.

Arthur Simpson Deighton sat, half bent over his desk, his head buried in his arms, weeping.

A distant voice seemed to whisper:

Strange. You treat some of them like pieces in a game, but you care about the others. It's most amusing, I suppose, and while I'm used to laws and rules shifting and changing, I never will understand the rules you live by, Arta Myrdhyn.

"I let myself care about him, Titania. About all of them."

You grow soft, old human. Weak. Your caring is distant, pointless. It's not at all amusing.

"It shall be neither distant nor pointless, someday."

Idle threats. Idle promises. You know what is necessary, but you have yet to do it. Coward. Crazy, useless coward. Now, you have another excuse to wait.

Arthur Simpson Deighton wept until his aching eyes were dry of tears.

Later, in Pandathaway: Slavers' Guildhall

"By the time we arrived, they were dead, every one. Before we were driven off, we were able to capture a couple of the Mel whores; they are outside, waiting your pleasure. They didn't see it, but they did report: Cullinane and a handful of his men took on more than a hundred of ours, and won."

"All dead? *All?*"

"Every one. The beach was scattered with rotting bodies. It was clear that many of them had died in some sort of gunfight, some in some kind of explosion. But the rest . . . there were those who had been killed by strangling, some with an axe, and some with a sword. I was trying to investigate further when the Mel attacked— yes, with guns."

"Captured from Ahrmin's party?"

"I don't know if it was our powder or that accursed Cullinane powder."

"Ahrmin and a score of good guildsmen and a hundred mercenaries were killed, the Mel have guns—and you say that there is *worse*?"

"There is. I know there's no word of Karl Cullinane returning to Holtun-Bieme—they seem to think that he's dead."

"You say that he *isn't*?"

"I say that nobody else has seen *this*. We found it nailed to the chest of one of our men; he had been hung by the heels and slaughtered like a goat. We were meant to find it; the Mel didn't attack until after we discovered it.

"The symbols on the very bottom seem to be the signatures. There are three of them. *Three*: an axe, a knife, and a sword. I think the writing on top is that accursed Englits of his, but you can see what's written in Erendra."

He held up a piece of sun-bleached leather, on which were written, in dark, dried blood, some English words that they couldn't understand.

And below the words they couldn't understand, also written in blood, were three Erendra words that they could:

the warrior lives

The Warrior Lives

Vol. 5 of

The Guardians of the Flame

For Sprague and Catherine,
role models

Acknowledgments

I'd like to thank the people who helped: Will Shetterly
and Emma Bull, who found me the place to finish this
book; Pamela Dean and Nate Bucklin, for the last-
minute proofreading; the rest of the Minneapolis SF
crowd, for reasons both trivial and profound; Mark J.
McGarry, who made it better, again; Felix Tang and
John Jaser and the other good folks at Logix Micro-
computer; Scott Raun, who quibbled a bit; Harry
Leonard, who quibbled a lot; my editor, John Silbersack; my wife, Felicia; and always, particularly, my
agent, Eleanor Wood.

PRELUDE

Laheran

Every man is like the company he is wont to keep.
                                            —Euripides

"You have to find him," said Slavers' Guildmaster Yryn. "You have to stop him."

Yryn looked old, and stoop-shouldered. His neck seemed to have trouble holding up his massive head, and his eyes were more of a dull gray than the sharp, piercing slate-gray that Laheran remembered from his apprenticeship in the guild.

As they walked through the garden, Yryn fondled the piece of sun-bleached leather, his nail-bitten fingers stroking it as if it were a magical talisman, which it wasn't.

There was little enough in the world to be sure of, Laheran thought, but the leather wasn't magical. It had been carefully examined by a competent wizard, a master in Pandathaway's Wizards' Guild, and while the wizards couldn't always be relied on—they were notorious cowards, for one thing—they could be trusted to know if something was magical.

The inner courtyard of Slavers' Guildhall was a quiet place, one for reflection. Marble benches surrounded a lawn that was always ankle-height, the garden guarded by cornered hedges, the precision of it all maintained each night by scissor-wielding slaves working under smoky torchlight.

Except for the flowers. A gardener, fealty-bound to the guild,

263

had the responsibility for their care. Flowers were different, Laheran thought, as he bent to sniff the rich fragrance of a blood-red rose. They required loving attention, not just fearful care.

Laheran liked the garden. It was the one quiet place in the city, the only place he could get completely away from the noise and the bustle and the smells of Pandathaway.

"You have to stop Karl Cullinane," the guildmaster said, as though Laheran hadn't heard him.

"You said that." Laheran held up an admonishing finger, hoping that Yryn would slap him down for his insolence, silently begging the guildmaster to assert his authority.

But the older man just nodded.

Laheran could have cried. The guildmaster was losing his grip on himself. Could his grip on the guild be far behind?

It was a bad time to be leaving Pandathaway. Perhaps Laheran oughtn't have any delusions about having a chance at the guildmastership—there had never been a guildmaster in his twenties, and damned few in their thirties—but as the youngest full master in the guild, it wasn't at all impossible that he could have some impact on the outcome of the contention.

If there was to be a contention. Perhaps what the guild needed now was stability, even if that meant that somebody would have to be the power behind the throne.

Laheran held out his hand to accept the piece of leather. It was about two handbreadths across, not of terribly high quality, probably cut from a leather food sack of some sort.

There was writing on the rough surface; Laheran recognized it as dried blood. He couldn't make out most of the writing, although he suspected it was in that Englits that Karl Cullinane and his friends were turning into a common trade language throughout the Eren regions and beyond.

But below the scratchings that he couldn't decipher, there were the words he could:

The warrior lives, they said. Beneath were three crude drawings: a sword, an ax, and a knife—a threat that Cullinane would kill them with whatever was handy.

It was the third such piece of leather Laheran had seen. The first he himself had brought back from Melawei; it had been pinned to the corpse of a brother slaver, a man who had been split with an ax from his brow almost to his waist.

The second had been discovered in Ehvenor, tied to the hilt of a sword that had been struck through three bodies; the killers had either discovered the slavers in a dark alley or drawn them into it, leaving them behind dead, dead, and dead.

This third one had been found in Lundeyll, in a rented room at an inn there, again pinned to the corpse of a slaver, this time by a knife that projected from the dead man's open mouth like a bloodied metal tongue. Nimyn was his name; Laheran knew him slightly. He was a journeyman on a routine trading mission, traveling down the coast toward Ehvenor with a string of a dozen well-tamed male slaves, most of whom were born into servitude. There were two other slavers with Nimyn, but they were left alone.

The guildmaster finally put it as a question. "Will you find him? Stop him?"

"Yes," Laheran said, stooping to pick a rose, twisting the stem loose from the bush with deft fingers that managed to avoid the thorns. He fixed it to the collar of his cloak with a long silver pin.

He wished he had a mirror with him; he was pleased with the way he looked. He knew what he would have seen: a tall, slim, elegant young man in blue and gray, his hair the color of autumn flax, his short, neatly trimmed beard only a few shades darker. A light, crimson cloak—more of a cape, really—fastened with a braided silver rope, hung elegantly from his right shoulder, the cut of his tunic and mid-calf breeches more elegant, more careful than was usual among guildsmen.

He rested his palm for a moment on the hilt of his sword, striking a pose. He knew he looked somewhat younger than his twenty-five years, and knew that his age and his foppishness tempted others to either underrate or overrate him. That suited him.

"I believe that I will," he said finally. "What resources do I have?"

"Come with me," the guildmaster said.

The two of them passed into the dark cool of the marble halls.

The walls were spotless and the floors only barely dirtied by the day's traffic, but there was a strange smell in the halls—beyond the usual stink of human sweat, of pain and fear—that never could be scrubbed out of the tiles. Whip a slave to death—although with the economics of slavery these days, that was the luxury of a bygone era—and he would leave his smell not only on the rough stone walls where you chained him, but throughout the rest of the hall.

But there was something else. As the two slavers passed by an open door, the scribes working at their desks in the room looked up, a quick flash of panic passing across their faces.

This was Slavers' Guildhall; there should have been no trace of fear on the face of a guildsman.

But there was: the place also stank of slaver's fear.

It somehow smelled different than the fear of a slave.

They all feared that Karl Cullinane would come for them, and not just outside, somewhere in the field. That would have been different. That was frightening, but acceptable. You had to learn to look over your shoulder when you were away. Raiding or trading, you had to sleep lightly, listening for the quiet patter of unshod feet on deck, the muffled whisper of a sword leaving its scabbard, the snick of a cocked hammer.

No, it wasn't only an assault in the field they feared now, but one in the guildhall itself.

Laheran followed Yryn upstairs into the master's meeting room, where ten men sat around the wide oak table.

None of them were master slavers, but they were all reliable journeymen, most of them well scarred: tough and blooded, men who made their business as raiders and tamers, not just as sellers.

The guildmaster introduced him around the table; Laheran exchanged guild grips with each man in turn. And each man in turn gripped Laheran's hand just a bit too hard, as though grabbing for reassurance, not simply confirming Laheran's guild membership, or returning his courtesy.

"I can have a hundred more men for you in two tendays," the guildmaster said.

Laheran shook his head. "No. The guild has tried that before. A small group this time, with a small, fast ship. We'll go quietly from Pandathaway, not loudly announcing who we are. We take his trail, find him, and kill him." There was no great rush. If it was possible to catch Cullinane—and it had to be possible to catch Cullinane—then Cullinane was headed north.

Possibly by way of Pandathaway and the guildhall? No, that was unlikely. There were too many defenses, both physical and magical, at Slavers' Guildhall. Cullinane wouldn't be able to get in here.

But, conceivably, he would stop off in Pandathaway and kill a slaver or two, hunt them down outside the guildhall. And that could work to Laheran's advantage: the larger the monster, the larger the reward for killing it.

Laheran eyed them all levelly. "We will find Karl Cullinane, and we will kill him."

The warrior lives, indeed. Perhaps Laheran was younger than all previous guildmasters, but perhaps that wouldn't matter if Laheran killed Karl Cullinane.

He smiled at Guildmaster Yryn.

"Leave it all in my hands," he said.

PART ONE
Holtun-Bieme

CHAPTER 1

It ain't over till it's over—and maybe not then, either.
—Walter Slovotsky

Wearing only a faded pair of Home denim jeans, Jason Cullinane bent over the washbowl beneath the mirror, scrubbing gingerly at his face. The early morning water was even icier than it should have been.

As he dried his face on a fresh-smelling towel—royalty hath its privileges, it occurred to him for not the first time—he felt at his chin. It was a bit stubbly, although he had shaved the day before. He tossed the towel aside and reached for the bone handle of the straight razor sitting on the sideboard, but as he eyed himself in the mottled mirror he decided that the faint stubbling made him look older. He let his fingers drop to his side.

A distant laugh sounded in his head.

Take on a few responsibilities and your beard starts growing, eh?

He didn't smile.

Your father would have laughed at that.

"Perhaps he would have." But he wasn't his father. He looked into the mirror. Through the mottled glass—Empire glassmaking wasn't even up to Home standards, and Home standards weren't high to begin with—under a shock of dark brown hair, two dark brown eyes looked back at him. Just the other day, U'len had told him that he was looking more and more like the Emperor. In particular, there was something about his eyes, she said.

I can't see it, he thought. They were just brown. He shook his head as he stared at himself in the mirror. He couldn't see it at all. He wasn't the giant that Karl Cullinane had been; Jason's jaw didn't even seem to have the firm resolve that his father's had had; there wasn't that I-can-handle-anything-that-comes-along look.

He shrugged. Maybe he didn't look so different, but everything else did. Things seemed so changed since his return to Biemestren. His room on the third floor of the residence tower felt smaller. Hell, even the castle seemed to have shrunk in his absence, although he couldn't quite figure out how or where.

His fingers reached up to his neck, the familiar feel of the leather thong and the small crystal amulet comforting. It wasn't that it prevented him from being magically located; he didn't have to hide in Biemestren, and if trouble came looking for Jason here, it would have the House Guard to deal with. The comfort came from its familiarity. The leather and crystal hadn't changed.

They're waiting for you. Hurry down.

Give me a second.

He took a fresh soft cotton tunic from where Elarrah had laid it out on top of his bureau late the night before and pulled it over his head, then padded barefoot across the rug to where he'd left his boots by the door. He considered the rising scratch marks in the age-darkened oak of the door jamb, from the cluster of six or so that were about chest-high, to the one that was on the same level as his eye, and the two close together a bit above.

He turned about and worked his heels closer to the wall, then set his hand on top of his head, resting his fingers against the door-jamb, before turning about to see that there indeed was a difference; his fingers were a good half-inch above the previous high mark.

He reached down to his belt, drew his knife and marked the spot.

Jason at seventeen, although just barely. He drew himself up straighter.

Let's try for at least eighteen. You had better move it: breakfast is being held for you, and you've got a workout with Tennetty in an hour.

"A workout? Today?" He sat down and pulled his boots on. He was leaving for Home and Endell in a few days; if he wasn't good enough with pistol and swords by now, he surely wasn't going to be a lot better by then.

Nonsense. You grow a little each day, Jason; you'd better learn a little each day.

True enough. He was nowhere as good with a sword as his father had been—

—and that wasn't good enough, at least once. Remember. You've got to outthink problems; you can't count on outfighting them. Even if you were as good as Karl was, which you aren't.

Again, true enough.

He went downstairs.

Breakfast in the castle had been an informal, catch-as-catch-can thing in the old days, despite Mother's claim that breakfast was the most important meal of the day, and U'len's insistence that he sit and eat a full meal instead of bolting down a sketchy breakfast. U'len tended to take what Mother said, as Father used to put it, like it came out of a burning bush.

Whatever the hell that meant. Another question he'd never be able to ask his father.

But it wasn't the old days. Too much had changed since Jason's return to Biemestren with the news that Karl Cullinane was dead. Mother and Bren Adahan had tried to minimize things with ceremony, trying to hide in some sort of formal arrangement of their lives the fact that the core of it all was gone.

Dead.

The dining hall fell silent as Jason entered. He gave a brief bow to the two dozen people in the room, then quickly walked to the head of the table, seating himself in *his* chair as though he belonged there.

"Please, be seated, all," he said. Mother still wasn't down, but they could be comfortable while waiting.

Doria Perlstein was already sitting; she didn't take to court manners. From her chair halfway down the table, she smiled a good morning.

He returned her smile. Strange, though. He knew she was as old as Father and Mother, but when she'd shed her Hand persona, she'd also shed all of what the years had done to her body, but not quite all that they had done to her face: her eyes weren't those of a twentyish girl. They seemed much older.

"Morning, Jason," Tennetty said as she took her seat at his right. Turning her chair to let her single eye sweep the room, the skinny woman scanned the assemblage with reflexive suspicion before deciding there wasn't anybody to kill, not quite yet; she relaxed into her chair.

With a "Good morning," a smile and the clack of heels striking the floor, Jason's sister Aeia stalked across the room and dropped lightly into her own chair by the foot of the table, rubbing at her sleepy eyes, then gathering her long hair behind her head and tying it into an improvised ponytail. She was dressed in a pair of tight leather trousers and a loose, ruffled blouse that was almost impossibly white.

"Going riding this morning?" he asked.

She nodded as she reached for a roll, then dipped it in a honey tub and took a huge bite. "I'm going to get all the riding in I can here." Back Home, what with teaching at the local school, Aeia had little time for riding, something she had grown to like.

Tell her she'd better watch the eating, Jason thought. *I think she's starting to put on weight.*

No, you don't.

Ellegon must have relayed the exchange; she chuckled and turned to Bren Adahan, who had taken his usual seat by the foot of the table, next to her. "My little brother seems to think I'm getting old and fat. You willing to disagree with the Heir?"

Bren Adahan nodded slowly. "On this matter, I am."

"Fair enough, Bren—but sit over here. We've got some stuff to talk about before the council." Jason beckoned to him, and waved at a seat next to his own.

The Holtish baron's thin mouth twitched in irritation, but then Bren Adahan studiously blanked his face for a moment before displaying an easy smile that looked genuine enough. He nodded briskly, then leaned over to whisper a few words to Jason's adopted sister before taking the seat Jason had indicated. He stroked idly at a small cut at the point of his square jaw. Adahan had cut off his beard a tenday before, and had taken to shaving twice a day.

Jason tried to conceal the fact that he didn't like Adahan. Maybe it was that Bren Adahan was more than ten years older than Jason, and carried his extra age as though it conferred both wisdom and respect.

Not fair. He doesn't get enough time with Aeia as it is.

I have to talk to him about some things. We might as well get it all settled during breakfast, Jason thought back, knowing that he was lying to himself. That was all true, but it wasn't the reason. Jason didn't like the way Bren looked at his sister, like he wanted to—

*He *does* want to. Humans are like that. It's all perfectly natural, as Elarrah could have told you two nights ago. Your sister is more than ten years older than you are, and knows what she's doing. And she is going to let him, eventually, on her terms. So leave well enough alone.*

Jason reddened. *Elarrah?* The fact that the upstairs maid was sneaking into his bedroom at night was supposed to be secret. He didn't want it noised about.

Relax; I'm reasonably discreet. But it's silly to leave her alone just because I'm around. I have been reading your mind, such as it is, since before you were born. The next time you want some privacy, just ask me to tune you out. Like your father used to.

I don't want to talk about it.

There was a distant chuckle. He couldn't tell whether he heard it in his ears or his mind.

Bren Adahan reached out and touched Jason's arm. "Are you all right, Jason?"

"No." He shook his head to clear it. "I mean, yes. I'm fine; I was just talking to Ellegon."

Bren Adahan nodded, and looked down the table at the two empty chairs near the foot. One was Danagar's, who was freshly returned from his travels through Nyphien, trying to find out who was behind the Kernat slaughter. While Danagar had only negatives to report, his trip had been much longer and far more exacting than Karl Cullinane had planned for him; he looked to be shy about twenty pounds.

At Thomen Furnael's urging, Jason had installed Danagar in a room in the residence tower, with orders that he sleep late—

And fatten himself up.

Although there was something strange about Thomen of late. Jason was tempted to ask Ellegon to peep him, but . . .

But that's not right. Your father used to tell me not to peep family and friends, and I'm beginning to understand how right his instincts were, at least on that. Either brace Thomen and insist he discuss what's wrong with him, or wait until he brings it up.

Jason nodded. That could be put off for a while; for now, they had a problem in the other conspicuously empty chair: Mother's.

Bren caught his stare. "It's getting late. You really should send for her."

Jason shook his head. "No. We'll start without her." He raised his voice. "U'len, you can start serving breakfast."

Half waddling, the fat woman brought the first tray out herself, setting it down between Jason and Bren Adahan before lifting a huge stack of oatcakes onto Jason's plate, following that with a fist-sized cube of ham.

He held back a smile. "I can't eat that much," he said.

She waved a finger at him. "Eat it you will, either for breakfast or as your dinner. You're leaving tomorrow, and I'm not going to have you going out and getting yourself killed with only the remembrance of road food on your mind. When you get your stupid head blown off, it's not going to be because you were too hungry to think straight. It's *not* going to be my fault," she said. She picked up the honey tub and poured the thick honey on his oatcakes as if she were pouring water on a fire.

"Just go away and leave me alone," he grumbled.

"Shut up and eat."

He loved the peevish old woman—she'd been watching out for him for as long as he could remember—not that either of them would ever admit it out loud. U'len wouldn't like that.

"I leave when you start eating," she said, crossing her arms over her massive bosom. "So eat."

He picked up his fork and set to work.

Everybody else followed his example; the room was filled with the familiar clatter of plates and tableware, and the sounds of low voices talking between mouthfuls.

I'm starting to get a bit concerned about Mother. Relay, please: everybody's down for breakfast except you.

I don't want to. It's not fun being in her mind. . . . Oh, very well. The mental voice fell silent.

What is it?

I don't want to tell you.

"What *is* it?"

Tennetty kicked back from the table and had a flintlock pistol halfway out of her holster before Doria laid a gentle hand on her free arm, stopping her.

Everybody was looking at him.

Jason shrugged a *pro forma* apology. "Sorry. I was talking to

Ellegon." *Please.* Deep inside, he knew what the dragon was going to say.

She's not in her room. She's in her workshop, bent over her bench, crying. Again. She won't answer me.

He started to push himself away from the table, but noticed that, once again, all the eyes were on him.

There was a long silence until Bren Adahan turned to him. "Please forgive me; I should have mentioned that I spoke to your mother late last evening; she said that she was going to be involved in some sort of work last night, and would probably sleep through breakfast, or get up early and go to her workshop."

He says, "That's the lie you should have told. Now attend to your responsibilities. We have an agreement on that score, Jason Cullinane."

"So we do," he whispered.

So keep it.

"In that case," Jason Cullinane said, "everybody please be seated, and let us finish our meal."

Unembarrassed, Tennetty seated her pistol firmly in its holster and herself in her chair, then picked up a bacon roll and began to eat as though nothing had happened.

Jason was grateful. He had to try to hold things together, but sometimes he wasn't sure that he could, even for the little things: they ate in silence, the hall empty of Karl Cullinane's booming voice.

CHAPTER 2
Andrea Cullinane

Walk wide o' the Widow at Windsor,
For half of creation she owns:
We have bought 'er the same with the sword an' the flame,
An' we've salted it down with our bones.
(Poor beggars—it's blue with our bones!)
Hands off o' the sons o' the Widow,
Hands off o' the goods in 'er shop,
For the Kings must come down an' the Emperors frown
When the Widow at Windsor says "Stop!"
(Poor beggars!—we're sent to say Stop!)
>   —Rudyard Kipling

One of the differences between Karl and me—and it's a
major one—is that I'm far too considerate to ever leave my
wife a widow. Guess I'll just have to live forever.
>   —Walter Slovotsky

Squinting in the bright morning sunlight, Jason Cullinane walked past the salutes of the two guards and out into the day. It was a pretty day, the sky above was—

Huh?

He turned. "Kethol? Durine?" What were they doing on guard duty?

Bringing his flintlock carbine back up to port, redheaded Kethol split his weatherbeaten face in a grin. "Good morning, sir."

Tossing his head to clear a shock of hair from his eyes, massive Durine nodded a good morning, bringing one huge paw up to scratch at where his rough grown beard really didn't end, and his bull neck really didn't begin. The man was built like a bear.

"Morning, sir," Durine echoed.

"What are the two of you doing on front door duty?"

Kethol shrugged. "Got into a bit of trouble last night with the general." A tall, rawboned man, he gripped his rifle with knuckles like walnuts.

"Doing what?"

"It was mainly my fault, sir." It was Durine's turn to shrug. "I had too much beer last night. Got into a little barracks fight."

Jason looked them over more carefully. There was a nasty bruise over Kethol's left eye, and the knuckles on Durine's left hand were almost raw.

"Over what?"

Durine shrugged again.

"One of the whores in town," Kethol said. "Pirojil's taken a fancy to her. Loryal's been bothering him about it."

"Loryal?"

"One of the new troops, from Tyrnael. Him and his three brothers joined up just before the Emperor and us took off for Ehvenor. When Piro punched Loryal, two of the brothers jumped him, then Loryal and another brother jumped *me* when I tried to come between them and settle things down." He broke into a toothy smile. "'Course, I was calling them poxy sons of a motherless cur while I was trying to calm them down. All Durine did was pull two of them off, while Piro and I settled things, two-on-two."

"Injuries?"

"Just a few." Durine shrugged, again. "Pirojil lost two teeth, and the Spider says some of Piro's ribs are cracked. He took a nasty bite in the ear; Loryal beat him kind of bad. Kethol's dance-partner is lucky the cleric got to him pretty quick, or he'd be singing lead tenor. My two got their heads cracked, just a little. All resting in the infirmary. The Spider put Piro's teeth back together, but left the rest. They all start their punishment tours when they're up and about."

Jason nodded. Valeran had given him long lectures about barracks discipline. What Garavar had done was sound economics, and even sounder discipline: use the minimum magic necessary to heal the combatants beyond danger or permanent damage, but let them ache for a while—the more, the better.

But to every rule there were exceptions. Durine, Kethol and Pirojil had been his father's companions on his last ride to Ehvenor. "I'll see Garavar—"

*As you *were*, Jason.* Ellegon's voice was firm. *Even when you're wearing the crown, you'd better have a better reason than that for overruling Garavar.*

He tried to cover the interruption with a cough, and wasn't at all sure he was successful. *But—*

But nothing. Now let's go see your mother.

"I'll see you later, then," Jason said, knowing that he hadn't covered his gaffe well.

Actually, you didn't cover it at all. They know you were going to meddle in Garavar's domain. But they probably won't say anything about it.

Jason left the path for the grass. It was shaping up to be a pretty day. A light, gentle wind blew in from the west, accompanied by only the fluffiest of clouds in the blue sky overhead.

The grass was up to his calves, trimmed that morning by sweeping scythes into a rippled sea of lush green. Jason breathed in the rich smell of the new-mown grass, enjoying it.

That was the thing about peace, *he* used to say; it gave people time and inclination to care about something as trifling as the height of grass on a lawn. There were limits to even an Emperor's powers; it was simple to forbid everybody except the caretakers to walk on the grass, but during wartime it was hard to find somebody to care for it.

He walked around to the side of the main residence tower, stepping from the softness of the lawn to the stones of the parade ground.

A huge, vaguely triangular head lifted from the warmth of the stones and stared at him.

"Morning, Ellegon," Jason said as he walked over to the massive beast. Father used to say that Ellegon was the size of a Greyhound bus, which Jason had never quite understood. Now, a bus was a kind of cart, but wasn't a greyhound a kind of dog, a small mastiff or something?

Ellegon was huge; Jason couldn't imagine a dog a twentieth that size.

Good morning, Jason, the dragon answered. With a deep

grunt, he got first his forelegs and then his rear legs underneath himself, then raised himself to his feet, his massive, leathery wings curling and uncurling almost spasmodically, while smoke and steam issued from nostrils the size of dinner plates.

The dragon's mouth sagged open to reveal rows and rows of teeth the length of a forearm . . . and an incredible miasma of dragon halitosis, painfully bad breath that reeked of decaying flesh and rotting fish. Ellegon wasn't fastidious about what he ate.

Jason gagged. "Turn your head away, *please.*"

Sorry. Scales creaking in the morning air, Ellegon turned his massive head away, clearing the air with a quick shot of flame.

It never really made sense to Jason, the way that others had to restrain a fear of Ellegon. It was like, well, like being afraid of Tennetty's swords. The universe was divided into two kinds of people, and only one kind was endangered by either.

They're not just afraid of being eaten. Humans don't like me because I know too much.

Way too much. It was one thing for Ellegon to save Jason from making a fool of himself in front of Kethol and Durine; it was another for the dragon to probe into . . . private matters.

I won't mention it again, the dragon said, although Jason could have sworn he heard a distant mental mumble: *Just like his father. Spends too much time thinking with what's between his legs rather than what's between his ears.*

"And you eat too much, too.—Let's go see her."

It was only a few hundred meters across the parade ground to the northwest corner—too short for Ellegon to bother with flying.

Jason walked quickly, the dragon lumbering along behind.

Normal humans like to steer well clear of working wizards; it's only prudent. Andrea Cullinane's workshop was far away from anything else within the walls of the castle. If it hadn't been for security considerations, everybody involved would have been more comfortable with putting it outside the inner curtain wall, or perhaps in Biemestren township itself.

But security considerations had been involved; Mother's Biemestren workshop had, as far back as Jason could remember, been in a low stone building in the northwest corner of the inner ward.

Jason knocked on the door. There was no answer. "Mother, it's me. Jason."

Nothing.

She's in there. Do you want me to try?

No. I'd better do this myself.

His hand trembled at the door latch.

One of the things he'd been taught early was not to interrupt Mother when she was working. It was one of the few lessons that involved switching; Mother hated hitting him almost as much as he hated it. She said that "don't disturb the wizard" was the This Side equivalent of "don't touch the driver," whatever that meant.

That was the trouble with dealing with the Other Siders, like his parents, and Walter Slovotsky, and Doria Perlstein—they kept talking in terms that nobody could understand. It wasn't just all this stuff about cars and planes and microwaves (and what *was* a microwave, anyway? Was it how an Other Side dwarf said goodbye?) it was that their frame of reference was, so often, so completely different from normal people's.

But while he couldn't understand the referent, the lesson had long since been driven home, and learned below the level of conscious decision. He *knew* that she wasn't really working anything dangerous: Ellegon would have warned him.

You got that right.

Still, his hand shook. Damning his traitor fingers for trembling, Jason lifted the latch and swung the heavy oak door slowly inward, slipped inside, and closed the door behind him.

"Mother?"

He sniffed involuntarily. The inside of the stone building was dark and dank, the thick air heavy with smells strange and familiar. There was a distant odor he couldn't quite place, although he could make out the rich, musky fragrance of marrhymh and the sharp tang of burning peppercorns. Mainly the smell reminded him of stale sweat.

The only light in the room oozed out of a crack at the junction of wall and ceiling; all that it revealed was the narrow entryway where Jason stood, and the dark hall beyond. Rows of black gauze curtains obscured everything beyond that.

"Mother?"

He pushed through a layer of curtains, and another, and then another. The curtains were dry to his fingers, but they seemed to cling wetly to his face; shuddering, he pushed inward.

"Mother?"

He could barely make out the light of a lamp through the last set of curtains. He pushed through to see the form of his mother, huddled over her workbench, making jerking, almost random jottings with her quill pen, while an oil lamp flickered above her. To her right, a crystal globe lay supported in the coils of a brass snake, its head impaled on the north pole, staring languidly at the world. At her left was a rough clay statue of a man standing with his arms crossed over his chest. Where his left hand lay on his arm there were only two full fingers; the other three were stumps.

The statue was still visibly wet; beyond it lay a clump of clay and a half dozen small knives, short sticks bearing wire loops, and other clayworking tools he couldn't readily identify.

"Mother," he said, "put it away."

She didn't answer, but continued to scribble.

"Mother," he said. "Put it away."

Nothing.

"I'm going to count to ten, and then take it away from you."

She shook her head, flinging stringy black hair back and forth. "No. I got closer last time. Maybe I can—"

The crystal glowed brighter.

"See!"

"That doesn't mean anything, not unless you can see *him*. Which you can't, because he's dead."

"You didn't see the body." The crystal grew yet brighter, and brighter still—

The light died, leaving the interior of the room lit only by the flicker of the oil lamp.

"No!" She pounded a fist on the table, then turned to face him.

He forced himself to repress a shudder. Her eyes were red, the lids swollen with tears and lack of sleep, and deep hollows had taken up residence in her cheeks.

"Mom. . . ." He took her hands in his, momentarily shocked at how feebly she pulled away. "Please. We—all of us—saw the explosion. Walter and Ahira stayed behind. He couldn't have survived the blast, but if he had survived the two of them would have brought him here by now."

Walter Slovotsky and the dwarf were still an open question. There wasn't any sign, not any word from them. While it would have been a bit soon for them to get themselves back to Holtun-Bieme, they should have reached Ehvenor by now, even if they were

traveling by Mel dugout; or gotten over the mountains, if they were
trying the overland route.

Where were they? That was the live issue. Father was dead.

"I'm still going to try. Until I can locate the body or until I
see him."

But he was blown to bits, he thought. He couldn't say it, not
to his mother, not to his father's widow. "Your spell isn't going
to recognize . . . what's left of him. Put it down, Mother, then go
change your clothes and wash up. We have council tonight, and
you're going to have to . . ." He let the words trail off.

You're going to have to look alive. That was what he meant, but
he couldn't bring himself to say it. Sometimes you have to live
on the silences.

"Mother . . . you know he's dead. There's one proof, beyond what
we all saw."

"Yes?" Her voice, usually a warm contralto, squeaked and cracked
at the edges.

"Father loved you. If he was still alive, there's nothing that'd
keep him away from you."

Her lower lip trembled. "He didn't even send a last message back
to me."

"He didn't need to; he told Tennetty that." Jason's eyes filled
with tears. "What could he have had us tell you? That he loved
you? Mother, didn't you *know* that?"

She turned away, and her shoulders shook silently.

Please. Jason is right. We have to carry on, Andrea. All of us.

Slowly, her crying stopped and her breathing slowed. She took
in a deep, ragged breath, then turned slowly, wiping her face on
her sleeve. "Just let me try a bit more. Please?"

"No. There are things to be done, and you've got to make
yourself . . ."

For a moment, her old smile peeked through. "Presentable? Less
like an old hag?" She shrugged. "Easy enough."

She pushed him back a few inches, and held her hands out in
front of her, muttering words that could only be heard and then
forgotten.

She changed.

The hollows in her tear-dampened cheeks dried and filled out,
the flesh growing firmer in front of his eyes. Her stringy hair
seemed to shed its oil, and gained body as she straightened

herself, her chest lifting, her body straightening, and just for a moment she was clear of eye and firm of step, the way she had always been.

"I *thought* that was what you've been doing." Doria Perlstein's calm voice cut through the dark; she pushed the curtains aside and stood next to Jason. "Send the seeming away."

For once, Doria didn't look younger than Mother did. She held herself like a much older woman—unbent by the years, but perhaps more weighted down with knowledge.

"Send it away, Andrea." Doria swallowed. "Or I will."

When Doria had shed her clerical persona, she'd lost the ability to gain more spells; all she had left—all she ever would have—were the few in her head. Exactly what they were and how many there were was a secret, but each was irreplaceable.

"Why does it matter?" Andrea's voice was rich and melodic, something out of Jason's childhood. "This will serve, as well as anything else, and better than most."

"Nonsense. It doesn't make you healthy. It just makes you *look* healthy, whether you are or not. That's all. It's like putting nitrites on salad—remember nitrites?"

"I don't miss nitrites. I used to be horribly allergic to them."

Doria returned her smile. "Even if you weren't, it was a bad idea to use them on food. They don't preserve the quality of it, just the color." She took Andrea's arm. "Send it away, now. You can take on a seeming, if you have to, to make yourself look worse; never cover up what's really happening to you. Jason, take her other arm."

He did, and it felt firm and supple in his hand, until his mother murmured a harsh word that melted in the air . . .

. . . and the arm seemed to shrink.

"You've been fooling yourself, and the rest of us." Doria *tsk*ed once. "You're just wasting away. We're going to build you up, okay?"

Andrea's grin was weak. "You know a lot about that?" Her voice creaked.

Doria's grin was strong. "I used to be a home ec major, remember? Training for my MRS, Walter used to say, when he wasn't accusing me of taking mommy lessons. Well, you need a mommy now. There is nothing really wrong with you—nothing that a lot of food, exercise, and rest can't help. You keep out of here, understood?"

"No." Andrea flared. "I've got to try, at least. I've got to locate him, if he's still alive, if he—"

Doria sighed, "He's dead, Andrea. Please try to accept it. Let's go get you some breakfast. Then we're going to see if I can walk you off your feet. Then some sleep, and then more food and exercise." Her smile returned. "Until you really do look as good as the seeming made you look."

"You're forgetting." Jason shook his head. "We've got a council tonight."

Doria glared at him. "You and Thomen are going to have to run it, then. Your mother has a date with a feather bed. Understood?"

I have two messages. One from your mother: "I'll make it down for the council; don't worry." She means it. The other's from Doria; she says: "Like hell she will. Act like you give a damn about somebody besides yourself." But she really only means it a little.

And what do you say?

I'm with Doria on this one. If you and Thomen can't handle things tonight, it's about time we found out, isn't it?

CHAPTER 3

Before the Council of Barons

Our swords shall play the orator for us.
—Christopher Marlowe

*I've always figured that talking beats fighting. And talking is
only about my third favorite thing.*
—Walter Slovotsky

Jason Cullinane sat alone in the great hall of Castle Biemestren,
looking at the place as if he had never seen it before.

In a sense, he hadn't. Not from this perspective. He'd had to
sit in Father's place at table—but there hadn't been any formal
dinners since Jason's return.

He walked over to the long oak table and sat in his own place,
his old place, to the left of Father's seat, then ran his fingers across
the dark surface that had been much battered from years of use,
and abuse. He rubbed his thumb across a slight depression, all that
remained of a little notch. He'd carved the notch in the table
himself, during one long, boring formal dinner, until Father noticed
what Jason was doing. Father, his huge hands gentle as always, had
taken the knife from Jason's hands and sighed in deep disappointment. Other fathers hit their sons, but Karl Cullinane had always
said that was wrong.

*A man whose profession is violence must never use violence on
his own,* he'd said.

Karl Cullinane had just sighed, and looked disappointed, and maybe older than he should have, and then dismissed everybody else from the hall. The two of them had gone down to the carpenter's shop to fetch a file, a sandcloth, brushes and varnish. He and Jason had smoothed out the notch, and then varnished over it, then cleaned and replaced the tools. All the while, Karl Cullinane had looked worn around the edges, a bit defeated.

Jason would have preferred it if Father had hit him.

Mikyn's father had hit Mikyn a lot.

At that, he shook his head. That was something still left undone. He'd have to face Mikyn and the rest of Daherrin's team. He could take that. Jason Cullinane might have run like a coward, but he'd hunted down and killed Ahrmin, just as his father had killed Ahrmin's father.

There was a lot left undone—like this damned Baronial Council.

I don't know how to run one of these things. I have to learn, I guess. But it wasn't right that he should have to learn on the job.

*That *is* dreadful. It's so incredibly unfair. I find it hard to think of a greater injustice in the history of the universe.*

Fire flared outside the far window; Jason walked over to it, pulled the shutters back and threw one hip over the sill. Below, Ellegon stood in the courtyard, his wings furling and unfurling; above, the night winked down, distant faerie lights pulsing in odd chords of color.

Jason forced a chuckle. "You wouldn't happen to be suggesting that I'm feeling a little sorry for myself, would you?"

Suggesting, no. Asserting, declaring, announcing, maintaining, stating, affirming and averring, yes. The dragon dipped its mouth to take a man-sized bite out of what was left of an ox.

"I guess that's what we keep you around for. It isn't because we've got a lot of cattle we need eaten."

There was a vague draconic chuckle, but then Ellegon's mental voice sobered. *I'll be back shortly; I'd best do my evening patrol before this council starts.*

He'd been alone for only a few moments when he heard a sound behind him.

He turned to see Thomen Furnael walking across the blood-red carpet toward him, his eyes missing nothing. He was about Jason's height, but his extra five years had filled him out: his chest and shoulder muscles were corded from frequent workouts. A trim black beard was full on his face, although it, like his short-cropped black hair, was speckled with silver. Furnael men turned gray young.

As usual, Thomen Furnael was dressed elegantly, befitting his status as baron and regent. His scarlet tunic was cut loose across the shoulders and tight at the waist. Trimmed with black leather along the seams and hem, it was laced up the front with a snaking of silver chain. A short black cape hung elegantly over his left shoulder, half-concealing his left arm. His black trousers were buttoned up the front with nacrestones; his square-toed boots were of finely tooled black leather.

Incongruously, it was a broad, plain weapons belt that held his tunic tightly around his hips, a cord-handled smallsword sheathed on the left side, rigged to stay within easy cross-belly reach of his right hand; an unadorned flintlock pistol stuck butt-first out of a plain holster on his right side.

"Jason, what are you doing here?"

"Just waiting. Figured I'd get here first."

Thomen shook his head. "No, you get here *last*. You make everybody sit around waiting for you, until it's time to make your entrance. Then you make them stand up while you walk in slowly and take your seat." He chuckled. "Helps to remind them who's in charge."

"And who *is* in charge?"

"You are. Or will be, if you keep reminding them of that." He pointed down, at one of the woven grass runners that protected the rug. "Ignore those, too—let everybody else stay off the rug."

Jason had never known Thomen's father, but Father had always spoken highly of him, and of Rahff, and once had declared that the three Furnael men he'd known were a counterargument to Tom Paine's claim that the trouble with hereditary aristocracy was that virtue wasn't hereditary.

"You're sure?" Jason said.

"Now, don't go Cullinane on me. Trust me. Or, if you don't, get yourself another regent, send me back to my courtroom—better, to my barony." His tone was light, but there was a serious undercurrent. Thomen's mouth twisted. "No, I don't really mean that. Right now, there's nobody else really competent to take over. Everybody's got his private agenda, except maybe Bren and Garavar, and old Gar figures that the best way to handle any threat is with volleyed fire. Bren wouldn't be bad, but the rest of the Biemish barons wouldn't stand for a Holtish regent."

"You would?"

Thomen nodded. "If it was Bren, yes. He admired your father almost as much as I did—as I do." He beckoned to Jason. "Come on. Let's get out of here before they start wandering in. We've a bit of time to kill; what do you feel like doing?"

"I want to talk about whatever it is that's been bothering you for the past few days."

What could it be? Mother had been distant ever since Jason returned from Melawei, and the return of Danagar was cause for relief, not concern. But the duties of regent seemed to be weighing unusually hard on Thomen's shoulders.

"Well, there is a problem." Thomen Furnael bit his lip. "Can I think about it a while longer? It's . . . a bit complicated, and I want to work out how to handle it."

Jason shrugged. "Fair enough. Tomorrow?"

"Sooner, maybe. It'll come up at the council."

"Shouldn't we talk about it before?"

"Not really." Thomen shook his head. "Now: what do you want to do until then?"

Jason smiled. Maybe he couldn't figure out the politics as well as Thomen could, but there was one thing he could do better, usually. "Two-swords. Best three points of five?"

Thomen Furnael nodded. "Might be a good idea to work off a bit of that energy that you always have too much of."

"Father used to say that when you're speaking English, you're not supposed to end a sentence with a preposition."

"Walter Slovotsky always used to say something like, 'Okay, let's work off a bit of that energy that you always have too much of, asshole.' "

They got the engineer on duty to open the armory, and while Thomen stripped off his tunic and boots and pulled out the practice swords and masks, Jason took a taper and went around the room, lighting lamp after lamp after lamp, until the low-ceilinged stone room was passably illuminated by the flickering yellow light. Hopping first on one foot and then the other, he pulled off his boots, tossed them aside, then accepted a steel mesh mask and two weapons from Thomen. The mask was basically a mesh bucket suspended from the headband inside. The first weapon was a very stiff foil, its tip protected by a welded-on cap twice the size of Jason's thumbnail; the second was a short wooden stick, about the length of his forearm, a substitute for the dagger that was the secondary weapon when fighting two-swords style.

Setting his weapons down so that he could hang his tunic on a peg on the wall, Jason worked his shoulders, trying to loosen them. He set the mask on his head, then picked up the weapons and tried a few practice lunges, still feeling the strain in his thighs from his earlier workout with Tennetty. But that was something old Valeran had taught Jason: the lessons that counted most were the ones that you got when you pushed yourself hard.

Thomen slipped on his mask, then quickly saluted and took up a fighting stance, his foil held out in his right hand, his practice dagger carried low in his left, by his side. "Start off with foil touches on saber targets, then switch to saber rules?"

"Sure. Saber rules always with the dagger, though."

"Of course."

Jason took a slow breath, let it out slowly, then repeated the process twice. It helped to settle the mind.

He was ready. Saluting, Jason took up the same stance that Thomen had been holding, then moved in slowly, first holding his place, stepping back as Thomen whistled the tip of his foil through the air and lunged in a classic high-line attack.

Jason brought his foil quickly across from left to right, steel ringing on steel as he brushed Thomen's foil aside; while the baron tried to retreat, Jason riposted, lightly touching Thomen on the chest.

"My point," Jason said. "One to nothing. Bad habit, Thomen; break out of it before it breaks you."

"What do you mean?" Thomen said, parrying, then retreating when Jason tried a lunging, low-line attack. The foils clashed, and when they broke Thomen scored a solid touch on Jason's right arm.

"One-one," Jason said. "And you know full well what I mean: you always make the first attack real simple, and let your opponent get in the first point while you're seeing how quickly he can move."

"You don't like that, eh?"

"Valeran would have bladed you for it. It's—"

Jason lunged, but Thomen riposted easily, stopping Jason's cutover as Jason pulled back.

"—a game technique. You don't want to get pinked in a real fight just to see if the other man's any good."

"But this is just a game." Thomen smiled. "I don't have to fight for real; I'm a member of the effete ruling class, remember? All I have to do is look pretty sitting on a judge's bench or a baron's throne. Or I can—"

They engaged again; this time Jason tried a quick cutover, and it was Thomen's turn to parry and riposte. Jason brought his left hand up to parry that, but Thomen disengaged, retreated two steps, then lunged again.

Jason could barely keep up as the foils whistled through the air.

Parry high, bind, riposte, then stop-thrust, never forgetting that the left hand carried a knife, too.

Thomen's high-line marching attack met Jason's lunge. Each tried for a parry, but their momentum was too great. As they came together, Jason kicked out at Thomen's knee—but it wasn't there. He was off balance for only a moment, but that was long enough for Thomen to score two quick touches on his chest.

"Only counts as one. Two-one. Saber rules?" Thomen asked.

"Sure." Jason beat Thomen's blade aside, hard, and flipped his sword at Thomen's head, but Thomen retreated a step, catching the foible of Jason's weapon with his forte, loosening Jason's grip as he beat Jason's sword completely aside and leaving him exposed from face to ankles, without enough time to bring up his dagger.

Thomen slashed once, a stinging blow that would have opened Jason from left shoulder to the waist, then stepped back and saluted. "Three to one. Mine."

Jason returned his salute. "Another best of three?"

Thomen shook his head as he walked to the washbasin in the corner. "No. By the time we sluice ourselves off and dress, they should all be waiting upstairs."

He was trying to hold it in, but Thomen Furnael was indecently pleased with himself. Jason could practically read his mind: Maybe the father had once kicked Thomen in the balls, but damned if he couldn't out-fence the son.

Jason would have felt pleased with himself, too, if only he'd deliberately let Thomen win.

Damn it, Thomen was *good*.

CHAPTER 4
The Council of Barons

*The fundamental purpose of the Baronial Council is to force
the Biemish barons to put themselves under my sword;
whether they walk out with or without their heads is up to
me, and depends on their behavior.*

*The Holts are a different case. They haven't been called in
for Council, yet, not because they don't "deserve" it or some
such nonsense, but because they're already under Imperial
control. Hell, the Holtish barons' military governors can
hang them first, and explain it to me later.*

*As we start to return Holtun to civilian rule, though, the
Holtish barons will have to attend council, too. It'll just
about double the council size. Which will at least quadruple
the amount of time spent in meetings.*

*I wish I knew British history better. Is this the way Parlia-
ment started?*

—Karl Cullinane

*Guy I used to know once said, "That government isn't best
which governs least—it's the best government that needs to
govern least." I'd swipe it as one of Slovotsky's Laws, but it's
just a bit too serious, and maybe a smidgen too true.*

—Walter Slovotsky

Jason stood outside the great hall, waiting, until he decided he'd
had enough of waiting.

At the door he stopped next to the ceremonial guard—a short, loud-voiced corporal named Nartham—wondering how he was going to be announced, realizing that he'd forgotten to arrange it. Nartham had presented Thomen with a loud "Thomen, Baron Furnael, the regent"—Thomen was here as both regent and noble, not as a judge—but what was right for Jason?

He rapped the butt of his halberd on stone three times to get everyone's attention. "Ladies and gentlemen, the Heir."

Jason walked across the carpet, trying to make it look slow and graceful, feeling more awkward than he'd ever felt before. Thomen had primed him for the council, but it just didn't feel right.

He paused for a moment at the foot of the table. Mother's chair. Standing next to it, Doria gave him a slight nod, then put her hands together and tilted her head, miming sleep.

Good. Aeia's eyes twinkled as she stood by her chair, her back just a bit too ramrod-straight, as though to say, *I used to change your diapers, Jason: I'm not about to take you seriously as a ruler.*

"Good evening," he said, keeping his voice level, as he took his seat—*his* seat!—at the head of the table. "Be seated, all. We have a full agenda."

The Biemish barons, each with a single adviser, seated themselves along the left side of the table, while Holtish barons, each save one with the military governor of his barony, took seats on the right.

Vilmar, Baron Nerahan, was conspicuously alone, as though to remind everyone present that his was the single Holtish barony released from direct Imperial government. The trim, compact man settled stiffly into his chair, then smoothed the pleated front of his immaculate white tunic before folding his hands genteelly in his lap and turning a vaguely interested but generally blank expression on the world, the eyes under the heavy brows missing nothing.

Still standing was Tennetty, who moved back and leaned against the near wall. Clad as usual in a mannish leather tunic and worn leggings, she hitched at her combo belt as though to remind everyone present that she was carrying a blooded saber, a Nehera-made bowie and two loaded pistols, instead of a formal smallsword.

Thomen leaned over and whispered in his ear. "I asked the dragon to be around in time for this, but he isn't back, yet. We'd best handle the simple items first. But you'll have to start with the matter of your mother." Thomen beckoned to the court secretary, a burly engineer who looked incongruous sitting at the writing desk next to the long table of the great hall. The red-bearded man looked like he'd be much happier taking a shift in the gunworks.

Thomen gave a slight nod.

"Very well," Jason said, rising. Thomen had been explicit: he must start on his feet. Tower over them, dominate the meeting, make it clear that he was in charge. Even if he wasn't. Particularly if he wasn't.

"Welcome, all, to the council. There's much to discuss tonight, so I'll skip any long speech about how much we all miss my late father, and let us get down to work. First item: the absence of my mother. She's been working far too hard lately, and has been ordered to rest herself for the next few days, until I leave."

There was a quiet rush of muttering at that.

Thomen spoke up. "We know that you'll all wish to pay your respects in person to the empress, so I've arranged for your quartering for the next few days."

Bren Adahan shook his head. "Maybe the rest can stay, but Ranella and I ought to get back to Adahan, by way of Furnael and Little Pittsburgh. Production's slipping, and we've got to find out what's behind it—from the reports, it sounds like there's supply problems in Adahan, but—"

An emperor, even an emperor-to-be, has to be obeyed. "Ranella can handle it. You'll do as you're told," Jason said.

The room was suddenly cold. Bren Adahan had spoken casually; he hadn't been ready for Jason to bite his head off.

"Your pardon, sire," Bren Adahan said. "You are quite correct; I shall do precisely as I am told. It was a figure of speech; I meant to inform you and the regent that there are urgent matters requiring attention in both my barony and in barony Furnael, and to suggest that Governor Ranella and I ought to handle them." He inclined his head perhaps a mite too deeply, then straightened, his expression stony.

Thomen momentarily rolled his eyes heavenward, while the others around the table stirred.

Flame flared in the windows.

Good evening, all, Ellegon said, announcing himself as he thumped to the ground in the courtyard outside. Leathery wings flapped in the breeze as the dragon settled himself in.

And good evening to you, Ellegon said, his mental voice taking on the timbre that told Jason the dragon was talking to him alone, *shit-for-brains. Looks like I got here too late.*

What are you talking about? And what kept you?

Nothing important. I just picked up a small party traveling later than seemed sensible, so I had to duck behind the next hill and wait until they pulled around the bend close enough that I could read them. They were clean.

The dragon's caution made sense. Ever since Ellegon had been shot during the Holtun-Bieme War, Ellegon had been careful of approaching humans. Much better for Ellegon to have some cover between himself and some unknowns than to try to fly low enough to deeply read them, and risk being taken by an assassin's dragonbane-tipped crossbow bolt.

Everybody was looking at Jason, waiting.

"Well," he said, "where were we?"

You're about to apologize to Bren Adahan. That's where we are. Now, Jason.

But—

Don't argue, just repeat after me: My apologies, Baron Adahan...

"My apologies, Baron Adahan—"

* ... you'll have to excuse me ...*

" ... you'll have to excuse me ..."

* ... but as you all know, I'm new to this ruling business, and I'm afraid it's set my temper a bit on edge—and you'd damn well better smile ingratiatingly here, asshole.*

"I'm ... really new to this ruling business, and I think it must have set my temper on edge."

He tried to smile ingratiatingly, but wasn't sure if it came off. Jason Cullinane couldn't ever remember trying to smile ingratiatingly before. He was one of the people others smiled ingratiatingly *at*.

It had worked, he decided, when Bren Adahan sat back in his chair, clearly mollified.

No, it didn't. What worked is that I just relayed privately, on your behalf: "Sorry I'm such a jerk; I'll apologize later—would you and Aeia meet me for a drink after the council?"

"The next item," Thomen said, "is the matter of the Heir's planned absence."

"If I may?" Ariken, the white-haired baron from Krathael, leaned forward, and continued at Thomen's consenting nod. "You have brought up an . . . important matter. This . . . leaving of yours we have been hearing about . . ." he said, in voice creaking with age. "I . . . respectfully, yes, always respectfully . . . counsel against it, and ask why you seem to find it necessary to leave at such a . . . difficult time. Until you've assumed the crown—and your full duties—it would seem, almost, perhaps irresponsible to leave the Empire, even for a short . . . period of time." He sat back hard in his chair, panting, his lined face ashen. "And it . . . does me good to see you, from time to time."

Isn't there anything that can be done for him?

Have you a cure for old age? There was nothing that could be done, either for the baron or the situation. Barony Krathael had been overrun by the Holts during the Holtun-Bieme war; the baron was fiercely devoted to Karl Cullinane, his rescuer, and to his heir. As long as he could run the barony adequately, it would both be and seem an act of rank ingratitude to force him to abdicate in favor of his son.

Arrifezh, the rapier-slim baron from Arondael, shook his head. "If he is going to spend time away, best to do so now. At least . . ."

"At least he isn't abandoning the Empire like his father did? Is that your charge, Baron Arondael?" Baron Nerahan put in. He was a cruel-looking man, his two shifty brown eyes staring out at the world from under heavy brows. His sharp nose and bristly mustache always reminded Jason of a rat's whiskers. During the Holtun-Bieme war, he had been directly responsible for incredible cruelties.

But since then, as your father used to say, he's been a Boy Scout. And while he's still trying to rout Arondael, he's trying to do it as your follower, so you'd best treat him kindly.

"Is that your charge?" Nerahan repeated. "Do you claim that the Emperor abandoned us?"

"It's *my* charge, if no one else has the nerve. *Yes!*" Tyrnael slammed his hand down on the table, dismissing Tennetty with a snort when she let her hand drop to the butt of a pistol. His chin set stubbornly, Listar Tyrnael tossed his head, clearing his unruly black hair from his eyes. "He abandoned us. His responsibilities were here, with us. He was the Emperor."

"Baron," Thomen said, his voice cutting through the murmurs. He pursed his lips, then drummed his fingers on the timeworn surface of the table. "It was his decision, not yours, and not mine. He paid in full for his decision, and did his best to see that we don't have to. Let it be."

Tyrnael wasn't inclined to let matters rest there. "There's a lesson in this, and I—"

"Baron, please." Bren Adahan spoke up. "He's right. For the sake of the realm, let it be."

At Nerahan's nod, Arondael's brow wrinkled.

"And," Thomen Furnael went on, "as to the Heir traveling to Home now, I do have a bit of news that might affect your views on that. But there are some matters to discuss first."

Tyrnael, still visibly bothered, subsided.

Kevalun, the military governor of Irulahan, sat forward at that. Perhaps he'd caught something in Thomen's manner. "News, Baron?" he asked, perhaps a touch urgently. It would have been easy to think of young-looking Kevalun as almost a contemporary, Jason reminded himself, but the general was into his fifties. In fact, Kevalun had a son in his thirties, and a daughter of about sixteen—a rather attractive daughter of about sixteen.

Just keep it in your pants and listen up.

"News, General. In good time, we'll get to it. Before we discuss the Home issues, and the matter of the Heir's trip," Thomen went on, "we have several items to go over on the agenda. Let's get to it."

The first item was the progress of the removal of Imperial troops from barony Nerahan, and the return of the barony to civilian rule. Predictably, the transfer of power was proceeding too slowly to suit the Nerahans and the Holts, and was both proceeding too quickly and was too abrupt to suit most of the Biemish.

After that, matters turned to appropriations: Ranella and Bren Adahan argued forcefully for increased development in the Little Pittsburgh steel facilities, while Thomen formally recused himself, on grounds of conflict of interest: the plant, although near the Adahan border, was in Furnael.

The consensus, surprisingly enough, was to spend the required money.

Not really surprising. Thomen's had bowies, made from samples of the new batch of steel, sent to each of the barons. It's good stuff, almost the quality of Home wootz. The promise of an endless supply of it, cheap, is worth some investment.

That led to the question of the railroad. While the barons had been almost unanimous in their approval of increased spending on the steel plant, they were—with the sole exceptions of Thomen and Bren Adahan—completely united in their opposition to any excessive spending on what Terumel, Baron Derahan, referred to as "this dubious Engineer magic."

Ranella looked over at Jason. She was a thick, plain woman, whose hands were always nicked and stained from some set of experiments that hadn't gone quite as planned.

She wants your support on this. Thomen thinks she's right, but he says that the barons aren't going to go for it.

Jason stood. "I'm very much in favor of a railroad," he said. "Just as the roads hold Holtun and Bieme together and link the two, a railroad can do more."

"Yes, yes, yes," Arbert, Baron Irulahan said, dismissing the obvious with a wave. "But this will involve huge revenues—tens of thousands of marks, just to start. When do we see the return on such an investment?"

General Garavar had sat silent so far; at this he stirred. "Immediately, if we build it correctly." He beckoned to his aide, who produced a map. "I've been giving this long and careful thought," he said as he spread the chart out on the table. It was a simple map of Holtun and Bieme and the surrounding countries. "Ranella wants to put the first line here, to link Biemestren and Little Pit-sa-burg," he went on, stumbling over the still-awkward English words. "There's much sense in that, surely; Biemestren is the capital. But I say we run it here, from Biemestren into barony Tyrnael, terminating here, at Kernat village."

Kernat village. The room fell silent. The matter of the Kernat village slaughter was not at all closed, despite Danagar's failure to fix the blame. Was it an attempt by the Slavers' Guild to provoke another war in the Middle Lands? Or was it a probe by Prince Pugeer of Nyphien, an attempt to see just how hard he could push the Empire before it pushed back?

"And the payoff?" Tyrnael raised an eyebrow.

"It's now a four day ride from Biemestren to Kernat village—perhaps three days, if I push the men. They'll arrive tired, their horses tired, their fighting ability limited until they've had at least a good day's rest. If we had a railroad it would be a one-day trip, and the men and horses would arrive rested, ready to fight.

"Put the railroad here, and I can put the entire Home Guard, plus cannons, into Tyrnael, ready to strike into Nyphien or repel a strike, within a day." He paused to let that sink in. "Put spurs out, spanning the country, and not only can we trade with ourselves easier, faster, not only can we move steel and grain from one end of the Empire to the other, but we can move soldiers more quickly."

"It's still an . . . awful lot of money," Baron Krathael said. "There's land to be cleared, some of it in my barony. How will I be compensated for that?"

The conversation degenerated into a discussion of right-of-way. There had long been precedent for the throne, both in Holtun and in Bieme, declaring a right-of-way for the purpose of building military roads. The owner of the land was always to be compensated, but there was no clear precedent as to how much would be paid.

Karl Cullinane probably would have said something like, *Precedent be damned—we'll figure out a reasonable way to handle it and then implement it.*

Ranella looked over at Jason. "If I may? A compromise: could I build just a demonstration line, run it from the castle out, say, half a day's ride? The local farmers could use it for bringing goods to market in Biemestren, and we could test its ability to move troops."

Jason knew that he should say something, but what could he say? Garavar and Ranella had made all the sound arguments; all that was left to Jason was pounding on the table, and that would have been silly.

Thomen took the initiative. "With the consent of the Heir, Engineer Ranella is authorized to build a demonstration railroad."

Nod, please.

Jason nodded. "I consent, of course."

Thomen looked down at the paper in front of him. "Next matter: Baron Nerahan has applied to have his soldiers trained with, and armed with, rifles. Baron Nerahan."

Nerahan rose, and made an impassioned plea. Jason would have been impressed with his depth of feeling—if Ellegon hadn't told him that Nerahan had expected to have his request denied the first time around, and was merely laying the groundwork for a future, successful request. That surprised Jason—that somebody might plead so hard for something he didn't expect to get was a bit bewildering.

Arondael, unsurprisingly, led the Biemish assault against Nerahan's request; the other barons' opposition was more *pro forma* than anything else. With one exception.

Thomen Furnael stood. "I'm speaking not as judge or regent now, but just as a member of this council." He paced the room as he spoke. "There are dangerous forces at work in the world. I'm not just speaking of the Nyphien problem, although we're going to have to face that soon enough, one way or another. I'm not just speaking of the rumors I've been hearing of late about strange things coming out of Faerie, either."

Strange things? I hadn't heard anything.

Thomen has better sources of news than you do. Well, that's not true: he has the same sources of news, but he listens somewhat more carefully to them. He works a lot harder than some people I could name.

Jason brushed the dig aside. *So, what's the news?*

Not much, not really. But there have been some bizarre killings around Ehvenor. The information isn't reliable, but there's talk of finding only the front halves of a string of six horses, the rear halves having been cleanly bitten off, and of finding dead humans, and of parts of dead humans, and of beasts that fly away like dragons, or other large creatures that run away, creatures that can't be seen when you look directly at them. The dragon gave a mental shrug. *How much weight should be given to all of this is a good question. Rumors are completely false some of the time and largely false most often.*

Thomen was still speaking. "—and part of that plan is to return as much of Holtun as possible to baronial rule as soon as possible. I understand that many of us aren't minded to trust Baron Nerahan, but I invite you all to consider the effect of not trusting him, not trusting any Holtish barons."

Baron Tyrnael nodded. "Given that, I'd prefer that we start this with Adahan, not Nerahan." Bren Adahan smiled tightly. "Baron Adahan has demonstrated his loyalty to the crown, and his . . . associations with the family are well known."

Aeia smiled tightly. "And what associations might those be, Baron?" Her voice was deceptively light, but Jason knew she was seething inside.

Family trait: you Cullinanes don't like having your, err, affairs discussed in public.

Tyrnael smiled. "You two are always seen together, Lady. If you spurn his company, that would not be so. And if Baron Adahan has *not* asked you to marry him, then will I recommend to the Heir and regent that they take his barony away from him permanently, and give it to someone who is not a fool."

"I'm not a fool," Bren Adahan said with a grin.

"My point precisely."

That pacified Aeia, although not Bren Adahan. "I'd rather . . . not resume day-to-day control over Adahan, not yet. For one thing, military government gives us a good reason to keep enough Imperial troops garrisoned near Little Pittsburgh to protect it, if necessary. For another, I've much to learn from the Engineer, and can't study with him while I'm in Adahan. 'For sage advice, go where the sage is'—I intend to resume my studies at Home." He looked to Aeia for just a moment, then looked away.

She nodded. "Think of what an engineer-baron is going to mean to Holtun, in the long run."

A muscle twitched in Tyrnael's jaw. "I am."

"Very well," Thomen said with a nod that dismissed Tyrnael's comment as a concession. "Which brings up the next matter, and it's something that you may find as distressing as I do." He produced a piece of paper. "We've received, via a Home trader, a letter from Lou Riccetti. The Engineer is talking about selling guns and powder to Therranj."

CHAPTER 5

The Silver Crown

Wealth I ask not, hope nor love,
Nor a friend to know me;
All I ask, the heaven above
And the road below me.

—Robert Louis Stevenson

I'm a simple man. All I want is enough sleep for two normal
men, enough whiskey for three, and enough women for four.
—Walter Slovotsky

"Much of the letter is personal," Thomen said into the silence.
"But of the rest, part of it reads:

> Lady Dhara is here from Therranj, again wanting to dis-
> cuss, as she puts it, "the status of the Valley of Varnath." I'm
> not sure that's really important to them, not anymore, although
> she offered me a package deal under which we're granted title
> to and sovereignty over Home, plus a rather substantial amount
> of metals (including gold, silver, and mercury!) and gems—she
> brought a small chest full of industrial-grade diamonds with
> her, as a gift. Nice stuff.
>
> In any case, reports are that things are heating up between
> Therranj and Melrhood.

Our part of the package, though, would be some guns and powder, plus—preferably—the secret of making gunpowder.

Given Ranella's new wash, that might not be a bad idea, if the price is right. Eventually, how to do you-know-what is going to be worked out; but how to do the other kind of you-know-what is a lot trickier, particularly when you come to the problem that the Brits ran into when they switched over too soon.

Ranella frowned as Thomen read, opening her mouth as though to interrupt, then sitting back when Bren Adahan touched her arm and shook his head.

In any case, can you spare a couple of tendays and take the Dragon Express out so we can discuss this? I've put the elves off for now, but they don't like it much, and I don't like that they don't like it. I prefer to get along with my neighbors.

I also need Ellegon out here. We've got a security problem: there's five new probationers out here who he hasn't mindprobed yet, and either he's going to have to do that before long, or we're going to have to work out something with Thellaren. Besides the fact that the Spiders can't probe as deeply as Ellegon does, Thellaren just isn't thorough, and I don't completely trust him.

Also, you and I have got to discuss communication security matters. It's been happening a bit slowly, but the other day an apprentice pointed out to me how English is quickly becoming the lingua franca for trade between species where Home is involved, and the practice is spreading. . . .

Thomen set the paper down and looked over at Ranella. "Can you explain this to us? What is this 'wash'? And this 'you-know-what'?"

"No," she said. "It involves a trade secret. I may not reveal it, except on orders of the Engineer himself."

Thomen nodded at that. "I understand. Still, this is the sort of thing that's known to both the empress and Doria Perlstein. Would you have us ask them?"

Ranella shrugged. "Go ahead."

Tennetty hitched at her pistol as she looked at Jason, as though asking who she ought to shoot.

Jason shrugged, then made a patting, be-still gesture, so that she wouldn't decide that his shrug was permission to shoot whoever she felt like.

He tried to puzzle it out. It had something to do with the secret of making gunpowder, and perhaps another kind of gunpowder—slaver powder, perhaps?—but only the Other Siders and a very few, very senior engineers knew how to make any kind of gunpowder at all. Surely, many juniors had some idea of portions of the process, but the whole of it was a trade secret. Even Jason knew that part of it involved the dirt from the uninhabited portions of the engineers' caverns—beyond the region that Lou Riccetti called the Batcave, for some reason or other.

Ariken Krathael cleared his throat. "Governor, are you telling us that you put your . . . obligations to this mayor of Home ahead of those to the throne of Bieme—of Holtun-Bieme?"

At that, a series of cross-arguments broke out, some barons raising their voices in criticism of Ranella, Bren Adahan almost shouting his own support.

Better get involved in this, or Ranella's going to be in trouble.

But what do I say?

Try pointing out that this is an additional reason for you to go to Home, as well as Endell.

So it was. "Excuse me," Jason said, rising.

The voices quieted, but they didn't quite die down.

Bang!

Tennetty lowered a smoking pistol, cocking her head critically at the hole in the overhead beam.

"A bit off the mark, alas. Guess I'm getting old." She drew another pistol and cocked it, not quite pointing it at anyone. "I think the Heir is asking for your attention?"

There was a thunder of footsteps on the stairs, and four guards rushed into the room, two with pistols drawn, a third with a naked saber, a fourth carrying a pike.

Tennetty grinned. "Nice response time, folks. End of test; return to your duties."

Thomen nodded, dismissing them with a wave and a glower.

Over at the door, the guard muffled a grin behind his hand. Aeia didn't bother hiding hers.

"I'm not sure I approve of firing warning shots indoors," Terumel Derahan said.

The smell of gunsmoke hung heavily in the air, a reek of char and sulfur.

Tennetty holstered the empty pistol and drew another, cocking it. "Neither do I. Now, when Karl hacked your father's head off, *that* was a warning. To his descendants. Heed it."

Ellegon—

I tried to shut her up, but she's not having any. Tennetty's not completely tame, you know.

I worked that out.

Tennetty was still talking. "See that dark spot on the rug? It's—"

Jason stood, swallowing heavily, and tried to summon up a command voice. "Tennetty, shut up. Right now."

"—what's left of your father, and—"

"*Shut up.*"

Her eyes met his for a long moment.

There was a taste of bile in the back of his mouth. Wasn't she going to back down?

Out of the corner of his eye, Jason could see Bren Adahan and Aeia slowly moving their chairs back, but he didn't dare drop his gaze. "Put the gun away, Tennetty," he said. "Right now."

Fire flared in the courtyard outside; the dragon roared. *Put it away.*

Jason didn't turn to look. He kept his eyes on Tennetty's. "*Now.*"

Swearing under her breath, she uncocked the pistol and holstered it. "You do his voice very well," Tennetty said. "But he wouldn't have used it like that on me, not when I was backing him. So maybe one day we'll see just how well you walk in his footsteps. Maybe real soon, one way or another."

With that, she turned on her heel and stalked from the room.

Jason found that his knees really didn't want to support him; he sat down heavily. "My apologies, everyone. Tennetty was devoted to my father, and she misses him. And my particular apologies to you, Baron Derahan. While it was your father who issued the challenge, my father should have given him a chance to reconsider."

Derahan didn't look mollified.

Why should he? You've now implied that his father was a fool for challenging yours. He was, mind, but that doesn't make it politic to say so. Now sit back and let Thomen change the subject.

"In any case," Thomen was already saying, "this does suggest that the Heir ought to travel to Home, in the company of Ellegon and perhaps a few others. Clearly, it would be wrong for the Engineer to give out the secret of gunpowder to the elves, no matter what the pay to Home. With the Emperor dead . . ."

" . . . I'm the best ambassador you've got," Jason said.

Smile, and repeat after me . . .

Jason smiled.

"Unless you think there's another who outranks me?"

"Unless you think there's another who outranks me?"

"I've got an idea." Bren Adahan chuckled. "Whoever thinks they outrank Jason gets to tell Tennetty."

"You've made a good point." Nerahan pursed his lips judiciously. "Gunpowder is the advantage that Home and the Empire share; it's valuable to both, but only as long as it is secret. Perhaps the Heir can persuade Lou Riccetti of that."

"Yes, yes, yes," Baron Hivael put in. "But why this other trip? This one to Endell?"

Jason opened his mouth to answer, *Because Walter Slovotsky told me to.*

But, actually, that wasn't true. Walter had told them to have Ellegon bring Kirah and the children to Holtun-Bieme as soon as possible. He hadn't said that Jason ought to go along.

But it was Jason's job to do it; it wasn't something he felt right about assigning to somebody else. Part of it would be to tell Kirah and Slovotsky's daughters that their father and Ahira were still missing. He just couldn't delegate that.

"Because I promised I would," he said. That was truthful, even if it wasn't the whole truth. He'd promised himself another trip away, before he settled down as prince of Bieme and emperor of Holtun-Bieme.

Jason rose. At the near end of the room stood the slightly raised podium, where the richly carved throne of the prince of Bieme stood. Next to the throne was a locked strongbox. Taking a large brass key from his belt, he knelt and unlocked the box, pulling from it a simple circlet of silver, the beauty of the mirror-polished metal more enhanced than overshadowed by the rubies, diamonds and emeralds that studded it.

"Warriors swear on swords. I've sworn on this," he said, adding privately, *as of now,* "that I'll take this trip, before I even consider assuming the crown and my full responsibilities. Who here would make me a liar?"

Surprisingly, at least to Jason, the murmurs ceased. Thomen gave him an admiring nod.

As the meeting tapered off, Jason turned to Thomen. *Relay, please: Well, how'd I do?*

Thomen frowned.

He says, "Pretty poorly, actually. The admiring nod was for my audience, not for you. But perhaps you didn't do too badly, for a beginner."

Jason put the crown away in its cloth bag, and then looked out in the courtyard.

And I suppose I'm going to be graced with your opinion, whether I want it or not.

Good guess. Below, the dragon was settling in for the night, neck stretched out so he could rest his chin on the ground, his legs tucked catlike underneath his body. *Me? I think Thomen was half right. The first half.*

Well, at least it was settled that Jason was going. Now, all there was to do was decide on a team. Best to talk that over with Tennetty; her judgment about these sorts of things was better than his. Even if she was ticked at him.

INTERLUDE
Laheran and the Dead Men

*Be not angry that you cannot make others as you wish them
to be, since you cannot make yourself as you wish to be.*
—Thomas à Kempis

The wind came across the Cirric, blowing across the guildhall
and the kennels, which, oddly enough, didn't smell of anything.
That was strange; slave kennels always smelled of shit and piss and
fear, and sometimes death.

There were a dozen people standing on the hot stones of the
courtyard of the Erifeyll guildhall, and most of them smelled of
fear.

Fear wasn't the only thing that the two ragged men and the girl
stank of; there were no baths to be had in Erif's dungeon. The
fools—didn't know how to handle merchandise. There was no way
for them to run, and nowhere to run if they did.

Not only were all three chained at the wrists, throat and ankles,
but a half dozen of Lord Erif's armsmen stood by, armed cap à
pied.

Erifeyll, just two days away from glorious Pandathaway.

"The entry was through the rear," a guard said. "Somebody
pulled the bars right out of the wall," he added. "But at least they
didn't get away."

Laheran ignored him. The idiot seemed to think that because
some of the slaves were recaptured, this wasn't a horrible defeat.

The details didn't matter. This was *Erifeyll*. Did that mean that Pandathaway was next? Probably not. That was too obvious. So, probably Pandathaway was next, because they'd think that the guild would think not. So probably not, so probably, so—

Laheran sighed. One thing he had learned as an apprentice was that when you didn't know how to solve a whole problem, it made sense to solve what you could while you were thinking. He turned to the slaves.

The girl whimpered and squirmed as Laheran examined her collar. Not guild work. There was a reason that most guild collars were dipped in gold, despite the cost. Gold didn't rust.

The iron of these collars was rusty, and like sandpaper. The rust had worn her neck raw underneath; at Laheran's nod, two of his men gripped her with practiced hands so that he could inspect her more closely. His probing finger came away with blood and a greenish pus.

"Idiots," he said. And: "Key."

The guard sergeant thought about protesting for a moment, then shrugged and pulled a key out of his pouch. Laheran quickly unlocked the collar and dropped it to the dirt.

The wound was festering badly.

Amateurs. As though the only way to treat slaves was with beatings and chains. The girl was twelve, perhaps thirteen. Her round eyes and sharp chin proclaimed her of Shattered Islander stock, clearly, possibly Klimosian or Bursosi. She could be almost presentable, quite attractive in a year or two, and might well respond better to kindness than the whip if she wasn't to be brutalized into scarred ugliness and sullen tractability.

Practiced fingers felt at her forehead—she was running a fever— then dropped to feel at the rest of her. Hmm . . . perhaps sooner than a few years.

He turned to Kelimon. "Take the three of them to the ship. A bit of healing draughts on the neck should be enough, but examine them all thoroughly; she may need more." Laheran turned to the guard sergeant. "They are all property of the Slavers' Guild; all were caught as fugitives."

But the majority of the dozen or so slaves in the kennels— Laheran would have to check the records in order to be sure just how many—had escaped, taking with them what horses and what money the guild had had here.

Still, there was nothing more that these three could tell him. They'd only seen the dwarf, who had hustled them outside through the rear window of the slave cage.

The guard shook his head. "I think Lord Kuryil—he's the keeper of the dungeon—expressed an interest in her."

"Then he should have had the sense to see that her health was attended to," Laheran said from between taut lips. "She is not for sale here. Take them away, Kelimon, take all three of them away. We'll drop them off at guildhall in Pandathaway."

Normally, Laheran would have taken the guard's comment as an opening for a negotiation. But if Kuryil was deliberately degrading the girl's condition in order to lower her price, he ought to be taught a lesson. Besides, Laheran was irritated with all of them. He was honest enough to admit to himself that that was the real reason he was rebuffing Kuryil—not to educate the lord, or even because he suspected that a bath, some healing, and a few tendays of gentle but firm handling might increase the girl's value.

The gray-robed wizard and his apprentice stood to one side, twin masks of indifference on their bearded faces. The apprentice looked like a painting of the wizard as a young man; Laheran could see where the squint-lines were beginning to form, tracks of a buzzard around the eyes.

"Shall I open it now?" the wizard asked. "Or shall we all stand out in the hot sun all day?"

Laheran stood in front of the door. As before, there were those awkward Englits scrawlings and the signatures were symbols—a sword, a knife and an ax—but the final words were in Erendra.

The warrior lives, they said.

And: *Don't open this door. A surprise for slavers waits inside. Preserve it for them.*

Laheran looked at the wizard and at the guards. "You take orders from Karl Cullinane, do you?" he asked, more rhetorically than otherwise.

One of the guards bit back a response.

"*Well?*" Laheran snapped. "Out with it."

"It cost Lord Erif a goodly amount of money to have it preserved for you, Master Laheran," the guard said. "He did it for you, as a gesture of cooperation with your guild, not because he takes orders from Karl Cullinane, or anyone else."

Laheran nodded. "There's truth in that. My apologies." He set his palm against the splintered wood of the door, but it didn't move. He pushed harder, and harder, but still there was no motion, not even the slight give of a bolted door.

He walked to a shuttered window, worked his fingers in between the overhang of the shutter and the wall, and pulled.

Again, nothing happened; the spell of preservation had kept the building sealed, just as the murderers had left it.

He sighed. Enough; it had to be done sometime.

"Release the spell," Laheran said.

The wizard stepped up to the door and lightly touched it with a split-nailed finger, quietly but carefully pronouncing three syllables that could only be heard and forgotten, not remaining on the tongue or the mind.

The shutter released and swung violently open, barely missing Laheran's nose. The slam of it against the wall sent hands reaching for swords.

He drew his own sword and, standing carefully to one side of the window, stuck it inside and waved it around.

Nothing happened.

One of the guards stepped forward. "I don't understand why all the delay," he said as he took a step forward and pushed on the door.

Laheran moved quickly, catching the guard across the waist in a leaping tackle, just as the door swung wide.

Thwup.

A feathered bolt bit into the guard's shoulder; the heavy man dropped his weapons and screamed.

Laheran rolled easily to his feet, brushing himself off. "Best take your man to the Spider," he said to the other guards, as one knelt over the pale form of the idiot who had opened the door. "There's nothing to interest you here."

Laheran stepped inside. It was as he'd thought: one of the dead men was Daviran. He'd apprenticed with Daviran years ago; Davi was one of Laheran's few friends.

And now clever Davi sat in a chair, his face pale in death, his throat slit from ear to ear.

There was nothing alive inside the kennel. He could see one body spread out on the floor, and there was another dead man sitting in a chair, and yet another tied upside-down to the top crosspiece of the slave cage, but a live man hadn't fired the bolt; a crossbow had been nailed to an open closet door opposite the entry, and an improvised rope and pulley arrangement set up to make it fire through the opening door.

Laheran knelt to examine the body under the table. The right hand was crushed, splinters of bones peeking through the bloody flesh, as if someone had run the hand through a wine press.

That hadn't killed him, though; his chest was crushed, the breastbone smashed inward, probably killing the man instantly.

That smelled of the dwarf, Ahira, and Davi's slit throat spoke of Walter Slovotsky.

And the poor, dead bastard tied upside-down to the cage was pure Karl Cullinane. Laheran let his hand rest on the short length of spear that projected from the dead slaver's chest.

He could just see the monster tying the guildsman upside-down, and then taking his time hefting a spear, only to throw it almost through the slaver.

The three of them would die, and that was all there was to it.

Laheran drew his knife and considered the edge. Was it really possible to cut a man ten thousand times without killing him? Ahrmin had been right: Cullinane was too much of a threat to be allowed to live. He had to die. And his friends with him.

Laheran looked once again at the parchment note on the door.

The warrior lives, you think? Not for long, Karl Cullinane. Not for long, you murdering animal.

Laheran tore the parchment down from the door and slashed it to ribbons.

CHAPTER 6
Tennetty

The business of the samurai consists in reflecting on his own station in life, in discharging loyal service to his master if he has one, in deepening his fidelity in associations with friends, and, with due consideration of his own position, in devoting himself to duty above all.

—Yamaga Soko

The difference between being a trusted friend and a devoted vassal is non-trivial. Me, I'd rather be the first; vassals tend to go to the well too often.

—Walter Slovotsky

"Come in," she said.

Her room, a small cubicle down in the dungeon level of the tower, was lit only by a flickering lamp set in a stone niche at eye-level. It was cold down below the ground, and it smelled of ancient mold, but that didn't seem to affect Tennetty as she sat tailor-fashion on her rumpled bed, considering the edge of a bowie, her face cast into shadow, hiding the patch over her missing eye.

"So," she said. "You let them talk you out of it?"

"What are you saying? That I don't want to go?"

She snickered. "You have a keen eye for the obvious." From somewhere in the darkness she produced a whetstone, spat on it, and began to hone the edge of the knife with slow, even strokes.

314

Jason didn't like that kind of accusation, and he didn't know how to deal with it. "I thought I proved something in Melawei," he said, not realizing how foolish the boast sounded until the words were out.

She eyed him evenly. "You proved that you could use a rifle, once. You did it when it counted, I'll give you that. But you didn't prove that you're a substitute for him, boy. You sit in *his* chair, and you expect all of them to look up to you like you're *him*. . . ." She spat on the stone and continued to stroke it down the edge. "Well, you're not. Not by me."

"Tennetty, I—"

With no warm-up, no hint that she was about to move, she lunged at him, springing from the bed.

"Guards!" he shouted, as he caught her knife-arm, trying for a kick to her kneecap.

She got her leg behind his and swept his feet out from under him, landing heavily on his chest, one arm trapped underneath him.

The tip of the knife flickered in the lamplight, descending—

—and halted an inch from his eye.

"Your *father* would have beaten me, Jason. You're just not as fast as he was, not as brave, not the ruler he was, not—"

A rifle-butt slammed against her head with an audible *thunk*. From the edge of his vision, a huge hand reached out and fastened itself around her wrist; another, somewhat smaller hand gripped her by the hair and lifted her up, not at all slowing at her muffled groan of pain. She struck out with a free hand but it was blocked, the sound like a fist slapping a side of beef.

"Take her, Durine," Kethol said, releasing his grip on her hair, stooping to help Jason up.

She tried to lash out with a savage groin-kick, but Durine, moving more gracefully, more quickly than any man his size had a right to, had already turned to catch the kick on his hip.

Like a mastiff with a rat he grabbed her, then shook her hand until the knife dropped from it. Durine yanked her toward him with one hand, punching her in the pit of the stomach with the other.

Retching, she staggered, and would have collapsed if Durine hadn't economically spun her about and thrown her to the ground, then knelt beside her, gripping both her hands in one massive paw, drawing a beltknife with the other.

He looked up at Jason, who was standing half-supported by Kethol. "Do you want to do it, sir, or should I?" Massive shoulders shrugged under his leather jerkin. "Makes not much of a difference to me."

Jason struggled to sit up. "Would you all—"

Tennetty snarled, a sound more animal than human. "Just testing him, I was just testing him," she said, the words coming out as a threat, not a plea.

"Let her up, Durine," Jason said. He straightened, a salty taste in his mouth; he reached to the bleeding corner of his lip. He couldn't remember how, but it must have been cut in the fight.

Durine looked at Kethol, who shrugged, as though to say, *It's up to him.* Reluctantly, the big man let go of her hands and rose, not sheathing his dagger. "I'd not go for that knife, Tennetty," he said, his voice casual, perhaps a touch embarrassed, as if he'd caught himself repeating a transparent platitude like, *Remember to dress warm when it's cold.* "It'd be sort of a foolish idea."

She nodded and worked her way over to the edge of her bed, pulling herself up to it, rubbing her hand against the side of her head. In the flickering lamplight she looked old, and about used-up. "I hear you."

"I think you've done enough testing of him." Kethol picked up her pistol belt from where it hung near the bed and slung it over his shoulder. "Well, young sir, what do we do about this?"

"I just came to ask her about the party, the one I'm taking to Home, and then to Endell." Jason tried to dismiss it with a wave. "We got into a disagreement about how ready I am, and she tried to prove a point."

Kethol's mouth twisted into a smile. The expression didn't look right. "With respect, sir: this is why you called for help? You were perhaps proving that you've mastered that form of self-defense?" He turned to Durine. "What do you think?"

Durine shook his head. "I don't like it. We haul her in front of the general, at least."

Kethol snorted. "After he told us that he doesn't want to see our ugly faces for the next two tendays? Maybe Captain Garthe instead?"

"Over an assault on the Heir?"

"I'll decide what's done about it!" Jason snapped.

Durine thought it over for a moment, then nodded. "Yes, sir.

We can discuss it with the general while you're gone, I guess. Long as you're not taking her with you. You give a dog one bite, not two."

Tennetty shook her head. "Wrong. I'm going with him. I'm as good as there is at what I do."

"Threatening royalty?" Kethol shrugged. "Who's going to keep an eye on you?"

She shook her head, then clearly regretted it. "If we're going to carry any cargo at all, we've got to keep the group down— remember, we've got to bring Slovotsky's woman and kids back from Endell. Bren Adahan and Aeia are bound for Home, and that means we can take maybe three more. Jason, me, and three more. I was thinking of Garthe, Teven, and maybe Danagar, if he can travel, but—" A spasm of pain creased her face and closed her single eye, leaving it watering.

"A corporal and two of the general's sons? Captain Garthe would be fine, but I've got a better idea," Kethol said, looking at Jason. "What would you say to me, Durine and Pirojil for the other three? I'd mean you'd have to talk the general into letting us off our punishment, and getting Piro healed up."

Which wouldn't bother Jason at all.

"Me instead of Pirojil," Tennetty said. "You either take me or kill me. Karl told me to watch out for you, Jason." Moving with exaggerated slowness, she rose from the bed and walked over to him. Durine glanced quickly at Jason, but Kethol's eyes never left Tennetty as she unstrapped her pistol and slowly, carefully, pulled it from the holster, handing it butt first to Jason.

"Cock it," she said.

Durine raised an eyebrow. Kethol shrugged, then nodded.

Jason cocked the weapon, holding it as he'd been taught, the barrel pointed toward the ceiling.

"Lower it now, point it at me." Again moving slowly, she reached out and pulled his arm down, until the muzzle was resting just underneath her chin, cold steel against her flesh.

"Either trust me or shoot me, now," she said, as though she didn't care one way or another.

"It's your decision, sir," Durine said. "Your father used to have a high opinion of Tennetty, but I don't know as you'd want to give her another bite. You give a dog one bite, not two."

"You already said that," Jason said.

"So I did. Well?"

Jason jerked his head toward the door. "Leave us alone for a moment or two," he said, not lowering the pistol. Was she really betting that she could beat the hangfire?

"We'll be just outside the door." Durine said. He and Kethol scooped up their rifles and left.

"What would you advise my father, Tennetty?" he asked.

She didn't hesitate. "I'd tell him to shoot. You can't trust somebody like me, not after I've come this close to killing you."

"Even though I know you won't do it again?"

"You *don't* know. You can't know. *I* don't know. Your father wouldn't give me another chance."

Jason nodded. "Maybe you're right." He pulled back the hammer, lowered the weapon and uncocked it, then handed it to her. "Then again, as you were so kind to point out, I'm not my father." He turned away from her and walked out of the room, his back feeling quite naked and completely vulnerable.

CHAPTER 7
Goodbyes

I've never liked cats' ways of taking their leave—the ungrateful little creatures just go without saying anything.
Not my way. Saying goodbye is something we humans do pretty well.

—Walter Slovotsky

Aeia escorted him into the bedroom. "Take it easy on Mother," she whispered. "She's not doing too well."

Doria was already there, her legs curled under her as she sat in an oversized chair by the window, a lapdesk and pen across her lap. As Aeia and Jason walked in from the outer room, she set the lapdesk on an end table and walked to them.

Andrea Cullinane was asleep in the bed, her face seemingly a little younger, a trifle less worn around the edges than it had been when Jason had seen her in the workshop. For a moment her breathing speeded up and her eyelids fluttered, but just as Jason thought she was going to wake up she turned over on her side and buried her face deeply in her pillow.

"She'll be fine, I think, but she's been overdoing it with the magic for a long time now," Doria whispered, her lips pursed in professional disapproval. "Just think of her as a recovering junkie and you'll have a good picture." She guided them out toward the hall, far enough away that the whispers wouldn't carry to the bed, but close enough so that the three of them could still see Andrea's sleeping form.

"'Junkie'?" Jason asked.

Doria's brow furrowed. "Drunk, then. Think of her as a drunk trying to give up drinking. The trouble is, she can't give it up; but she has to cut it down to the point where it's not going to hurt her."

Aeia shook her head. "But she's going to be okay?"

Doria didn't answer for a moment. "Remember that I'm not what I was, but—"

"But you've still got a feel for the way of things," Aeia said firmly. "That's what Andrea says," she added, when Doria seemed about to protest.

"Perhaps," Doria said. "But . . ." She shrugged it away. "In any case, I don't want her to have any more shocks, not right now. When she's well, she's a lot stronger in body and soul than most people are, but—"

"How do you know that? This 'feel' of yours?" Jason was skeptical. Doria had lost her persona as a Hand healer when she'd defied the matriarch in Melawei. He was grateful to her—hell, she'd defied the matriarch by using her spells to save Jason's life— but that didn't blind him to what she'd given up.

Doria's face went stony. "Because after the two of us were gang-raped," she said calmly, levelly, almost mechanically, "she recovered from what sent me into catatonia. She was able to deal with it and, not too much later, to resume a normal sex life with your father. That takes a kind of strength of character that I doubt *you* have, boy," she said, her whisper momentarily vehement. She fought for control of herself, and found it. "But she's not at her best right now, which is why both of you are to play this up as an easy little vacation before you settle down to marriage and work or whatever—"

"Doria?" Andrea's sleepy voice interrupted itself for a yawn. "What is—oh, Jason, Aeia," she said, sitting up in bed and smiling. She held out her hands to them.

Awake, she looked dreadful. Her eyes were puffy and red, and there were crusts at the corners of her mouth and eyes. Jason took one of her hands in his. Hers were dry and hot, the skin loose as an old woman's. But Mother couldn't be getting old, could she?

She smiled at them. "The two of you will watch out for each other, now. And be careful."

Or maybe she could.

He shrugged. "Nothing to it. Just a quick jaunt on dragonback, and a pickup in Endell. Nothing to it," he repeated.

Why did the words sound insincere in his ears? That was about the size of it, in fact: it was just going to be a handful of days away from Biemestren, that was all.

Andrea didn't seem to hear him. "I haven't seen Janie for years and years. My, she must be as big as you are. And I only know about little Doria Andrea from Walter's and Kirah's letters." She smiled at Doria. "Although I did notice that you got top billing."

"Then again," Doria said, "naming her 'Andrea Doria' would have been a—"

"No, don't say it!"

"—it would have been a disaster."

The two Other Side women giggled like a couple of girls. He didn't understand it; he spread his hands to confess ignorance when Aeia looked at him curiously, then shrugged as though to say that she didn't understand it either.

But their laughter was infectious, and Jason and Aeia soon found themselves laughing, too. Laughter made the goodbyes easier.

Doria caught up with them in the hall. "She's not in the best shape. She's been substituting seeming for real health for too long, and that's an awful trap. So I want her to rest, and not worry. . . . And I also want both of you to get back when you're supposed to. Understood?"

Aeia hugged her. "Understood, Aunt Doria."

Jason nodded. "I'll miss you, too."

She bit her lip and smiled. "There is that, too, boychick. Take care."

PART TWO
Home

CHAPTER 8
Outside of Enkiar

Miscellaneous is always the largest category.
—Slovotsky's Laws

The night was clear and bright above, dark and threatening below. Off to port and perhaps a mile below, the murk of the Enkiar streets was relieved only by a precious few lanterns, and by the glowing coals of three garbage fires at the town's western perimeter.

The stars flickered brightly, while distant faerie lights pulsed in a lethargic adagio of scarlet and cerulean. Again, Jason tried to look straight ahead, past the straining neck of the dragon, as the rush of air beat tears from his eyes. He wiped at the dampness at his temples and let himself ease back into the straps.

A massive hand gripped his shoulder. "It shouldn't be too much more," Durine said, his voice pitched to barely carry over the wind and the flapping of wings. "Any time now." He gave Jason's shoulder a reassuring squeeze.

Behind Durine, half-hidden behind tied-down canvas sacks, the others were strapped in their saddles, Kethol, still wide-eyed, looked down with more than a little apprehension, Tennetty watching everything with active indifference. Aeia took flying as a matter of course—she'd ridden on dragonback since before Jason was born—while Bren Adahan kept his expression under strict control.

They weren't at the first of the usual campsites, Ellegon reported. *So we'll try the next one.*

While Enkiar was militantly neutral, and the Home warriors were free to make camp in the forests to its west and north, the enforcement of that neutrality was sometimes more theoretical than actual outside the city proper. Though Lord Gyren's troops enforced the neutrality in the city itself, the discipline tended to fade toward the edges.

There were advantages to all that. Enkiar's neutrality didn't stop the Home raiding teams from gathering information. A few times, Home warriors had managed to parlay that information into the ambush of a slaver caravan. It worked both ways, though; once, slavers had managed an ambush of Frandred's team, an attack that had left twenty of his warriors dead. So Home raiders never camped twice in a row in the same spot, and always kept a good watch.

Rising on a pillar of smoke and flame, a signal rocket flared green ahead of them.

Nope. They're at number five, Ellegon said. *They have a dwarf standing guard.*

How could you tell?

Think about it. At this distance, the dragon said, *human eyes couldn't spot me against a night sky. Dwarves are different.*

The dragon's wings slowed as Ellegon swooped down, then broke into a furious flurry as the ground came up quickly.

"Torches!" a familiar gruff voice called from below.

Daherrin, what are you doing on watch?

"We was short of dwarves," came from the darkness.

Three shadowy shapes ran up in the darkness, holding bundles of unlit torches in front of them; Ellegon's flame flared briefly, judiciously, lighting the brands one by one.

Jason quickly unfastened himself from the saddle and dropped heavily to the dew-slick grass, flexing his knees to take up the shock.

As the torches cast their flickering light around the meadow, Jason found himself face to face with Daherrin and Mikyn. Mikyn was Jason's age; they'd been friends since early childhood. Now Mikyn looked older, a bit world-worn since Jason had last seen him: his sparse brown beard just a touch fuller, the hollows under his eyes darker, and the bones of his face more prominent in the flickering firelight. If Jason hadn't known better, he would have put Mikyn's age at perhaps twenty-five, maybe thirty. Old.

The big change was in his expression; Jason's childhood friend was looking at him as if he were a stranger.

"Jason," Daherrin said, his voice shockingly cool, no tone betraying warmth or anger. The dwarf hadn't changed in the many tendays since Jason had last seen him: a solid, seemingly unchangeable stump of a person, almost as wide as he was tall. While Daherrin's head barely came to the top of Jason's chest, his shoulders were every bit as broad as Jason's father's had been. Above a mouse-brown beard shot with gray, two beady eyes peered out over an absurdly aquiline nose.

The dwarf's lined face was unreadable in the flickering torchlight.

Then he broke into a smile so broad it would have torn apart a human's face. "Jason," Daherrin said, hugging him so hard bones threatened to break. "Jason, boy, it's good to see you." He released Jason and stepped back. "*Damn* me if you ain't a bit less skinny across the shoulders." His face sobered. "Heard about your father, and I'm sorry."

Jason nodded. "So am I."

Mikyn didn't say anything; he watched Jason.

The dwarf slapped Jason across the shoulder, almost bowling him over. "I also heard that you did for Ahrmin. Nice going." He smiled. Killing didn't bother Daherrin; it was by way of his business. "You sure the bastard's dead? I recall that your father thought he'd killed him once."

Jason returned the dwarf's level gaze. "I saw his brains."

"Good man. Betcha your mother's proud a' you." The dwarf started to turn away. "One more thing?"

"Yes?"

The dwarf turned toward the dragon. "Hey, Ellegon, keep a lid on things for a minute, would ya?" he called out, then turned back to Jason.

I'd rather you didn't—

"Chew on *this,* fucker," the dwarf said. A huge fist caught Jason on the cheek; the world came up and slapped him in the back, knocking the wind clean out of him. He tried to sit up, but curtains of darkness threatened to enfold his mind.

The distinctive clicks of rifles being cocked cut through the darkness.

"Tennetty, ta havath," Durine said. "I say ease up, all of you."

"Shove it up your ass," Tennetty shrilled. "You're ready to kill me for fucking putting my *hands* on him, and you're going to let—"

"Tennetty, shut up. Everybody put your weapons down, *now,*" Aeia shouted into the night. "Ellegon!"

Everyone, be still. There's nothing going on that's worth dying over. Dragonfire brightened the sky, penetrating through the haze around Jason's brain. *He's fine. —Jason, get up.*

Mikyn looked down at him. "That didn't square things. But maybe, just maybe, it's a start." He offered Jason a hand.

Jason took it, and for a moment considered kicking his boyhood friend in the balls. Twice. Hard.

But he dismissed the idea and accepted Daherrin's and Mikyn's help to his feet.

"You coulda gotten half my team killed." The dwarf's nostrils flared as he gripped Jason's hand with painful strength. "I should give everyone a paddle and make you run the gantlet over bare coals, and if you was anybody but the future fucking Emperor, that's exactly what I'd do. But you are, so I can't, so we're all going to have to live with the way you fucked up.

"You can be Heir, or boy Emperor, or *his* son, or whatever you wanna be, but you never, never do that again, or what I'll do to you'll make you think this was like the kiss on the butt your mother used to give you when she was done changing your diapers. You hear me, Jason Cullinane?"

"I hear you." Jason released their hands and stood, wobbly.

Everybody, calm down. There has been no harm done.

Off in the darkness, Tennetty and Kethol still faced off against Daherrin's three warriors, Aeia and Durine standing between them. Guns and swords were drawn, but there hadn't been any shots fired or blood spilled, or damage done.

No harm done.

The dragon loomed above them all, whisps of smoke issuing from his nostrils. *Tell them that.*

"Ta havath." Jason raised a hand. "Everybody, ease up, eh?" He took a step and reconsidered. Except for his head; he had a bitch of a headache.

Close to a hundred warriors gathered around the campfire as Daherrin's quartermasters divided up Ellegon's supplies. The supplies were divided into three categories: clothes, weapons, and miscellany.

Clothes were plentiful. There was a change for everybody. Warriors would pick up fresh clothes and disappear into the night down the lamplit path to a nearby stream, soaping up, then shivering as they sluiced off in the cold water and changed into fresh clothes to return, damp and cold but clean, to bag the dirty laundry for washing at Home.

There was plenty of powder and shot to go around, and a few spare rifles to be exchanged for ones damaged beyond field repair.

Miscellaneous was, as Walter Slovotsky used to say, the largest category. There were: spare lamps, sewing kits, a few precious flasks of healing draughts, leather thongs, coils of rope, bundles of arrow stock and fletching equipment, a small bag of mail... but no food. While raiding teams were expected to buy staples and fodder locally, dried meat and fresh vegetables were a great treat on the road.

Not this time.

Daherrin swore softly. "An' it's real good to see you," he said to Aeia, his voice only a trace sarcastic, "and your noble baronship," he added, with a too-deep bow toward Bren Adahan, "and all that, and Durine's a real treat for the eyes...."

The big man chuckled.

The dwarf expectorated into the fire and considered the sizzling gobbet of spit for a moment. "But I'd have rather had your weight in carrots and prunes than all of you."

His second, a lanky man who was missing most of his front teeth, shrugged. "Well, sho we shend shomebody in to town tomorrow to pick up shome more shupplies."

"We could. But—" The dwarf considered it for a moment. "I don't like facing the slavers if we don't have to."

Jason raised an eyebrow.

"Slavers in town." The dwarf spat again. "Big caravan—too big fer us ta take right now. But they are headed back toward Pandathaway, and I've got a runner off to Frandred; mebbe we'll join up and jump them around Metreyll, if they take that route."

A large caravan? Ellegon's wings fluttered nervously.

Large slaver caravans almost always meant a lot of dragonbaned crossbow bolts.

The dwarf nodded. "Yeah. Which is why, if I'm sending somebody into town right now, Enkiar being neutral or not, I'd like you to hang around until tomorrow. Fly up into the hills and get lost fer a day; but we might need some quick rescue."

Steam hissed from between the dragon's teeth. *But if I'm that far away, I can't mindtalk to anyone, and I can't even get distant thoughts and impressions from anyone except Jason.*

Thanks a lot.

"Jason." Daherrin toyed with his beard. "You got a problem with going into town?"

Not again, he thought. *I'll not run again.* "There's no problem, Daherrin." Jason shook his head. "I can handle it."

Tennetty nodded. "Right. I'll watch your back."

"No." Bren Adahan said.

Heads turned toward him in surprise.

"I don't recall asking your opinion, Baron," Tennetty said.

Bren Adahan waved her objection away. "You're too well-known. Anybody sees Karl Cullinane's one-eyed attack bitch and they'll start looking at who she's protecting. Jason will be safer if he's less visible—just him, and a few others. Jason will be just one of the crowd."

"The baron's making sense." Durine nodded. "Count us in."

"No." Bren Adahan shook his head again.

Kethol cocked his head to one side. "What's your problem with that?"

"Mixed teams. Do you like working with mixed teams? It's better if Jason is protected by a team that's used to working together. They're used to working in concert; they can read signals from each other that you and Durine and I would miss."

Kethol bit his lip, and then nodded. "You may be right. I don't like it, but you're right. Rather have Daherrin work with his own people—Jason will be safer that way."

"It's my call, not any of yours," Daherrin said. "I go in with my people, plus Jason. Jason, me, Mikyn, Arrikol and Falherten. Now, what do we call you? Any name you prefer?"

"Taren," Jason said. "I'm used to answering to it."

The dwarf raised his voice. "Okay, everybody—this is Taren. You all get used ta calling him that, and just that. Five extra watches and a twentieth-share penalty on the next haul for the first one who miscalls him. Double the penalty for the second. There won't be a third." He slapped his meaty hands together. "Okay. Let's get this shit unpacked."

CHAPTER 9
"The Warrior Lives"

Fundamentally, every bar is the same as every other one, if it's the kind you're drinking in, to end a sentence with a preposition, which I haven't.

—Walter Slovotsky

On the road ahead, a soldier at the guard station began working the wooden arms of a pair of signal flags. A tall, lanky man, he moved easily, as though the weight of his steel helmet and rusty chainmail didn't matter, or couldn't be allowed to matter. The red and white cloths fluttered madly as the long wooden arms clicked and clacked in the warm noon air, then halted for a few moments, only to start up again.

Jason, sitting astride a big brown gelding, caught Daherrin eyeing the motion intently. "Can you read that?"

Daherrin nodded briefly. "A bit, Taren." He shrugged. "'Nough to know that's not one of their danger signals. Alarms tend to be short. We shouldn't have much trouble; Enkiar's an open city, remember?"

"We don't usually have any trouble in Enkiar, Taren," Mikyn said. Like the others, he was giving Jason's assumed name a thorough workout. Jason hoped that would all wear off before they ran into anybody; folks might wonder why it was Taren-this and Taren-that all the time.

"You still in touch with the dragon?" Daherrin asked.

Jason shrugged. It was hard to say. He *thought* he could feel Ellegon's distant presence, but he wasn't sure. Besides, it didn't matter if he could now; the issue was whether he could if and when things went sour in Enkiar.

A better question was whether that would do any good at all. It would take Ellegon at least a few minutes to arrive in response to even the most plainly heard call for help; it took only a moment to turn a live person into a corpse.

They rode in slowly, hands away from weapons, although none of them was heavily armed: each of the four humans carried only a beltknife and sword, while Daherrin sported a bastard combination of a short staff and a mace. There were five rifles in the flatbed wagon that Falherten drove, but those were props, not intended for use; real rifles weren't brought into Enkiar.

The outer guard station consisted of a pair of low stone buildings that might have concealed as many as twenty men each, no more. No more than a bowshot beyond that was the curtain wall surrounding the town, the only visible access an open gate.

Daherrin was known in Enkiar, certainly by one of the guards, possibly by the half dozen manning the station; it took only a few moments, a palmed coin and a handshake to get them inside, after the most cursory of examinations. They did have to surrender the guns, but since the only ones they were carrying were the five slaver blunderbusses that required the magically compounded slaver powder, leaving them behind presented no problem. Slaver powder wasn't particularly a secret, not for years; it was just horribly expensive.

"Besides," Daherrin said, tucking their whittled-bone claim tokens into his pouch as they rode through the gate and into Enkiar proper, "it gives 'em something to think about." His ugly face split in a grin. "Let 'em wonder if we're really using Home powder, or if that secret died with you-know-who's father."

That didn't make any sense, none at all. The making of gunpowder was an Engineering secret, known only to the Engineer and his most senior and trusted subordinate master engineers. All the other Other Siders probably knew something about it, but none of them except the Engineer knew the details of what everybody knew was an incredibly detailed and difficult chemical process.

He thought he was keeping his own counsel, but something must have shown on his face. Mikyn snorted. "I don't think so either, but there's lots of folks who think he could do anything."

"Maybe he could, Mikyn." Arrikol said. He was a tall blond Salke, his hair twisted into a single thick braid, seaman style. He clicked his tongue against the roof of his mouth as he reached across his waist, nervously pulling his sword a fraction of an inch out of its scabbard, then slipping it back, pumping the steel a few times like a piston before he caught himself and stopped.

Falherten, sitting on the narrow bench of the flatbed wagon, clucked at the horses and twitched the reins gently. "The market's the other direction, Daherrin; you're going the wrong way."

The dwarf smiled. "Gotta be sure that they know we're here, Fal. If we don't let them see how confident we are, they might get the idea that we're worried or something. Not that we are, eh?"

Falherten didn't return his smile.

Jason swallowed, hard.

The main streets of Enkiar, easily wide enough for two carts to travel in each direction, were paved with ancient cobblestones, their tops worn smooth, the spaces between them packed with the dirt of years. It was more like riding down a good dirt road than a cobblestone street: there weren't any ruts.

It was midday, and a pretty day, and the streets were filled with life. Seemingly endless crowds of ragged children played tag, weaving in and out of the streets and onto the sidewalks in a restless dance. A thickset woman in the ragged gray dress of a peasant walked down the road, a plump, nut-brown chicken struggling under either arm; her stringy hair was bound back with a kerchief of dissonant scarlet.

Over in the smithy, a fat man worked over his anvil, his face greasy, his bare chest and massive belly sweaty from the heat of his forge, the coarse black mat of hair covering his torso broken in perhaps half a dozen spaces where white scars peeked through, announcing that he had been clumsy or careless with hot metal perhaps half a dozen times.

At a nearby stall, a willowy woman crouched over her iron brazier, dipping a brush into a bowl of sauce. She basted the skewers of meat and vegetables on the grill, then exchanged the brush for a paper fan, gently fanning the coals. The scent of broiling lamb and onion and garlic spread across the air.

Two compact men in flat, broad hats leaned toward each other over an empty barrel of grain, one repeatedly shaking a small leather purse, the other shaking his head and repeatedly shouting, "Not for that, not for that," spraying the first with spittle.

Just a normal market day.

"Farmers' Market's down this way, Taren," Daherrin said.

Beyond the last of the low stone buildings began a series of low pens for animals; it stank of cattle. Jason hated the smell of cattle; he'd ridden far too long downwind of it on a cattle drive from Metreyll to Pandathaway.

There was a leisurely sale in progress; a trio of brawny men Jason took to be innkeepers were spending as much time consulting with each other as they did bidding on the half dozen animals in the pen, little to the delight of the auctioneer.

Beyond the cattle pen were pigs; beyond pigs were the chicken cages. Beyond the chicken cages were three steel cages, each big enough to hold perhaps two dozen humans.

There were three guards at the door of the cage, none of them in the red and brown livery of Enkiar's Prince Gyren. Slavers.

They didn't look evil; they just looked like three swordsmen in iron and brass and leather. Nothing unusual, unless you looked closely at the way one of them narrowed his eyes.

You couldn't always tell evil by looking at it. Maybe that was part of why Gyren of Enkiar kept Enkiar non-partisan in the war between Home and the Slavers' Guild. Gyren the Neutral, he called himself—proudly, as if there were something to be proud of in being neutral in a fight between Good and Evil.

Well, maybe Good wasn't good all the time. Jason wasn't good, noble, right and proper all the damn time. He'd been a coward once, and been afraid a lot. But at least he didn't own people.

The middle cage was empty, the other two nowhere near capacity. One held perhaps ten glum men, ranging in age from early teens to middle fifties; the other contained five women, all plain and unadorned.

But could any of them be from Kernat village? Jason kicked in his heels and rode over toward the cages, calling out, "Are any of you from Kernat village? Any Biemish among you?"

One of the slavers reached toward the signalling horn at his waist, desisting only when another shook his head. "Ta havath," he said, holding up a palm toward Jason. "You're an Imperial?"

Jason nodded. "By origin, if not profession, at the moment," he said.

Behind him, Daherrin's horse pranced impatiently, snorting. "Ta havath, Taren," the dwarf said. "You're a Home raider these days, not an Imperial." The dwarf eyed the slavers carefully, his broad smile more than vaguely insulting. "My name's Daherrin, slaver. You heard of me?"

The slaver nodded. "I recognized you from descriptions."

The dwarf nodded back. "Then why aren't you sweating like that one is?" he asked, indicating another of the slavers with a jerk of his head. "Or shitting yourself the way your other friend's about to?"

"Because there's nothing to worry about." The slaver smiled back. "Never heard you were stupid, never heard you were stupid enough to start trouble in Enkiar and end up with the city being closed to you." He turned to Jason. "We don't have a problem, young Taren. These aren't Imperials; they're all from the Shattered Islands. I haven't seen any fresh merchandise from Holtun or Bieme for years." His words had the ring of conviction, and none of the sullen slaves seemed to be stifling an objection; possibly he was telling the truth.

Daherrin had been trying to catch Jason's eye, but Jason had been deliberately ignoring him. "Taren," Daherrin said, snapping out the word like a lash. "That's enough."

Jason turned his horse away, the others falling in beside him. "Sorry, Daherrin," he said as soon as he was sure they turned a corner and left the slave markets behind. "But I had to know."

"We can talk about it later," the dwarf said. "Later." He shrugged. "No, damn it, we can talk about it now. You don't *ever*," he said, "*ever* go independent on me again. You're not in charge here; I am. If I'm out of it, command goes to Falherten, then to Mikyn, then to Arrikol. You're only in charge if you're all alone 'cause the three of us are dead."

Jason's ears burned.

"What you just pulled, boy," the dwarf went on, "is the sort of shit that your father always used to. But he could get away with it. You're not him. He could have taken all three of them all by himself; you couldn't."

"So?" Jason couldn't resist protesting. "It was my risk."

"Bullshit," the dwarf said. "Not when you're part of a team. Part of *my* team. When you do something, you're counting on the rest of us, just like we're counting on you. There's plenty of room for independent thought, but you don't act like you're on your own, 'cause you're not."

They rode in silence for a minute.

"They're mostly ugly," Mikyn said. "Like usual."

"Eh?"

"I've always heard Walter Slovotsky talk about all the beautiful women he'd freed."

"There is something to that. Aeia's awful pretty, for a human," Daherrin put in.

"But most of them look like that," Mikyn said, jerking his thumb toward the cage. There wasn't a beautiful slave girl among them; they all looked like overworked domestics.

"Way I understand it," Daherrin said as they rode on, "ugly humans hurt just as badly as pretty ones." The dwarf clucked his tongue, once, twice, three times, urging his pony into a faster walk. "Not that there's shit we can do about it here. Let's go buy some supplies."

It didn't take long to get the oats that they wanted—although Daherrin spent five times as long haggling over prices as Jason would have—and it took much less time to load the sacks of grain onto the bed of the wagon. That would have gone even more quickly if Daherrin had participated, but the raiding team leader didn't always make a practice of dirtying his hands.

The ritual was repeated at each of the stalls. Negotiate, pay and load. First the grains for the animals, and then a few sacks of dried beef and, finally, apples, carrots and turnips for both people and animals.

But, finally, the last copper was exchanged between Daherrin and an apple seller, the last sack opened and examined, the last sample apple removed (via a slit in the bag, from the middle of the bag, while the dealer's back was turned), then peeled, quartered and offered to the dealer, Daherrin seemingly by accident failing to put away the beltknife he'd used for paring the apple, the apple seller biting into the fruit without so much as a surprised glance, perhaps having dealt with a suspicious dwarf before . . . and then, with the apple seller's bite, munch and swallow, they were done.

"So. I guess we head back to camp," Jason said.

"You guess wrong, again. He used to call it 'showing the flag,' "

Daherrin said, "even though he didn't like to do it. Scared him as bad as it scares me. Which don't mean shit." He looked Jason over carefully. "You're thinking that I'm about to take a risk, just like you did. The difference between what we're doing now and what you did a while ago is that I'm deciding this. Understood? Calculated risk, not an empty-headed impulse."

"Do what?" Jason asked, as Daherrin levered himself into his saddle and kicked his horse into a canter.

"What we're gonna do now, Taren," the dwarf said. "What I'm gonna do now. Can't let the traditions die."

... *With him.* The unspoken words hung in the air between them. "There's a tavern, over this way," the dwarf said.

Falherten had a bit of trouble getting the flatbed turned around.

The tavern was a one-story wattle-and-daub building, differing from any of the dozen others on the street in, first, the huge pewter tankard, easily a quarter of Jason's height, that hung over the door like a boast, and, secondly, in the persons of the thirty or so soldiers in the livery of Lord Gyren, crowding the street in front of the tavern.

Their leader, a jowly man with a long, oily mustache that curled down the sides of his face and under his chin, held up a restraining hand as Daherrin dismounted, signaling for the others to wait.

Daherrin put an easy grin on his face. "Greetings, Captain . . . ?"

"Asklans. Greetings, Daherrin."

"Oh? We met before?"

The captain nodded. "A few years back. Some of my men and I applied to join the Home raiders. It is perhaps as well you didn't take us; this is working out acceptably. The pay isn't good, but there's less blood. We would like to keep it that way."

"Hey, Fal," the dwarf said, gesturing at Mikyn and Arriken to dismount. "You and Taren watch the wagon. We're gonna buy the captain an ale or three."

Jason looked at Daherrin. *Relay, please: I'm not going to let you keep me out of things,* he started reflexively, then remembered that Ellegon wasn't close enough.

But the dwarf relented anyway.

"Belay that," Daherrin said. "Taren, you look too thirsty to be standing on the street."

Jason tried to feel at the corners of his mind. Yes, the dragon was there, if need be, and perhaps was wondering something—perhaps how things were going?

He tried to broadcast a feeling of cautious reassurance, but wasn't sure that he was even capable of feeling that, much less transmitting it. Shrugging, he followed Daherrin into the tavern, Asklans and a half dozen of his soldiers following behind.

There was probably an exception to the rule about taverns looking the same—near as Jason could figure, there were exceptions to all of Slovotsky's Laws—but this one wasn't it: it was a dark and smoky room, too few lanterns sending too much smoke and too little light into the stale air.

It was crowded, too: there were easily forty men sitting on stools around the rough-hewn tables, most of them looking at Daherrin and his three companions, and at the soldiers following them in. Most of them were locals, some in the clean broadcloths of merchants, others in the rough gray tunics, breechclouts, and leggings of peasants, their tunics belted with rope, not sword belts—but a dozen of the men were armed, some with their swords belted on, some with them propped against the walls.

"I smell slavers," the dwarf said, sniffing loudly. "The Slavers' Guild doesn't need to make its members wear uniforms, not when slavers stink up a room."

The room got very quiet, very quickly. At one of the low tables, four peasants looked from one to another, then rose, leaving their ale and bread unfinished as they headed out the door.

One of the slavers reached slowly, carefully toward his sword belt, not pausing when Asklans held up a restraining hand, desisting only when another slaver shook his head twice, quickly, his face expressionless.

Daherrin seated himself at the nearest of the tables, his eyes never leaving the slavers.

The innkeeper—a thickset man with the customary beer belly and big hands—scurried over, wiping his hands on a rag. "Drinks? Or drinks and food?"

"Just ale," the dwarf said. "Four tankards. Go help him pour, Arriken."

"That won't be necessary," Asklans said, taking up a position behind the dwarf. No apparent signal passed from him to his troops, but the six men spread out, two of them taking up parade rest positions in a far corner, two others near the door to the kitchen, the final two walking to stand behind the slavers in the far corner of the room.

Daherrin didn't turn as he answered, "Maybe it isn't." But he didn't say anything to Arriken, who followed the innkeeper into the kitchen, returning with four pewter tankards, each brimming with foam. Arriken sipped each one in turn, setting the first in front of the dwarf, the second in front of Mikyn, the third in front of Jason, and taking the last for himself.

"Drink up, Taren," he said. "If things go to shit, you may as well have a last brew in your belly." He sat down next to the dwarf and gulped his own ale, the foam staining his full lips and beard.

Nobody in the room spoke for a long time, until one of the slavers stood. Daherrin shook his head fractionally, and Mikyn, who had looked as if he were about to launch himself across the table, relaxed to the same degree that Jason did: not much.

Jason didn't like it. Slavers were supposed to look evil—Ahrmin had looked like cruelty incarnate—but this one didn't. He just looked like a normal, twentyish man in the tunic, breechclout and leggings combination that was the common dress in the Eren regions. His sword was at the left side of his waist, the scabbard rigged to keep the hilt canted forward at a comfortable angle for a cross-body draw.

His face wasn't pinched; his eyes weren't sunken hollows. Just a normal-looking brown-haired man, with perhaps a too-easy grin on his broad face. But it wasn't much of a grin.

"Greetings," he said, seating himself opposite Daherrin, Jason and Arriken, both hands on his tankard. "Willem, senior journeyman of the Slavers' Guild. You are?"

"Daherrin," the dwarf said, returning the human's gaze levelly. "Home raiding team leader."

"Arriken, raider," Arriken said.

"Taren, raider," Jason said.

"Death," Mikyn whispered, his voice barely audible.

"Mikyn," the dwarf snapped, "ta havath."

"I'm your death," Mikyn repeated. There was a tight grin on his lips, a smile that wasn't at all reflected in his eyes. "I'm what you see before it all ends for you." He whispered the words gently, almost lovingly.

When just a child, Mikyn and both his parents had been taken by slavers. He and his father had been freed in a raid by the team headed by Karl Cullinane. His mother had never been heard from again.

"*Mikyn*," the dwarf repeated. "Ta havath, I said. We're just here to show the flag," he went on in English, "not to get our heads broke in a fight. Ease off, boy."

Mikyn wasn't having any. "Remember me," he whispered. "Always remember me."

There was a metallic taste at the back of Jason's mouth: the taste of bile, the taste of fear. *Ellegon!*

There was no distant reassurance.

Asklans clapped his hands together three times. "So be it. Enough of this; we're not going to have a fight here." He nodded to one of his men, who stuck two fingers in his mouth and gave out a three-part whistle, which was repeated from outside.

Jason, Daherrin, Mikyn and Arriken found themselves quickly surrounded by easily a dozen soldiers, each with a drawn shortsword; across the room, the slavers were similarly surrounded.

"Enkiar is neutral," Asklans said. "Enkiar will remain both neutral and peaceful, if I have to butcher a thousand slavers and raiders. By the authority of Lord Gyren, you both are to leave Enkiar— Daherrin, you and your team will head out in the morning on the Home road; Willem, you will inform Master Lifezh that all of you are to leave tomorrow, heading toward Khar."

"Such was our intention," Willem said. "Such was our intention."

Soldiers began to crowd Daherrin and his group out the front door, while others pushed the slavers toward the back.

Then there was a low cry from one of the peasants in the dark of the room. "The warrior lives," the harsh voice whispered. "The warrior lives."

Jason couldn't see who said it, but he did catch a glimpse of Willem's face before the soldiers pushed him out the door.

The slaver's face was white.

The warrior lives? What did that mean? And why should it scare the slavers so badly?

"You'll be on your way by sunset," Asklans said. "By sunset, do you hear?"

"We hear," Daherrin said. "I'm not sure we understand everything, but we hear."

CHAPTER 10

Farewells

"My idea of an agreeable person," said Hugo Bohun, *"is a person who agrees with me."*

—Benjamin Disraeli

Arguing is one of life's greatest pleasures, even if you have to argue with yourself. 'Course, I could enjoy the other side of that argument, too.

—Walter Slovotsky

There's no enemy in range; I'm coming in.

Ellegon swooped down out of the late afternoon sky, the backblast from his fast-moving wings drawing nervous neighs from the horses and sending sparks from the dying campfires swirling off into the grasses.

That had happened before, and the half dozen of Daherrin's warriors on fire duty were ready for it; five of them stomped out the sparks, while the sixth wielded a canteen, for insurance.

The dozen Enkiaran soldiers down by the road had good discipline: although several of the horses pranced their nervousness, none of the horsemen let his mount get away from him. Enkiar's neutrality apparently applied to nonhostile dragons, too.

As long as none of them have dragonbane on their bolts, Ellegon said nervously.

I would have assumed you mindprobed them.

341

*Assume all you want. All I can tell is that none of them *knows* he has a poisoned bolt. I doubt that would do me a lot of good if their fletcher's primed one without telling them. Let's get in the air. Now.*

Durine was already tightening the dragon's rigging and helping first Aeia, then Bren Adahan into their places.

I'll be just a minute.

While the others got aboard, Jason took a moment to brace Daherrin. "What was that about a warrior living?"

"Who knows?" The dwarf shrugged. "Wouldn't make too much of that. Probably another freelancer put a scare into them, even if they have been scarce for the past few years. If so, he'll—most likely show up at Home, sooner or later."

Mikyn led his horse over. "I don't know about that. What say you send somebody on their trail to find out?"

The dwarf shook his head. "No. Just no. There's a full hundred slavers, and I don't like those odds at all."

"Then make it just me," Mikyn said. There was a strange note in his voice, a suggestion of something that could have been resolve, could have been fear. "I have to."

"No," the dwarf said. "The bastards've gotten better over the past coupla years—they been putting rear guards on their backtrail more often than not."

"Then set me up as a roving tradesman—we've got the traveling farrier outfit all ready to go—and let me go."

"Shit, Mikyn, we discussed this a tenday ago, and you said then that the traveling farrier disguise is wearing a bit thin, and—"

"Mikyn," Jason said, "what is it?" Jason had thought at first that Mikyn had just been trying to spook the slaver, but there was more to it than that.

"I remember the voice. It was his voice. When we were sold. I heard his voice."

The dwarf snorted. "Not bloody likely. That was twenty years ago; he ain't a lot older'n you."

"Then it's a brother, or a son, or a fucking *cousin,* or it's one of the bastards that just happens to sound like the one who . . ." Mikyn's fists clenched. "But he's *mine.* You hear me, Daherrin? He's mine. You're right: the team can't take their trail. But I can."

Jason, we have to go now.

Just a moment. "Daherrin, it's your team, and I wouldn't think of interfering with how you run it . . ."

"Right." The dwarf actually laughed. "The usual Cullinane opening to interfering with how I run the company. You think he should go get his liver sliced open?"

"No. I don't think you should let him go. Not unless you want to, upon reconsideration." *Relay, please: but I think he will, no matter what you do, and you're better off giving your blessing than having a deserter gone in the night.* "And unless Mikyn promises to keep his head down. My father took out a lot of slavers when he died."

"He did, at that," Mikyn said, a thin smile peeking through his beard.

"But we'd all be better off if he'd lived." Jason gripped Mikyn's shoulder tightly. "All of us would be."

Mikyn hesitated, then nodded fractionally.

He's still going to go. But the dwarf says: "Okay, kid. Get going; I'll pretend to think about it, and then let him slip away tonight, after we're moving."

"Take care, Jason." Daherrin clasped Jason's hand. "Hey, I know you're planning on settling down after this, but if you ever change your mind, I've got a job for you. Pay's low, and the working conditions range from bad to terrible, but at least the food sucks."

CHAPTER 11
Wehnest

Lord, give me the wisdom to distinguish between unnecessary brutality and brutal necessity. At least some of the time.
—David Warcinsky

Probably the most difficult decision real humans have to make is whether something is necessarily brutal or unnecessarily brutal. I wish there was something funny about that, but there you have it.
—Walter Slovotsky

Wehnest was usually Ellegon's last stop before Home. Partly it was because it was a solid day's flight from any of several of the usual rendezvous locations; largely it was because there were often extra trade goods remaining after the resupply runs, usually consisting of leftover Nehera-made blades that were marketable anywhere.

This wasn't a usual trip; but they stopped in Wehnest anyway.

The ground rushed up in the dark, more felt than seen; Ellegon's flailing wings battered the air so hard that Jason couldn't keep his eyes open, but he felt the ground coming up as though it was reaching up to knock them out of the sky, until, at the last moment, their downward momentum slowed and the dragon landed with a thump that rattled Jason's teeth.

Everybody down, the dragon said.

They all alighted in the dark. By arrangement, Tennetty and Durine slipped off into the trees, on watch.

Everyone was silent for a moment, then Ellegon snorted. *We can light a fire; there's nobody around.*

The clearing that Ellegon had chosen was just short of a thinning stand of tall pines and stumps; beyond the trees, a fallow field stood in the starlight, a ragged rug of weeds proclaiming its idleness. Over the rise in the other direction was Wehnest, but it would be safe to start a small fire anyway; the light breeze was blowing steadily into the forest, and the smoke of a fire wouldn't be visible before daybreak, still several hours away.

Jason smiled as they quickly gathered and stacked firewood. At least he wouldn't have to light it. Karl Cullinane had insisted that Jason learn to light a fire with flint and steel—a laborious and downright boring process. Lighting this fire would be easy, what with Ellegon around, but gathering wood took no less time.

I still say you should just skip Wehnest, the dragon said. The purpose of this trip is to pick up Walter's daughters and wife, not to trade in some blades.*

Aeia stooped over a fallen tree, grabbing an out-thrust branch with one hand and neatly detaching it from the tree trunk with three quick chops of her hatchet. "The trouble with that is that we're doing more than one thing," she said. "We're also checking into the Kernat raid."

Jason dropped an armload of wood on the charred spot near the center of the clearing. Aeia was right, as usual. Still, the chances of learning anything in Wehnest were minimal; Wehnest was one of Home's main trading partners, and likely the ground had been gone over repeatedly by Home traders.

But the difference between likely and certain was important; Jason would probably never learn what had happened to the people who disappeared from Kernat village, but he had to try. It came with the job.

As defined by your father, the dragon said. *Not every ruler thinks he has to look into everything himself.*

Firstly, it wasn't everything. Karl Cullinane had felt perfectly comfortable in sending Danagar, General Garavar's son, out spying—about this very matter, in fact.

But, secondly, Karl Cullinane had established the point that the

Emperor of Holtun-Bieme wasn't going to be afraid to get his hands dirty, and that was rubbing off, much to the better. Bren Adahan was along on this trip only partly to chase after Aeia; he'd long since accepted Karl's notion that a ruler was supposed to be in contact with the world, not sitting in a castle in luxurious isolation.

Thomen Furnael had picked up on that, too, Jason thought with a smile. Although the last time Thomen had tried something clever, Father had sent him home with a groin kick that Gashier had described in glorious detail. The kick had been to teach Thomen another lesson: opposing Karl Cullinane wasn't a good idea.

All that's true, the dragon said. *But I don't have to like it. Getting too involved with the world is what got him killed. You Cullinanes aren't unkillable, you know.*

That was true enough. Although . . . there had been a time when it had been thought that Karl Cullinane was unkillable, that nobody could take him on. There were legends that had grown up around Jason's father, about the time that he had single-handedly freed his wife-to-be from a thousand slavers.

And, like all legends, there was a germ of truth in that: Karl Cullinane had freed Andrea. But it had been from a scant dozen slavers, and Walter Slovotsky had been along, softening them up with several crossbow bolts fired out of the night.

Filling a legend's boots was going to be hard. Piling firewood for Ellegon was a lot easier.

"I think that's about enough," Jason said, dropping a final armload on the pile. He stood back. Ellegon's cavernous mouth opened fractionally, and then a quick tongue of flame issued forth.

The wood only broke into a smoky smoulder; Ellegon tried again.

It's too damp, the dragon said with a petulant sniff. He raised his head again and exhaled a huge mouthful of flame that not only set the stacked firewood burning, but sent flaming embers shooting off into the night, some of them threatening to start minor fires which could, if unchecked, quickly grow into a major blaze.

Aeia stomped out one incipient ember; Kethol and Durine, both giggling incongruously, pissed on a second and third, while Jason ground out a fourth.

Nice going, Ellegon, he thought.

I can't control everything, the dragon said.

Still, it did make a good campfire.

Tennetty and Durine had first watch; Jason slept like a dead man.

The first thing to do the next morning was to head into Wehnest and get some horses. While Wehnest was smaller than, say, Biemestren, it was spread out, and some of the places Jason wanted to go to were a fair walk from each other.

Besides, it gave him the chance to look up a friend. Of sorts.

Pistols close at hand but not in evidence, Tennetty, Kethol and Durine spread out, watching the street, while Jason, Bren Adahan and Aeia walked up to the stables.

He heard a distant mental question from Ellegon, and sent back reassurance. Everything was fine. The stables were better kept than they'd been the last time he was here; the straw covering the dirt floor was freshly changed, and while the place reeked of horse piss and horse shit, most of it seemed to emanate from the exercise yard outside, not the stables themselves.

The hostler was bent over, busy examining the left front hoof of a small brown mare.

"I'll need the use of half a dozen horses for two or three days," Jason said, slapping a silverpiece on the railpost. It rang brightly, a musical tone that announced that it was too much money by an order of magnitude.

The hostler, surprised, dropped the hoof and straightened, looking him in the face.

He was a short, fat, bald man whose eyes held traces of fear and pettiness, perhaps, but no cruelty. Or maybe Jason was just projecting; he had reason to know that the man wasn't cruel, was in fact more softhearted and sentimental than a hostler, or anyone else in this world, had any business being.

Maybe.

"*Taren*," Vator the hostler exclaimed. A smile broke across his face. "Taren, boy," he said, clapping his hands to Jason's shoulders. "Or should it be Jason?"

Bren Adahan stiffened, but Jason held up a hand. There was no reason to worry. Jason had fled as word spread that Karl Cullinane's son was on his own in the Eren regions, alone and vulnerable. He hadn't expected his cover to fool Vator then, and he certainly hadn't expected the cover to be intact by now.

As Walter Slovotsky would have said, you can't be just a little bit exposed.

Jason eased his rucksack from his shoulders and then, practiced fingers undoing the knots in the leather drawstring, drew out a winesack.

"A drink for luck," he said, straightening, uncorking it. "Jason Cullinane, heir to crown and throne of Holtun-Bieme, wishes you well." He tilted back the skin. He hadn't drunk out of a wineskin for too long; some of the lukewarm liquid ran down the side of his cheek, down his neck, into his tunic. He handed the skin to Vator.

"Vator, the hostler, of Wehnest, wishes you well," Expertly the fat man tilted back the wine, then handed it to Aeia and Bren Adahan, who introduced themselves and drank.

"Now," the hostler said, "you want some horses?"

Jason nodded. "And saddles. Just for two days, maybe three," he lied reflexively. It would be one day at most, that was all the time they'd need, but it made sense to let even someone as trustworthy as Vator think that there was plenty of time to arrange a betrayal.

The hostler nodded. "The silverpiece will be fine," he said, tiredly, as though announcing his resignation to a long session of bargaining.

"Agreed," Jason said.

The hostler looked every bit as disappointed as surprised, but he turned to the stables, calling out, "Gachet, Gachet, where are you? Are you sleeping again?"

"No, master, no I'm not," floated down from the hayloft. "I was just cleaning up here."

"I should flay you within a handbreadth of your life, but just saddle six of our best—yes, yes, the white gelding, I said the best, didn't I?—just saddle six of the best and I'll forget it all, I'll forget it all."

A man in a ragged tunic and black iron collar clambered down from the hayloft and disappeared into the stables.

Jason felt the smile fade from his face; he looked the hostler over coldly.

Vator seemed taken aback for a moment, but then he shrugged.

He didn't have any reason to be afraid; while Home warriors were almost always willing to take on slavers, slave-owners were a different matter. Home couldn't afford to take on every slave-owner in the Eren regions; the policy was to not free slaves in the hands of private parties, unless the private parties were acting on behalf of the guild.

Aeia's smile seemed genuine. "Jason never mentioned that you were doing so well when he was through here."

Vator smiled weakly. "I arranged a trade, when some guildsmen came through here, looking for the boy from Home. I gave them his direction and they gave me a slave. An acceptable deal, eh? Of course, there was the problem of telling them where you'd gone. I had no intention of putting them actually on your trail, so I sent them toward the Healing Hand Tabernacle."

"Which is where I told you I was going," Jason said.

"Yes, yes," Vator said, with a nod, "but I knew you were lying." He gripped Jason's hand tightly. "I'd not betray you, Jason, then or now. —Let me help Gachet saddle your horses."

Their first concern had been the possibility of slavers in town, but there weren't any; the slave trade was at a virtual standstill around Wehnest, as the cost of hiring labor was so much lower than buying it.

And, since there was no sign of fresh slaves, there was therefore no sign of any slaves who had been taken in the Kernat village raid. That part of the mission was, so far, a failure.

Still, the Nehera blades had gone for a nice price, Jason thought, hefting the small bag of silver and listening to the coins tinkle pleasantly. He'd have to tell Nehera first off, once they got to Home; the dwarf would be pleased that authentic Nehera blades were still so valuable.

"It could be Ahrmin," Durine mused. "He was always tricky."

"If that little bastard was behind the Kernat raid," Tennetty said, the index and middle fingers of her free hand drumming a random tattoo on the front peak of her saddle, "it's not impossible that the people they seized were simply killed."

"Then why take them at all?" Kethol asked.

Jason nodded. That didn't make sense either. There was some Other Sider's principle that Walter Slovotsky had told him about, something about not making explanations any more complicated than necessary to fit the facts. Somebody's . . . knife, was it? No, not knife. But something similar. Knife, blade, sword, dagger, razor, cleaver. Cleaver. That sounded familiar. Beaver's Cleaver—that sounded about right.

"We don't get to understand it all," he said, as they rode back to the corral outside Vator's stables, dismounting one by one.

Gachet, Vator's slave, ran to take their reins and led three of the animals into the corral while Jason, Aeia and Bren Adahan led their own horses.

Jason's skin crawled. He hadn't had much experience around slaves—the only kind of slaves in Home and Holtun-Bieme were *former* slaves—and he didn't like it much. He remembered the Slavers' Guildhall in Pandathaway, and the crack of whips and parting of flesh.

Inside the corral he let the reins drop and dismissed the horse with a light slap on its solid flank. Not quite the animal that Jason's big gelding, Libertarian, had been—but not a bad mount, at least for the day.

The slave led the horse away.

Slave. . . .

Jason's fist clenched.

Jason. The distant voice held concern and alarm.

I'm fine, he sent back.

There was nothing he could do about it, then or now. Wehnest was neutral, and there were no slavers here; he could hardly take Gachet away from Vator.

That was the trouble, he thought, as Vator walked over to him, concern creasing his sweating brow. "Is there a problem, Jason Cullinane?" the hostler asked.

Beyond Vator, a few children and an overweight, stooped woman were working in the stables. The woman mucked out one of the stalls while one of the children brought fresh hay for the horses and another helped Gachet unsaddle and wipe down the horses.

It wasn't the same thing as in Pandathaway, Jason thought. Vator was the sort who would threaten to beat the slave within an inch of his life, but he wouldn't do it. He didn't mean it. Vator's wife and children probably worked every bit as hard as Gachet, and Vator himself surely worked harder.

"Gachet," Jason heard himself saying, "do you want to be free?"

The slave paled. He looked from Vator to Jason, then opened his mouth, closed it, opened it again, and then closed it again.

Over in the stables, the woman bent down to whisper to one of the boys, who took off down the road behind the exercise yard, bare feet pounding on the bare dirt.

Kethol looked over to Jason, as if to ask, *Do I chase him?*

"It's your play," Tennetty said. "Call it, Jason."

Durine looked from Jason to Tennetty to Kethol, and then nodded.

Bren Adahan took a step toward Jason, but stopped when Aeia grabbed his arm. "Leave it be," she said. "Pick us up, and hurry," Aeia muttered.

Don't do anything stupid, the distant voice said. *I'm on my way.*

Vator faced him. "There's no glory to be won here, Jason Cullinane, unless you can find some honor in six of you cutting down one unarmed man." He spat on the ground between them.

"Perhaps we don't have to do anything to the one unarmed man," Bren Adahan said. "Perhaps you will simply free Gachet of your own will."

For a moment, just a moment, Jason thought Vator was going to back down. It would have been the logical, the reasonable thing to do. Resisting didn't make sense; they had him outmanned, and Vator was no warrior.

"You'll not take what's mine, Jason Cullinane," Vator whispered. He had a knife in his belt; anyone who works around horses and stables finds a hundred daily uses for a knife. His hand dropped to its hilt.

Tennetty cocked a pistol with an emphatic click. "Don't even think about it." She extended the pistol and sighted down her arm.

"Lower your gun, Tennetty," Jason said. He was the center of everything, but he couldn't hold it all together. It was all falling apart, and there was nothing he could do about it.

Except try for a way out.

Come pick us up, and hurry.

Hang on, please, the distant voice said. *Just a few more moments.*

"Sure, I'll put the gun down. Soon as you draw your sword. I'm not going to have to tell your mother that I let him stab you to death while you stood there with a scabbarded sword."

"She's right, sir," Durine said. "Get your blade out. Please."

Compromise. There had to be a compromise.

Jason drew his sword. "Change your mind, Vator. Let him go, of your own free will."

"Go into the stables, Gachet," Vator said quietly, his eyes never leaving Jason's.

"As you are," Bren Adahan said, as he and Aeia each took one of the slave's arms; Gachet didn't resist as they moved him away.

"Dur—around the other side," Kethol said, breaking into a sprint for the stables. He came out a moment later; dragging Vator's wife by one arm and holding a crossbow in his free hand. "She was trying to load this."

Vator's eyes never left Jason's as a dark form rose above the trees. With a flurry of wings and a gout of flame, Ellegon's massive form appeared over the stables and hovered momentarily, sending dust and leaves swirling into the air before the dragon dropped heavily to the ground.

Vator's wife screamed; tearing her arm loose from Kethol's grasp, she fled for the stables.

Let him go, Vator, the dragon said. *There's no shame in being defeated by an overwhelming force.*

Vator's eyes never left Jason's. "You'll not take what's mine."

"Get aboard, everyone," Jason said, "Kethol, help Gachet get aboard."

"Let's move it, people," Tennetty said. "I can hear the hoofbeats from down the road, and even if they don't have dragonbaned arrows, my hide isn't as thick as Ellegon's."

Vator shook his head. "Not this time, Jason Cullinane. Not this time." He drew his knife and lunged at Jason.

"*No!*"

Two guns fired at once. One bullet missed entirely, another smashed into Vator's knee. The fat hostler opened his mouth to scream, but the blade of a thrown knife flew past his lips, becoming a hideous metal tongue.

The hostler fell dead at Jason's feet. A stench rose into the air as his body voided itself, leaving him without dignity even in death.

There was no need for it. Jason might not have been the swordsman his father had been, but even Jason could take on an overweight hostler wielding a utility knife. It wasn't necessary.

We have to get going, the dragon said. Tennetty scabbarded his sword, and then Durine half-helped, half-carried Jason up to his seat.

Fasten yourself in. Now.

Distant fingers buckled him into place.

"Let's get out of here, Ellegon," Tennetty said.

Wings flapping madly, the dragon leaped into the sky. Gachet screeched as the ground dropped away, stopping when Tennetty told him to shut up.

Below, a young boy, standing over the dead body of his father, looked up into the sky.

They flew in silence for a few moments, until Tennetty snorted, briefly. It could have been a laugh.

"What's so funny?" Aeia asked, her irritation audible.

Tennetty sighed. "Reminds me of the old days, that's all. Just remembering something the dwarf once said in the old days, about how we seem to leave most towns just ahead of the cops."

CHAPTER 12
Home, At Last

I judge impetuosity to be better than caution.
                    —Niccoló Machiavelli

Niccoló Machiavelli was an asshole.
                    —Walter Slovotsky

It was sundown when they landed in the front yard of the New House, the house where Jason had spent most of his time growing up, before the move to Biemestren.

As they circled in, a crowd of people gathered below, their elongated shadows playing across the grass: a few warriors from Frandred's team; some farmers in from their fields on business; Petros, the deputy mayor; and Lou Riccetti. The Engineer was grim as death as he stood, fingers twining impatiently, thin lips pursed perhaps in sorrow, perhaps in irritation.

There's news, the dragon said as he *thunk*ed to the ground. Ellegon's mental voice held a quaver of excitement. *About your father.*

"Jason," Lou Riccetti said, "quickly: how many did you leave behind you in Melawei?"

"Two. Ahira and Walter Slovotsky."

"Then," Lou Riccetti said, choosing this words slowly, carefully, "I think your father might be alive. I may have a lead on where he is. Come with me inside; we've got to talk to Aldren."

CHAPTER 13
"All Men Are Created Equal . . ."

*We boast our emancipation from many superstitions; but if
we have broken any idols, it is through a transfer of idolatry.*
                                    —Ralph Waldo Emerson

*I find that we all get more legendary as time goes by. "Leg-
end" means, basically, "bullshit."*
                                    —Walter Slovotsky

A trader had brought word of Karl Cullinane's death just the
tenday before.

Lou hadn't been sure whether or not to believe it.

Then Aldren came Home.

"As far as I know, I was the last one out searching for you,"
Aldren said as they sat in the living room of the New House. "I
was posing as a mercenary soldier looking for work." He sat back
in the big leather chair next to the fireplace and drank more from
his big pewter tankard of ale. In the light of the crackling fire,
he looked ordinary enough: fortyish, gray hairs streaking a roughly-
cut brown beard, a few scars on his hand and a few laugh lines
around his eyes. "I must have hit Pandathaway about three tendays
after you all left; and I figured that if you'd gotten as far as
Pandathaway by the time Ahrmin left, you'd likely be chasing after
Karl.

"Which, it seemed to me, made the search for you pointless.

355

But, just in case, I headed north, up the coast, on the grounds that it might be a good idea to scout out Guild strengths in some of the coastal cities; we don't like to work that close to Pandathaway, but maybe we're going to have to, way pickings have been.

"In any case, I found that there were fewer guildsmen around than there ought to have been—skeleton crews everywhere, and they looked scared."

He drained his ale and signaled for more; Riccetti himself refilled it from the hogshead in the corner.

"I'm not the best swordsman around, and I'm not too good with a gun. But there's two things I'm real good at: I can blend into the furniture, and I can drink any two men under the table. I got a couple of them drinking, and then drunk. And they started talking.

"Seems that Ahrmin and all of his shorebound force died in Melawei."

That didn't surprise Jason; Walter Slovotsky had said that he wouldn't let anyone kill Karl Cullinane and live to brag about it.

"When their relief force got there, they were stinking in the sun. And there was a note left behind, pinned to one of the corpses, part of it in a language that the slavers didn't understand and part of it in Erendra. There were three signatures to the note. The part in Erendra read: *The warrior lives.*

"Scared the shit out of the slavers, but what could they do?"

Jason swallowed. *The warrior lives.* The same thing somebody had said in the Enkiar tavern. He walked to the mantelpiece and ran his fingers along it, the heat from the fire beating against his legs, even through his trousers.

Outside, leathery wings rustled in the night.

What do you think?

I don't know. What do you think?

There was no answer as Aldren went on: "Then, about six tendays ago, a guildsman in Lundeyll woke up next to one with his throat cut. Another note, also with three signatures. The word is that a dozen men, several of them Mels—but not all of them— caught a ship out of there the next morning, just ahead of Lord Lund's proctors."

"Shit." Tennetty slapped her hand down on the arm of her chair and laughed. "He could be alive. Leaving town just ahead of trouble is the Cullinane family trademark, Jason."

Lou Riccetti's smile and nod were distant. "Lundeyll was the first town we fled from, on This Side." His smile vanished; he shook his head. "Your namesake died there," he told Jason. "He was my best friend." Riccetti bit his lip. "I'm sorry—go on, Aldren."

"Another note, also with three signatures." Aldren reached for a map. "In Wehnest, on the way back, I picked up news that it's happened again, on Menelet. In any case, the slavers believe that your father and his two comrades are somewhere in the Shattered Islands, or maybe on Salket. Every guildsman is either hunkering down, hoping they'll hit somewhere else, or trying to hunt them down."

Lou Riccetti leaned forward. "Aldren just got in yesterday. I was putting together a team to go hunting for them, too. But your arrival suggests another idea."

Kethol nodded. "With Ellegon to place us, we've got a good chance of getting to them before the slavers do, particularly if we can figure out where they'll hit next."

Thanks for the vote of confidence. But it all depends on where they're going to hit next, and on how well we can guess.

Aeia smiled. Jason had to admit that his adopted sister was lovely when she smiled. "We know where they're going," she said. "Just draw a line. They're headed for Endell. Probably Ahira's idea; when they get close to dwarvish territory, they'll be safe. If the slavers don't catch up with them or cut them off first."

That seems to be generally true, but I doubt that Karl or Walter are going to draw a straight line for the slavers to follow.

"We have to know." Jason began to pace back and forth. "We have to tie it all down, and quickly."

Lou Riccetti raised an eyebrow. "Before the slavers get to them?"

"It's not that." Jason dropped heavily into his chair. It was like ripples on a pond, like the skipped stones. When Jason was a boy, his father had little time to play with him, and after they moved to Holtun-Bieme, that time had dropped off to virtually nothing.

But he remembered a day, when they were back visiting Home on some business, and an evening, as the sun set, when his father took him down to the lake and taught him how to skip a stone across the water. The trick was to pick the right stone, to curl your index finger around it, then throw it sidearm, just right, and it would bounce five, six, seven times across the still, flat water, each bounce sending out a circular, expanding ripple.

Word that Karl Cullinane was alive was spreading after the strikes, like the splashes of the stone that day.

"If he's alive, he can handle all the slavers in the world," Jason said. "It's not that; we have to nail this down, tight, before word of this reaches my mother."

He stood. "My father's death hit her hard." *Harder than any of you know, or are going to know.* "I won't have her hopes raised and then dashed. We have to settle all this and get back to Biemestren before word reaches Holtun-Bieme. We find out if my father's really alive, and we find out fast."

Ellegon spoke up. *I can drop you off along the coast and rendezvous later, but I have a run that can't wait forever. Daven's team is not going to be able to hold out without a resupply.*

And more; Ellegon might be needed to extract Daven's team, a few at a time.

There was another matter. *I want you to check in on my mother, and stay with her if necessary.*

Doria was a good—Doria *had been* a good healer, but she wasn't a healer anymore, and she couldn't read minds.

True. But I don't like picking her brains. It's not like with you.
Do it anyway.

Still, it shouldn't take many of them. They had more of a Walter Slovotsky job than a Karl Cullinane one: Locate, find, make contact and extract. Get them to a rendezvous with the dragon and get them all out. And back to Biemestren.

"Best to start from the other end," Tennetty said. "Endell; work our way south, hoping that we don't pass them by, or if we do, that we pick up a live trail."

Kethol nodded. "Just you, with Durine and me to keep an eye on your back. Small and fast. We find them, rendezvous with Ellegon and lift out."

"And me," Tennetty said, quietly. "You can't leave me behind. Not for this."

"And Tennetty," Durine said. He studied her with a curious intensity. "But that's all."

Lou Riccetti nodded. "That makes sense. Take tomorrow to rest up—there's some things I want to get ready for you—and you can leave the day after."

"No," Aeia said. "That is not all. I have to know. I have to go. He's my father, too," Aeia said. "Or isn't my blood Cullinane enough for you?"

"*Definitely* not." Lou Riccetti shook his head. "Not you, Aeia. You have to stay here. You're needed; the matter is closed."

As she opened her mouth, he raised a palm. "I can't—force you to stay here. But Ellegon won't carry you into danger—not this time. Until it's proven otherwise, we have to hope that Karl is alive, but assume he's dead. If Jason's going into harm's way to find him, then we have to consider who the Cullinane heir is. You think Andrea's likely to have any more children?"

Aeia shook her head.

"Then who else will produce the Cullinane heir, if Jason doesn't come back? Which is why you stay, too, Bren Adahan."

For a moment, Jason thought that Lou Riccetti was going to prevail, but then Bren Adahan shook his head.

"You may be correct, Mr. Mayor," he said slowly, choosing his words carefully, like a man picking his way barefoot across sharp stones, "that, if Jason dies, the Cullinane heir has to come from her womb—but I don't have to be the father. I would not be the father. I'm still a Holt. The Biemish barons would not stand for the father of the Heir being a Holt, or the son of a Holt." His fists clenched. "While I resent these private matters becoming subjects for public comment, let me point out to you that my only chance at having Aeia for my wife is to keep Jason Cullinane from getting killed. He will *stay* alive." His fingers curled around the arm of his chair, their knuckles white.

He looked Jason square in the face. "Which is why I am coming along, Jason Cullinane. I will see to it that you stay alive, no matter what it takes."

Tennetty stood. "Everybody drink up, then hit the sheets. Tomorrow, we pack; we leave the day after."

Jason couldn't sleep. It would have been nice if there was somebody to hold his hand while he slept, but there wasn't, not anymore. Valeran was dead, and so was Chak. Mother was too dependent on him, even if she didn't know it. Doria wasn't here, and Karl Cullinane was dead.

Maybe. Maybe not.

Everybody died on him. Chak, Valeran, Father, even Vator. The bastard. Why did he have to die in a fight over a slave? Was it worth his life?

Shit. It just didn't make any sense. None of it made sense.

Jason sat in a weathered wooden chair on the porch of the New House, carving idly at a scrap of pine and staring out at the starlight, watching the slow pulse of faerie lights off to the west. Somewhere in the distance, dicalas chittered in the trees.

A dark shape passed overhead: Ellegon on the last leg of a patrol. The wards around the valley prevented anyone from bringing in magical implements, but couldn't react to creatures unencumbered by spells. While the dragon spent little time here these days, the resident raiders appreciated being able to reduce the guard on those few days when he was around. A night's sleep was a precious thing.

Are you out there? That didn't make any sense, either. If Karl Cullinane was alive, nothing in the world would have kept him from his wife. If he was alive, what were Walter Slovotsky and the dwarf up to? Sure, it made sense to prevent the slavers from returning to Pandathaway to brag of having seen Karl Cullinane's dead body—but they couldn't possibly be counting on maintaining that kind of deception. The word would eventually get out.

But maybe he wasn't dead. Jason hadn't actually seen his father die; all that any of them had seen was a wounded Karl Cullinane leaving them behind, and then an explosion.

Could he have triggered the explosion from far enough away to have survived it?

It wasn't impossible. Or was it?

He could be alive. In which case Jason wasn't going to have to take the crown, not yet.

That felt good. As if a weight had been lifted from his shoulders. Or as if, maybe, a weight was now being lifted; he couldn't tell, yet.

But it felt good.

The door behind him yawned open, light splashing through and pushing the edges of darkness away, although only a little. Jason turned to see Lou Riccetti, an undyed cotton robe belted tightly over a pair of Home jeans, a pair of wooden clogs on his feet. Riccetti had a wooden box and a mottled glass bottle under one arm; in his other hand he held a lantern. He set the lantern on a table.

"What are you doing up at this hour?" Jason asked.

"I was going to ask you that." Riccetti chuckled. "You should go to bed." He pulled out the bottle's wooden stopper with his teeth, then spat the stopper carefully onto the tabletop. He set the box on the table at Jason's elbow. "Maybe some of the Best will help." He tilted back the bottle, wiped his mouth with the back of his hand, then handed the bottle to Jason.

Jason sipped the fiery liquor out of politeness. It tasted horrible—but then again, he'd never developed the Other Siders' taste for corn whiskey. No, that wasn't fair. It wasn't just the Other Siders; Home was doing a modest trade in Riccetti's Best, although other distillers were springing up all across the Eren regions and into the dwarvish north and elvish east.

They sat in silence for a few minutes, passing the bottle back and forth.

"The council wants me to talk you out of doing business with the elves over powder," Jason said. "But will you listen to me?"

"I will listen, but I'll do what I think best. Don't count on persuading me." Riccetti shook his head. "You don't have the information I do. Or the feel for what happens next."

"You sound almost like Doria," Jason said, chuckling.

Riccetti laughed. "Maybe I do. Been a long time since I've seen her. When you get back, tell her I want a visit. Maybe she could bring your mother, and whenever Slovotsky shows up, we could all play some bridge."

My father played bridge, too. It was one of the Other Side innovations that just hadn't caught on. Like the shower.

"About the powder . . ."

"Yeah. The powder." Riccetti opened the box and pulled out a small leather pouch. He opened it and tilted half a dozen tiny brass buttons onto the table. "Step the next. We strip the frizzen and pan off the long rifles and put on a metal nipple leading into the end of the barrel. Then modify the hammer to snap down tightly over the nipple. Nehera can do ten a day; lesser blacksmiths can do at least four or five.

"Come here." He picked up one of the buttons and walked a few paces off the porch and down to the first flat stone in the walk. He set the button down carefully on the stone. "Give me your knife."

"Eh?"

"Your knife, your knife."

Jason drew his beltknife and handed it over properly, hilt first.

The older man squatted in front of the stone. Taking careful aim with the hilt, he slammed it squarely down on the metal button. It flashed into a quiet snap of flame and a small puff of smoke that shattered in the light breeze.

"Primer. Hit it hard enough, it flashes into fire. Just like the priming powder in the pan."

They returned to the porch and sat back down, Riccetti laying Jason's knife down on the table.

Jason picked it up gingerly. The metal was blackened where Riccetti had struck the primer cap, but the carbon rubbed off on his thumb.

"Advantages: no hangfire; reloading goes a bit more quickly. Also more reliable—no more worry about breaking flints. That's what we do as soon as is politic, after we sell the secret of powder-making to the elves."

It made sense. Just stay a pace or two ahead of everyone else . . . but Jason still didn't like it. Eventually, the Nyphs could end up with guns. The barons wouldn't like that. And justifiably so.

"Not enough of a step?" Riccetti said. "You're right. I have a present for you." He tapped his fingers on the box. "This was going to be for your father, but I guess you inherit it, too." He opened the box. Inside was a plain leather holster, rigged in a peculiar way. Riccetti set it aside.

In the light of the lamp, the two nested guns looked strange, but even more strangely deadly. The pistols had unusually long barrels, but there was some sort of cylindrical thing over the trigger, where the frizzen and pan were supposed to be. The pistols were encircled by a square of brass pegs mounted in holes in the box.

Riccetti picked up one of the pistols and quickly did something with his hands that made the pistol click and the cylinder swing out to one side. "It's modeled on the old Colt Peacemaker—but I'm a better engineer than old Sam Colt," he said. Jason wasn't sure how much the Engineer was talking to him and how much he was talking to himself.

"These are called cartridges," Riccetti said, pulling out one of the brass pegs. "Everything in one—bullet here, resting on charge, inside here, primer cap here." He tapped the gray tip of the . . . cartridge. There was a hole in it, like the head of a penis. "I've drilled about halfway through the bullet. When this hits meat it expands, mushrooms almost like it's exploding. It *will* do damage."

He worked the pistol; the cylinder slipped to one side. Riccetti slid the cartridge into a hole in the cylinder. "Fits in here like so," he said, tilting the weapon up, letting the cartridge fall back into his palm. "Six holes; six cartridges," he said, fitting five of them in, "but carry it with an empty chamber here, under the hammer. Don't want it going off when your horse takes a bouncy step."

He tilted the weapon back; the five cartridges slipped back into his palm, looking oddly innocuous and even pretty in the lamplight. "Save your brass. We can reload it here, if it's not too badly bashed up—and if it is, we can always use some scrap. If a bullet misfires, drop it to the ground and bury it shallowly, with the toe of your boot. Don't pick it up."

He snapped the empty barrel back into the gun and pointed the weapon out into the night. "You can pull the hammer back like this," he said, thumbing it back until it locked into place with a solid click. "The empty chamber under the hammer rotates out of the way, bringing a cartridge into line. Then fire slowly, squeeze carefully—it's easier than what you're used to; there's no perceptible hangfire." Riccetti smiled, lowering the hammer carefully.

"Or you can just pull back on the trigger. Double action, it's called."

The hammer rose, then snapped down. "Hammer rises, then falls. Hammer hits firing pin, pin hits primer, primer fires charge, charge shoots bullet. Different gunpowder—different principle. And when we sell the secret of the old stuff to the elves, it won't teach them how to make this kind—or how to make it safe when you do. But Ranella and I can do it."

Jason smiled. "I don't even know how the old gunpowder is made." It was something he'd have to be trusted with eventually, but certainly not until he took the crown.

Riccetti ignored him. "You'll find it smokes a whole lot less than you're used to. Smells different; not as much like the fires of hell. In any case, you pull the trigger again and the cylinder turns, bringing a new cartridge into line. Hammer hits firing pin, pin hits primer, primer fires charge, charge shoots bullet." He dry-fired four more times, quickly.

"Like five pistols in one," Jason said.

Lou Riccetti smiled. "Or better." He picked up a thin, flat, round piece of steel, about half again the diameter of a Biemish copper mark, but perhaps a fifth as thick, and fitted six cartridges snugly into it. He snapped a cover over the primer end of the cartridges, holding them tightly into place. "Break open the cylinder, like so, dump out your old brass and slip this in, tight." He snapped the cylinder closed; the cover went flying to the ground. "Loaded again. Fire six times more; repeat as necessary. Strip off your tunic."

"Eh?"

"Get to your feet," Riccetti said, doing just that. He picked up the holster. "Strip off your tunic."

Jason did just that, and Riccetti helped him shrug into the holster. "The rig fits around your back, regardless. It can go on over the tunic—a good idea, if you're wearing a cloak or coat over the tunic—or under, like this." He handed the gun to Jason; Jason slipped it into the holster.

It slid almost under his arm, but not quite, and hung with a comforting weight. The butt was canted forward far enough for an easy draw with the right hand, and a clumsy one for the left.

Jason reached across his waist to where his swordhilt would have been; the gun didn't interfere with a cross-body draw.

"It won't give you away—as long as you don't show it. A lot of folks carry a hidden knife strapped about there, and more and more slaver pistols are showing up."

He tapped a stubby index finger against the pistol. "Right now there's exactly six of these in existence, and only two thousand rounds of ammunition. In a year, Ranella is going to be making them in quantity in Holtun-Bieme; we'll keep the ammo manufacture here, where I can keep an eye on it. In ten years, not only will every Imperial soldier be equipped with long guns that can fire faster and farther than this pistol, but you'll have a limited number of weapons that can fire more than two hundred rounds per minute. You have the opinion of the Engineer on that." He smiled. "Now, how scared are you of a bunch of elves with single-shot black powder guns?"

Jason didn't like it—damn it, gunpowder was *their* secret, even if he wasn't privy to it yet—but the Engineer wasn't going to be deterred.

"I guess we do it your way," he said.

Riccetti knocked back another hefty gulp of Riccetti's Best. "You guess right, Jason Cullinane. Like your father used to say: 'All men are created equal. Lou Riccetti made them that way.' "

"I . . . don't understand."

Riccetti handed him the bottle. "You will, Jason. You will."

Jason took a sip, and then shrugged. "I'll take your word for it."

"Two more things. If he's alive, you find him and you tell him thanks from me." Riccetti hefted the bottle as though to drink from it, then set it back down on the table. "I don't think I ever got around to saying thanks to the big bastard," he said, shaking his head. "Damn it."

"He knew." *Or knows.* "And the other thing?"

"I'm not a warrior," Riccetti said slowly, deliberately. "I'm very good at what I do, I'm very happy at what I do; I'm as good in my way as your old man was in his.

"But just this once, I wish I was a warrior. So you do it for me. If it can be done—you do it." Riccetti picked up the pistol and placed it in Jason's hand, folding Jason's fingers over it. "This is an iffy sort of thing, but if your dad is dead, and if Slovotsky and the dwarf screwed up and didn't kill the one who got him, and if you get the chance—no heroics; don't get yourself killed—you take this pistol," he said, squeezing tightly, "you walk up to who-ever killed him, you stick the barrel in his navel, you say to him, 'Lou Riccetti says hello, asshole,' and then you pull the trigger until all you hear are clicks. You blast his belly out through his fucking spine—you do it for me."

The Engineer's eyes were wet; he turned away.

PART THREE
The Search

CHAPTER 14
The Test of the Dwarf King

The nobly born must nobly meet his fate.

—Euripides

When the Black Camel comes for me, I'm not going to go kicking and screaming—I am, however, going to try to talk my way out of it. "No, no, you want the other Walter Slovotsky."

—Walter Slovotsky

At the end of the corridor there was another of the peculiar doglegs, this one more difficult than the last. As the passage jogged off to the left, the ceiling inclined sharply downward, leaving a narrow space that took a bit of doing even for a dwarf to fit through. That made it much more awkward for a human: Durine had to leave his weapons with Tennetty and Jason and worm himself through in an awkward half-squat.

Getting in to see King Maherralen of Endell was getting to be a definite pain in the ass, Jason Cullinane decided.

Jason handed Durine's combo belt through, then passed along the big man's shotgun and his own swordbelt. One of his pistols was inside his tunic, a comforting weight; the other, along with the gear that they had left behind, was outside the main entrance to the old warrens, under the watchful gaze of Ellegon, Bren Adahan and Kethol.

As Bren Adahan had put it, the locals were moderately friendly allies, but there was little point in tempting either their friendliness or their moderation.

That had made sense to Jason; besides, it gave Bren Adahan the chance to haggle with a stableman over the price of a few horses without Jason around. Jason didn't make a good haggler; he was too impatient.

"Watch your head, young sir," Durine said, perhaps too solicitously, as the big man accepted Jason's gear.

"Just move yourself along to keep up with Nefennen, human, and let us worry about those following," said Ketherren, the guard captain. He was a half-head shorter than any of the other of the dwarves, and perhaps two handbreadths broader across the shoulders.

Jason worked himself through, then straightened and stretched.

Again, the room beyond the dogleg was yet another one of what Durine had named "trap rooms." The wide, low door beyond was thick oak, its blankness broken only by three arrow loops; a man's height above, another stone-rimmed balcony loomed threateningly.

Behind the five of them, the rest of their dozen dwarvish escorts mumbled to themselves, while the three leading them waited impatiently in the room beyond.

Jason tried to reach out with his mind to Ellegon, but he couldn't read the dragon; they were too far away, too deep inside the mountain.

He hadn't known what to expect when the three of them were herded into the warrens, but it had been something roomier than this. The further they'd been led into the depths of the Old Warrens, the lower the ceilings had become, as though the long-ago ancestors of these dwarves had started tunneling as giants, shrinking as they bored into the cold stone.

The light breeze that always seemed to come from ahead of them was cool, but not uncomfortably so; it was the grim demeanor of the dozen guards that chilled him.

The hall ahead jogged right, then left again, the gloom more moderated than alleviated by the faint blue light of the overhead glowsteels.

Then the corridor widened and the ceiling retreated, until the passage was again comfortable for humans to walk through.

A few dozen yards down the corridor, a massive door blocked their way. The two guards in front of it bore short, thick polearms.

There was no exchange of passwords; the leader of their dwarvish escort ran ahead to whisper into the ear of one of the guards, who then rapped a staccato tattoo on the panel with his thick knuckles.

Rusty hinges protesting loudly, the doors swung slowly open; Jason's party was ushered into the room beyond.

"Your majesty," their escort announced in thick, guttural dwarvish, "Jason Cullinane and his party."

Tennetty snorted. "I think you like the sound of that too much."

"Shut up," Durine said, moving a half-step closer to Tennetty.

The ceiling of the hall of the mountain king was high, easily sixty feet over their heads. A roast was being turned slowly in front of the open fireplace at the far end of the hall, the smoke adding to the gloom.

There were a dozen dwarves gathered around the long table, although it could easily have accommodated twice as many. Unused plates of polished stone stood stacked, and waiting, while a trio of husky dwarf women prepared the meal. One basted the roast, another stirred a pot, while yet another used what looked like an oversized pair of tweezers to move twenty or so vaguely spherical objects, which looked more like stone loaves than anything else, around in front of the fire.

"Greetings," the dwarf at the head of the table said in thickly accented Erendra. He rose from his chair and walked toward them. "I am Maherralen, son of Mehennalen." The shortest of the dwarves, he was a barrel-chested creature, almost as broad as he was tall, but there was nothing small or insignificant about the strength of the oversized hand that gripped Jason's.

"The human does not look any too impressive to me," a bent-nosed dwarf sitting at the table muttered in dwarvish, as Maherralen released Jason and waved them all to seats. "Too skinny. Emaciated. Maybe they don't eat enough."

"You do not impress me, either," Jason answered in the same language, "with either your wisdom or your manners. Would you be happier if I made a few more insulting comments about you?"

There was a moment of silence, while the dwarves, including the cooks, looked to the king for a signal.

Maherralen smiled as he reclaimed his seat. "Perhaps you would impress him more if you did. But that would make you a poor guest."

"You speak dwarvish?" Bent-nose asked.

"It seems that he does, Kennen." Maherralen cracked a thin smile. "Although I can't place the accent. Heverel, perhaps?"

Jason nodded, reaching down to unclip his bowie from his belt, but not unsheathing it as he laid it on the table. "Nehera the smith taught me. That, and other things."

Another dwarf smiled. "A smith you are, too?" The way it had been explained to Jason, smithing was the most respected profession among the dwarves. It stood to reason: the tools that the smiths forged made it possible for the dwarves to tunnel through stone, both giving the dwarves a secure place to live and providing access to seams of hematite and the other minerals that they could turn into metal, the source of their stock in trade.

"I wish I could say I was." Jason shook his head. "I just know a bit of smithing."

Apparently that was the right answer; some of the frowns dissolved a trifle.

The day was dragging on outside, and there was a no-doubt-impatient dragon out there; Jason leaned forward. "In any case, we are here to—"

"Yes, yes, we know. Our messenger carried your request in," Kennen said. "But you are here, human, not elsewhere, and you will discuss things at a reasonable pace, not in an indecent human hurry."

Jason frowned. "I don't understand."

Maherralen nodded. "That's correct. You do not understand."

"We're just here to—"

"—take the Slovotsky women with you," Kennen said.

Well, that was true as far as it went; they were there to load the Slovotsky women on Ellegon-back, and dispatch them to Holtun-Bieme, as per Walter Slovotsky's instructions.

Jason said as much.

"But can we trust you with them?" Kennen said.

It's not your decision, Jason thought. It was Walter Slovotsky's. If Kirah or the girls wanted to go against Slovotsky, that was a family matter; Jason wouldn't try to force them to come along.

But they weren't here. Tennetty leaned over and whispered in his ear. "I get the impression that the Slovotsky women may not even know we're here."

"That is quite true," another dwarf spoke up, his deep voice gentle. "I am Neterren, son of Kedderren. I request that you don't think so unkindly of us."

Jason nodded. "I will hear you."

"Ah." Neterren's smile broadened. "You know something of formal argument. To begin," he said formally, his gravelly voice taking on a sing-song quality, "I was with Kirah when she gave birth to Doria Andrea," he said, spreading his hands in front of him. "I held her when she took her first breaths. To continue, it is important to me that I know she is going into good hands."

"Or? Would you keep them here against their will?" Tennetty snapped.

Neterren smiled sadly. "No. We couldn't do that," he said. "We—"

"It's all I can do to understand the filthy idea," Kennen said. "Sure."

"Tennetty, hush," Jason said, turning back toward Neterren. "To respond to your beginning," he said in dwarvish, pacing his words with traditional slowness, "your friendship with the Slovotsky family is noted, and accepted. To respond to your continuation, it is important to me, too, that the wife and daughters of my father's friend go into good hands. Walter Slovotsky designated mine."

Maherralen shook his head. "Your word on that is not sufficient, and I am yet unpersuaded. You must convince me. I'll simply not let them know that you are here, if we decide not to trust them to your hands." The dwarf spoke sadly. "I like few humans, but I've grown attached to these three. Four, if you include their father."

"They were left in our care, Jason Cullinane," Neterren said. "We'll not simply hand them over. Not without being sure that it is right." He stared at Jason unblinkingly.

It felt something like when Ellegon probed Jason, but there was no mindtouch; it was as though the dwarf thought that by looking at Jason he could judge his essence.

But the moment passed. Neterren shook his massive head. "I can't decide. Not just from looking at you."

"Then they will be tested," the king said. He snapped his fingers at the nearest of the dwarf women, who glowered back and vanished through the curtains, returning with two large, silver drinking horns brimming with foaming ale.

"I am Wellen, son of Gwellin." Another of the dwarves stood.

"I drink." He took one of the horns from the dwarf woman, gesturing with it to where Jason and the two other humans sat.

The dwarf tilted back the horn and began to drink. Both his capacity and speed were amazing; only a few gills of the brew dribbled down the sides of his mouth, running into his beard as he downed it all. He tossed the drinking horn end over end, high into the air, then caught it, slamming its mouth down on the table.

"Nicely done," the king said.

The dwarf woman walked over and handed the horn to Jason.

It was huge. There was no chance that he could possibly down it all.

"Wait," Durine said. "Is the test just for him, or is it for all of us?"

Neterren smiled. "You pass the first test; you ask a good question. Yes, Durine, the test is for any and all of you. We shall decide what is success and what is failure."

"Not you," Kennen snapped.

Durine stood. "Then *I* drink," he said with a smile. "I can drink real good." He took the horn from Jason, then moved a few steps away. Durine tilted the horn back and drank.

The first few swallows went quickly, but then Durine seemed to flag, to almost choke on the no-doubt bitter ale, but the big man pressed on, finally lowering the drinking horn.

A brief smile flickered across his face, then he, too, tossed the horn into the air, the few drops of liquid that remained spinning off into the gloom.

He reached up to catch the horn as it fell, then slammed it down on the table just as the dwarf had. He stood, wobbling a bit, and belched hugely.

"Nicely done, Durine," Tennetty said. "What's next?" She patted her belly. "Eating?"

"I am Belleren." Another dwarf stood. "I wrestle," he said, stripping off his leather tunic and boots, leaving himself in only breechclout and leggings.

"You're mine," Tennetty said, standing, reaching for the laces of her tunic.

"We don't wrestle women," Kennen said. "It's embarrassing enough for Belleren to have to face a human in the first place."

Durine hadn't taken his seat. "I'll wrestle you," he said.

Jason stood. "No you won't. I'll do it." Durine wasn't drunk, but he would be in a matter of moments; that amount of beer on an empty stomach would go quickly to his head.

Jason stood and stripped off his tunic, then unbuckled his holster, handing it to Durine. "What are the rules?"

"Two falls out of three. Just proper wrestling, for me." The dwarf shrugged. "For me, grips only; for you, no weapons. Punch me, stick your fingers in my eye, throw me; anything. You can even keep your boots on and kick me. If I let you hurt me, I deserve it."

On grass, Jason would have kept his boots, but their leather soles could skid too easily on the stone; he sat down to take them off.

"Let me." Tennetty smiled as she squatted in front of him and unlaced his boots. "I think you've drawn the hard one," she whispered. "How much do you want to bet the next dwarf says, 'I fuck'?" She snorted.

Jason shook his head. Tennetty always found herself diverting.

"Watch your ass," she said.

He'd been right to take off his boots: the stone was gritty and cold under his feet; it was like walking on sandpaper.

There was the metallic taste of fear at the back of his mouth as they moved to a clear space on the stone floor and squared off. Jason knew that a human with normal strength had no chance of beating a dwarf. But that wasn't the test. Or if it was, he had already failed. He'd failed tests before; it didn't kill you. Jason worked the muscles of his shoulders.

It wouldn't kill him to fail this test unless the dwarf wanted to kill him. Once those hands closed on Jason, it wasn't up to him. The dwarf could throw Jason on his head—or just twist Jason's head off.

There was a derisive laugh from one of the dwarves.

Belleren moved in, reaching for Jason's arm.

He remembered Valeran going on about unarmed fighting. *You never have to be unarmed,* the old captain had said. *You've got feet and hands and elbows and a head—use them.*

He snapped a kick at the dwarf's groin, but one of his opponent's hairy hands clamped down on his ankle, lifting it up, pushing Jason off balance.

The dwarf smiled; there were several gaps in the rows of yellowed teeth. "Not good enough."

He lunged for Jason, but Jason dodged to one side, lashing out with his foot and connecting solidly with Belleren's knee. The dwarf staggered to one side, his vulnerable back to Jason; Jason leaped on him to finish him off.

The dwarf stank of the unwashed sweat that slickened his back and bull neck. If Jason could get one arm around Belleren's throat and brace himself, he could choke the dwarf. Dwarves had stronger muscles than humans but that didn't make the arteries in their necks any more resilient. Cut off the supply of oxygen to the brain and—

—he was grabbed, lifted and slammed down hard on the stone floor, the force of his fall knocking the wind out of him.

He left a dark patch on the stone, where skin and blood had rubbed off against the floor. He clenched his jaw, turning his scream into a high-pitched groan and fighting for breath as he fought his way to his knees, bent over, trying as hard as he could not to puke on the cold stone.

Both Tennetty and Durine were on their feet. He knew he was supposed to, he was expected to wave them back to their seats, but it was all he could do to fight for his next breath, to force himself not to scream at the white pain throbbing up and down his back.

Belleren waited for him to get to his feet. He wasn't even breathing hard.

Jason could breathe again, a little; he forced himself to his feet, his hands clamped over his belly, trying to force more air into his lungs.

"As soon as you're ready, we start again," Belleren said.

"No, slam him down *now*," Kennen hissed. "Two falls out of three."

"As soon as you're ready," the dwarf said again, waiting patiently.

Still clutching at the pit of his stomach, barely able to breathe, Jason staggered toward the dwarf.

"No." Belleren caught him by the shoulders, not ungently. "I'll wait until you're—"

Jason gave the back-handed shot everything he had, and caught the dwarf solidly on the windpipe.

"Gack," the dwarf said, his fingers tightening on Jason's shoulders.

"I'm ready now." Jason hit him again, in the same place, harder.

"Gack." Belleren released Jason and staggered back.

Jason didn't have much strength left, but he reached down and fastened his left hand on the belt holding Belleren's breechclout, and then smashed his right fist as hard as he could into the dwarf's groin. And again, and again.

"*Grmph.*"

Jason let go of the dwarf and tottered away, as Belleren fell first to his knees, then to his face, clutching his crotch.

"If your dwarf can't get up?" Tennetty asked. "Jason wins?"

"Yes," Maherralen said. "There was nothing said about the giving of quarter; he need not wait for Belleren to recover."

Jason staggered toward the dwarf, who had gotten to all fours. All he had to do was jump onto the dwarf's back and fix a chokehold before Belleren got to his feet. All he had to do. . . .

He couldn't. If it had been a fight to the death, that would have been one thing; if lives hung in the balance, he could kick a man who was on his knees.

But Belleren had given Jason quarter. He had to wait, even if that meant losing.

And it didn't matter if that was the right or wrong answer to the dwarves—it was Jason's right answer. He forced himself to stand straight.

"I'm sorry I hit you when you weren't expecting it," he said. "I'll wait for you, Belleren."

CHAPTER 15
Janie

Those not present are always wrong.
—Destouches

Being right all the time is a real expensive habit.
—Walter Slovotsky

A wet cloth lightly slapped his face.

The cool dark reached out with vague fingers for him again, and he reached for them. It was much better to fall back into the murk, much easier than dealing with all of the pain.

The cloth slapped his face again, harder.

"Go 'way," he tried to shout, but it only came out as a mumble. This time it was a hand—not slapping him; tugging at his arm.

"Go *away*." He slipped back into the dark.

"That's the thing about Cullinane men," Tennetty's harsh voice said from a long way off. "They don't wake up easy."

Another voice laughed, a sound of distant silver bells. "So Dad used to say. Can you do anything more?"

"I have done almost all I can do," a deep dwarvish voice said. It took a moment for Jason to place it: Neterren, the least hostile of King Maherralen's court. "He needs sleep now."

"He can sleep in the air," Tennetty said. "If you don't want to wake him, I will." Metal slid against leather, flesh thunked against flesh and steel rang on stone.

378

The darkness swam toward him, but he pushed it away, far away, and forced his eyes open, swimming up into the harsh blue light of the glowsteel hanging overhead.

Durine had Tennetty pinned against the stone wall. The room was small, and crowded; the other two had backed away to give Durine room. Durine had both her wrists in one of his hands and—

"Stop," Jason shouted. It only came out as a harsh whisper, but that was enough. "Let her go."

Durine shoved her away, hard.

"That's two, shithead." Tennetty eyed him stonily. "I was just going to touch him with the knifepoint. Wakes you up real quick."

Stooping to pick up the knife, Durine shook his head. His eyes didn't leave hers for a moment.

Jason's first reaction was to reach for his weapons. His fingers went to his side, to where one pistol lay, wrapped in his tunic. He slid his fingers inside the tunic, letting them rest on the cool steel.

Naked from the waist up, Jason was lying on a mattress bag of some sort—much softer than anything he was used to—which rested on a wooden frame. He forced himself up on an elbow, and found to his surprise that he could.

Rising to his less than majestic height, Neterren smiled down at him. "Feeling better, young Emperor?"

Actually, he was. He reached his hand to where he'd scraped half of the skin of his back off against stone, and touched only flesh. It was overly sensitive, like the skin under a scab that had just come off, but it didn't hurt at all.

"You're a healer?" he asked, as Neterren felt at Jason's wrist.

"A keen eye for the obvious runs in the Cullinane family," Jane Slovotsky said as she moved around to where he could see her. There was something unusually graceful in her walk, something like a warrior in a fighting stance.

He'd only seen that kind of walk a few times before: it was the kind of studied grace possessed by a few of the more prominent members of a traveling acrobatic troupe that had passed through Biemestren a few years before. Both men and women always walked with perfect balance.

It was the same kind of grace that Walter Slovotsky had. Balance ran in the Slovotsky family, it seemed.

She was dressed in leggings and a mannish brown cloth tunic, long enough to be more of a shift, belted tightly at her waist to reveal a slim but definitely female figure. Her light brown hair was cropped short, framing a face with high cheekbones, ever-so-slightly slanted brown eyes, and thin lips bent into a smile that was partly friendly, partly mocking. He knew that she was fifteen, about to turn sixteen, more than a year younger than he was, but her appraising look made him feel like he was being examined by somebody at least five years older.

"When you're done checking me out, maybe we can re-introduce ourselves," she said. "I don't know how well you remember me, but we were kids together ten years ago, I'm Jane Slovotsky."

He reached for something clever to say. "You grew up." That wasn't it.

She laughed again, and he wasn't sure whether she was laughing at him or with him.

Neterren released Jason's wrist. "You'll feel better in the morning; it would be best if you rest for the remainder of the day, though." He turned to the humans. "He could use some more sleep."

Jane shook her head. "I'll be short."

"Just a *little* time, eh?" Neterren smiled.

"Got a few things to talk over with Hero, Junior, here." She folded a blanket over into a cushion, dropped it to the stone floor next to the bed and seated herself on it, tailor-fashion.

Neterren's eyes twinkled. "Then I'll be sure you don't tire him."

Tennetty shrugged. "We might as well leave." She turned to Durine. "I'll keep an eye on him while you go tell the others, outside."

Durine shook his head as they walked to the door. "I'll be outside, young sir, if you need anything. Tennetty will brief the others." He closed the heavy wooden door behind him.

"How did I do?" Jason asked.

Neterren's brow furrowed for a moment. "Oh. The third fall. Belleren picked you up and slammed you down, in less time than it takes to say it. Bunged you up fairly heavily, too."

"I thank you for healing me, Neterren," he said formally, as he'd been taught to give thanks.

"You can thank him for the use of his room, too," Jane said. "Such as it is."

"I don't need much, Jane," the dwarf said. "The cell serves my needs."

"I mean," Jason went on, "did I pass the test?"

Jane snorted. "Think it through, hero. You were being tested, among other things, to determine if you're good enough to protect me. You lost—and to an opponent you could have beaten. Maherralen doesn't impress too easily, and that didn't do it."

But the dwarf king had said that if Jason didn't pass the test the Slovotsky women wouldn't even know that he was there. He said as much.

Neterren smiled. "Jane has run through these warrens for ten years; she knows them as well as any Endell dwarf does. She also knows the *hazvarfen*, the echo paths, better than anybody else." The dwarf gave her an affectionate pat. "She was listening. The Slovotsky women are free here, young Emperor. We aren't . . . constituted so as to be willing to hold them here by force. It is still my opinion that you shouldn't go, Jane," the dwarf said.

"To begin," she said formally, in dwarvish, only cheating a little on the gutturals, "I do not rely upon Jason to protect me. That big ox of his looks like he would be better at such a thing. To continue, if he does protect me, it's going to be with a gun, knife, bow or sword—I do not think that any matters of importance are dependent on his mastery of the art of wrestling, no matter how highly the Moderate People rank that art. To continue further, any issue of danger aside, it seems to me that I must go along. I invite discussion." She waited.

The dwarf nodded. "I respond to your beginning: I am concerned about your well-being. I respond to your continuation: I am concerned about your well-being. I respond to your further continuation: I am concerned about your well-being, and—"

"You are stalling," she said in Erendra. "You won't hold us here by force, but you would prolong the conversation forever." She threw up her hands in exasperation.

Neterren chuckled. "Very well, little one. I'll be back to check on you later, Jason."

The dwarf left, shutting the door behind him.

"So," Jason said, "you're going back to Holtun-Bieme with Ellegon?"

"That's what I wanted to talk to you about." She shook her head. "No." She swallowed heavily. "Mom and Dorann are going there. I'm going with you."

✧   ✧   ✧

There was something Father had once said about what he called his "command voice," about how if you said something, if you gave an order with perfect and complete faith that it would be obeyed, then it *would* be obeyed.

I will be obeyed; she will do what I say. "You are not," he said, willing himself to believe that he would be obeyed. "You will go to Holtun-Bieme on Ellegon's back. With the others."

She pursed her lips for a moment, then took a quick chew on her lower lip, and just for a moment he thought she was going to give in.

But then she shook her head. "Look, I don't like it any more than you do. Less—I'd much rather stay here, shooting blanks. But—"

"You will—"

"*You* will hear me out, shithead." She slammed her hand down, hard, on the bed. "No—I'm sorry. Wrong approach." She closed her eyes and formed her hands into fists, then relaxed them and her whole body. "Let's try it this way: hear me out, please?" she said, softly, her eyes resting on his eyes, her hand resting on his hand.

It couldn't hurt to listen. "Go ahead."

"You're going under the assumption that the three of them—both our fathers and Ahira—are alive and carving a swath through the slavers, heading this way. Sort of like that last run thing he used to talk about, except that it's an announcement that your father's alive. Correct?"

He nodded. "It's just an assumption."

She returned his nod. "But it makes sense. There's a lesser probability that this is some scheme of the Slavers' Guild to get you out of Holtun-Bieme and chasing after ghosts, but if that had been the case they would have been ready to jump you in Enkiar.

"It sounds a lot like your father. I've been re-reading his letters; Karl Cullinane has been champing at the bit for years, wanting to get out from under that crown. This is just the sort of thing he'd try to pull, particularly since he'd know he'd have to settle down after it."

"But what does that have to do with—"

"Listen to me! Think it through, damn it," she said. "Who do you think's running the operation? *Your* father? Look, I've been raised to think highly of the great and powerful Karl Cullinane, but if they've survived this long, it's because they're doing something tricky. A lot of tricky things—you think the slavers looking for them are all idiots? You think that they can't track a team consisting of a dwarf, a big man and a bigger man with seven fingers? It has to be something tricky.

"And tricky isn't something your father is. Or was. Ahira can be subtle, but this whole thing smells of craftiness." She dipped two fingers into her belt pouch and produced a copper coin. "Look," she said, slipping the coin into her right fist, then holding both fists out in front of her. "Quickly, which hand is it in?"

He shrugged. He'd seen the sleight before. If it had been done well—and it had—there was no way that he could tell which hand held the coin.

"The right," he said, picking one at random.

"Nope," she said, as she opened her first, revealing an empty right hand. "Guess again."

"The left," he said, then realizing that since she was letting him guess again, it couldn't be in—

"Wrong again." She held up an empty left hand. She picked the coin out of her lap. "You think like your father. I think like mine.

"This is my father's show. If you haven't latched onto that by now, it's because you don't think enough like Dad. There are only two people I know who can follow his thinking, convoluted as it is. One of them's Ahira; he and the dwarf have been working together since before I was born." She shrugged.

"And the other one's you?"

"Good guess, Jason. Have Ellegon drop us off outside Elleport and we'll hire a boat and find them. Trust me, I'll find them for you. There's just one thing I want you to do."

"Yeah?"

"Keep me alive while I'm doing it," she said. She swallowed, hard. "You may not understand about this, but I've got to tell you that I'm scared shitless."

He knew something about being scared. He knew a lot about being scared. But it wasn't something he was yet brave enough to admit to a pretty girl, not if he didn't have to.

She stuck out a hand. "We got a deal, Cullinane?"

He took it. "We've got a deal, Slovotsky."

CHAPTER 16

Elleport

All the rivers run into the sea, yet the sea is not full.
—Ecclesiastes 1:7

There just isn't any pleasing some people. The trick is to stop trying.

—Walter Slovotsky

Ellegon dropped them off before dawn, near the Orduin just north of Findarel, a small riverfront village less than a day's ride from Elleport and the Cirric. They were too close to the dock area to risk a light, so it took longer than usual to unload their gear from the dragon's back, and then get Kirah, little Dorann and Kennen aboard again.

The dwarf didn't like any of it, and while they were unloading he stood by, explaining to all and sundry how much he didn't like it.

He loathed riding on dragonback, he abhorred the idea of Kirah going to Biemestren, he found idiotic the idea of Doria Andrea going to Biemestren, he thought the idea that he was going to Biemestren was detestable—

Why not just tell him to shut up or you won't take him to Biemestren?

Because I wouldn't mean it, the dragon said, *and I don't like making phony threats. If I don't take Kennen to Biemestren I would

384

have to leave him with you. Either that, or abandon him. Abandoning him would not sit well with King Maherralen, and I'd prefer not to be met with a hail of bolts the next time I stop off in Endell. So I'll just bear up bravely under the weight of the irritation.*

And be a fine, fine example to me, Jason thought.

—and Kennen very particularly was not fond of the idea of Jane going off into who-knew-what kind of trouble with a bunch of spindly humans, and he loathed the fact that the saddles were rigged for these oversized excuses for persons, and he was angry that the lap-belt chafed him, and he thought it was absolutely ridiculous that it was taking so long to get everybody and everything unloaded and then get the three of them reloaded, and—

Shut up, Kennen.

The dwarf took a long look at the dragon and started complaining again.

—and it was incredibly stupid that Kethol couldn't work any faster than that, how the—

Shut up or I'll roast you, the dragon said, slightly parting his reptilian jaws, letting just a whisper of flame escape from between his teeth.

The dwarf shut up.

Oh. I didn't think of that. I should have said, "Try threatening to burn him."

Sarcasm ill becomes you. There was a distant, draconic chuckle that held the sharpness that meant it was only for Jason.

But, finally, Jane's mother, Kirah, and her sister Doria Andrea were strapped back into their places on the dragon's back, and so was the dwarf. All of the goods for Jason and the company had been unloaded, while both the Slovotsky family possessions and the trade goods destined for Biemestren were safely lashed into place.

They were done. It was none too early, either; the blackness of the eastern sky was turning into dim darkness, threatening to brighten into a new day, and the dragon had to be away.

Jane's mother called down a last urging to be careful, her voice carefully balanced between her own fear for her older daughter's safety and the need to continue to reassure her younger daughter that there was nothing to worry about, and wasn't the ride on Ellegon's back fun? And wasn't it just wonderful that they were going to get to do it again now!

Three tendays, Ellegon said. *On Pefret. I'll be there; I hope you are. Preferably all of you, and our three friends.*

"Preferably." *Just keep things quiet.*

Ellegon shrugged. *We don't have much longer until word reaches Biemestren, but even when it does, we'll keep it from your mother, just as long as we can.*

"Please," Kirah called down, "be careful."

His pounding wings sending leaves and sticks and dust flying about, the dragon leaped into the air, leaving behind Kirah's gentle words to her daughter, Dorann's shouts of excitement, and a few stray oaths from Kennen.

Tennetty already had her rucksack on her back. "Saddle up, people," she said. "I want us to catch the first barge out of Findarel."

She could have passed as a trader, if you didn't know her. She had her glass eye in the empty socket, and it could pass a cursory inspection. Jason hoped she would pass; her identity was too good a clue to his own. The charm that the Spidersect cleric had placed on the eye kept it moist in appearance, and slaved it to the motion of her real eye.

Her sword was stowed with the common gear—women wearing swords were enough of a rarity to be suspicious—but she could protect herself somewhat with the oversized bowie at her waist and with the two pistols she carried, one in a holster under her left armpit, the other tucked into the top of her right boot.

"Move it, people," she said.

Durine looked at her, long and hard, as though to say that she wasn't running things here, and that as far as he was concerned she'd never run things; but Kethol must have caught Jason's headshake out of the corner of his eye, and nudged the bigger man, who subsided.

Jason swapped a trade knife for passage for all six of them, and got the chief bargeman to throw in two meals and the use of his tent. Durine, Kethol and Bren Adahan were tired; they hadn't gotten much sleep the day before.

Tennetty was unimpressed. If she had been negotiating, the bargeman would have thrown in some local coin, and thanked them smartly for the bargain. Or so she said.

Jane, on the other hand, wasn't visibly bowled over by

Tennetty's claim. She tilted her head toward Jason as they leaned against the forward rail, watching the river bend and turn in the distance.

"The other possibility, of course," Jane murmured, "is that Tennetty would have pushed him so far, so hard that he would have called for the local armsmen." Which was entirely possible.

Still, maybe Tennetty would have gotten a better deal. Space wasn't at a particular premium today: the bags of grain and barrels of dried beef weren't piled more than shoulder high anywhere on the barge. There were only a dozen or so chicken cages with their clucking birds idiotically eyeing the outside world as they floated gently toward somebody's stewpot. There was even enough room for the bargemen to have all four of their mules on board, carefully hitched and hobbled at the rear rail, instead of trotting along the mulepath on the riverbank, the same path they would take to haul the barge upriver.

Riding or walking, downriver was easy on the animals, although it was a bit trickier for the bargemen. Instead of using their poles simply to keep the barge far enough from the riverbank to avoid grounding it, the four brawny men, their torsos gleaming with sweat, worked in almost silent coordination to keep the massive craft well toward the middle of the river. The current was fastest there, and business waited for no man. Still, they had to keep the ungainly craft under control, anticipating the turns of the swollen Orduin.

Which were, granted, familiar to them. But the work was hard; all four of them were heavily muscled, and the chief bargeman's hand had been hard and strong when Jason had shaken it.

The day wore on, and with a changing of the guard it was Jason's, Tennetty's and Jane's turn to nap in the shade of the tent, with Durine posted just outside. Tennetty unbuckled her belt and lay down flat on her back, folding her hands over her belly as she shut her eyes.

Jason decided that he was tired; when Janie unselfconsciously stripped down to bare skin and slipped into her blankets, he barely noticed.

Just as he was stretching out and deciding that he really couldn't sleep, that he had a responsibility to keep an eye on everything, tiredness overcame him and he dropped off to sleep.

✧　　✧　　✧

Durine woke him when they were only a short while out of Elleport; the other two were already up and out of the tent.

Jason rubbed the backs of his hands against his gritty eyes and scratched at where the bugs infesting the tent had bitten him— all over, basically—and took a few moments to dress, again checking his pistols to make sure that both of them, the one in his shoulder holster and the one in his rucksack, were loaded, which they always were, and turning the cylinder until the chamber under the hammer was the one just ahead of the empty one, then dryfiring each pistol once to make sure that the mechanism still worked, which it did.

Valeran, his teacher, had taught him to handle firearms ritualistically; adapting to a new ritual wasn't difficult.

In only a few moments the pistols were checked and ready and stowed. He walked out into the afternoon.

As the barge rounded the final bend, the bargemen swung the craft out into the river to avoid a pair of barges bound upriver, then bent their backs and their poles to bring it back into the quiet water near the banks, so that it wouldn't be carried away into the Cirric.

Beyond the banks the fields stood idle, expanses of rotting cornstalks proclaiming that they had been harvested neither recently nor long ago, but somewhere in between.

"There's the docks, over there," one of the bargemen said, indicating a direction with a jerk of his chin as he once again bent his back to his pole. It took longer for them to maneuver the barge over to its berth than Jason would have thought it should, but only a few moments for the waiting dock crew to grab the expertly thrown lines, pull the barge in tight against the dock and tie it firmly in place.

Still, the sun was getting low in the sky as they left the barge, making their way across the floating dock to the shore, all of them staggering a bit as they got their land legs back.

Bren Adahan took the lead. "The first thing we should do," the baron said, "is to find some lodgings for the night. Tomorrow we get to find out what's going on."

"Or," Jane put in, "at least what the locals think is going on."

CHAPTER 17

Questions and Answers

Kindness is within our power, but fondness is not.
                              —Dr. Samuel Johnson

A little gentleness goes only a short way. Ladle it out gener-
ously, and often, when you can.
                              —Walter Slovotsky

Jason, Jane and Bren Adahan made their way through the farmers' market, toward the docks and the Slavers' Guildhall. Elleport
wasn't exactly Pandathaway, but the markets had some charm.

Just goes to show that you can waste a lot of time and effort doing
more planning than is necessary, Jason thought. As it turned out,
"the Warrior" and his two companions were the talk of the market, and the rumors were flying thickly. Too thickly: the story was
growing in the telling.

Jason and the others had made some changes to their appearance: with their gear stowed in their rooms under the watchful
eye of Kethol, they could tolerate a careful search. Jason and Bren
wore the raw leather of Wehnest cattlemen, and Janie was in the
ragged shift and rude iron collar of a slave. The fact that the collar
had a secret catch that not only allowed her to take it off, but
brought out a slim blade that could easily slice through leather
or flesh, was not apparent.

That she had very nice legs, however, was. When they'd stopped to get directions toward the guild pens, they'd gotten several offers on her.

They stopped at an appleseller's stall, Bren quickly negotiating for three shiny apples, each about the size of his fist, then handing one to Jason, tossing the smallest to Janie, and biting into the third himself.

The appleseller was a short, wan man, vaguely toad-faced, yellowing teeth showing for just a moment as he eyed Janie in her shift and collar. Jason muffled a glower, while Bren Adahan shared the appleseller's smile.

"Had her long?" the merchant asked, while Bren Adahan eyed a basket of apples as though pretending to consider buying more.

"A while," Bren Adahan said. "I picked her up in Wehnest, to make the trip more pleasant."

"I can imagine."

Janie didn't blush, although she did lower her eyes.

"Cooks, too," Bren Adahan said. "But I've had better. I thought I'd sell her here, but I'm beginning to suspect that the market isn't good right now."

"Not from the guild," the merchant said, "although a private sale might bring you some good luck." He shrugged. "You might try Emmon the silversmith, over on the Street of the Dead Dog—he always seems to have some extra coin, and a keen eye for flesh. Though that ax-faced woman of his'd probably make him resell her."

"Not the guild?"

He shook his head, then shrugged. "The slavers are nervous about buying, what with the Warrior and his friends running around slitting their throats and then vanishing." He picked up and hefted an apple, the shiniest of the lot, and then polished it still further on his apron, before calling out to the baker across the way and tossing the apple in a practiced high arc that brought it almost exactly into the baker's outstretched palm.

The baker threw a quarter of a head-sized loaf back; the appleseller tore off a hunk and nibbled at it.

Jason forced a slow nod. "Where were they last seen?" He bit into his apple again.

The merchant looked him over thoroughly. "I wouldn't, young man. The hilt of your sword may be well-worn, but trying to take on Karl Cullinane isn't something for an amateur. Particularly not one who enjoys a good apple as much as you do." He raised his hand in a brief salute of dismissal. "I'd like your business again."

The three walked off.

"Too much information," Jane murmured.

The Warrior and his men had been spotted in Lundeyll, and on Salket, and on half a dozen of the Shattered Islands, and in Enkiar, and Nyphien. Slavers had been found dead in Pandathaway itself, and on ships bound for Ehvenor. There were three of them, armed with nothing more than swords and knives; there were a score of them on a stolen slaver ship; hundreds of them could appear at any time. They were nowhere and everywhere.

The rumors were just beginning to make a splash here. In a few days, or a few tendays, it would be old news, but now it was all flying fast and furious, and there was no way to sort the truth out from the noise.

If there was any truth to be sorted out.

Damn.

Janie had the only good idea that occurred to any of them all afternoon: since they wanted to know who was killing the slavers, the best place to go was the guild section of the market.

The Slavers' Guildhall was ahead; the steel pens outside held only half a dozen people, although there was ample room for a hundred.

Bren Adahan leaned toward him. "What do you say we skip this? We already have enough information. Too much."

Jason nodded. "Just what I was thinking."

"Then why didn't you *say* it?" Jane whispered, irritated.

"More beer, if you please," Durine called out.

There was no immediate response.

He pounded his fist on the table. Tankards and platters rattled on the battered wooden surface, spoons, knives and spicers dancing for a moment. "More beer, if you please," he repeated, his voice almost a whisper.

"My pleasure, sir. My pleasure," the innkeeper called back, scurrying out with two fresh tankards of what was probably the worst beer Durine had tasted in years. The stocky man across the table started to glare at him, but clearly thought better of it; he decided that the watery stew in his bowl was interesting to watch. "Your food will be ready in a moment, or right now, if you'd like," said the innkeeper.

"No rush," Durine said, sipping at the beer. Awful stuff. Was it as bad as the beer they'd had in the barracks a couple years back, from the barrel where they later found a drowned mouse? It was a close call.

Tennetty pursed her lips, inclining her head slightly toward the nearest of the three skinny men with seamen's pigtails who were seated together, down the bench from where she and Durine sat. Her ears were sharper than his; she'd heard something that suggested the sailor knew something of interest.

The dining room of the inn had probably been the outside not too long ago: the long room ran across the front of the inn, as though it were an enclosed porch; the door that led inside was large, thick and weatherbeaten.

At the far end of the room, a pair of ragged children of indeterminate sex—the older perhaps seven, the younger perhaps five or so—took turns slapping at each other and stomping on the treadle that turned the spit over the cooking fire. A heavily freckled, moderately pretty girl in her early teens occasionally paused in her dicing of carrots and onions to ladle some more brown sauce over the leg of lamb on the skewer, then waited a few moments for the sauce to burn in a bit before slicing off another few pieces of meat and stacking them haphazardly on a platter.

There was definitely some wild onion in the sauce; Durine could smell it from where he sat.

But just as the cook finished preparing a plate for the two of them, the sailor mopped up the last juices on his plate with a slab of bread, crammed the dripping slice in his mouth and stood, pushing his plate away, resting his hand for a moment on the shoulders of one of his comrades to steady himself. He turned to leave.

Tennetty tilted her head closer to Durine's. "He was saying something about 'the Warrior' and some island." She rose and he followed, ignoring the way the innkeeper looked curiously at them, then decided that it wasn't any of his business why they had decided not to eat the food that came with their rooms.

Durine and Tennetty followed the sailor out into the daylight.

The business district was crowded as they followed him toward the docks, through streets filled with sailors from the boats in the harbor; with merchants bringing dried meat and bagged grain down toward the docks, or returning from there with their hands pressed to the sides of their tunics, accompanied by a guard or two watching the crowd nervously for pickpockets or robbers; with ragged children playing their endless games of tag through the cobbled streets; with horses standing hitched in front of flatbed wagons, pissing noisily on the road.

Every city was the same.

"Try to look a bit less conspicuous," Tennetty said. "You're not built for following people."

"No," Durine said, "I'm not." He was every bit as tall as Karl Cullinane, and while his physique was the middle-heavy one of a wrestler's, he was heavy with muscle, not fat. He wasn't as pretty as the Emperor or Kethol were, or even as pleasantly ugly as Pirojil was—

But he wasn't supposed to be pretty, or inconspicuous. He was supposed to be large and dangerous. That was what the Emperor had kept him around for, and that was what he was good at: breaking things, and threatening to break things, whether the thing to be broken was a stout door or a thin neck.

Tennetty had a thin neck, and one that probably deserved breaking. But Jason had said not to, and even if the boy wasn't emperor yet, he was the closest thing to it. Besides, Bren Adahan had said she ought to be kept alive, and even if the baron was a fucking Holt he was a tame one, long as Aeia was leading him around by his—

He suddenly realized that he was alone, that while he had been woolgathering Tennetty had slipped away. He scanned the crowd for her, but there was no sign.

Still, the sailor was ahead, pausing at an alley to loosen the drawstrings of his trousers and relieve himself in the gutter. Fastening himself up, he seemed to see something ahead, and vanished into the alley.

Durine quickened his pace.

The narrow alley between the two three-storied buildings was nearly blocked by a man-high pile of dirt; there seemed to be some sort of excavation going on in the cellar of one of the buildings. There was barely enough room for Durine to squeeze by.

By the time he did, Tennetty already had the situation well in hand. She was standing over the bound form of the sailor, who was making only quiet noises around the wad of cloth she'd jammed in his mouth. A nice decoy; although one would expect a sailor to know better than to follow a strange woman into even a well-lit alley. Then again, Elleport was a well-policed town, within its limits.

Durine bent over the man.

"We know you know about the Warrior," he said, talking quietly, slowly, patiently, knowing that when a man as large and powerful as he talked just that way it could chill the blood. "Let me tell you what is going to happen: I'm going to take out your gag, and you're going to quietly, quietly, answer all our questions." He dug two fingers into his pouch and came up with an imperial quarter-mark, a small silver coin the size of Durine's little fingernail. "After that, I am going to give you this, and you're going to walk away, and forget this happened, and never, never mention it to anyone."

Tennetty slipped her eye patch over her glass eye and smiled at the way the man's face whitened even further as he realized who she was.

"Take the patch off and go stand watch," Durine said.

She thought about it a moment, then moved off to do just that. He was getting tired of her habit of hesitating before complying, and he wouldn't have minded doing something about it, but Jason had said no.

Durine worked his fingers for a moment. It wouldn't be fair to take out his frustration on the sailor, so he just seized the man's face in his right hand, letting the sailor feel just a trace of the strength in his fingers. "Don't worry about her. Worry about me. If you don't do exactly what I've told you, if you lie to me, if you call out, if you ever tell anyone anything about this, I'm the one who's going to find you, wherever you are, lay hold of you by the back of your head, and grind your face against the palm of my other hand until you don't have a face anymore. Do you have any difficulty in believing me?"

The sailor tried to shake his head.

"Good."

From over by the mound, Tennetty laughed. "We are *not* nice people," she said.

The sailor talked at length.

The others had their ways; Kethol had his.

He followed the woman past the unblinking eyes of the house's bouncer, upstairs to her crib. The room was tiny, barely big enough to hold the pallet on the floor and a pitifully small wooden chest that probably contained all the whore owned. There was a large iron padlock on it, and he had spotted the poorly hidden pocket in the collar of her thigh-length shift where she kept the key.

She unbelted her shift and dropped it to one side. Underneath she was glistening from her bath; Kethol had insisted that she clean herself first. There was enough filth in the world, and on the road.

Damp and naked, she reached for his tunic, but he pushed her hands away. "I can undress myself," Kethol said.

For just a moment, her eyes widened. Perhaps she'd heard a trace of threat in his voice, and while there were limits to what he could do to her, he had rented her for the night and nobody would complain about a few bruises. That came with the rental, too.

He nodded his head toward the pallet, and she obediently slipped under the thin blanket.

He undressed swiftly but unhurriedly, folding and stacking his clothes carefully, leaving his scabbard on the floor where he'd be able to reach it in the dark, then blew out the lamp and joined her under the blankets.

She reached for him, but he gripped her wrists.

"Please," she said, "I'll do whatever you want. Anything."

"I've paid for the room, and for you, for the night," he said. "I decide what we do."

"Yes sir," she said as his grip tightened.

"First," he said, "you'll tell me how you came to be here."

She told him a long and rambling tale that began on Keelos island, where she was sold into slavery when her father lost the farm, and continued with her being freed by a Home raider team, and with her decision to try to return to her home, and how there was nothing there, and how she hadn't any skills, and what could she do, and . . .

"And about the Warrior . . ." he said, interrupting.

While he held her wrists in his hands, she told him everything she knew. Karl Cullinane and his two companions—or maybe his twenty companions, or perhaps his hundred companions; nobody knew for sure—were everywhere at once. There had been raids throughout the Cirric and along the shore of the Cirric. Everywhere.

"That's all I know, sir, really."

His grip relaxed.

"How do you want me, sir? Do you want me to—"

"Shh," he said, letting her go. "I just want you to hold me. Gently. All night long." He was paying for the night; he could have whatever pleasure he wanted. Being held made him feel almost alive.

INTERLUDE

Laheran

Where the lion's skin will not reach, you must patch it out with the fox's.

—Plutarch

The rooms in the Triple Hamlet Inn were clean, but Laheran paced them like a caged beast. This was the place to wait, but waiting came hard.

Salket was only a matter of time, Laheran had decided. The question was, where? Salket was a big island; there were four guildhouses spread out across its length.

Cups-and-coins was not Laheran's favorite game. Children played it with walnut halves and walnut shells; in the streets of Pandathaway, jugglers sometimes played it for copper and silver and gold.

The principle was the same: put one coin of silver and two of copper under three small, identical cups. The juggler would move them around the polished surface of the board he held across his lap, fingers dancing deceptively, until you were thoroughly confused. If you set your coin, be it of copper or silver or gold, in front of the cup with the silver coin in it, you won a coin equal to your bet; if you failed, the juggler kept your coin.

There were many swindles, of course. Sometimes you might think that you'd heard the *tink* of the silver coin against one cup, and gleefully set your coin in front to it, only to find a copper underneath; the clever juggler had merely tapped a ringed finger against the side of the cup, mimicking the sound of the coin.

Wherever you looked, wherever you *knew* the silver coin would be, it wouldn't be. If you guessed randomly, your chances were one in three; if you tried to guess wisely, you had no chance.

Laheran was tired of playing cups-and-coins. The writ of authority that Guildmaster Yryn had given him had been useful; Laheran had ordered the other guildhouses on the island shut down, leaving only the one house in the Triple Hamlet open. And well-defended.

Some of the defenses were obvious. Laheran and two dozen guildsmen had taken rooms down the street from the guildhouse, and were—some of them openly, some of them covertly—keeping a tight watch on both the town and the house.

Some were subtle; Cullinane wasn't the only one who could set a trap. The locks on the heavy doors to the slave kennels had been booby-trapped; turning a key to the left, the normal way to unlock a sprung lock, would release a deadfall that would crash through the ceiling from the room above, crushing whoever stood in front of the door.

Other precautions had been taken with the approaches to the rear, barred windows; the most important safeguards had been taken with the slaves themselves, with the poor wretches locked in the cage. It was hard, but guildsmen had to make sacrifices.

Laheran paced back and forth. The waiting was the hard part.

CHAPTER 18
Aboard the Gazelle

The dawn speeds a man on his journey, and speeds him too in his work.

—Hesiod

That glowing red ball hanging just over the horizon had damn well better be the setting sun, bucko.

—Walter Slovotsky

About the time that Elleport disappeared over the horizon, Jason came up on deck, one pistol seated firmly in his shoulder holster, a thong holding it firmly into place for extra security on the rolling deck. His sword was belted tightly around his waist, along with his Nehera-made bowie.

The real giveaway, though, were the Home-made shirt and button-front blue jeans.

It was a clear afternoon, the sun just beginning its fall toward the horizon, the ship rolling lazily as it quartered the waves. Jason's stomach didn't like the rolling gait, but it wasn't complaining emphatically.

Bren Adahan was stretched out on a blanket on the deck by the rail, sunning himself, wearing only a towel tied sarong-style around his waist.

"We didn't discuss this," he said, raising himself up on an elbow.

398

He caught himself. It really didn't matter whether they had discussed it or not, not anymore. A group of a half-dozen people traveling to Klimos to exchange trade knives for nacrestones might be well-armed—given that Klimos wasn't entirely civilized, they'd better be—but it was unlikely that they'd have both guns and Home apparel . . .

. . . unless they were from Home.

No longer lolling idly at the tiller, Thivar Anjer's eyes widened. His creased face, walnut brown in the bright sunlight, wrinkled into a scowl as he started to turn toward Bothan Ver, the grizzled old sailor who was the *Gazelle*'s only crew, but stopped himself.

"A time for truth, it seems," Anjer said.

"So it seems," Durine said. He was seated cross-legged at the stern, near the captain. Stripped to the waist, the big man dipped the bathing ladle over the side and into the water, then brought it up and poured the water over his head, giving himself a sketchy sponge-bath. His thick hands rubbed at a hairy torso crisscrossed with pink scars, rivulets of flesh through a forest of hair.

"Durine," Jason called out, sniffing at the cake of soap he'd retrieved from his rucksack. It was real Pandathaway soap, made from Mel copra and who knew what else, smelling of flowers and sunshine. "Catch." He tossed the cake to Durine, who quickly wiped his left palm dry on the deck and reached up to let the soap smack into his palm.

Durine smiled a quick thank you, then began to lather his massive chest and belly.

Kethol was stretched out on the narrow free space at the bow, shaded by the jib, his eyes closed, hands folded over his stomach, apparently asleep. "Makes it easier," he said, his eyes still closed, not moving, "not to have to keep up a disguise."

Which was why Jason had done it. Besides, if he didn't, Tennetty was going to.

Tennetty came up from below, squinting in the daylight, now in her leathers, her hands patting her guns and the hilts of her sword and knife as though for reassurance. Balancing easily on the deck, she eyed the horizon, then reached down to help Jane Slovotsky up through the hatch. "Too bad," Tennetty murmured, "that Ganness wasn't in Elleport."

"Avair Ganness?" Jane Slovotsky raised an eyebrow. She was wearing a white blouse and a tight pair of Home denim shorts;

incongruously, she had heavy shoes on her feet. Nice legs, though. Maybe a bit too skinny. But not much.

Another wave broke below the bow, spattering them all, making the metal cooking box hiss. Jane raised a hand to wipe the sea water from her face, the light, golden hairs on her forearm glistening with sun and spray. "Tennetty, you really expect that any time we need transportation by water, Avair Ganness is going to be around?"

"You haven't ridden with Ganness."

"No, but I have heard about him. Cullinanes and their friends seem to keep getting him in trouble, costing him ships."

"They do, at that." Tennetty laughed.

Jason liked that. He hadn't seen her laugh, not much, not since that night on the Mel beach, the night that Father died, or didn't.

The wind caught the peak of another whitecap, spraying them all again.

The rear deck was crowded, and Thivar Anjer didn't like it much. He glared at them while Bothan Ver went forward to where the half dozen needle-nosed rapentfish their nets had scooped up that morning were grilling over the steel cooking box.

"So. We're seeking Karl Cullinane," the captain said, not really a question. "What will happen when we find him?"

Jason opened his mouth to say something about how all the captain would have to do was drop them off at the rendezvous with Ellegon, but Bren Adahan beat him to it.

"You will go your way, and we will go ours," Bren Adahan said. "We'll use his transportation."

"If he and his friends have any," the captain mused. "Very well— I'll go my way with double the money, and all of the trade knives."

"Oh?"

"I used to know an Avair Ganness, captain of the *Warthog*. He used to talk at some length about how dangerous it is to get involved with Cullinane. I don't mind taking risks, but I won't do it for a few silvers. Nor will I do it without you all swearing on your blades that my ship and I will be released unharmed, and that you won't stop me running in the face of a fight." He gestured around. "I'm no warrior; this is not a warship."

"You'll be free to go. If you don't betray us. Or try to," Tennetty said.

"Agreed. Have we a bargain?"

"Yes, you have a bargain," Bren Adahan said.

"No. Not you." Thivar Anjer turned to Jason. "Young Cullinane, have we a bargain?"

"We do."

"Cullinanes don't break their word, do they?"

"No, we don't," Jason said.

Jason couldn't sleep. The hold was dank and musty, redolent of rotting fish, decaying wood and a distant, acrid stench that Jason couldn't quite identify. The smells, combined with the constant, albeit gentle rocking of the boat, had him vaguely nauseated.

He dressed and climbed the ladder, clearing his throat as he did so that Kethol would know it was him and not be surprised. That was one of the many things Valeran had taught him: never surprise a guard accidentally.

Bothan Ver was half asleep next to the bound tiller, only occasionally coming half awake to take a quick glance at the sky and water, perhaps make a slight, drowsy adjustment to tiller and sheets, and then stretching out again in his steersman's chair.

The night was chilly. Kethol crouched next to the cooking box, warming his hands over the banked coals. Straightening, he handed a waterskin to Jason, who took a quick swig for politeness, then handed it back.

Klimos lay ahead, somewhere off the bow. Just another of the Shattered Islands, a cluster of dirt-poor islands in the Cirric, where the people supported themselves by fishing and farming in good years, by selling off their children in bad years. They'd evolved a complex set of rules as to when and why some children were saleable and others weren't, but it still sucked.

Tennetty, sleeping lightly in her bag belowdecks, had been born on one of these islands, sold into slavery by her parents.

Jason shook his head.

Some problems didn't admit of easy solutions; Home raiders didn't often travel into the Shattered Islands. Being caught at sea by a slaver ship was always a possibility; like the Pandathaway-based Slavers' Guild, the Home raiders hadn't established themselves in the Outer Kingdoms, on the other side of the Cirric.

Besides, what could you do? Kill all parents who would sell a child? And what then? Pull food and money from the air?

He knew what Tennetty's answer was to that. Killing was her

answer to everything. But Jason didn't know what his was. Not yet.

"At least I didn't get left behind this time," Kethol said. He knit his fingers together and cracked his knuckles.

"Eh?"

"Your father left the three of us in Ehvenor. The three of us who survived. The trip cost us some good men, sir."

And the trip wouldn't have been necessary if Jason hadn't panicked the first time he'd been around shots fired in anger. He wanted to lash out, but the rebuke was justified.

Kethol looked at him, then shook his head. "Not what I meant. Not what I meant at all. Would have happened eventually. You keep juggling knives, you're going to get cut. We all juggle knives."

Kethol had another swallow of water, and the two of them were silent for a while, watching the dark sky and the sea.

Far off, toward the horizon, a ring of perhaps a dozen faerie lights pulsed excitedly in sequence, blue chasing red around and around, the blue becoming brighter as it closed in on the red, fading when the red took on a tinge of orange and speeded up. And then, without warning, the lights stopped cooperating and spread across the sky, their pulsing color changes becoming random, lethargic.

"Do you think he's alive, Kethol?"

The lanky warrior took a long time answering. "Yes. And no. And maybe it doesn't matter, young sir." Kethol shook his head slowly, blunt fingers toying with his beard. "Yes, because he's what he was. Fastest man with a weapon I ever did see. Didn't matter what weapon—sword, staff, bare hands, anything. There maybe was a better swordsman here or there, and maybe somebody as good with a staff, but your father was a . . . wizard with everything.

"So: yes, he's alive, because of what he was, and because the Empire needs to be held together by somebody who knows what he's doing, and I'm not sure you do, not yet." The way he looked at Jason wasn't either friendly or hostile, just appraising. "No, that's not true. I'm sure that you don't, yet. You don't know when to be hard and when to be soft—which your father did. I don't think you know when to be direct and when to be subtle—which your father didn't. Doubt you've got the strength of will and the strength of body to carry off being direct all the time. Which he had.

"So yes, he's alive. We need him." Kethol leaned forward on his elbows and sighed. "But, no, I don't think he's alive, because nobody could have lived through that explosion that you and Tennetty described. Perhaps it doesn't matter, because perhaps it's all for nothing anyway."

He chuckled, a thin laugh that rattled in his throat like small, dry bones. "Only one thing I'm sure of, young emperor-to-be, and that's that you'd better decide who you are. If you're going to be just one of the fellows, then you'd best not expect us to follow you blindly into combat. If you want to be above us, keep yourself apart."

"And if I don't?"

"Well, then you'd better hope that your father is alive. In either case, you'd best not spend the night asking a simple soldier what we'll find at the end of the trail.

"Go to sleep, Jason."

CHAPTER 19

Klimos

*A timid person is frightened before a danger, a coward during
the time, and a courageous person afterward.*
—Jean Paul Richter

*Slovotsky's Law Number Thirty-One: Get scared right
away; avoid the rush.*
—Walter Slovotsky

Elleport to Elevos, and there were nothing but rumors; the
markets were full of them. The Warrior had just struck at Menelet,
but he'd been killed there. Or was it on Millipos?

Or he hadn't been killed. And it wasn't Millipos. It was Bursos.
Besides, did you see that thing that flew overhead last tenday? It
looked like a dragon, perhaps, and what are dragons doing in the
Eren regions?

The trade in dragonbane was brisk.

The Warrior? Who cared about the Warrior when something,
some *thing* had struck on Heshtos, leaving half the village dead,
before it slipped into the sea? The village wizard? He was among
the dead. The surviving villagers had sold two dozen children to
the Slavers' Guild for the hire of a Pandathaway wizard, promising lavish treatment, anything, if he would only live among them
and protect them.

The Warrior? No, not Heshtos. No, he and his dozen companions had raided Millipos, or was it Deddebos? It couldn't have been Filaket; perhaps it was Salket? No, it wasn't Salket, or Salkos, but maybe it was Bursos, and it was a hundred companions. No, two—another human, and a dwarf. A dwarf at sea? Don't be ridiculous. Dwarves don't sail; if they were to fall overboard they would sink like stones. Idiot.

There was a guild factor in residence in the only village on that tiny island, but they kept Tennetty on the *Gazelle*, and Kethol, Bren Adahan and Durine maintained a disguise as bounty hunters, seeking the Warrior, and they let the slaver's man live.

Elevos to Millipos, and as night fell Bothan Ver's sharp eyes saw something in the sky, something large and black, flying. But it was flying west and they were sailing north, the sun was setting and they couldn't quite make out what it was.

It wasn't Ellegon, that's all that Jason was sure of. It wasn't Ellegon.

Landfall at Millipos, and there were nothing but rumors. Yes, the Warrior had struck at Klimos, but he had disappeared. There were too many hunters on his trail; he had vanished into the air. No, he hadn't vanished into the air: he had attacked the slaver factor there, but had been driven off.

There was a tavern in Millipos that catered mainly to sailors, some drinking up their pay between trips, others looking for work. Kethol and Bren Adahan bought drinks, and listened.

Nothing since Klimos. But did you hear about . . . ?

They passed up the first rendezvous; they were a good three days' sail from Pefret, and there was no reason to hit Pefret. Next rendezvous, they hoped.

But now it was Millipos to Filaket, and there were nothing but rumors.

Try Klimos. He was there, and there hasn't been any rumor of him since. But he's still around; he kills slavers in their sleep, and he has two—no, twelve, no, a score of companions.

Slavers, *here?* With the Warrior about to step out of the night and skin anything resembling a slaver? Are you mad? Well, yes, we had a factor here, but look at the rice in the granaries—we don't have to sell anybody. What kind of monsters do you think us, that we would sell our children when we don't have to?

The smudge of smoke on the horizon grew as they approached Klimos, the *Gazelle* pointed high, running close to the wind, heeled over hard.

As he stood by the rail, there was a coldness, a tightness in Jason's belly, as though the bread and cheese he'd eaten earlier had changed into stone.

"Okay, people," Tennetty said, clapping her hands together for attention, "enough looking around. I want all guns loaded, all pans primed, all hammers on the half-cock. Bren Adahan and Durine, load your crossbows; Kethol, get your longbow strung."

Bren Adahan shook his head. "We are at least—"

"Shut your mouth and do as you're told," she said. "I've got more experience in running a raiding squad than anybody else here. So that puts me in charge of everything and everyone, which includes you, Baron Adahan "

Jason found all of them looking at him.

It's not fair, he thought. *I shouldn't have to make this kind of decision just because I'm my father's son.*

And why not? Why was Tennetty making a fuss when they were easily an hour from the island? The smoke indicated some possible danger, sure—but why bring things to a head now?

He thought about that for a quick moment, and decided that if there had to be an argument over who was in charge, now was the time for it. Maybe Tennetty wasn't quite as crazy as everybody thought.

Everybody was still looking at him.

What would his father have done? That was easy: Karl Cullinane would have trusted Tennetty. But Karl Cullinane could have relied on Tennetty. Jason didn't know any such thing.

He'd pretend that he did. He tried to keep his voice level. "You're in charge, Tennetty. Everybody load up, prime and half-cock."

"Oil patches, everyone," she added. "Save your spit. And, Durine," she said, "use a slug load in the big smoothbore."

"Mind if I overload it a bit?" the big man asked, as he carefully tied his short-barreled shotgun to the railing, then reached for the smoothbore.

"It's your face it'll blow up in."

"It's not much of a face, anyway." Durine tipped a heavily-rounded measure of powder down the muzzle of his big shotgun, pushed a hunk of wadding after it, then took a greasy bullet almost the size of his thumb out of his pouch and shoved it down into the barrel.

Jason belted his second holster tightly around his waist, then got his other revolver out of his bedroll gear, checked to see that it was loaded and that the empty chamber was under the hammer, and strapped it tightly into the shoulder holster.

He slipped the lacing out of his tunic front, leaving it open to his waist, tying the leather thong around his forehead partly just to put it someplace, partly to see that he didn't get any stray hair in his eyes. He was beginning to need a haircut, but this wasn't the time to do anything about that. He took out his kit and started working on his rifle, pleased to see that his fingers were faster at it than Bren Adahan's. At least there was something he could do better than the baron.

"This is not a warship," Thivar Anjer said, considering the smoke. "That appears to be trouble ahead."

Bren Adahan had finished priming his pan, and snapped the frizzen down into place with a sharp snick. "You've been here before," he said to Thivar Anjer.

"Yes, yes, of course I have, but—"

"Where does it look to you like the fire's coming from?"

"It's damn clear where the fire's coming from—it's Lehot's Village, over on the lee side of the island, and it's burning. It looks like your Karl Cullinane has been here again."

Tennetty snorted. "Everything that goes wrong anywhere in the Eren region is Karl's fault? Besides, we knew that he was here, that he killed some slavers here some tendays ago—you think he'd be stupid enough to come back?"

Jane opened her mouth, then closed it. Jason squatted next to her.

"What is it?" he asked. As they talked, his hands kept working at his rifle: wrap the bullet in an oil patch, seat the patch firmly with the short-starter from his pouch, slip the short-starter into his belt while he trimmed the patch with his beltknife, put the knife back in the scabbard, take the short-starter back in hand and seat the bullet firmly, replace the short-starter in his belt, slip the ramrod out from underneath the barrel to ram the bullet solidly home, replace the ramrod, take the vial of fine priming powder out of his pouch, tip a measure into the pan, snap the frizzen down.

She shook her head. "Tennetty's right, but for the wrong reason," she whispered. "I don't know that your father might not think it was tricky to double back and hit the same location twice. But *my* father's too clever for that. The slavers will have to worry about the possibility, anyway. That means that they'll have to watch out at places that the three of them have already hit—and Dad isn't going to let your dad hit them where they're watching."

"So?"

"So if the reports are right that the three of them hit the slavers here, then whatever this is, it isn't them. I say we get out of here," she said. "I don't like it."

Bren Adahan gestured at the smoke. "If you bring us around to the windward side, come around the island, and then cut across the path of the smoke, can we make a fast escape if we have to?"

Thivar Anjer shook his head, his mouth creased into a contemplative frown. "Better to sail straight in, in any event; I should be able to sail two, three points closer to the wind than a warship, if we have to run. But I am not willing to bet my ship and my life on that."

Bothan Ver studiously pulled in the mainsheet, as though a thumbs' breadth more or less slack was an important difference.

Bren Adahan licked his lips. "We have to investigate. This is our best clue to Karl Cullinane."

"Ah, a clue," Thivar Anjer snorted. "What will you have to suggest should the clue consist of a three-masted slaver raiding ship?"

"Don't worry about it," Jason said. "We can outrun a warship if they've taken some sail damage. Jane, would you dig up a couple of the signal rockets and the launching rod?"

"Sure." She smiled. "You're thinking like a Slovotsky, and I like it." In a few moments she was back on deck with two of the slim, short-finned cylinders and the launching rod.

"This is supposed to be set in the ground to launch a signal rocket," she said, "but we can tie it to the railing, pointing backwards, and fire it off at any ship chasing us. If we can hit their sails—and if you can steer your ship, I can hit their sails—they'll be too busy dealing with their burning ship to give us any difficulties."

Durine rested his hand on the captain's shoulder. "Besides," he said, "it would make Tennetty very unhappy if we ran away from no threat at all."

The captain frowned. "Your logic has persuaded me."

All the preparations for fight-or-flight seemed unnecessary when they pulled around the island. There were no ships to fight or flee from, just a dozen or so small boats, none more than two-thirds the length of the *Gazelle*—fishing boats, suitable too for traveling to close islands, not really big enough to travel out in the Cirric.

But something had happened.

Two of the boats had been capsized; another lay on the sand with its mast splintered. What had been houses and sheds up at the edge of the sand were now just smoking ruin; pilings like blackened matchsticks stood where the dock had been. Black smoke still hung over the trees, almost obscuring the path up from the water.

Thivar Anjer spoke up. "It would seem sensible to leave. Whatever has done this is dangerous."

"You've got another lead to Karl Cullinane?" Jane Slovotsky asked gently.

"Does that mean you think we ought to check it out?" Jason said. "I thought you were for skipping this island."

"Any law against changing my mind?" She shrugged. "Either check it out real quickly, or not at all. I wouldn't want to wait in the dark for whatever did that."

"The dock is gone," the captain protested. "I will not ground my boat."

"There's a rowboat over there, still looks whole," Tennetty said, not taking her eyes off the water as she stripped down to her bare skin, belted her bowie around her naked waist, then tied her hair tightly behind her.

There was nothing even vaguely lewd about her naked body; it was all muscle, skin and scars. "I'll get it. Jason, keep me covered." She vaulted over the side, splashing feet-first into the water, then swam for the rowboat with swift, sure strokes.

He ought to say something constructive. "Durine, if you see anything in the water near her, shoot it." He could almost hear Ellegon in his head, saying something like, *Sure, sure. He would have, like, yelled *boo* otherwise.*

But there had to be something else to have them do. He reached up to his shoulder holster and drew his pistol. It had a faster rate of fire than anything—but Kethol's longbow would be a good second. "Kethol, use your bow."

"A good idea, young sir." Kethol smiled as he set aside his rifle, lashing the barrel to the railing with a practiced slipknot. "I've done some bowfishing, too. Remember, you've got to aim long. Things under water seem closer than they are."

He worked his shoulders under his tunic, then nocked an arrow and drew it back experimentally, the feathered shaft held easily in his knuckles. He slowly relaxed the tension on the bow.

"I'm ready," he said.

What next? There had to be some useful order to give, to remind everyone—particularly Jason—that Jason was in charge.

But nothing happened as Tennetty swam to shore, retrieved four paddles scattered across the rocks and sand, and threw them in the flat boat before launching it and paddling out to the *Gazelle.*

There was easily room enough for six people, even with weapons. He should go first, Jason decided, tying it fast as it scraped against the *Gazelle's* side.

"Okay," he said, "after me."

"Like hell," Tennetty said, half-dressed already. Her damp hair clung to her face like black vines. "We do this in two transfers. First Durine, the baron, and me establish a position on shore, and then I paddle back for you, Jane and Bothan Ver." She wiped her nose on her arm. "Kethol and the captain can stay—"

"We have your *word!*" Thivar Anjer hissed. "I will not send Bothan Ver ashore with you, and I'll not come with you myself."

The captain was right. Jason had given his word, and the word of a Cullinane wasn't to be taken lightly. "No, Tennetty. They stay here."

Tennetty shook her head vigorously, flinging drops of water. "That was before we—"

"*No,*" he said, trying to speak with his father's voice. "No, Tennetty." She would have listened to his father; he tried for Karl Cullinane's command voice, speaking each word slowly, emphatically: "They stay here."

"Shit." She spat on the deck. "We don't have time to argue. Kethol, you stay on watch, and don't drink or eat anything. If there's trouble, send up a signal rocket and get out of here. Send up another one when you want a rendezvous."

"Understood, Tennetty." The redheaded man smiled, teeth starkly white against his red beard. "Although you'd think we don't trust our new friends here."

"Hey, guys?" Jane Slovotsky raised a hand. "If somebody's going to be left behind, I wouldn't mind if it's me. I can light a signal flare real good, and my Dad's explained to me that Slovotskys don't like to stick our faces in the way of the ax. Although I could have worked that out myself," she added.

Durine and Bren Adahan smiled at that.

Tennetty snorted. "I've been watching the way these two have been watching you, and I'd sort of like to be able to introduce you to Karl as at least one woman of our acquaintance who hasn't been raped. We do it my way."

Getting ashore was tense, but uneventful. In just a short while they were all on land, the boat carefully beached.

Nothing stirred around them. It was still, the silence more accented than interrupted by the gentle slap of the waves on the rocks and the crackling of the smoldering wood.

"Keep it quiet, people," Tennetty whispered. "Let's move out."

There was only one clear path off the shore: a wide dirt road leading up, into the woods.

With a quick hand signal, Tennetty had them spread out. She took the point herself, with Durine on the right side of the road, behind her, Bren Adahan on the left, his rifle slung, a two-pronged fishing spear in his hands.

While everyone carried an extra pistol or two, Durine practically bristled with weapons: his heavy saber dangled from the left side of his belt; he carried the big smoothbore shotgun in his hands, a short rifle slung over his left shoulder, a rucksack over his right. The wooden butt of a flintlock pistol stuck out of his boot, and there was another brace of them in his belt, on the right side, leaving room for him to reach across his belly for the saber on the left.

Jane Slovotsky, the most lightly armed of the party, was in the middle, carrying a flintlock rifle and a single pistol, while Jason brought up the rear, his own flintlock heavy in his hands.

The wind changed, bringing more smoke their way, stinging their nostrils, carrying distant sounds to them; the crackling of the fire and something else, a dull roar that Jason couldn't quite make out.

Ahead there was a break in the trees. "Should be a village there," Tennetty said as they gathered around her. "In this part of the world they tend to keep trees between themselves and the Cirric; helps to break up the wind. There was—"

A distant scream cut her off. It was high and ululating, a cry of agony.

"Slow and easy, people. Slow and easy," Tennetty said.

They crept around the bend.

Where the trees broke, there had been a village. It was now burning and smoldering; some of the wooden houses had been smashed, and that had probably set off cooking fires, the sparks leaping from house to house.

There was another scream and some more cries; their source was clearly further down the road.

"Easy, easy," Tennetty whispered as they rounded one of the few remaining houses.

"Oh, shit," she said.

The cleared area beyond had apparently been the center of the village, where folks came to talk and trade together. Now they were even closer together; in the very center of the clearing, a hundred men, women and children huddled tightly.

Except for one: a short, wizened man in gray tattered robes stood between the humans and the creature. His left arm hung limp and bloody by his side, but his right arm was thrust out in front of his body, as though supporting the mass of light that stood between him and the creature.

The light and the lightning pushed it back, but the creature launched itself in the air for the wizard, only to be knocked back again.

It was a huge black beast, its body covered by tight fur that gleamed blackly in the sunlight. It was easily twice the size of a horse, its flat, triangular head vaguely lupine.

It had been wounded, at some point; a dozen arrows stuck in its shoulders and flanks, like feathers in an almost-plucked goose. Dirt matted a raw wound on its right foreleg; something had managed to cut through its hide.

Again it lunged, and again light and lightning issued from the cloud, knocking it back.

It crouched and screamed its defiance while it gathered its breath.

Maybe he tripped, or perhaps he panicked, but one of the

villagers stumbled away from the rest, and then started to run when he realized he was alone and exposed.

The creature leaped and growled as it snatched at the fleeing man, pinning him to the ground with one paw, then dipping its head to pick up its victim, shaking its head like a dog shaking a rat, then flinging the now-limp form into the air. Then the monster turned back to the wizard.

Screams and cries filled the air, along with the deep growl of the creature as it tried and failed to reach past the cloud of light and fire.

Still, with each bolt of lightning, each blast of light, the glow seemed to dim marginally, as though its power were being drained whenever the creature slammed into it.

Jason had never seen anything like the monster before; but he remembered rumors of strange things coming out of Faerie. Could this, whatever it was, be one?

It didn't matter. He couldn't let it kill a village full of people. He cocked the hammer of his rifle and brought it to his shoulder.

"*No,*" Tennetty hissed. "It's not our fight."

"*Yes,*" he snapped back. "Would my father run away?"

"You're not your—shit, shit, shit," she said. "Fucking Cullinanes never listen." She brought her rifle to her shoulder and fired, all in one smooth motion.

Perhaps the bullet hit, but all that Jason could see was the creature dropping to all fours, then turning to face the new threat.

He took careful aim, trying for the base of the creature's neck. A head shot was risky; if you got the angle wrong the bullet could just ricochet off the creature's skull.

But if you could tear open any of the arteries leading to the brain, if you could smash the trachea. . . .

A gun crashed to his right, and then one to his left.

One shot missed, but the other became a splash of blood over the creature's right eye and a bestial scream of pain as its huge mouth sagged open, and it turned to see where the sound and hurt had come from.

The bullet had torn a gouge across its skull, but the creature wasn't seriously injured. It turned and leaped, covering half the distance between itself and Jason, settling its hind claws into the ground as it braced itself to spring and rush.

As it pushed itself into the air, Durine's smoothbore went off with a bang and a cloud of smoke, smashing the creature's right eye into a bloody mess, leaving it half-blind and fully maddened.

It fell to the ground only a few meters from Tennetty, who calmly fired one of her pistols into its side, only to be batted aside by a massive paw as she dropped her hand to her waist to grab another pistol. She tumbled through the air, falling to the stones, battered, broken like a child's discarded toy.

Bren Adahan, his pistols empty, his fisherman's trident lying bent on the ground, held his saber out in front of him with both hands, as though that narrow needle of steel could deflect claws and teeth. The monster batted him to one side, then stooped to bite, stopping only when gunfire from somewhere to Jason's left shook its body.

It's up to me, Jason thought.

It was just like in Melawei. It was always up to him, and he wouldn't fail, he couldn't fail, not when it counted.

He placed the sights on the creature's throat as it raised its head to snarl at him, then squeezed the trigger slowly, carefully.

The creature's remaining eye glared balefully at him as it braced itself for another leap.

The hammer sparked down on the frizzen; the butt of the rifle slammed into his shoulder; and a gout of flame from the barrel of the gun tore blood and flesh from the side of the animal's neck.

But the animal didn't slow, didn't stop, didn't fall down and die like it was supposed to.

Jason dropped his rifle to one side and snatched at the pistol in his belt holster.

"It happens sometimes," Valeran had once told him, the old man's eyes glazed, his voice slurred with drink, "that when the whole world is going to shit around you, time does funny things. Freezes, like ice, and you've got from now until forever. Don't smile, boy. There's nothing good about it." The battered old warrior leaned back and took another long pull on his bottle. "Only trouble is, you're fastened into place, too, like a roach frozen in an ice chip. Won't do you any damn good. Doesn't ever do you any damn good."

The monster didn't stop; it leaped at him. Jason took it all in, sights, sounds, and smells: the woody scent of smoke in the air;

the musky reek of the creature; the cries of the villagers; Jane's shrill shouts from behind him; the pop of a pair of pistols, and the blood and gore splattering the creature's side; the tight fur on the creature's muzzle, terminating in a wet, leathery snout.

His peripheral vision was clear as fine crystal and the light was heady as wine, taking on an almost golden glow. In that glow Bren Adahan was on his feet again, blood streaming from his mouth and nose, his saber in his hand, all skills and training forgotten as he raised the sword over his head, as though preparing to hack down on the huge beast.

Durine had his rifle up to his shoulder; his brow was furrowed in concentration, his bottom lip caught in his teeth.

Jason bent time, forced his slow right hand up and pulled the trigger, once.

Fire and smoke nipped off a corner of the creature's ear, that was all.

And then lightning spoke, once, from his right, and the world crashed down on him.

He wasn't sure if he'd been unconscious, but the world was a black pit of pain. He tried to breathe, but the black mass crushed him down against the ground, blinding him with the weight of the stinking fur, the immense burden grinding the mass of the pistol in his shoulder holster into his chest.

There was blood and grit in his mouth. He forced a little air into his lungs, feeling broken ribs grate, moving in his chest in sharp, agonizing counterpoint.

From a distance, he could hear them.

"Move it, move it, get it the fuck off him," Tennetty said. "You— use that spear as a lever. All of you there, push."

A single shot rang out, and Jane Slovotsky's clear contralto cut through the sound and pain. "Do it, now, please," she said.

The weight lifted, marginally, and he felt strong hands clawing at his ankles. When they pulled on his left leg the pain in his knee drew a scream from between his clenched teeth, but they didn't stop dragging him painfully across the rocky ground. Bones ground in his knee.

He tried to gasp for breath, but couldn't draw any in.

Somebody forced the mouth of a bottle between his lips, glass knocking hard against his teeth.

The too-sweet taste of Eareven healing draughts washed the taste of blood from his mouth, giving him enough strength to swallow.

He did, and as the liquid warmed his throat and chest the familiar miracle happened again: he healed.

One of his ribs had shattered, broken in half a dozen places, splinters of bone ripping into his flesh with every breath. The splinters became pieces and the pieces snapped into wholeness with a flurry of sound like corn popping.

He could breathe again and the air, even though it tasted of blood and dirt and shit, was sweeter and richer and tastier than a fine puff pastry.

Bruises unbruised; as he brought his right hand up before his face, a deep gash across his palm closed, ragged edges sealing themselves together until what had been slash became a red line that turned pink and vanished before his eyes. His broken right knee closed in on itself, blood vessels expelling tendons and bits of bone, ruined nerves reasserting themselves, while ruptured muscle, tendon and bone knitted and strengthened.

Dozens of villagers crowded around as he lay on the ground, next to the mountain of fur and flesh.

He could see Jane Slovotsky and Bren Adahan out of the corner of his eye; she stood arrogantly apart, one hand on her hip, another holding a cocked flintlock, while Bren Adahan leaned against the vast bulk of the dead creature, tilting back the bottle of healing draughts to drink from it.

"Durine. . . ." It felt as if he were shouting, but all he could hear was a thin croaking. Recovery was draining; there was a limit to what the healing potion could do.

The big man knelt at his side. "I'm right here, young sir," he said. Tennetty stood next to Durine, the left side of her face caked with blood.

"Ten? Are you—?"

She smiled through a mask of blood and dirt. "They got to me first with the healing draughts. I'm all right."

"She's fine," Durine said. "Everybody is fine, young sir."

"Your bullet?"

Durine nodded, as he rested the butt of his rifle on the ground, leaning on it. "Best shot I ever made. Cut right through the spine, killed it instantly."

"Luckiest shot you ever made," Tennetty said. "Or were you really aiming between the vertebrae?"

A sense of strength and power hummed in Jason's head, like strong whiskey; he rolled to his knees, waving off a score of helping hands.

He forced himself to his feet, but his new legs wouldn't support him; if Durine hadn't caught him, he would have fallen.

"Who . . . ?" he tried to say, he couldn't get the words out. "Are all of us okay?"

"We're just fine," Durine said.

Jason had failed, but they hadn't failed. "Bren?"

The baron was quickly at his side, smiling broadly, although the front of his tunic was bloodstained and he was mopping at his bloody face with a wet cloth that a villager had provided.

"We're all alive," he said, his voice quietly triumphant.

They were surrounded by a hundred smiling villagers, ranging in age from a scattered few infants to the old wizard who stood apart, watching them.

Something pulled at Jason's tunic. A barefoot, brown-haired little girl, five or six years old, dressed in a torn shift that had been made from a grain sack, held his pistol with one hand and tugged at his tunic with the other. "Is this yours?" she asked. "Sir?"

He accepted it, and stored it away in his belt holster, patting once at his other gun. "Yes, it's mine."

She smiled up at him, quickly hugged his waist, then vanished into the crowd.

Something caught in his throat; he couldn't speak for a moment.

Tennetty snickered. "Very nice, very nice. But is it worth getting killed?"

"Shut up."

Other villagers had gathered together their gear and piled it on the grass, not far from the dead beast. What had terrorized the villagers was now just a pile of fur and flesh. Two boys, one maybe ten, another perhaps a year or two older, were poking at the body of the beast, one with a short wooden stick, another with the hilt of a broken sword.

Bren Adahan's scabbard was empty. Jason drew his own sword, rapped the flat of it smartly against his now-solid knee, hard enough to make the steel ring with the distant sound of bright bells.

"Borrow mine," he said, reversing his grip and holding it out to the baron, who gave a quick salute with it, then slipped it into his scabbard. It was a loose fit; Bren's preferred saber was longer and heavier than Jason's.

The gray-robed wizard stood apart from the rest of them, watching them with eyes that didn't seem to blink. "I am Dava Natye," he said slowly. "We are in your debt."

Tennetty snorted. "Bet your fucking ass you are." She gestured at the beast. "What was that?"

The wizard shook his head. "I do not know. Traders have brought rumors of strange things coming out of Faerie. The Warrior spoke of—"

"The Warrior?" Jason asked. "He was here?"

"Two tendays ago," the wizard said.

"Describe him," Tennetty hissed.

The wizard shook his head. "I only saw him for a moment, outlined against the flames of the burning shack of the slaver, Nosinan. A big man; I can say no more. He told me to be gone, that this was a matter between him and the guild.

"He left a message, and then he vanished." The wizard spread his hands. "I never saw his boat, nor his companions. But they were here; and now they are not."

"The message," Tennetty said, taking a step toward the wizard, then stopping herself. "He left a message for us?"

"Not for you. For the slavers. He shouted at me, 'Tell them,' he said, 'tell them that the warrior lives, and tell them I am coming for them.' Then he shouted at his companions to meet him and the boat, and gave the body of Nosinan a final kick . . . and then he was gone."

Several of the villagers nodded in unison; one of them, a thin pock-faced man with deep-set eyes, spoke up. "It's just as Dava Natye said. It's just as we told Laheran, of the guild."

CHAPTER 20

Comfort

Be cheerful while you are alive.

—Ptahhotep

Grab what comfort you can, however you can, whenever you can. The ride gets real rocky 'way too often.

—Walter Slovotsky

Bren Adahan had decided that Jason and Tennetty, still recovering from the shock of their wounds and the healing, needed a good night's rest. Jason wasn't in the mood to protest.

So they spent the night ashore, explaining to the villagers that it would not be a good idea if anybody from the village came up on them at night. They camped out on the grassy fringe just above the rocks, in clear view of the *Gazelle*, where it floated at anchor. The others preferred to sleep under the stars, but Bren Adahan and Jason each pitched a small raider tent.

Jason was asleep when something touched his foot. He woke suddenly, reaching for his pistol.

"Easy, Jason," Jane Slovotsky's voice whispered from the mouth of the tent. She tapped him on the foot again. "You were crying out in your sleep."

There was a bitter taste in his mouth, and his head felt as if someone was regularly jabbing a dull icepick into the back of his head. He brought himself up to his elbows.

"It must have been a dream," he said. But the dream was gone now. Something about wading through knee-deep rivers of boiling blood, holding a crying baby girl over his head. It had been distinct, sharp as the edge of a knife . . . but now it was gone.

He wiped sweat from his forehead and stretched, his blankets damp and musty around him. "Thanks for waking me." Her outline was vague in the dark, and then it was gone. She was gone.

His mouth still tasted sour as he checked his weapons. There was no waterskin near his head; he'd forgotten to put one nearby. As far as he knew, Tennetty had the only bottle of Riccetti's Best on the island. He needed a drink of something, and his bladder was full, tight as a drum.

He didn't like waking Tennetty. Not only did she need her rest, but she always came awake armed. Two or three times the *Gazelle* had taken an unexpected pitch or roll and he'd found himself bumped up against Tennetty, the slim woman coming awake wide-eyed, a knife in her hand.

He had slept in his jeans, but unbuckled the waist for comfort; he buttoned himself up, slung his holster over his shoulder, then crawled out and stood up in the night.

Tennetty was asleep a few yards to his left and Jane had returned to her blankets and sleeping canvas, to his right.

Tireless Durine was on watch, sitting on a rock down by the water. The big man raised his hand in greeting.

Bren Adahan's tent was a stone's throw from Jason's, and beyond that was the forest; Jason took the traditional twenty steps beyond the farthest sleeper and urinated against the nearest tree. He buttoned his fly and walked back toward the camp.

Beyond the charred bones of the waterfront buildings, beyond where gentle waves stroked the shore, the *Gazelle* stood at anchor, supported by a sea that seemed built more of reflected starlight and faerie light than of water. It caught the twinkle of the million points of light overhead, and mixed it with the pulsations of the distant faerie lights.

There were light footsteps behind him—bare soles on dirt.

Jane Slovotsky cleared her throat. She stood there in the dark, wearing loose drawstring pants and a shirt, holding a pair of clay bottles. "Pretty, isn't it?"

"Yeah."

"Which do you want? Whiskey, water?"

"Both," he said, accepting the whiskey bottle first.

"You're not exactly your father," she said. "He wouldn't have let me sneak up behind him."

"I heard you."

"Sure."

He uncorked the bottle and took a swig. Lou Riccetti's corn whiskey might not have been as important a development as guns and gunpowder, but it had its points. Still tasted like horse piss, though.

"Easy on that," she said. "You had a bit of a shock today. Don't push yourself."

His first reaction was to bristle, to tell her that he was capable of judging how much he should drink and that it was none of her damn business . . . but she was right.

"Good point," he said. He exchanged bottles with her, and she took a quick swallow before recorking the whiskey.

A cold wind blew out of the west, but her smile was warm in the darkness.

The water was cold and fresh. It tasted good, particularly clean and bright tonight. Valeran had once said something about the value of almost getting killed: it did tend to sharpen the senses.

He handed her the water bottle. "Thanks."

"Mind if I ask a question?" she said as he started to turn away.

He shrugged. "Go ahead."

"Why haven't you made a pass at me?" There was a curious lilt in her voice, a note he hadn't heard before. "Is it me, or is it you, or is it some combination?"

"Has every man you've ever known tried to get you to sleep with him?"

She smiled. "Almost. Since I turned fourteen."

He looked down the slope toward the others, and she nodded.

"Sure. All three of them. Durine was kind of cute about it. Bren's being kind of a nuisance."

He shook his head, once. "Bren Adahan says he wants to marry my sister," he said coldly. "I'm not sure I like that."

"No harm done." She snorted. "I said no. Besides, I didn't know that it fits in only one," she said. "Yours shaped like a key?"

There wasn't anything to say to that, but he did anyway: "Do you have to talk like that?"

"I don't know." She shrugged. "Runs in the family. A lot runs in my family. . . . Did you ever ask yourself why my father sent you after me?"

"Because he wanted you and your mother and your sister to relocate to Biemestren," he said.

She snorted. "You *do* need a keeper. Didn't it occur to you that he thought that the two of us might pair off? Or don't you have all the parts?"

"No." It hadn't occurred to him. He swallowed. Why was she bringing this up? Just to make him uncomfortable. It should have occurred to him, though. Back in Biemestren, around court, there had been constant subtle pressure from most of the barons to pair him off with a baronial daughter. Any baron who had a daughter had no difficulty seeing her as the next empress. Why should Walter Slovotsky be all that different?

"Oh, that's too bad," she said half-mockingly. "You don't have all the parts, eh?"

"You know what I meant."

"Yes, I do."

He didn't remember her putting down the bottles, or moving closer to him, but suddenly she was in his arms, her hands locked behind his back, her mouth warm on his.

After a while she let go of him, moved a few inches away. "About time, Cullinane."

Durine had been watching the whole thing casually from his place by the water. Jason wasn't sure, but he thought he saw Durine smile before he turned away.

"He knows," Jason said.

She shrugged. "So what? Doesn't your tent have enough room for two?"

"Y-yes," he said, biting his lip in frustration at the way his voice shook for a moment. He was the man, damn it; he was supposed to be smooth and sophisticated. "But, why?"

"Didn't your father ever tell you not to look a gift horse in the mouth?" She laughed quietly, then kissed him gently on the lips when he frowned. "No, no. I'm not laughing at you. It's because, like, you're irresistible, maybe?"

"Try again." His smile didn't feel entirely genuine. Maybe Jane Slovotsky saw herself as an empress at court, too, eh?

"Who knows?" As though she was reading his mind, she nodded. "It won't bother me that from the morning on, it'll get easier to keep Bren's hand off my ass. That's getting real tiresome. But mainly it's because of my father."

"Your father?"

"Something he said. Something about what almost getting killed does. Or doesn't it make you horny, too?"

CHAPTER 21

To Salket

The logic of the heart is absurd.

—Julie de Lespinasse

Lying, like eating, can be overdone.

—Walter Slovotsky

Klimos to Geverat, and they hadn't been there, but maybe on Menelet? No, no, the raid on Menelet was tendays ago. It was Klimos. The three of them, the dozen of them, the hundreds of them, had struck on Klimos, burned everything to the ground.

And did you see that thing fly by last tenday? I don't know if it was a dragon, but you wouldn't have any essence of dragonbane to sell, would you?

Geverat to Heshtos, and Jane thought that might be it, so they fired off a signal rocket that night and lay anchored offshore for a night and a day, supposedly rerigging the mast.

A boat came out to investigate, but it was only some local fishermen: Did you see those strange faerie lights last night? And have you heard about the Warrior? He could be anywhere—I hear the slavers are pissing down their legs any time they hear a loud fart.

They went ashore, but there was nothing but rumors.

424

❖   ❖   ❖

Jane Slovotsky knelt by the map. "Salket," she decided, tapping the parchment, then resting her hand on Jason's leg. "It feels right." Her hand was warmer than it had any right to be.

"Two days," Bothan Ver said, hauling in the mainsheet, nail-bitten fingers directing the rope precisely, delicately, like a puppeteer pulling on the strings of his marionette. "Perhaps."

"If the wind holds," Thivar Anjer added, leaning on the tiller, squinting at the distant horizon. "Which it might."

"We'll find him there," Tennetty said, stropping her bowie against a whetstone. "And maybe only one or two of us will die."

"Everybody dies," Kethol said quietly. "Some of us a little piece at a time."

"It's your play, Jason," Durine said. "You're the Heir."

"That you are," Bren Adahan said. "And may one inquire why you're glaring at me?"

"You and I will have a talk about my sister," Jason said. "After Salket. And give me back my damn sword."

INTERLUDE

Ahira

The world is a vast temple dedicated to Discord.

—Voltaire

The dwarf was tired, dirty, and sore as, still on the back of his gray pony, he was hurried past the guard stations, into the inner bailey of Biemestren castle. The tendons in his thick neck burned like hot wires and a hot gray film had taken up residence behind his eyes. His right shoulder was a constant dull ache. It never went away, not even when he slept. The skin around the edges of the wound was raw and red.

After he had been picked up near New Pittsburgh, riders had been sent ahead, bringing word that he was on his way. So it was no surprise that they were waiting for him on the grass.

But it was still good to see them; it had been too long.

He dropped heavily to the ground and tossed his weapons to one side.

Kirah, D.A. in her arms, ran over to him. She dropped to her knees, burying her face against his good shoulder, and wept.

"Ta havath, Kirah, ta havath," he said, awkwardly patting her on the back. "Walter was fine, last I saw him." But that was too damn long ago.

He'd taken a bolt in his shoulder three weeks before, but he ignored the pain as he scooped up little D.A. She balanced easily on his forearm for a moment, then planted a wet kiss on his wet cheek.

"I love you, Uncle Ahira," she said, clear as a bell.

He folded the little girl in his arms and held her gently, carefully, in arms that could, that *had* snapped a man's ribcage like matchsticks. Fingers that had crushed, fingers that had destroyed, fingers that ripped flesh, toyed with her pageboy-length hair. "Got a new haircut, eh?" he said.

She nodded and smiled, practically bubbling. "Aunt Doria and Auntie Andy did it."

They surrounded him, Doria, looking as she did in his dreams sometimes: young again, if you only looked at the arms and neck and face, and didn't quite notice the eyes.

Still holding D.A. in his right arm, he wrapped his left around her waist. "It's good to see you, old friend," he said, damning the quaver in his voice. "Is Ellegon here?" he asked, although he'd been shouting with his mind for the dragon for hours.

"No." Doria shook her head. "He's trying to rendezvous with Jason and the rest in Mipos. He'll be back—maybe with them— in a day or two. I hope." She bit her lip.

Thomen Furnael stood a few yards apart, his face creased in concern. He was dressed informally: trousers, a light shirt, a black robe tucked over his arm. "We have to know, Ahira: is he alive?"

Andrea's face was a mask of grief. She didn't have to ask.

God, she looks old.

The dwarf shook his head. "Of course not. He blew himself up in Melawei, just like Jason and the others must've told you. Get me a drink, and get me into a hot bath, and we'll talk about it. We've got a day or two before we can do anything. If we can do anything."

The water was already hot in the officers' bath, over by the barracks. Ahira crouched in the oaken vat, the water up to his neck, steam rising from the surface.

It had been forever since he'd had a hot bath.

He sat back and tried to ease his muscles; he was strung tight as a lute's treble strings.

It had made sense, when Walter had proposed it on the beach at Melawei.

"Look," Walter had said, "he's dead, and there's nothing we can do about that."

"Except gather together what we can for burial," Ahira said, kneeling in the hot sun over Karl's hand.

It was Karl's left hand: the three outer fingers were just stumps.

Miraculously, the hand had survived intact, severed almost cleanly at the wrist, although it had been thrown easily a hundred yards from the center of the explosion.

Ants were already crawling on it, but Ahira couldn't force himself to reach out and pick it up, or brush them off.

Damn it, damn it, damn it.

"We can't bring him back to life," Walter said. "But we can keep him from dying."

"You're getting clever, Slovotsky," the dwarf said. "Sounds like a bad idea to me." But he didn't mean it, not really. It was just a reflex, after so many years.

"First thing we got to do is bury the hand, plus any other parts of him we can find. Or parts of the slavers that might be him. We can't let the Mel see that hand, and work it out. The official story is that Karl left."

"And then?"

"We've got to kill us some slavers." Slovotsky's smile was broad in the sunshine. But it wasn't really Walter Slovotsky's smile.

It was Karl's.

"When the Mel came back down from the hills, we—well, Walter, actually, lied his head off. Karl had left aboard Ganness's boat, we said, and we were to follow, once the slavers were dead.

"Old Wohtansen wasn't any too happy about that—I think he still remembers the time Karl punched him—but some of the Eriksen men volunteered.

"Didn't like the trip much. If anybody ever asks you if you want to face a storm on the Cirric in nothing more than an outrigger canoe with the sloppiest lateen rigging the universe has ever seen, tell them no.

"We hit them in Ehvenor. And then Lundeyll, and then Erifeyll, careful to leave evidence of three of us at all times.

"Walter and I split up in Erifeyll. The next part of the plan called for some time at sea, in the Shattered Islands. I'd be too conspicuous. A dwarf sailor? No; better they look for two humans and a dwarf. And just in case the legend of Karl Cullinane were to reach here, and raise false hopes, I was to hie myself back, fast as possible."

Ahira leaned back in the water and toyed with a cake of pear-scented soap, blunt fingers gently stirring up lather on its translucent surface. He tried to loosen his tense muscles, but that didn't happen. He fastened his hand around the bar of soap and squeezed. The soap flowed between his fingers like wet clay.

"I ran into a bit of trouble. Tell you about it sometime."

Doria felt at his shoulder, dry, practiced fingers touching impotently at a wound that was only partly healed. "We've sent for a healer," she said. "Spidersect."

He shrugged. "Walter's hopping among the Shattered Islands now, working his way—as indirectly as possible—to Elleport, then back up the Orduin toward Endell. He may head there, or he could change his route and head toward Home."

"Islands?" Garavar's voice sounded like gravel.

"Yes, yes, islands. He hires on as a sailor, and spends some time in the taverns across the islands, talking up the Warrior, and how he's been heard of here, there and everywhere. With his two, or twenty, or two hundred sidekicks. He should be finished soon; by now there'll be far too many hunters on the Warrior's trail, and Walter won't want to run into them." The dwarf sighed.

"Or, maybe he won't be finished. Not if he sees a Home signal rocket. He'll have to investigate that, which means that he's going to be looking for the kids just as hard as they're looking for him. Say, about half as hard as the slavers are looking for the Warrior."

Doria's fingers gripped his with surprising strength. "I'll come with you."

The dwarf shook his head. "No. Just me and the dragon. We'll try the next rendezvous that Jason and Janie set up, and if that doesn't work we'll try to find him."

"No," Andrea said. "No. It's you, Ellegon and me. I can find them."

"How do you expect to do that?" Doria was angry.

"I have my methods, Doria. Magic." Andrea muttered a few quick syllables that could only be heard and forgotten. She held out her right hand, and sparks danced between her fingers. "I know you think I use too much magic, but don't you think it's worthwhile for this? For my son's life?"

The sparks grew more violent, more frenzied, snapping like whips between her thumb and forefinger. Andrea's skin flinched where the sparks touched her, but she didn't shrink from it. Her lips moved silently, and the sparks grew louder, the flashes brighter and sharper, until with a quick flick of her fingers she dismissed the light and sound into nothingness.

"I know a bit about magic." Doria pursed her lips. "Sure, you can make a model of Jason, but you can't break through the protection spell of his amulet, no matter how much power you use. Magically, he isn't even vaguely similar to any form, not while he's wearing it."

"You're quite right." Andrea smiled thinly. "I can't. And I can't find Bren Adahan, or Tennetty, or Walter. Not while they're wearing their amulets. But Kethol and Durine aren't wearing amulets, are they?" She stalked out of the bath house, her skirts flaring as the breeze caught them.

And then she was gone.

"I don't like her using magic," Thomen Furnael said. "But I don't see any good way around it."

Or of stopping her, Ahira added silently.

Doria kept her thoughts to herself.

There was nothing to do, for the moment, but lean back and soak in the hot water, and rest.

He closed his eyes.

CHAPTER 22
Steer's Head Inn

All hell broke loose.

—Milton

Tell me again why it's a good idea to take a lot of chances.
—Walter Slovotsky

The storm moved in as the day was moving out. The sun hung just above the horizon, but the sky was dark with oncoming thunderheads. The damp wind whipped grass and leaves into the air around Jason as he stood on top of the hill.

Jason shivered and pulled his cloak around him, then bent to pick up the signal rocket. "Set the launching pole," he said.

Durine firmly shoved the thin metal pole into the bare ground, canted just a bit into the wind.

Jason straightened, then carefully slipped the rings on the side of the signal rocket along the launching rod. He knelt to unwrap the base of the rocket; it had been covered in waxed paper to keep the damp out.

It seemed to have worked just fine; his fingers couldn't feel a trace of wetness. The roll of fusing he took from a canvas bag was another matter. Something or other had gotten to it, and it was soggy.

It would probably burn, but perhaps not. Best not to fool with it. They had already taken that possibility into consideration; Jason

431

had a flintlock pistol stuck into his belt, its tamping rod protruding from the barrel.

Dragging the heel of his boot to carve a shallow trench in the dirt, Durine kept his eyes on the road below.

Down there, Bren Adahan waited with their rented transportation: two saddle horses and the flatbed wagon, drawn by a pair of ragged mules. Janie and the others were a day's ride away, at Tesors, the port village, with the boat.

Durine handed him a powder horn, and Jason carefully tipped a trail of the powder into the trench, leading up to the signal rocket. He finished up with a heaping spoonful under the base of the rocket.

That ought to get it going.

"Okay, now, head on down there. I'll be with you in a moment." He could move faster than Durine, and while it was unlikely that the rocket would blow up, there was no sense taking a chance on it.

He waited for Durine to get to the base of the hill, and noted with approval that the big man had the horses' reins held firmly in his hands.

Standing at the far end of the trail of gunpowder, Jason took the tamping rod out of the pistol and stuck it carefully in its slot below the barrel. He primed the pan, then snapped the frizzen down, cocking the pistol before he aimed it carefully at the snaking trail of black powder.

Why was he aiming? He didn't need to aim. He knelt and set the muzzle against the end of the trail of the powder, and pulled the trigger.

The flintlock pistol spat fire, lighting the trail of gunpowder, sending a line of fire sizzling toward the rocket.

Jason didn't wait to see if the rocket would launch safely; he was already partway down the slope, out of line of sight of the rocket.

A vast cloud of smoke billowed from the base of the rocket, the reek of sulfur sending Jason huddling into his cloak, in a coughing fit.

He straightened, his eyes tearing, as the rocket roared away, leaving behind smoke and sulfur. Rising on a pillar of smoke and fire into the darkening sky, it climbed faster and faster, the fire growing more and more intense, as though challenging the brightness of the dim stars themselves.

The rocket's propellant charge burned out. The flame died, only to be replaced a few seconds later, a few degrees higher in the sky, by a bright green flash that expanded into a globe of fiery points, and then was gone.

Jason climbed back up, donning his damp leather gloves so he could pull the launching rod out of the soil. Heated by the flames of the signal rocket, it hissed against the gloves.

By the time he made his way back to the road, the others were saddled up. Bren Adahan had finished nailing a piece of parchment to the tree. They'd thought of using paper, but the parchment ought to wear better.

They'd thought about the date, too. With the increasing popularity of English numbering over the Erendra addition-based notation, it was entirely possible that somebody might decode the date. So they'd spelled that out phonetically, and followed it with a short message in English, similar to other notes that they'd left in various places across Salket over the preceding tendays.

It read:

> *Mother's health delicate; it's important that you abort this and reach Holtun-Bieme before word reaches her. We are heading into the Triple Hamlet; others waiting aboard a single-master, the* Gazelle, *at Tesors, until this Tenthday. Rendezvous, with Ellegon on Mipos, next Ninthday. Next rendezvous, with Ellegon, two tendays later, outside of Elleport.*
>
> *Be there.*
> *—Jason*

Jason tossed the launching rod into the back of the flatbed, and stripped off his gloves.

"Let's go," Bren Adahan said. "I want to be a good ways away from here before we make camp for the night." They'd be in the Triple Hamlet tomorrow, and see what could be found there. Apparently that was the only Slavers' Guildhall left on Salket; the others had been closed down.

If Karl Cullinane, Walter Slovotsky and Ahira were hunting slavers on Salket, they'd be hunting them there. If.

"You're too impatient, Baron," Jason said. The baron wasn't the only one who was too impatient. As Jason climbed into the saddle, his mare whinnied and took a prancing sideways step. He tightened the reins firmly, then patted her gently on the neck as she settled into a slow walk.

"You think they saw it?" Durine asked Jason.

Why was Durine asking him? What did Jason know? "I hope so," he said. "Even if we had another rocket, we wouldn't get any benefit from setting it off, not with that storm moving in. And I hope they're here, and if they're here, I hope . . . I just hope."

He shrugged it away, and gave another hitch to the reins.

The storm had long since broken when they rode into the Triple Hamlet of Kalifeld, Bredham, and New Runsek.

While lightning flashed across the sky and thunder crashed in his ears, cold rain clawed at Jason like an animal, icy fingers clutching at his face, his neck, his shoulders. Rivers of water ran down his back; he hunched forward, over the pistol under his tunic, trying to shield it with his body. He doubted that it was working, but maybe the rounds in his saddlebags were dry.

His trembling fingers, twisted tightly in the reins, were wrinkled from the wetness, and his jaw ached; the only way he could stop his teeth from chattering was to clamp his jaw tightly.

He was thoroughly cold and thoroughly miserable. But he couldn't complain. Bren Adahan and Durine, every bit as utterly water-logged as he was, didn't say a word. They just rode on, Durine stolidly ignoring the water that ran down his neck, Bren Adahan pulling his sodden cloak around him, a single hand emerging to handle the reins of the flatbed.

The road had been dirt; it was now a treacherous, clinging, stinking mud that clawed at the legs of their tired mounts, pulling the horses down.

Only the mules seemed unaffected. Despite the way the mud threatened to cover the iron-rimmed wheels up to the hubs, the mules simply put down their heads and trudged on miserably.

An oilskin tarpaulin covered their gear in the flatbed; Jason hoped that the water hadn't gotten to everything important, although he was sure that the rifles were soaked, and would have to be carefully dried and oiled when they stopped, lest they rust through their blueing.

Thankfully, at the crossing leading into the villages, the mud turned to cobblestones, and the horses' steps ceased to be a sullen, leaden plodding. Their hooves, cleaned somewhat as they walked through the pools and rivulets and streams that coursed over the cobblestones, actually resembled hooves now, instead of muddy stumps.

But the rain intensified, almost blinding him.

"Ahead, there," Bren Adahan called over the crash of thunder, and, sure enough, Jason could see the sign of an inn ahead, a piece of hammered silver that waved in the wind, beckoning them. It looked like a silver mushroom.

Across the road and further along it, another tavern's sign, this one a mounted cow's head, seemed to nod at them. But the Silver Mushroom Inn was the closer, and that was where Bren Adahan got down from his horse, tying it to the hitching rack.

Jason and Durine were quickly at his side. The three of them walked up the steps, and on to the covered porch, out of the rain.

Jason had been fantasizing about getting out of the rain, but it didn't help much. He was still wet and shivering, and thoroughly miserable.

The thick door was closed. Durine lifted the heavy brass goathead knocker and slammed it down twice.

There was no answer, but warm light peeked out through the shuttered windows, and Jason fancied there was a distant whiff of hot soup in the air. He tried to dismiss it, but his mouth began to water.

The door swung partly open; a fat, red-bearded man stood there, wearing a pullover cotton tunic, blousy pantaloons and a grease-spattered apron. He eyed the three of them for a long moment before he spoke.

"There's no room at the Silver Mushroom," he said. "Try the Steer's Head, down the street."

Bren Adahan started to turn away.

Voices whispered inside. "There's three of them, but the big one's kind of fat. N' if one of them's a dwarf, it's the biggest fucking dwarf I ever saw."

"We'd best be sure. About all of them."

"Hold one moment." The innkeeper swung the door open and beckoned them in. "The lad is shivering. You should at least come in for a mug of hot wine," he said. "I wouldn't want you to think unkindly of the Mushroom."

They walked inside. The entryway of the inn was a conventional mud room, barely lit by an overhead lamp; boot scrapers mounted on the floor to make a first pass at the mud, grass mats farther in to catch the remnants.

Jason was shivering; he stood on the stone floor, water running off him in rivulets. Bren Adahan, his finery a sodden mess, leaned against a wall, brushing his hands down his arms, trying to get some of the water off.

Only Durine seemed unmoved: he stood to one side, silently, indifferently, methodically scraping the mud off of his boots, looking more like a corpse fished out of the river than anything else.

Two men walked quickly through the inner door, one holding two pairs of steaming silver tankards; the other, a tall, slim blond man, held only his own tankard.

The first was almost a caricature of a guild slaver: he was a sullen, thick-jowled man, a crop tucked into the left side of his belt, a truncheon into the right, his bulging belly threatening to slop over both weapons.

The other, a small-boned man who stood half a head taller than Jason, smiled gently at Jason and Durine before turning his attention to Bren Adahan.

"My name is Laheran," he said, striking a pose. He was slim, and studiously elegant, from the silver pin stuck through the collar of his short cape, down to the polished, pointed toes of his boots. A light rapier hung from the left side of his waist, and while the scabbard was trimmed in silver and shell, the weapon's basket hilt was wound with simple cord and brass; it was a weapon that advertised itself as something that was to be used, not merely displayed.

Jason kept his hands away from the hilt of his sword as Laheran set his tankard down on a dressing table, then passed out the steaming mugs of mulled wine.

"I th-thank you," Bren Adahan said, his teeth chattering. He stripped off his leather gloves to accept a mug of spiced wine, then started to raise the mug to his lips.

"*No*, Trader Hofna," Jason said. "Durine. Mix them, if you please."

Durine blankly accepted the mug from Laheran, then walked over to the table and picked up Laheran's, pouring wine from his tankard into the other's and then back. It was very quiet for a moment while Durine offered Laheran a tankard.

The slaver smiled as he accepted it, then drank. "Laheran wishes you luck," he said. "Although your precautions are excessive," he said, tilting his head to one side, as though idly considering the matter. "The guild doesn't drug or raid here."

"Durine wishes you luck," the big man said, "although I try to make my own. Perfunctory apologies," he said, "but Taren and I have been hired to guard the trader, here, and we do our job." He accepted the tankard from Laheran.

"So I see."

"Taren wishes you luck," Jason said, drinking.

"Why did you do that?" Bren Adahan hissed as soon as they were back outside, in the rain. "If you thought that the wine was drugged or poisoned—"

"I wouldn't have accepted it at all," Jason said. He hadn't been warned about that; the locals wouldn't let the slavers simply go around poisoning or drugging travelers at random. The time Uncle Chak had been tricked was a special case; he and some other mercenaries had been decoyed away from Pandathaway, off the trade routes, and then drugged, chained and sold. "I didn't want to seem to be too eager to please," he said. "They're already suspicious there; that would have raised their suspicions."

Durine's massive head nodded slowly, heavily. "It was just the right move."

The three of them sat on the floor facing the fireplace, each with a steaming mug of tea next to him.

Jason reached up and felt at his hair; it was only slightly damp. He was finally getting dry. It would be good to be dry, if only for a short while.

Their room in the Steer's Head Inn was cold and drafty, the air smoky, the straw-ticked bedding musty and bedbug-ridden, but the fire was hot and so was the tea. It tasted mainly of sassafras, Jason decided, although there were definitely overtones of ferique and cinnamon. Too much honey, though. Still, on a cold, wet night, who was going to complain about that?

The thing he liked best of all was the private bath off the room, the kettle-like tub elevated over an iron stove that vented to the outside. A hot bath would be wonderful.

It had once been a more elegant place, perhaps long ago. The oaken columns at all four corners of the room were carved to resemble towers of dwarves, each standing on the shoulders of the one beneath. Under the smoky residue that covered the walls, Jason could make out the outlines of ancient murals depicting deer frolicking in a woody glen.

The chill was relieved by a massive fireplace on the wall opposite the glass-paned doors to the balcony; the fireplace was crammed full of blazing logs. To the right of the fireplace, their clothing, both what they'd been wearing and what had been in their bags, hung on a cast-iron drying rack. Jason could actually see wisps of steam rising from his sodden jerkin.

A blocky iron rested on a heating plate by the fireplace, and a heat-scarred oaken ironing board stood in front of a woven-grass kneeling mat, but none of them had used it, either to press the clothes or to finish drying them.

The clothes could wait. Their gear had all survived, but it was all soaking wet; it would be late evening before they'd be finished with it all.

Durine looked more silly than threatening as he sat on a floor cushion, the hair on his face, chest and belly sweaty from the fire, his skin reddened, a woolen blanket wrapped around his waist, his big smoothbore on his lap as he worked over it with a few hand-fuls of cotton batting and a mottled green bottle of olive oil. The latter was one of the nice things about Salket; olive groves stood all over the island, and there was always good oil, reasonably cheap.

Jason had finished oiling the second of his revolvers, and had it pretty much squared away. But the cartridges, spread out on the blanket like nuts fallen from a tree, were a problem. Water wasn't going to harm the lead bullet, or the brass casing, and the built-in igniters were sealed, too, but the powder itself was suspect.

Would it fire? Best to be sure.

He took a pair of pliers from the tool kit on the floor between him and Bren Adahan, and setting a round backwards in a quickloader for leverage, carefully pried the bullet out, then tipped the powder on the worn floor boards in front of him.

It didn't look a whole lot different from the usual Home powder, although it was finer. Just black dust, seemingly dry.

He took a spare flint from Bren Adahan's kit and, taking his now-oily bowie from the blanket where it rested, stroked the flint down the length of the knife. The bowie was awfully oily; it took three strokes to get a spark.

The powder flared into fire and smoke and then was gone, leaving behind only an acrid smell and a lot less smoke than Jason would have expected if he hadn't fired a few rounds at Home.

Bren Adahan and Durine were all eyes, but neither of them said anything. Everybody knew that the Engineer had given Jason some new pistols, but they'd been secret, up to now.

They were for his use. And *his,* if he still lived.

Jason shook his head. That didn't make sense, not now. The purpose of guns was to kill people who needed killing, not to be a Cullinane family secret. Both Durine and Bren Adahan were trustworthy, within their limits; Ellegon had sworn to that.

"You said my instincts were good when we braced the slavers," Jason said.

Durine nodded. "Yes. They were. Some of him has rubbed off on you."

That was arrant nonsense; Valeran had a lot more to do with how Jason turned out than Karl Cullinane did. But maybe the old soldier had taught Jason well—before he'd fallen to the ground, the smooth wooden hilt of a throwing knife projecting from his eyesocket.

"Then they'd better be good now. I want to lend you these. If I don't come back, they're yours to use. Return them to the Engineer; he'll decide what to do with them." He checked to make sure that the cylinder was still empty before he clicked it into place, then dry-fired the gun half a dozen times, the barrel carefully pointed away from either of them. "They are operated like this—"

"Excuse me?" Bren Adahan's brow furrowed. "You're giving us your guns?"

"I can't risk any gunshots, so I shouldn't take them with me." Jason shrugged.

"You don't mean to say that you're going out into the rain?" Bren Adahan shook his head. "To what end?"

"Think it through, Baron," Jason said. He was glad that Adahan had missed the obvious; it gave Jason a chance to lecture him. "Salket has been left conspicuously alone by this warrior and his men. Jane—and she knows her father better than anybody else—thinks Salket is next.

"So do the slavers; they've closed down their other houses on the island, leaving this one as the only target. This whole place smells of a trap within a trap. We ride into town, and the largest inn is completely taken over by slavers, who are advertising who they are, in case we missed it. Can't you smell a trap?

"And we've put them on guard, brought their alertness 'way up. You think they haven't noticed the signal rockets? Whether he's

seen our notes or not, the rational thing for Father to do under
the circumstances would be to give Salket a bye.

"Now, somebody real subtle would let them rot here forever,
waiting. Let them spend tendays waiting here for an attack that'll
never come.

"But Father's not that subtle. He's always figured that the right
way to scare slavers is to kill them. He'll go for it. Somebody's
got to see where the trap is."

"Walter Slovotsky is with him," Durine said. "He can do a better
job of reconnoitering than you can."

Jason shook his head. "But not if he's not here yet. Tonight I've
got a storm to hide in; tomorrow he won't." And Jason might not
have too long to hide in the storm, at that. A storm that moved
in fast could move out fast, too.

Durine nodded, rummaging through his gear for a moment
before coming out with a long strip of black cloth. "You'd best
blindfold yourself until you go; give your eyes a chance to adjust
to the dark."

Jason nodded. "Good idea."

Bren Adahan shook his head. "You're going back out in that?
To see if you can find where the traps are?"

No, Jason wanted to say. *I'm seventeen years old, and I'm so fucking
scared that it's all I can do to not shit all over the floor. But the first
time I ever faced real danger I ran away, and I can't ever let myself
do that again. I've got to be* Karl Cullinane's *son, and that means that
I do what's necessary, in cold blood, whether it's hacking a rebellious
baron to death or putting my own ass on the line.*

His father was a legend. A legend was, above all, a lie. And Jason
was the son of a legend. But maybe lies could become real, maybe
you could twist the universe, bend it to shape, and make the lies
real, if you could only keep your voice from shaking, your hand
from trembling.

"Of course I am, Baron," he said, as he stood, drawing the damp,
smelly, woolen blankets around him as though they were robes
of state. "I am a Cullinane."

The baron didn't quite know how to take it, so Jason forced
himself to meet his gaze until the baron looked away.

"I guess you are," Bren Adahan said.

CHAPTER 23

A Tap on the Shoulder

Am I a god? I see so clearly!
                —Johann Wolfgang von Goethe

His clothes had been uncomfortably damp until he stepped out into the rain, but his belly was warm, his tongue and throat still aching with the taste of a last cup of almost scalding tea.

Now his clothes were simply soaked again as he splashed down in the waterlogged grass behind the Steer's Head Inn, then stepped back into the cover of the balcony.

Between the flashes of lightning the night was dark, the darkness broken only by lamps in the windows of the buildings that vanished into the distance in the rain and the gloom. Most places, that was enough light to see by, but just barely.

He stood silently next to the shingled side of the building. Wiping the back of his dripping hand across his eyes, he took a moment to get his bearings.

The inn was to his back and to the south. Immediately to the east were the inn's stables, where their horses waited under the none-too-watchful gaze of the stablemen, both of whom had reeked of cheap wine. To the west, further up the street, were three residences, clearly of upper middle-class merchants, and then the stables of the Silver Mushroom Inn. The Mushroom itself was across the street from its stables.

Two streets over and three down was the Slavers' Guildhall. That

441

was Jason's ultimate target for the night, but it was hours away, at least. When you're on a stalk, move slowly and carefully, Walter Slovotsky had said. Move not at all, if possible; wait for the prey to come to you.

Well, that wasn't possible here.

He'd have to keep away from open spaces. Dressed as he was in wet, dark clothes, he would be invisible in the shadows, but in a flash of lightning he could easily be seen if somebody happened to be looking the right way.

On the other hand, immediately after a flash of lightning would be a safe time. He closed his eyes and waited. When brightness flickered through his eyelids and thunder crashed in his ears, he opened his eyes and stepped off into the night, adjusting the coil of thin climbing rope that ran diagonally over his left shoulder.

With every step, his boots would sink ankle deep into the muck. That did no harm, but they made sucking sounds when he pulled them out. Nobody would be able to hear it very far, not over the sound of the rain, but it did carry a few yards.

Jason hid in the lee of an old oak tree, leaning against it, the wet bark painfully rough against his back even through his tunic. He pulled off first one boot, then the other; he tied them together with a thong from his belt pouch and slung them over his shoulder, then used another thong to tie them to his chest.

A stone bit into the ball of his right foot with his first step; the edge of a rock cut into the side of his left foot when he hopped to one side.

Shit. This wasn't going to make it. He leaned back against the tree and felt at his toes. This had the makings of a disaster, but you had to do the best with what you could. That was the rule.

Rinsing his feet off as best he could in the muddy water, he untied his boots, then pulled them back on, mud squishing between his toes. With his first step, something gave beneath his right foot; he tripped and fell flat on his face in the mud, the fall knocking the wind right out of him.

Some hero.

Face down in the mud, he fought to get his hands underneath him and push himself out of the mud, struggling both to not breathe in the cold goo and to get some air.

Finally he was able to force himself up to his hands and knees, and draw a jagged, shuddering breath, before he almost fell over in a coughing fit. He knelt again and wiped as much of the mud from his mouth, eyes and nose as he could.

There was nothing to do but press on. He staggered to his feet and off into the night as quietly as he could, a taste of mud and grit between his teeth, shivering, miserable, exposed, cold, dirty and utterly alone.

The first four buildings he checked turned out to be just what they had appeared to be: the homes of middle-class merchants, or noble merchants—it was hard to tell which, in Salket. Jason guessed that one was an ironmonger, another an olive dealer, the other involved in the sale of dried fish, but he could have been wrong, and couldn't guess what the owner of the fourth house was.

What the houses weren't were barracks, and that was what was important.

Was the rain starting to ease, or was that just his imagination? As if in answer it beat down harder on his head, the wind picking up, driving the icy water into his face.

He moved on.

The Silver Mushroom Inn had been built primarily for comfort, not security; each of its several suites seemed to have its own balcony, lower than those of the Steer's Head Inn. Ladderlike trellises supported trails of ivy.

Above his head, a narrow shaft of light from a gap in the curtains cut into the night; laughter and the rattle of dice in a cup suggested what was going on. Jason waited under the balcony until he could count at least four different voices, although he thought it was probably more like half a dozen. He moved on to the next balcony; the window above was dark.

He thought for a moment about climbing the trellis, but that was just too tempting, and too dangerous. There could easily be some sort of trap, some sort of alarm cord hidden beneath the dripping leaves.

Still, that was the sort of thing that it was best to find out about. He stooped to check one of the rungs of the trellis, one at his knee level. He carefully inserted his fingers in the gap, gently probing for anything suspicious. Nothing. He stiffened his fingers and arm, and then rested part, then all of his weight on it.

The rung didn't give at all. Not surprising; the Salkes were known for building things to last. Still, the wood was old and splitting. He thought about splinters, and about pulling on his climbing gloves, but decided that good touch was the better part of valor here.

He tested another rung, and then another, and then slowly, carefully began to climb. He reminded himself again: patience on a stalk wasn't preferable—it was essential. You had to master time, not let it be your master.

Haste was dangerous.

It was fifteen rungs to the balcony; slowly he put some weight on it, until he was standing on the ninth. He reached up to close his hand on the railing and pull himself the rest of the way up—and then he caught himself. He couldn't see it, and he'd better see it before he put his weight on it.

He put his hand on the top rung, and started to draw himself up, but it gave fractionally. Slowly, slowly, he withdrew his hand, then felt around, slowly, carefully. Pretend that there might be sharpened razors hidden behind the trellis, at any moment, that was the trick. There might be.

He didn't find any razors, but his fingers found a hinge on one side of the trellis rung, and a cord running from the other side. Some sort of alarm.

He pushed a vine aside far enough so that, in the dim light coming from the next balcony over, he could see that the floor of the balcony was empty. There was nothing but water there, and not much of that; the floor was ever-so-slightly convex, like the lens of a magnifying glass, allowing water to run off the side and into the vines.

His probing fingers found nothing on the rain-slickened marble of the railing. Not a likely candidate for some sort of pressure switch; he pulled himself up and over the rail.

The panelled glass doors to the balcony were locked, and probably stronger than they looked, perhaps constructed like the panelled doors to the balconies at Castle Biemestren: what appeared to be criss-crossed wooden support members were actually wrought iron covered by thin wooden slats.

He unstrapped and drew his bowie, and tested the point against one of the criss-cross members; the sharp point sank easily a quarter-inch into the wet wood, but touched metal beneath. Just like home. There was no easy way inside, at least not through this balcony.

Jason slipped his knife back into its sheath and tied it into place.

He moved to the other side of the window; the curtain didn't quite cover there. Beyond the wet glass, light came into the room through the door leading to the bright hall beyond. He could see four tightly crowded sleeping pallets, two of them containing dim forms, and a rack of eight rifles, certainly slaver-powder rifles, set up near the door. It was a fair bet that this was a sleeping room for at least eight slavers. Multiply that by the six other balconied rooms in the inn, and he could guess that there were about fifty slavers in the Silver Mushroom Inn alone.

The next step was to—

A creak from inside the room froze him solid. His hand dropped to the bowie at his belt, but that was silly. There was nothing he could do with a bowie that wouldn't reveal him.

He stood next to the door and unwound the twin wooden handles of the garrotte from his belt. The thought of killing again made his hands tremble, but if the door opened he'd have to. Slip the thin strand of woven sinew over the neck, tighten and pull, and then ease the body to the ground and get the hell out of here.

His fingers tightened on the grips when there were low murmurs from inside the room. He couldn't quite make out the complete sentences, but caught a few fragments: "Your turn . . . awake this time . . . yeah, sure, if it don't rain."

Pressing his ear to the door, he could hear the sounds of somebody dressing, then stomping out of the room, while somebody else undressed, boots hitting the floor.

Then the thump of somebody dropping, dead tired, to a sleeping pallet. Jason waited until all he could hear were snores before climbing gingerly down the trellis. The rain was still coming down hard enough to make him miserable.

The Silver Mushroom Inn stables were next. There were only twenty horses in the stable, which wasn't in accord with his estimate of fifty slavers in the house. But there you had it: twenty horses, and one drunk stableboy sleeping up in the hayloft.

Next would be the guildhouse itself, and he'd have to be very careful there. It was only two streets over and three down, but walking down the cobblestone streets wasn't a good idea, dressed as he was. If they had any watch out at all, he'd be spotted.

He stuck to the service alleys behind the rows of houses. They were muddy, but there were more places to hide.

✧   ✧   ✧

This business was miserable and dull, and when it wasn't dull it was dangerous. Something slippery under the mud behind one of the houses shot his feet out from him, landing him on his side, something biting into his back, just below his right shoulder blade.

He reached back, and pulled a piece of wood from his flesh. It was a splinter as long as his finger, and his back hurt like hell where it had gone in. He had a small metal bottle of healing draughts in his pouch, but it wasn't for minor injuries; he had to save it for something that really hurt.

While the wind was getting colder and colder, the rain was starting to ease up, and, from the top of a hill, he could even see the stars through a distant break in the clouds. If he was going to check out the Slavers' Guildhall, he'd best hurry.

Standing in the lee of the wall surrounding the Slavers' Guildhall, it occurred to him that there must not have been a lot of warring going on in inland Salket, not for a long time. The houses, once they'd gotten away from the port area, had seemed to be designed for comfort, not security: there were windows at many levels, albeit often barred; few of the homes were surrounded by a protective wall. While the houses of the poor were of the familiar wattle-and-daub, the homes of the wealthy were built of brick, not thick blocks of stone.

The Slavers' Guildhall, though, was an exception, as were the buildings to either side.

Just to the west of the slaver compound was a wooden stable, more of a barn, really, probably property of the slavers: there was a covered walkway between the two. To the east was what had been a stately, three-storied home, but it had suffered fire damage. While the local lord's firemen had clearly put out the blaze before it spread, the house was ruined and hadn't yet been repaired or replaced; part of the facade was ripped clean off, up to the third story.

The slaver compound hadn't been damaged by the fire. It was two-storied, built of stone, not brick, and completely surrounded by a ten-foot-high wall topped with a railed walkway, with two guardposts at the rear corners of the wall, although neither of them seemed to be occupied at the moment.

It wasn't a castle; it wouldn't withstand a siege, or a large-force assault, but it was intended to stand up to anything less than that.

It was reasonably new, too; the edges of the stone were still sharp, not worn smooth by hundreds of years' exposure to the elements, as were the walls at Biemestren Castle. Jason would have been willing to bet that it had been built out of fear of an attack by the Home raiders, and only finished perhaps ten years before.

But it could be taken. You could take anything, if you had the means. Batter hard enough against any wall and it would come down. Fire enough bolts, enough arrows, enough stones, enough bullets into an enemy mob, and they'd run or die.

The slavers had gone to the expense of mounting mirror-backed glowsteels on poles at each of the four corners and halfway down each of the walls, and while their blue glow was dim—either the spells were initially weak or they badly needed refreshing—it was enough to see by.

The slavers hadn't thought of everything, though; a huge oak tree spread its leaves and branches almost against the west side of the wall. He walked to the side of it and checked carefully around the bark for anything out of place, some tripwire, some pressure plate. There wasn't anything.

He shrugged. Could they have left such a hole in their defenses? At the same time as they were beefing up their defenses by stashing anywhere from twenty to fifty extra armed slavers at the Silver Mushroom Inn? That didn't make sense. Still, from where he was he could see that there wasn't any other tree near enough to overlook the wall.

Best to take a quick turn around the wall before he tried anything. He wouldn't want to risk checking out the streetside door, but that left three sides of the square.

Staying near the wall, though, was probably not the best idea. He crossed to the other side of the alley and, his back to the wooden fence that ran along the edge of the neighboring property, he worked his way toward the next corner, moving slowly and silently in the rain.

There was a slaver in the guardpost at that corner, after all. Muttering something or other under his breath, a dark form leaned out into the night.

Jason froze.

In seconds that felt like minutes, like hours, the guard leaned back in. He hadn't heard anything. Jason waited a dozen heartbeats, then moved on.

As he turned the northwest corner, something touched his shoulder.

CHAPTER 24
Walter Slovotsky

He who has patience may compass anything.
—François Rabelais

Valeran used to say something about how, in a combat situation, it was about sixteen times better to do something useful and violent right away than to wait and figure out something even more useful and violent later.

Jason spun on the balls of his feet, his left arm coming around to block, while his right hand snatched at his belt, his fingers falling on the wooden handles of his garotte, not his bowie.

It didn't matter; better something than nothing. He struck out—
—and let his fist drop.

Walter Slovotsky was standing a few feet away from him, dropping a crooked stick to the ground.

"Easy, kid, easy," Slovotsky whispered, beckoning him into the shadows. "Just your Uncle Walter, who doesn't want to get killed. Now or ever."

Jason could see enough of him in the light of the glowsteel to see that he looked different: thinner, older, more shopworn. His beard was thicker and longer than it used to be; a shock of graying hair that badly needed cutting framing his lined face.

But it was still Walter Slovotsky; his all-is-peachy-keen-in-any-universe-clever-enough-to-contain-Walter-Slovotsky-smile was intact, although barely.

"What the *fuck* are you doing here?" Slovotsky whispered.

"Where are the others?" Jason looked around. "Ahira, Father—"

Walter Slovotsky's brow furrowed. "Your *father*? We need a long talk," he whispered, "and this isn't the place. You got a place around here?"

The rain had started to let up; as though bidding a farewell, a flurry of distant lightning bolts crackled to the ground.

Jason nodded. "The Steer's Head Inn. Two—"

"—streets over and three up." Slovotsky nodded. "You want to lead the way, or want me to take it?"

"Me first." It wasn't just that the rain was letting up; it must have been getting warmer, too; Jason didn't feel quite so cold anymore.

So Father was dead. He felt as if he should be crying, as if he was supposed to be crying, but he didn't feel like it. He had already mourned his father once, and perhaps once was enough.

Or perhaps not. Maybe the tears would come later. It was hard to tell about things like that. Try to lay down a rule, try to reduce what you do feel, should feel, ought to feel, will feel. . . . You try to turn that into some sort of formula, and you fail; emotions just didn't work that way.

Damn, damn, damn.

"Shit, folks," Walter Slovotsky said quietly, his hands cupped around a steaming mug of herb tea, "you weren't supposed to buy the bullshit." He frowned at Jason. "You were *there*, Jason. Nobody could have survived the explosion, and Karl couldn't run far." He shook his head, then tossed it to clear the stringy wet hair from his eyes. He had called the toss, and won the first bath.

There were lines at the corners of Slovotsky's eyes that Jason didn't remember from before, and his eyelids were puffy and red from lack of sleep. "Yeah," he said. "I know I look like death warmed over, and not too well warmed over, at that." He sipped his tea. "The only reason I sent the dwarf off toward Holtun-Bieme was to get him out of the way. I couldn't take to the Cirric with him along, and he's every bit as much of a potential martyr as your dad was. Always has been, from well before we faced The Dragon."

He looked like he was going to say more, then decided not to. There wasn't anything they could do about Ahira right now, and right now was the problem.

"How firm's your rendezvous with this *Gazelle* of yours on the tenth?" Slovotsky asked.

Durine shrugged. "They'll be there."

"Good. Then you be there, and I'll see if I can make it to the next pickup. Got to finish this, first." He chuckled. "That daughter of mine is something, isn't she? She's right that I wouldn't have insisted on finishing things off with Salket—this is a tough nut—but Karl would have. Particularly if he had a couple of dozen men with him." Slovotsky smiled. "They're ready for a major assault. They're not ready for me. There's both too many of them and not enough of them."

Bren Adahan shook his head. "From yours and Jason's description, it sounds too difficult. Even if you can climb in by way of that tree—"

"Which you can't. It's booby-trapped—there's at least four tripwires hidden on the branch you'd use to get to the top of the wall. Jason, didn't you see the other stumps?"

"Stumps?"

"Fucking Greek chorus—yes, stumps. They cut down all the other trees near the wall and left that one. Didn't you see?"

Jason was going to protest that he had been about to do a full recon, and that he would have noticed the stumps, but that would have sounded like an excuse.

Besides, Walter Slovotsky, himself an inveterate liar, wouldn't have believed him anyway.

"You can't do anything about it, so get out of here. It's mine." Slovotsky shrugged, his shoulders working their way out of his blanket. He pulled it tightly around him. "Those damned signal rockets of yours have the slavers stirred up like a bunch of angry bees."

"Perhaps your killing them has something to do with it as well," Durine said gently.

Slovotsky laughed, but it was a tired laugh. "It might, at that. I don't see any way to get all the slaves out, but I can take out the watchers in the two other houses on the street. . . ." He raised an eyebrow. "You *did* notice that they've got watchmen in the loft of the barn, and in the garret of the burned-out house?"

"Don't be silly. Of course I did." Jason forced a smile to match the lie. "Would I miss something as easy as that?"

"You are your father's son, at that. Sometimes I forget." Slovotsky smiled back. "Okay, so I take them out, get inside, leave behind a few deaders, get the cages open, and then start enough of a fire, create enough of a distraction to give some of the poor bastards a chance to get away, and then vanish. I don't need you around for any of that; you can't disappear into the woodwork like I can. Even if they hadn't seen you, which they have."

Most of the escaped slaves would be rounded up by the citizenry, of course, which was one of the reasons that Home raiders eschewed the cities—much better to get the slavers where there wasn't much of a local population to handle, either way—but some might be able to grab clothes and weapons, and perhaps enough money to buy themselves passage at one of the ports. Salket, like many areas in the Eren region, was a loose federation of small baronies, the barons meeting occasionally to settle internecine disputes, but without a unified government. It was in everyone's interest that, say, a hostler in the Triple Village return to Beteran of Tesfors a horse whose lip bore his tattoo; it was another thing to return an escaped slave who might, at least in theory, be related to the hostler.

But there was one problem with Walter Slovotsky's plan.

Jason leaned forward. "And what are you going to do when twenty to fifty slavers—armed with rifles and whatever else they can get their hands on—run over from the Silver Mushroom Inn, surround the place and shoot whoever or whatever comes out the door or over the wall?"

Slovotsky eyed him coldly. "I didn't know about them. You didn't tell me."

"I didn't think you'd miss something as easy as that." Jason smiled. "Besides, you were too busy talking."

After a long moment, Slovotsky smiled. "I was, at that. Let me think it over for a moment." He sat and drank some tea, staring into the flickering flames in the fireplace, as though he could find some wisdom there.

Finally he shook his head. "Can't be done. Shit. There's somewhere between a dozen and eighteen of them inside. We could probably kill the watchmen and a few of the guards and be gone, but we don't have anything near the manpower or the firepower to knock down a dozen quickly if it all hits the fan." He raised an eyebrow. "How're you fixed for money?"

Jason shrugged his shoulders. "We're fine. Why?"

Slovotsky scratched at himself. "Well, tomorrow afternoon see if you can rent about half a dozen horses, and station yourselves a ways down the road. I'll catch up with you, and we can get well ahead of any pursuit by switching mounts a lot. We should be able to make it to your boat half a day ahead of any chase, and be over the horizon by the time the slavers show. We hit the rendezvous with the dragon, and hit the air." He rubbed at his eyes with the back of his hand. "I'm burning out, boy. This shit takes a lot out of an old man."

Jason sat back and watched the older man carefully. It wasn't supposed to be like this. The Other Siders were supposed to be special, particularly Walter Slovotsky, a man who tossed off clever sayings like Lou Riccetti spun off new inventions: carelessly, casually, easily.

Walter Slovotsky was supposed to be something special, something more than just an exhausted old man, growing more tired and older by the moment. Slovotsky was into his forties, practically ready for the grave, and he looked every year of it as he drained the last of his tea and then staggered over to a sleeping pallet, dropped first to his knees, then to all fours. He sagged down into the straw mattress, seemingly asleep by the time he was fully horizontal.

Bren Adahan stood and stretched. "I would prefer it if you take first watch, Durine."

Durine nodded. "Very well."

Jason went over to the bath room and tested the water with his hand. It was warm, and that'd have to be enough; his eyes were sagging, and he didn't want to go to sleep filthy. Durine had washed his cuts, so they weren't in much danger of becoming infected, but it felt as if the grit Jason had slopped through had worked its way into every pore of his skin. He dropped his filthy clothes to the floor and mounted the step ladder, then lowered himself gingerly into the water.

Walter Slovotsky's plan would have to do, he decided. They didn't have the fire—

He stood up straight. "Walter, wake up—Durine, wake him up," Jason said, quickly rinsing himself off and getting out of the tub.

"What the fuck is it?" Slovotsky said after Durine had shaken him awake. He rubbed the back of a hand against reddened eyes.

Jason held out the two revolvers. "You said we didn't have enough firepower," he said, flicking open the cylinders. "You know what these are?"

"Where did you?—fucking Lou," Slovotsky said, holding one of the guns in his hand, cradling it like it was a child. He bit his lip for a long moment, and then straightened. "Fucking Lou," he repeated, his voice firmer, younger. "That hairless son of a bitch did it again." He didn't seem so tired, not anymore. "Yeah. I know what this is. How many rounds you got?"

"Two hundred. No, one-ninety-nine. Now, have we got enough firepower?"

Slovotsky stood silently for a long moment, so long that Jason was going to speak up, but thought better of it.

"Yeah," Slovotsky finally said. "That we do." He cocked his head to one side. "Your father used to get more mileage out of people than I would have thought they had in them. Including me, come to think of it. Looks like you inherited that from him, too." His eyes twinkled. "Get some sleep. Tomorrow we write the note, the one that says the Warrior lives."

Durine smiled. "I didn't think you wrote them on the scene."

Slovotsky laughed. "Hope I don't look that stupid. We write the note and rest up tomorrow, and tomorrow night, and the day after." He smiled, his face framed with a beard that somehow didn't seem quite so gray, not anymore. "And then we hit them." He cocked his head to one side. "Jason, you look like there's something you don't understand."

"I guess it's not important."

"Give it a try. You've got a problem with the assault plan?"

Jason shook his head. "It's not that. What I don't understand is about all the rumors. It took years for the story about you and Dad taking on Ohlmin and the slavers to, well, inflate like it has. But all this stuff about the Warrior running around with dozens, sometimes hundreds of men—those rumors have exploded."

"And you're wondering why?" Slovotsky nodded. "Couple of reasons. For one thing, your father was already legendary; these new rumors have just piggybacked on his legend. There are already dozens of stories of Karl Cullinane floating around; for the Warrior to build on them wasn't difficult." He rummaged through their gear and found the clay bottle of Riccetti's Best, pulled the cork, and took a heavy swig. "The stories would have spread quickly, even without the other thing."

"The other thing?"

"Well," Slovotsky grinned wolfishly, "I've been hitting damn near every tavern and hookshop in the Shattered Islands. I've been doing my best to spread the rumors myself."

Jason laughed. If anybody could find something heroic to do in every tavern and bordello in the Shattered Islands, it would have to be Walter Slovotsky.

CHAPTER 25
In Cold Blood

*My men, yonder are the Hessians. They were bought for
seven pounds and ten pence a man. Are you worth more?
Prove it. Tonight the American flag floats from yonder hill or
Molly Stark sleeps a widow!*

—John Stark,
before the Battle of Bennington

The way Walter Slovotsky explained it, most of the problems
were front-loaded; if things went to hell early, they should be able
to break off and get out before it all fell apart.

Two days of rest had Jason feeling human again as he crouched
near Durine, hiding in the dark next to the fence, with the walkway
to his left. The slaver compound was behind him. In front of him
was his target: the stable next door.

He was stiff, and his knees and lower back burned with pain; he
longed to straighten up, but it was almost twelfth-hour and the
guard should be changing shortly. That was the time to hit the
slavers; it gave Jason and his companions as much leeway as possible.

With a creak of protesting hinges the door opened and a blocky
man marched quickly toward the stable, someone behind him
closing the door. He was dressed in a metal cap and chain mail,
a slaver rifle and pike over his left shoulder, a hooded lantern held
high in his right hand.

He passed perhaps fifteen feet from where Jason and Durine hid, and it was tempting to take him now, but it would have been wrong; his relief would be watching a marked candle burn down, and would be both expecting him and would be expected shortly by whoever was on the other side of the door.

They let him pass.

After waiting to be sure that the door to the compound was closed, Jason and Durine rose and followed the guard into the stable. Best to let his light lead the way.

The stable was as Walter Slovotsky had described it: a three-story building, two partial floors surrounding an open space. At each corner of the building, stairways led up to the top level, where another man waited for the slaver they were following. It smelled of rotting straw and old horseshit.

The horses could smell them; a large roan threw back its head and whinnied, its hooves beating a heavy tattoo on the floorboards. They ducked into an empty stall, knowing that the two slavers would attribute the sound of the horses to the disturbance by the relief watchman.

Jason took a deep breath and let it out. "Wish me luck," he more mouthed than whispered as he crept off toward the stairs.

Walter Slovotsky had done a thorough recon of the stable the night before last; and he had tested Jason's memory on which stairs didn't squeak.

Jason worked his way up the far stairway to the second level while the relief watchman called out a password that he couldn't quite make out. He seemed to take the responding grunt from above as a matter of course, and then put his weapons in a wooden box that was suspended from the ceiling via a rope and pulley arrangement. He pulled on the rope, raising them. The pulley needed greasing; it made enough noise to cover any sound that Jason would have made going up the stairs, although he was only able to get halfway up the second staircase before the weapons carrier reached the top.

The slaver pulled it in with a long crook. The rattling sounds suggested that he was replacing the new guard's weapons with his own; it was enough noise to cover Jason's careful creep up the second set of stairs, avoiding the eighth, eleventh and twelfth steps.

Finally he was on the top floor. He waited for the weapons carrier to creak and shudder its way to the ground, and then he drew his garotte.

And waited, while the sound of the retreating footsteps of the off-duty watchman diminished, then disappeared.

The watchman over by an unshuttered window had been waiting, too. As soon as the other was gone, he set his metal cap down on the floor and then took off his chain mail overshirt and dropped it to one side, chuckling to himself as it clanked and clicked to the floor. Mail is heavy stuff; he sighed as he worked his shoulders, then picked up his pike and leaned on it, looking out into the night.

Jason was right behind him and quickly, gently, slipped the noose of his garotte over the slaver's head, jerking it tight, dragging the man backward to the floor as he kicked and shuddered, then voided himself with a horrible flatulence and an awful stench.

Jason held the garotte tightly while the slaver gave one final jerk and then went limp.

Jason stood over the body for a moment. It was strange. He didn't feel anything; this was just another slaver who had gotten in his way, and now it was a dead slaver. It just didn't matter.

He whistled twice, softly, and was relieved to hear three short whistles back. In a few moments Durine was at the top of the stairs, lowering his gear to the floor: four heavy crossbows and a windlass to wind them, plus a dozen bolts. While Durine quickly loaded the crossbows, Jason put on the dead slaver's steel helmet and stood in front of the window, holding the pike.

Across the way, the garret in the burned-out house was dark. Jason wondered if Walter Slovotsky had done his job and taken out the other guard.

Apparently he had; there was something moving in the dark under the far guard shack on top of the wall.

"He's fast, that one," Durine whispered, handing Jason one of the crossbows and taking the other for himself. They were just backup; if everything went right, Walter Slovotsky would take out the guards on the wall. If everything went right.

If he hadn't been looking for it, Jason wouldn't have seen the rope snake up and around the pole supporting the glowsteel and mirror next to the guard station. Jason dipped the pike twice to the left, and then to the right.

At that signal, Walter Slovotsky climbed quickly up the rope and disappeared over the side. There was silence for a few moments, and then a dark form slumped out of the window of the narrow guard shack at that corner.

"Guard," Durine hissed. There was movement at the near guard shack.

The door to the shack opened and the guard stepped out onto the walkway.

"Now." Two bolts hissed into the night, vanishing in the darkness. Jason was sure it was Durine's that pinned the slaver's throat to the wall of the shack.

The man struggled feebly and Durine put another bolt into him, this one piercing his chest squarely.

"Let's get downstairs," Durine said, quickly reloading the crossbows, then tying the windlass and a quiver of bolts to his belt.

It was a bit awkward walking down the stairs with a cocked crossbow in each hand, but in a few moments they were at the rear door. It slowly opened, just far enough to admit the two of them.

Walter Slovotsky stood there, smiling in the dim light of the overhead glowsteels. He hitched at the pistol at the right side of his waist.

"Now?" Durine asked.

"Now, we go kill some slavers in their beds."

Sick to his stomach, Jason returned Slovotsky's smile.

They stood in front of the locked door to the slave pens while Jason fumbled with the keys.

It had all gone bloody, but well; they'd killed six sleeping men, Walter Slovotsky slitting their throats while they lay in their sleeping pallets, while Jason and Durine had stood in the doorway, ready to put a bolt in anyone who woke up.

But none of them woke up; Slovotsky had slit six throats, with no sound except for gurgling gasps.

They'd walked through the sleeping room, the floor slick with blood and shit, and through a swinging door into a kitchen, where five men, sitting around a table, drinking wine and talking, had sprung up, only to fall beneath hissing bolts and swords.

Three of them had shouted and leaped to their feet, reaching for weapons. One had whimpered as he tried to parry Slovotsky's lunge, only to be spitted on a sword, and another had thrown up his hands and begged for his life; Durine had hacked through his neck like a woodsman chopping down a tree.

Just numbers. That was all they were: six men sleeping, five men sitting, three shouting, one whimpering, another begging, eleven men dying. Just numbers.

Finally Jason found a key that fit into the lock of the knobless door. Durine stood behind him, ready to kick the door open if necessary.

Walter Slovotsky's brow furrowed; he held up a hand. *Wait,* he mouthed, running his fingers along the frame, up to the top of the door.

As his fingers tested the oak timber above the door, his face broke into a smile.

He gestured Jason to move away. Slovotsky took a small metal rod from his pouch and inserted it into the hole in the end of the key, tying the lockpick into place with a quick twist of string. He tied another length of string to the end of the pick, took a few quick turns around the key, and stepped back.

Slovotsky beckoned the two of them over. "That timber above the door isn't a timber," he whispered, his voice barely audible even inches away. "It's a deadfall. My guess is that if we turn the key counterclockwise, the way you usually would, it'll slam down. But I want to hedge my bet; it might be set to fall when the door opens, so when you do the door, Durine, get your leg out of the way, quick."

Durine nodded, and took up a position in front of the door, no longer quite below the timber.

Jason drew his pistol, opened the cylinder and thumbed a cartridge into the empty chamber, while Slovotsky did the same. If there were other slavers behind the door, this was a place for guns; a sixth round in the cylinder might make a difference.

Slovotsky pulled on the string. Slowly the key turned in the lock. Something *snick*ed inside.

Durine, his sword in his right hand, his left arm wrapped in a cloak and left hand holding a lantern aloft, drew back his foot for a kick.

Slovotsky nodded. Durine's booted foot kicked the door, hard; wood splintered and shattered as it slammed inward.

Missing Durine's foot by only inches, the deadfall timber slammed down on the stone floor, splitting lengthwise with a pistol-like crack. Hopping over it, Slovotsky was first through the door: he broke left as he skittered inside in a half squat, the pistol held out in front of him.

Jason followed him in, breaking right.

There were shouts and cries, and Jason brought the pistol around, looking for targets.

There were targets in front of him: behind the bars, half-naked men crouched and shouted, some of them flinging hands up in front of their faces.

His wrist wavered, seeking a target. His finger tightened on the—

No. Those were the slaves in the cages; there were no slavers, no targets in the room.

Durine was smiling. "We're all set." The big man hung the lantern on a hook by the door, and left. He'd be keeping watch for a midnight relief party of slavers from the Silver Mushroom Inn.

Slovotsky was already straightening. "Ta havath, all of you. Shut *up.* You're being freed, assholes," he said, sticking his pistol into the front of his belt. He drew his knife and rapped on the bars with its hilt. "There's clothes upstairs, and you're welcome to what money and weapons you can find," he said, as Jason tried to stop the pounding of his heart.

Jason sagged against the coolness of the stone wall while Slovotsky released the slaves, ten unsmiling men in collars and filthy, ragged breechclouts, some of them standing in the front of their cage as though not sure what to do next, some of them still inside. They didn't appear to be ill-fed, but the slave kennels reeked of unwashed sweat; it was almost as bad as the charnel house outside.

Jason's lungs ached for the taste of fresh air.

"You'll find tools over there for getting the collars off," Slovotsky said as he worked the keys in the lock of the second cage. "The Warrior's next door, finishing off the guards in the stable. Help yourself to horses and saddles. I'd suggest you grab some food and weapons, and then get out of here. You're on your own."

One of the slaves, a skinny man, nodded briefly at another.

There was something very wrong here. The metallic taste of fear filled Jason's mouth, clutched at Jason's gut with icy fingers. Jason stepped away from the wall.

One of the slaves was having trouble getting up; Slovotsky took a step into the cell.

"*No.*"

A black-bearded man reached out and pulled Jason off balance while strong fingers grabbed at Jason's left arm. Instinctively, Jason jerked on the trigger.

The blast was impossibly loud in the close confines of the kennels, the gun kicking hard in his hand, flame lancing into the ceiling.

A blow to the head set the world spinning, sent him reeling back, but he brought the pistol down and shoved the cold metal barrel against an unwashed belly.

The hammer rose and fell. The gun kicked hard against his hand. A warm, salty spray and awful stench splattered Jason's face as the man staggered back, two more rushing to take his place.

Jason shrugged off one attacker and pulled the trigger again, flame lancing out, spearing a slaver in the neck, sending him stumbling back into the bars.

A hairy arm snaked around Jason's throat, but he had already drawn his bowie with his left hand and stabbed backward, slicing into flesh, twisting his knife out when he hit bone. The man's scream deafened Jason's right ear before fading off into a sobbing whimper as he fell away.

"Back *off*," Jason screamed, shooting another one. Three shots; three to go. "*Back off.*"

It was all obvious, now; these weren't slaves. They were the trap within a trap—slavers, masquerading as slaves.

Three of them had wrestled Slovotsky up against the bars, and one of them had gotten his knife, setting it against his throat while another clawed at the butt of his pistol. But Slovotsky, his eyes glazed, pressed his belly hard against the bars, trapping the pistol.

"Put it down. Put it down, or he dies," the slaver said, digging the point in for emphasis. "Do it now." Slovotsky's teeth clenched around a groan.

Fuck you, asshole, Jason thought as he brought up his pistol and shot the slaver in the right eye.

Slovotsky elbowed the other slaver away, drew his pistol and shot him, then picked up his sword and quickly speared two of the moving injured.

Jason had holstered his pistol and drew his own sword. He crouched, his bowie in one hand, ready to block, the point of his saber weaving, searching, hunting.

But they were all dead, all lying on the stone floor that was slick with the blood and the piss and the shit, and not only didn't it bother him, he liked it that way.

"'Put it down or he dies'?" Jason spat on the body of the slaver who had said that.

Durine was in the door. He took it all in with one quick look, then turned to Jason.

"Go get the horses ready," Jason said. "And fire the place. We'll be along."

Walter Slovotsky faced him, his face and beard speckled with blood, not all of it his.

"You could have shot me, Jason," Walter Slovotsky said.

"You complaining?"

"Not at all. Not at all." He pressed a hand tightly against the side of his neck, staggering.

Jason was quickly at his side, supporting the older man. He dug a flask of healing draughts out of his pouch and handed it to Slovotsky, who pulled the cork out with trembling fingers, then drained it quickly.

"Let's get the hell out of here, kid," Walter Slovotsky said, his voice deepening, strengthening. "We can skip the note this time."

"Like hell." Jason was already untying the strings of Slovotsky's pouch; he fumbled out two speedloaders, then quickly loaded both his and Walter's pistols, careful to put the spent brass back in Slovotsky's pouch. He'd leave the bastards only dead bodies and a note to remember him by.

He took the note out of his own pouch, and stuck it in the mouth of a dead man. "Like the man says, the Warrior lives."

He kicked the body in the face. "And we are not nice people," he said. He clapped a hand to Walter Slovotsky's shoulder. "Come on, old man. *Now* we get the hell out of here."

CHAPTER 26

Laughter in the Dark

You know how to win a victory, Hannibal, but you don't know how to use it.

—Maharbal

Jason couldn't sleep. The hold had been dank and musty, and the constant, albeit gentle rocking of the boat had him vaguely nauseated. Again.

Whatever I'm good at, it isn't sailing, he thought. Again.

At least he wasn't alone, and hadn't been all night. He'd taken a turn with the tiller, letting Bothan Ver and Thivar Anjer get some sleep. With the search for the Warrior behind them, and with Salket long vanished over the horizon, tight muscles were beginning to loosen.

They'd made it away, again.

As long as the wind held steady it was easy, and Thivar Anjer had made it easier on Jason by lashing a rod to the starboard rail; he didn't even need to use the compass. From Jason's seat in the cockpit, all he had to do was keep the pole star, high above, over the rod.

Jane Slovotsky had taken the first turn with him, just sitting alongside him on the steersman's bench, his free arm around her, the back of her head resting against his chest. Her hair smelled of soap and sunshine.

"You got any bright ideas about what we do when we get back?" she asked, toying with his fingers.

"Not really."

"You don't want to, like, get married and start making babies and stuff?"

"Nah." He touched his lips to the top of her head. "Maybe later."

She laughed. "Well, that's good, 'cause I don't, either."

"Besides, you've probably got to work your way through most of the young barons-to-be around court."

"Jason *Cullinane,*" she said, half-pretending to be shocked. "What kind of girl do you think I am?"

"You're Walter Slovotsky's daughter. And what's the matter— does only one fit?"

They both laughed.

Jane had gone below to sleep, and Durine had come up on deck a bit later, to noisily urinate over the side for longer than Jason would have thought humanly possible.

After he fastened himself up, Durine had started to go below, then shrugged. "Would you mind some company, young sir?"

"Not at all, Durine."

He sat down across from Jason and spent some time with him, not saying much. They just watched the stars and the night sky, and the distant pulsing of the faerie lights, until Durine yawned and got to his feet.

"I don't suppose," he said, "that you and I will be seeing much of each other after this, young Emperor. I just wanted to say that I'm glad to have been with you."

"Getting maudlin in your old age, Durine?" Tennetty's head poked through the curtains covering the hatchway.

Durine shrugged, his massive shoulders working beneath the thin cotton of his tunic. "A bit, perhaps."

She dropped to the deck, squatting tailor-fashion next to Jason. "Walter's been talking a lot about you. He says you did good. Real good."

"Yeah, but he lies a lot."

Tennetty's smile warmed him in the dark. "Pretty pleased with yourself, aren't you?"

Durine started to bristle, but Jason touched him once on the arm; he subsided.

"Yes, I am," Jason said. "I am very pleased with myself."

"You should be," she said. "None of us got killed on this one."

"I noticed." Although that wasn't true. Vator had died, and Vator was Jason's friend, even if Tennetty wouldn't think of him as one of them. But dead was dead, and there was nothing that could be done about it. Next time he'd do better.

He hoped.

She was silent for a long time. "You're not Karl, you know."

"I know."

"But you are a cold-blooded little killer. You'd slice a man open from crotch to his sternum, and then slit his throat for dirtying your boots with his blood and his guts."

He didn't remember drawing it, but his bowie was in his free hand. "Bet your ass, Tennetty," he said. "And not just a man."

She laughed. It wasn't a pleasant laugh, but that was fair enough, because she wasn't a pleasant person.

And he laughed back the same way.

Durine just looked at them as if they were both crazy.

Bren Adahan hadn't taken a turn, but he had come up on deck to relieve himself, too. He started to go back down, but then shrugged and sat down across from Jason.

"I want to talk to you about your sister."

Jason thought about telling him to go away, but Bren Adahan had been a good hand with the horses, had them at just the right spot down the road. He'd had them wait a few minutes while he walked back down the road and fastened a blackened rope across the road, at about the height of a rider's neck, and he'd even insisted on riding in front, his own sword drawn and held in front and to the side to at least give them a chance to catch any similar trap that had been set for them.

So Jason said: "Good idea."

"I'm a product of my time and place, Jason Cullinane. Don't judge me harshly. In Holtun, a baron has the right to ask. Besides," he added with a smile that was clearly man to man, "Jane is awfully attractive, at that."

"What are you asking me?"

"Don't mention anything to your sister. It wouldn't do any good."

Jason pretended to think it over, then nodded. "Perhaps I won't," he said. *I will,* he thought. Let Aeia decide whether or not she wanted to take official notice of it. "No problem, Bren. Go to sleep."

Betrayal? No. Aeia was family. Family came first.

As dawn broke over the horizon, he felt a familiar presence in his mind.

Jason, are you all right? Ellegon was just a speck on the horizon, but the speck grew.

I'm fine. But this thing about the Warrior—

I know—I've got Ahira and your mother with me.

Jason stood. "Okay, people. Everybody, wake up," he called out. He stood, more tired than a sleepless night accounted for. "It's time to go home."

PART FOUR
After the Search

CHAPTER 27

"The Warrior Lives"

A Roman, divorced from his wife, being highly blamed by his friends, who demanded, "Was she not chaste? Was she not fair? Was she not fruitful?" holding out his shoe, asked them whether or not it was new and well made. "Yet," added he, "none of you can tell where it pinches me."

—Plutarch

Jason stood outside the great hall, waiting, until he decided he'd had enough of waiting. It didn't take long for him to have enough.

There were three ceremonial guards at the door tonight: Durine, Kethol and Pirojil.

"Let's do it," Jason said.

Pirojil started to protest that it was too early, but Durine shook his head and Kethol rapped the butt of his halberd on the stone.

"Ladies and gentlemen, the Heir."

Jason walked across the carpet, uncomfortable in his velvet finery. It didn't feel right.

But that didn't matter. Got to keep a sense of proportion about everything. Control what you can, and let the rest go.

He paused for a moment at the foot of the table. Mother's chair. He rested a hand on her shoulder for a moment. She was stronger every day. Just have to keep her away from that damn magic that threatened to drive her crazy. Her fingers gripped his with surprising strength.

469

Ellegon, tell my mother that I love her— He stopped himself. She knew it.

To her right Walter Slovotsky and Kirah sat; to their right was Doria. A few days' rest had done Slovotsky a world of good; he looked a decade younger, and his I'm-so-clever-to-be-Walter-Slovotsky smile was perhaps a degree wider.

Ahira sat next to Doria, and the dwarf smiled broadly at him. He raised a clenched, hamlike fist to chest level, for just a moment, as though to say, Be strong.

Count on it.

Aeia was next to the dwarf. Jason had already talked to her about Bren Adahan; he didn't know what she'd decided to do about it, but that was her decision.

Flame flared noisily in the courtyard outside. *We all have to make our own decisions.*

That we do.

Thomen is upset that you haven't discussed anything with him.

Tell him to sit still.

"Good evening," Jason said as he walked to his seat at the head of the table. He looked over the assemblage of Holtish and Biemish barons, and their advisers. "Be seated, all. You have a full agenda; I have a short one. I'm going to stand.

"Tennetty—" He tossed her the large brass key to the strongbox. "Get it, will you?"

"Your high—"

"Shut *up*, Thomen," Jason said. "I'm going to speak my piece, then you can talk all you want.

"First item of business," he said. "Thomen, you've got too much to do, what with managing the Empire, sitting in court and all. I'm taking your barony away from you."

It was just as well that Thomen's mother, Beralyn, wasn't there. Of course, that wasn't by accident—Jason had ordered that she absent herself from council. Probably the last time he'd be able to do that.

Thomen Furnael was white-lipped. "And who are you giving it to?"

Tell him to keep his mouth shut, and make him.

As you wish, Jason.

"Me. It's Barony Cullinane, as of now. I've always wanted a barony. I'm going to have Lou and Petros send over a team of engineers to manage it for me. And—oh, thank you, Tennetty," he said, taking the bag containing the crown and tossing it casually to the table. "Garavar, I'm releasing Durine, Kethol and Pirojil from their oaths to you and the crown, and hiring them. I want to have them around me when I'm there.

"Next matter," he said. "The Other Siders." Slovotsky pushed his chair back. "Go ahead, Uncle Walter."

Walter Slovotsky drained his wine glass and stood. "You folks expect a lot of us Other Siders," he said. "Which is fair enough. The ones that Deighton sent over are all pretty special, and I've long since given up on believing that there's any coincidence in that.

"But we can't do everything. I don't build things. Ahira can't work magic—and you'll notice that the Engineer doesn't go around trying to get his ass killed, the way Karl used to. Andy came close to burning herself out by pushing her abilities too far too fast.

"We can't do everything, but you've been expecting that we can. It's one of the reasons that I was able to keep the legend of Karl alive longer than we could keep Karl alive. The kind of magic that lets somebody do everything doesn't exist." Slovotsky sat down. "It's all yours, kid."

"Which leads us to the last thing on my agenda," Jason said. "I can't do everything, people. And neither could my father. He tried to be everything—prince, emperor, father, husband, warrior— and he fell flat on his face too often.

"His mistake was letting you people put the crown on his head. How many times has one of you said to him, 'An emperor has no business doing this or that?' Garavar, how many times?"

The old general muffled a smile.

He's figured it out.

"But you didn't really believe it, Garavar. It was a joke to you, sometimes. You thought he could get away with whatever he did. You were wrong. He couldn't do everything, and neither can I. The difference is that I'm going to pick what I do. And I will do it very well."

He unwrapped the crown and stood. "Thomen, you've been governing the Empire since my father left to try to save my life. You put the realm first." Jason let his fingers run across the polished silver, resting lightly on the coolness of the central emerald. "About time we stop pretending that it takes a Cullinane to govern." He faced the barons. "Any of you Biemish who thinks this means the Empire's abandoning the plan of raising the Holts to full citizen status had better think again; it was Thomen's idea in the first place. Any of you Holts who think now'd be a real good time to revolt can speak now," he said, letting his hand drop to the butt of his pistol.

Jason waited in the silence. "I didn't think so."

"And what are you going to do?" Tyrnael asked.

"Change the world, Baron," Jason said. There was a friend of his, somewhere out in the Middle Lands, looking for the man that had enslaved him and his family. That was a good place to start.

"I've got some partners to work with, some teachers to learn from," he said, nodding toward Slovotsky and the dwarf, who smiled back as they pushed their chairs away from the table and stood.

Slovotsky shrugged. "I'm going to start by teaching him how to drink," he said.

"Sit still, Thomen," Jason said, placing the crown firmly, not at all gently, on Thomen's head.

Thomen eyed him for a long, long time. "You're not giving me much choice, are you?" he whispered.

"No, I'm not giving you *any* choice." Jason walked to the foot of the table and stood there for a moment, looking from face to face, fully ready and willing to kill anybody who objected. "Don't fuck with him, people. It wouldn't be a good idea."

But there were no objections.

It was time to go; he turned and walked out of the grand hall, Slovotsky and the dwarf beside him.

He paused at the door to shake hands with Durine, Kethol and Pirojil. "See you out at the castle," he said. "And don't get into any fights."

Tennetty was waiting next to Ellegon in the courtyard, leaning against the dragon's bulk, her arms crossed.

Ellegon's wings furled and unfurled. *How does it feel not to be Heir anymore? Just a common baron.*

Jason laughed. "Hey, I'm used to having a title. Can't give it up all at once. —Let's get out of here."

"You're not going without me," Tennetty said.

"Of course not," Ahira said.

"Wouldn't think of it," Jason said.

Slovotsky chuckled. "I wouldn't want to be the one to stop you."

She smiled. "I haven't heard any invitation."

Jason shrugged. "Well, what would you say to coming along with us? We've got to settle Walter's family into Castle Fu—Castle Cullinane, that is, and then we've got some things to do."

I heard something about changing the world.

Bet your scaly ass on it.

She nodded, and hitched at her belt. "What would I say?" There must have been some dust in the air, or something. She rubbed at her eye. "I'd say that the Warrior lives."